MARIANA'S SECRET

Katori Chronicles Book 2

A. D. Lombardo

ALSO BY A. D. LOMBARDO

Katori Chronicles Book 1 · The Half-Light

ACKNOWLEDGMENTS

Completing my second book changed me as a storyteller. My editor, Keith, encouraged me to challenge my hero. He taught me the best characters have flaws and make mistakes. As my characters grow, so do I.

I especially want to thank my son, Connor, for his early reading and honest opinion. Constructive criticism from my biggest fan came at a heavy cost. He reminded me the delete-key is the most powerful weapon in my arsenal; unfortunately, for one character, it was detrimental to his existence. Here's to you, Gino—may you live on in a future story.

Special thanks to my family and friends for your continued enthusiasm. Thank you for being my fans. It's a real dream to share this part of myself with each of you. Your perseverance and faith give me strength.

One significant honorable mention is my devoted husband. Over the shoulder, reading has become his pastime. Thank you.

Mariana's Secret

The Katori Chronicles Book 2
A. D. Lombardo

This work is a work of fiction. Names, characters, organizations, places, events and incidents are either products of the author's imagination or are used factiously. Any resemblance to actual persons, living or dead, or actual events is purely coincidental.

Published by A. D. Lombardo
ISBN (Paperback): 978-1-7333376-2-5

Cover design by A. D. Lombardo
First Edition 2019

www.ADLombardo.com

CONTENTS

MAPS

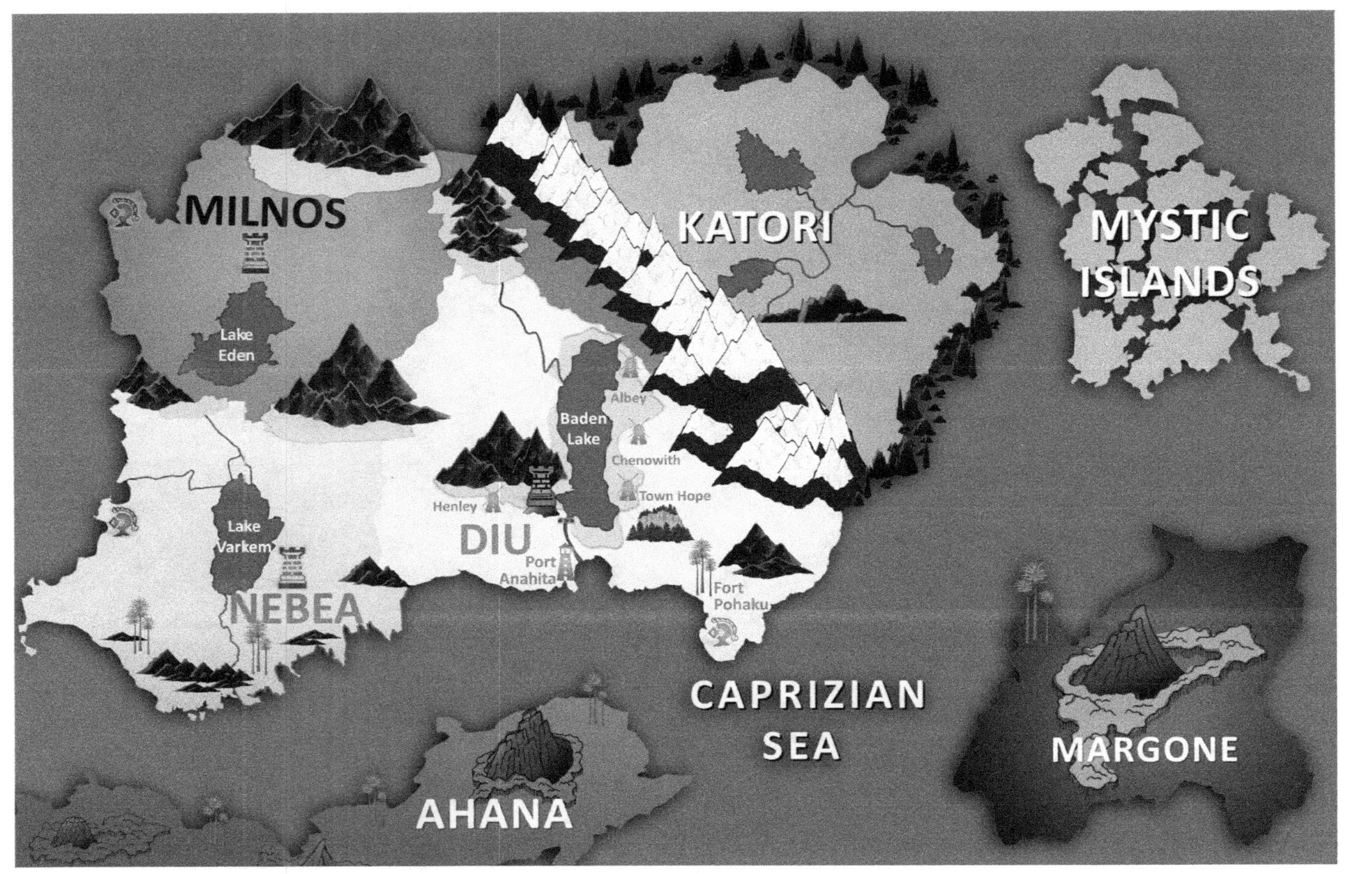
MILNOS
Lake
Eden
KATORI
MYSTIC
ISLANDS
Albey
Baden
Lake
Chenowith
Town Hope
Henley
DIU
Lake
Varkem
NEBEA
Port
Anahita
Fort
Pohaku
CAPRIZIAN
SEA
AHANA
MARGONE

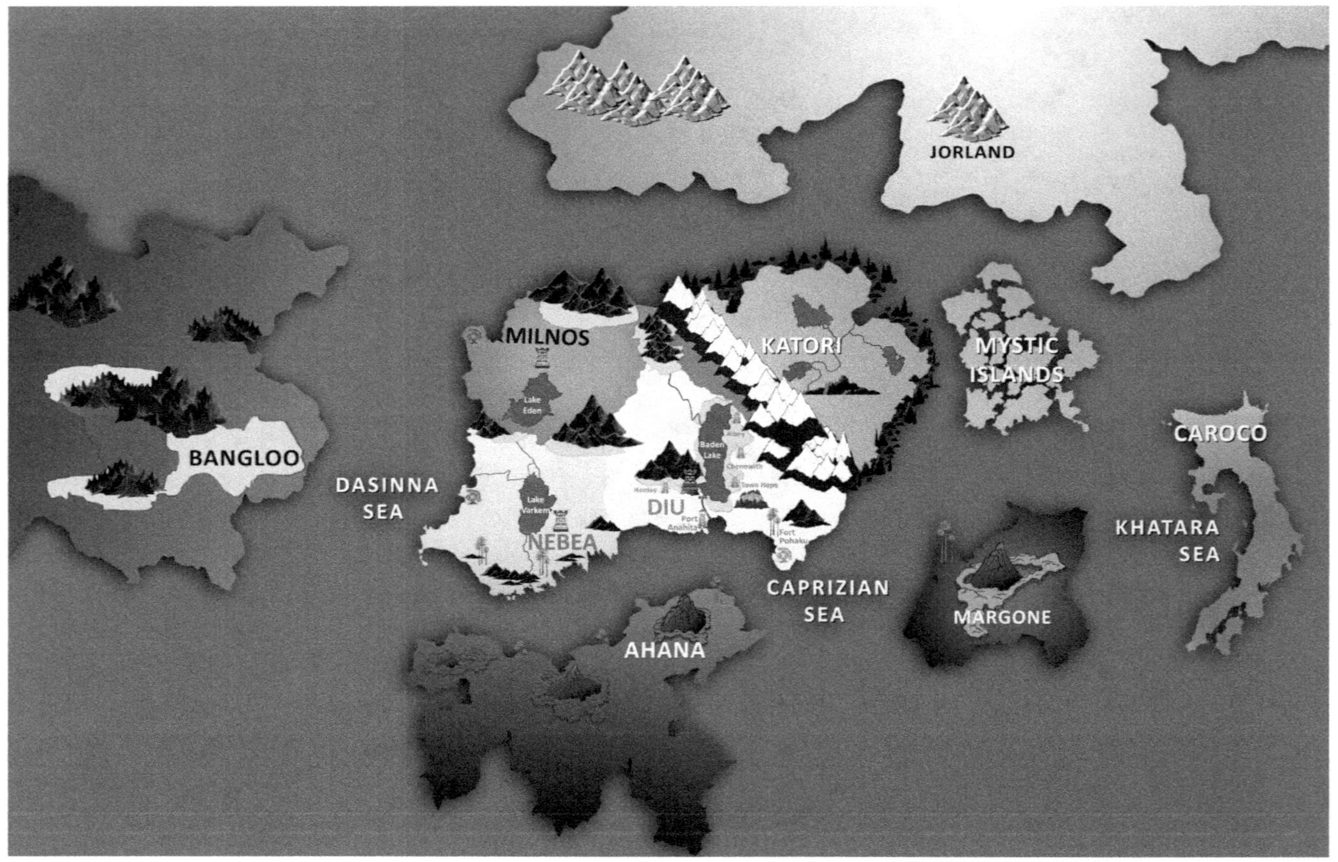
JORLAND
MILNOS
KATORI
MYSTIC ISLANDS
CAROCO
BANGLOO
DASINNA SEA
Lake Eden
Lake Varkem
Baden Lake
DIU
Port Anahita
NEBEA
Fort Pohaku
CAPRIZIAN SEA
MARGONE
KHATARA SEA
AHANA

PROLOGUE

Keegan's snarl quivered with anger. Tears streamed down the face of the man in front of him. The mercenary captain pressed his palm against the embossed star on his chest plate. No amount of begging would change his fate. He was a dead man. Still, the captain pleaded for his life. "I am not a thief, please... It was merely a trinket."

Keegan eyed the crew. The crew stepped back, fear swirling around them.

The wind whipped through the sails of the Caroco ship, and its flag—a black star on a field of red—snapped in the breeze. Keegan wrapped his hand around the man's neck. He applied very little pressure; he didn't need to squeeze. A tiny light emanated from a black crystal around Keegan's neck. The life of the captain shriveled away with Keegan's touch.

It wasn't enough to run the man through with his sword—no, Keegan wanted him to suffer. There was enjoyment in his eyes as he watched the lifeforce drain from the captain's face and limbs.

Keegan cast the man aside; his lifeless skin-and-bone corpse rattled on the deck of the ship. No words were spoken. His crew knew not to make eye contact when Keegan was on a rampage. With the wave of Keegan's hand, the mercenaries started stowing the cargo they had stolen from the now-sinking ship at their portside.

Two men heaved the corpse of their dead captain overboard. A foolish man who lost his life to greed. But then the crew spent their days plundering silver, gold, and gems from every ship they crossed without challenge. Temptation was everywhere. The Khatara Sea was a dangerous place, and none willingly ventured too close. Keegan and his pirates dominated the high seas taking everything that ventured close to Caroco.

The second wave of Keegan's hand set the ship in motion. It surged forward through the rolling ocean waves along with three other vessels. The Katori Weathervanes on each of Keegan's vessels worked their magic, their stylized movements shaping the wind and bending it to their purpose.

Outside the entrance to Keegan's quarters stood three terrified women. Their once-genteel nature was now gone, lost in the horrific slaughter of everyone on their ship. They clung to each other for comfort, their golden locks fluttering in the wind. Tears streaked their refined faces.

Keegan's gaze panned the figure of each woman. He grabbed the youngest girl and pulled her toward the cabin door. In protest, the older woman pulled her back to their huddle. "No, not her. Please, not her," she begged. "Take me instead."

Pleasure danced in Keegan's eyes. "She means something to you. Your daughter, perhaps?" The corner of his lip curled upward.

The three women clung to each other. Their sobs fluttered away on the wind.

There was no malice in his expression, only pure delight. "You're right, I don't need all three of you." With the flick of his wrist, the girl's lifeless body dropped to the deck.

Horror smacked the two remaining women in the face. The mother dropped to her dead daughter, sobbing. Keegan grabbed the hair on the older woman's head, hoisting her to her feet. He shoved her toward the door.

Weary and broken, she opened the cabin door and entered.

Keegan made to follow her, but before he could even take a step, a wave of energy smacked him back. One word echoed in his mind—*Mother.*

It was stronger than anything he'd felt before. The Weathervanes above stumbled, and the shift in energy reverberated through the whole ship. The wind died in the sails, and the bow pitched downward with the sudden change in speed.

Somewhere, far from here, a Katori was lighting up the world. And Keegan had felt it.

A wide-eyed Keegan ascended the stairs and shoved the helmsman aside. The Katori Weathervanes stepped to his side.

"Such raw power," he muttered, still in disbelief. He spun the ship with its remaining momentum. "Not since Mariana have I felt such power. Could it be she is still alive? How did you trick me, my love? I must have you back..."

CHAPTER 1

Facing the Past

Prince Kai sat cross-legged on the floor across from Kendra. She offered her open hands to him. "It has been months since we have sat together," Kendra motioned. "I would like you to try and reach out again. I believe you can glean outside the city. The more you practice, the better you will be. There are layers in our gifts. Explore and challenge your boundaries."

Kai took her outreached hands. "I can already glean the entire city. Like you said, it's been a while. I want to learn something new. You once said I could remember a past event, see the truth of a moment. I want to remember what happened the day my mother died. I have waited long enough—I will be sixteen this spring. Twelve years is long enough to wait for closure."

Kendra looked down. Her heavy sigh told Kai she was unsure. "Are you sure?" She hesitated, her eyes turning to worry. "The more you know..."

"I need to know what happened."

She squeezed his hands. "It will change everything. And I don't even know if you can do this. Half-Lights can't..." she paused to look at him, "they can't glean. You should not be able to do this."

It had never occurred to him he would not be able. He wondered why Kendra was having a change of heart. She had offered to show him the truth before, so why was she so scared now that he wanted to remember? Then he thought of the horror his mind had hidden from him all those years ago. Could he handle seeing it any better now? Probably not, but the burden of her death hindered every relationship, and the weight of blaming himself and others for her loss held him back. The anger held him back. He needed to be free. He must face her passing, or it would consume his future.

"Please, Kendra. Help me let it go. I know there is nothing I can do to change what happened, but I need to know the truth. Why can't I remember?"

She chewed her bottom lip. "I suppose you are ready." Her tone sounded hollow. "I can only hope for both our sakes it is not as I have feared. Promise me you will protect our secret."

What could she mean? Had he not proven capable? Were they not just as much his secrets? Why did he have to hide his ability to glean, bond with animals, and his incredible speed and strength? "Please, Kendra, you can trust me," he begged again. "I need to do this. I've had another dream. This time there was something new I remembered."

Kai felt the warmth build in his soul. He let the power grow, and he felt his eyes change color.

Kendra gasped in surprise. "Your eyes... No matter how many times I see them turn green, I can't believe it. You've gained control over the shift." She shook her head in disbelief.

He squeezed her hands. "I need to move past her death. I have done things you thought impossible being only a Half-Light. Show me my past. They are my secrets, too."

Lips pursed; Kendra slid her hands around his wrists. "I've waited a long time myself to know the truth. Since you have visions, you must be attuned to the energy within time itself. Only a few other Katori can do this—remember a moment in a waking vision."

The anguish in her eyes told him this was as important to

her as it was to him. "It is time her memory no longer haunts me." Kai nodded.

"You will need to be in the moment," she said slowly. "An observer, reflecting on the past without being controlled by your emotions. You must let go of your fear to see what your mind has hidden. Let your spirit guide you. Separate your heart from the event."

Eyes closed, Kai relaxed his breathing. He let go and felt peace as Kendra spoke.

"Think back to the moment in the gardens—feel it in your soul." She paused. "Let it pull you into a waking dream."

Kai pushed through the silence into his memories. The darkest part of his soul was a locked box he'd always feared opening. Kendra's voice was a distant echo in his mind. "You were calling to your mother." Kendra rubbed the back of his wrist with her thumb. "See her, but step outside of the child you were. See the child. Remember, you are only observing. Uncontrolled emotions can cloud the vision. Heed my warning, Kai. Don't get consumed by your childhood memory. If you lose grasp on time, you could break the link, leaving your mind trapped in the past version of yourself."

In Kai's mind, he recalled the garden maze. He heard his mother's laughter. A young Kai stomped with disappointment. Pink and white flower petals dropped on his shoulders. "Mom!" the younger version of him cried.

Kai gasped.

Kendra lightly squeezed his wrist and whispered, "Observe. Calm your breathing. Whatever you see, it is not happening now. Do not grab at the wave of time you are viewing."

Remembering Kendra's warning, he slowed his racing heart. He followed younger Kai around the small sundial, and they ran past the pink-and-white flower bed. Little Kai turned the corner. Mariana was doubled over in pain, grabbing at her sides. His mother turned, her face visibly caught between surprise and fear. She spoke, "I am sorry, Kai. I should have told you."

Mariana grabbed at her head. Pain and agony twisted her sounds. Little Kai stepped towards his mother. "Kai, stay away… Run away… Please. I can't hold it back much longer. It is coming. I am not in control…"

Mariana screamed in pain. Her fingers changed into large claws, tearing her dress. Pieces of fabric fell to the ground. "NO! Please. How can this be?" Her eyes bulged in fear. She held her breath, and the claws disappeared. Her hands grabbed at her head, and she fell to the ground.

Observing, Kai felt heat build inside his body. He clenched his hands around Kendra's wrists. "I want to help her!" he cried, tears streaming down his face.

Kendra whispered. "I am here with you. Let yourself see what your mind has hidden, see the truth. Remember, this is the past. You cannot change what happened. Don't get lost."

Once more, he slowed his breathing. He stared at his mother as she writhed on her hands and knees. Tears filled her eyes. Again, she laid her hand over her heart and screamed. Her body curled inward, and then she flexed her arms outward. With a burst of light, she turned into a giant blood-red dragon —with scales, horns, and wings. She had become as large as the banyark tree nearby.

The dragon screeched and sprayed fire into the sky. Then it fixed its amber eyes on little Kai.

Stunned, he held his breath. Little Kai fell to his knees. "MOMMY!" he cried. His voice trembled between sobs. "Please come back!"

From the opposite side of the garden maze, a guard entered the central clearing. He drew his sword and yelled. "Run, boy, run! RUN AWAY!"

The guard lunged at the dragon; his blade held high. In an instant, the dragon turned its angry eyes toward the guard and screeched. Terrified, the guard stepped back, but it was too late. Through screams of terror, the dragon ripped him to shreds. The ground was now covered in blood and pieces of his mother's dress.

Kai remembered the terror he felt in the presence of the dragon. The confusion of her transformation. Even now, he could not comprehend how this could be real. Little Kai shouted. "Mommy, please, no, no… NO!"

The dragon flexed and flapped its wings. A massive gust of wind sent little Kai backward against the maze hedge. Older Kai watched his mother fly away. His younger self curled into a ball and sobbed. The garden flooded with guards, all gawking skyward.

Kai let go of the moment and opened his eyes to look at Kendra. His heart throbbed with adrenaline. "Did you know?" He paused, studying her face. He gasped as the realization came to him. "You DID! You knew all this time, and you didn't tell me!"

Fury flooded his mind. He yanked his hands away. "My mother is the red dragon. It didn't kill her—it *IS* her." Anger consumed him, and tears welled in his eyes. Tears from years of needless suffering.

Kendra wept. "Kai, please, you must understand." She lowered her head and cupped her face with her hands. "I wanted to tell you, but it's… complicated."

Kai watched as she wiped the tears from her face. Her confident demeanor had turned remorseful. "What other secrets have you been keeping from me?" he seethed. "Be honest, for once."

"Kai!" she responded, shocked by his tone.

Anger welled in his throat. His words were meant to hurt. "You dole out little secrets about my heritage, but only after I discover my gifts on my own. I am only privy to Katori secrets when I prove I can do something that risks exposing you."

He clenched his fists tight and continued to glare at her. Everything in his life was secrets and lies. Did Kendra care about him, or only about keeping Katori secrets? "Why not share the possibilities and teach me?"

Kendra reached toward him. "You know we guard the Katori secrets with our lives. Since you are a Half-Light, we never expected you to be able to glean. Meditation should only provide clarity of mind—or at the most, perhaps enhanced focus. Anyone can meditate. We had no idea you would have the gift of sight like all Katori do. Your gift with animals is as good if not better than any trained Beastmaster." She looked at him as if she were seeing him for the first time. "You are an enigma to us."

Kai's thoughts twisted in all directions. "All you see is a Half-Light—half Katori. Nothing more. Why bother with me at all? I am not a thing. You kept this from me. Why? Why let me suffer? Why let me believe she was gone?"

She took several deep breaths. "You were Mariana's son." Kendra tilted her head to catch Kai's gaze. "I spent years trying to find a way into Diu palace. I gave up my life to be near you. My own husband disagrees with my choice, but I came anyway. Now, you mean the world to me. The truth is, my elders still guide me. They never wanted me to come here. If I ever wish to return, I must heed their warnings. They only allowed me to stay after I convinced them you might know something. I was asked to watch you. Test your abilities and report back."

"Report back!" Kai huffed. "Am I an experiment?"

"No, but Half-Lights have no gifts, but you do. If someday you remembered what I hoped was true—you would know one of our secrets anyway. Besides being able to connect with animals, some Beastmasters, like your mother, can turn into animals. Outside of the risks behind the world discovering what we Katori can do, the danger for your mother is more serious. She is very powerful. I wanted to know if she was alive, the elders wanted to know what you knew."

"And still you kept this from me. How could you?"

Kendra wiped the tears from her face. "I was trying to protect a Katori secret, we don't want to become weapons, slaves or worse—hunted." She wrapped her arms around herself. "You're right, I knew no dragon would ever attack her, without cause—unless someone was sent to attack her. I feared your memory would reveal her death was real. Keegan is a vicious man…" her words faded into tears.

Her words painted a new picture in his mind. The fear he'd had his entire life coursed through Kendra's eyes. She was as relieved as he was. His mother's death was a fear they both shared. "But now we both know the truth," Kai said. "She did not die—at least not that day." He reached for Kendra and shook her shoulder. "How do I turn her back?" he demanded.

Hesitation filled the space between them. Kendra's eyes welled with new tears. "If she has been a dragon all these years, I am not sure you can. Her original form, her true mind, and spirit are lost to us now. She may be permanently trapped in dragon form. Only the elders will know if she can be restored. We need their help. I must tell them she did not die. Keegan did not kill her. They may search for her once more."

Deep down, something snapped. An uncontrollable rage consumed him. It was difficult to accept this new memory of the past. His heart pounded, and he found it difficult to breathe or think straight.

"I will find my mother. And you will help me." Then an idea exploded in his mind. "I don't know why my mother left or where she went, but I do know I can sense others close to me. Maybe she is close. The Katori people are like beacons of light. You've said if I focus, I can find a specific person. You said my mother could search for a person. Teach me, please!"

"I cannot," Kendra shook her head. "There are risks if you light up the world. If you do this, it will reveal your location, something I believe your mother was protecting. I want her back too, but not at the risk of Keegan knowing you exist, or what level of power you possess. Besides, Mariana could be anywhere in the world. There are a rare few who could search in this way—glean to find a specific person."

One word stuck in his mind. "Who is Keegan?"

"A violent and dangerous man. Your mother feared him. We all do. I cannot teach you what you want to learn."

Her words bounced off his hardened heart. He was no longer willing to listen to half-truths and deception. "Get out," he demanded. "If you will not help me, I will have to do it myself. Like everything else."

Astounded, Kendra reared backward. "Kai please, let me explain."

"No, you had your chance to explain. Three years' worth of opportunity. I will find her on my own." Kai pointed to the door. "GO."

She rose to her feet and stepped into the hall.

Kai slammed the door behind her. His heart ached at Kendra's refusal, and tears raced down his face. The agony of his past twisted his soul.

CHAPTER 2

The Mind Master

T he more Kai opened his mind, the stronger his abilities became. The day of his mother's death had long since been a storm cloud over his mind, a burden. The freedom to explore his gifts without the looming darkness opened new possibilities.

Despite Kendra's warning, Kai spent much of his free time trying to glean for his mother. He was desperate for a clue, but no matter how hard he tried, he could not locate her. His range was limited, and without Kendra's guidance, he had no idea how to expand it or search specifically for his mother. There had to be a way to reach out. He wished Haygan was not away all winter with Simone in Katori. Maybe he could help when he returned.

What Kai needed most was a distraction. Riome's training would be the perfect opportunity to focus his talents productively. Like most evenings, he descended the east spire. Tonight, there would no combat training. Instead, he was on a mission. Riome gave him very little information about the reasons behind his assignments. Most were tests in the field. Break into a home, inn, or warehouse and collect something— a book, trinket, or information. Occasionally she had him return the item the same night. Simple tests.

Other nights he followed people and reported back. However, something about tonight's mission felt more important. Riome spent extra time preparing his disguise and reminding him how to follow without being noticed. She covered the importance of memorizing the details of a room before searching. And she told him speed was his greatest asset—think and react before the other person. Something they had in common—exceptional speed.

His attire was well-worn dark pants, a white shirt, and a reversible jacket. His face was bedecked with faint freckles, and his hair was reddened with some sort of dust Riome swore would wash out. Around his wrist, a dirty white rope bracelet, worn by sailors. Stuffed inside his boot was a small dagger, and a large sailor's knife with a braided rope handle was strapped conspicuously to his hip.

The tunnel below the palace that opened into Hightown's warehouse district was warm and musty. Kai was happy to exit into the fresh air. His route took him deep into Rimtown. He was given a warehouse location and a brief description of a man he was to follow. Kai kept his expression stern and his arms free at his side. He worked his way briskly through the city to his pickup point, a warehouse near the outer wall used by fishermen.

A brute of a man exited the warehouse as Kai rounded the corner. The cauliflower ears and the milky white eye identified Kai's mark. Kai walked straight passed the man, crossed the street, and turned the corner. He also took note of the brute's enlarged knuckles. This man was a fighter.

Once out of sight, Kai concealed his white shirt with the dark coat he had been carrying. Back on the main street, he resumed his pursuit. Within minutes, Kai was close enough to his man to pick his pocket. As Riome taught him, he studied the man's stride to identify any hidden weapons. The hitch in the man's walk and the crinkle in his pant leg meant he had a knife in his left boot.

The stiffness on his right side and the lack of a swinging

arm suggested a second weapon concealed one on his right. The bulky black bag weighing down his left shoulder suggested unknown possibilities. Kai backed off and crossed the street behind the next oncoming carriage. From the other side, he followed.

When the man turned the corner, Kai removed his dark coat and flipped it inside out, revealing a tan version of the same jacket, then he darted to catch up. Taking a chance, he crossed the street and quickened his pace. Kai had an inkling about the man's destination, and he wanted to get there first.

The Drunken Dragon had a particular reputation. One thing it didn't have—guards. Anyone who chose that establishment did so because they were looking for a good time, or they wanted to avoid Diu guards. Kai assumed the man he followed preferred the latter.

In the fading sunset, Kai grabbed the pub door. Two men stumbled outside. Out of the corner of his eye, Kai saw the man cross the street. His instincts had been right. Inside, Kai approached the barkeep and purchased a room. The barmaid slid a key across the counter as the brute entered the tavern. Kai ordered a drink before slipping the key into his pocket.

From a table near the stairs, Kai watched the brute. He too purchased a room, but he went straight upstairs without ordering. Unsure what else to do, Kai sipped his ale. A young barmaid approached his table. "Your meal, sir." She slid a bowl of stew over to him, even though he had not ordered one. "Please inspect your room thoroughly. Let me know if you find anything out of place. Enjoy your meal, complimentary with your room." She nodded toward the stairs.

The woman in front of him may have been a stranger to everyone else, but Kai knew who she was—Riome. He didn't have to glean through her disguise to realize it was her. He'd seen this outfit in her vast collection of costumes. Plus, she'd used this accent around him before. Clearly, she wanted him to know she was there.

And he knew what her message meant: *when the man re-*

turns to eat his meal, search his room, but leave no trace—take nothing. Beneath his coat, Kai's heart pounded. He hurried through his meal and waited. Thunderous footsteps echoed down the stairs. At the bar, Riome poured ale and played her part. The man stepped off the last step, and Kai slid from his seat and scurried upstairs.

Six rooms. Four open doors, two closed. Kai's key had the number four etched into the handle. He stood in front of his open door. Two sconces flickered on the wall above a small fireplace. The room looked clean but felt stuffy. There was a single bed, armoire, desk, and chair. Behind him, giggles and grunts told him bedroom five was occupied. Room six, next to his, had a closed door. *Six must be the brute's room.*

With his own door closed and locked, he opened his window. A refreshing breeze blew back the curtains. The alley behind the inn was dark and gloomy. Kai leaned out his window and saw curtains from room six flutter in the night. A candle flickered.

There was not much time.

Before Kai knew it, he had one leg out the window, searching for the timber frame running around the outside. The edge of his foot felt support, and he eased his other leg outside. Using both hands, he held tight to the roofline and slid his foot forward along the wooden ledge. Getting another handhold, he slid closer to the open window. He dared not look down.

When he wrapped his arm around the adjacent window and slipped inside, he almost collapsed under shaky knees. Uncertain how much time he had, Kai began to search the room.

Two lit sconces illuminated the room, a mirror image of his own. The desk drawers were both empty. The armoire bare. He ran his hands around the back corner of the cabinet— nothing had been stuffed behind. The porcelain basin was dry, the water pitcher full. The bed smooth and untouched.

Underneath the bed skirt, Kai found the black bag. Stuffed between several rumpled articles of clothing, he found a well-worn book. The aged honey-colored leather was cracked and stained with dried blood and ink. He opened the clasp.

Kai flipped page after page, memorizing as many details as he could. What he saw both shocked and disgusted him. Bloody fingerprints dotted the corner of nearly every page.

The owner is a bad man, he shuddered.

The sound of laughter in the hallway reminded him he had little time. He read more entries, then he gleaned the downstairs pub. The brute gulped the last of his ale, pushed his bowl and mug to the barmaid, and rose from his stool. Kai was out of time.

Swiftly he flipped through the remaining pages, making mental notes. The man was on the stairs. Kai closed the book, secured the latch, and returned it back to its rightful place. He knew he did not have much time, but he couldn't help but take a quick look through the satchel. The bottom was filled with knives, metal and wooden batons, a leather strap, and a chain. The scabbard on one blade bore the Milnos raven.

The brute climbed the stairs. Kai closed the pack, shoved it under the bed, and smoothed the bed skirt. One last scan of the room—everything looked correct. Kai climbed out the window back onto the wooden ledge. In his mind, he gleaned the brute opening the door as Kai slid between the gap spanning the two windows.

Heart pounding, he edged ever closer to his window. He inched along, hand over hand. He watched the brute slide his pack from its hiding place. After a search of the contents, he tossed the bag on the bed. Kai hooked one leg over the windowsill of his room, desperate to get inside. The man approached the window. Kai heaved himself inside and collapsed on the floor as the man leaned out his window.

◆ ◆ ◆

Alone, Kai walked back through the city. Hidden by shadows, he leaned against a Hightown warehouse to watch the guards patrol. He waited for Riome one street down from an old grate—the access point to the old armory where he trained with Riome and Dresnor. He knew where to go, but he was told to wait, so he waited. The streets of Hightown emptied. Still, he waited—for hours.

Down the street, Kai heard the click of shoes on cobblestone. He gleaned the area. The darkness faded. Ambient light illuminated the road. One figure strolled in his direction. Her brilliant light bloomed with his gleaning—a Half-Light. Happy to know it was Riome, he relaxed.

He heard a young woman's voice. "Hey, sailor. You mind walking a girl home?"

"My pleasure, little sister." He extended his elbow to Riome.

Riome stepped up to him, wearing a new dress with blue lace, and her hair pulled into a tight bun. A hefty bag hung from her shoulder. He assumed it carried the barmaid dress from the Drunken Dragon.

"Little sister? I am what, six or seven years older than you," she feigned displeasure.

Kai looked down on her. "Yes, but I am taller—little sister."

They strolled together down the street. "Why won't you tell me about your past?" he asked her.

"My secrets don't matter, Kai." Riome patted his arm.

Mystery and intrigue surrounded her like a warm blanket. She was the perfect spy. Kai wondered what she knew about their common heritage. Her inner light gave one secret away, whether she liked it or not, she was like him—a Half-Light.

Kai nodded to a passing guard. When the path was clear, they entered the grate-covered tunnel he used earlier. The tunnel was humid and warm from the water drainage pipes.

In the armory, Riome had Kai shake out the red dust from his hair before having him rinse the remaining dye in an old washbasin. Once the water ran clear, he changed into regular clothes and met her outside the Master General's tower. Kai's visits to Cazier had become so commonplace that no one gave him a second glance.

"What did you discover?" Cazier questioned.

Riome motioned to Kai. "You first, Kai."

"The man carried clothes, weapons, and a logbook, which read like a laundry list of torture. Entry after entry—date, punishment, and result. Whoever the prisoner was, the brute has been unable to break his character." Kai surmised. "Based on the date of the first entry, this prisoner has suffered nearly two years of physical and mental torture compounded by periods of sleep and food deprivation. The log details everything. Months of regimented beatings followed by hours of interrogation. The brute even logged dates of recuperation required before resuming, noting he feared killing the prisoner several times."

"Any notation about who the prisoner is or where?" Riome probed.

"I'm afraid not," Kai answered. "There was no mention of the prisoner's name or the information this prisoner was meant to divulge. If the brute was the torturer, according to his notes, he was sufficiently disappointed that he was unable to break the prisoner in question. The last entry mentions a pending transfer and a note to the prisoner's next jailor. The last summary stated: 'The prisoner refuses to submit—your mission—break him—befriend him and lead him to betray his country.'"

"To where?" Riome begged.

"Didn't say," Kai sighed. "Only gave a transfer date of six months from now. Although, now that I think about the exact words used, the brute mentioned the prisoner will need time to recover before he is ready to be moved to the port. Maybe he means to move the prisoner by ship."

Riome motioned to the door. "Good report, Kai. You may go."

"Wait, I want to know what you know." Kai looked between his cousin and Riome. "Who do you think this person is? You cannot shut me out."

Cazier said nothing. Riome shook her head no. Kai bolted to his feet and leaned over his cousin's desk. "So, I am a tool. You use me and toss me away. Why not use one of your other spies —unless you can't?" Kai studied their glances.

"It's not a matter of trust, Kai," Cazier insisted. "But you are correct. You are the only other person I could use for this mission. Riome understands the danger. I trust you—you are family, Kai. There can be no mistakes. We cannot miss our opportunity to rescue…" Riome tugged at Cazier, halting his monologue.

Kai stared at them both. "Please, I risked my life for the answers you wanted. The danger sure felt real while I dangled out a second-story window—twice."

"You know nothing of real danger and risk." Riome clenched her jaw. "This was a simple mission. I've spent years teaching you the craft, testing your skills. You still have a lot to learn. But you asked for this—to be a spy. We don't always get to know why we risk our lives. If you must know, we three are the only ones involved. This is not a highlight in your journal, Kai."

"I know better," Kai promised.

She only pondered her decision for a moment. "After you went upstairs," Riome explained, "a second man came into the pub, purchased a drink, and sat in the corner. He stared at the brute, as you call him. This new man looked like a scholar. He was entirely out of place in the Drunken Dragon. After your man went upstairs, I watched the newcomer. His face was familiar, yet different. Then you left. I meant to follow, but the brute came back downstairs. He sat with the scholar and handed him the honey-colored book you described.

"Naturally, I had to follow the scholar. Outside, I watched him enter a Hightown carriage and ride away. I was unable to keep pace," she concluded.

"So, let me ask again, who are you looking for?" Kai pressed. "You must have an idea who they have, even if you don't know where. Why do you care about this man?"

Riome's eyes turned away. Cazier waved his hand to steady her. "I care because he is my brother, King Andrew of Nebea," Cazier said. "We have been chasing news, or rather rumors that he is still alive. He's being held prisoner, but we don't know where or by whom."

"But we held a funeral for Andrew." Kai's brow furrowed together.

"What matters is I accepted the rank of Master General of Diu over becoming King of Nebea because I wanted access to the spy network my father developed here. My father was a strategist with the ability to see what is not evident to the average mind, as do I. If I were king, I would be forced to remain in Nebea, my brother Ashwin would be here. He lacks discernment."

"I hate to repeat myself," Kai leaned forward, "but Andrew died at sea. With his dying breath, your father said he saw Andrew fall overboard."

"True," Cazier nodded, "but, then there were rumors of an asset who was capable of breaking our ciphers and privy to our spy list, among other secrets. We heard this asset was being sold by the slave traders in Bangloo. The only person who would have all the information they mentioned is Andrew. I must save my brother. I serve your father because our two kingdoms are intertwined. We live, work, and fight as one."

There was sincerity in his cousin's eyes. Cazier was desperate to put his family back together. Kai knew what it meant to feel helpless to help those he cared for. Kai had only met Andrew a few times, but he remembered his kind eyes and sturdy handshake—simple but powerful memories of a great man. He continued to listen to Cazier.

"The trail went cold over a year ago, until now." Cazier waved his hand towards the fireplace. Kai presumed he motioned to a clue burned up in the flames, as was the Master General's way to conceal information delivered to Diu. "We heard an interrogator—your brute—was coming here to meet the Mind Master, Riome's scholar. We must root out the truth, if there is news about Andrew or this Mind Master, we'll find it."

While Kai listened to Cazier, he watched Riome tap her lips. He could see her eyes searching her memory. Then her eyes widened. "I do know him. He has changed significantly over the years. This Mind Master was an interrogation expert in Bangloo. I knew there was something familiar about him."

Kai thought about the details in the brute's book. The dates would certainly align with the attack at sea. Could Cazier's long-lost brother still be alive, a prisoner? He watched the Master General, his cousin, and Riome, the spy and his mentor. It felt good to be on the inside of their plans.

CHAPTER 3

Reflection

Stubble grazed across Prince Kai's knuckles as he ran his hand around his jaw. He stared at his reflection. *I should shave.* Yet he left his bathroom avoiding the task. Heavy-hearted, he pushed open his balcony doors and searched the predawn sky for answers he knew were not there.

At this early hour, only a few tiny lights dotted the waking city. He let his eyes scan the gardens below. Even from his corner of the palace, he still managed to see a portion of the great banyark tree. He was pleased that the tree no longer haunted him. Now it stood as a reminder; just as it reached for the sky, he would reach for his mother.

Kai thought about his life and the people closest to him. In two years, he would marry Amelia and move to Milnos. The concept overwhelmed him. He rubbed his forehead and tried to stop his overactive mind.

There were too many concerns to deal with. Duplicity loomed around his father's household, making it difficult to know the true nature of those closest to him. His stepmother Nola's motives concerned him the most. Her unnatural control over his father, not to mention his own experiences with her, made him wonder what she was planning. Was she involved with King Andrew's disappearance? He'd caught her more than once whispering privately with Regent Maxwell from Milnos. Cazier insisted Kai needed physical proof before accusing someone of treason. So far, it was his word against hers—his burden to bear.

Then there were his dreams. His Katori ancestry gave him many gifts, but unfortunately, not all were controllable. Visions either came in flashes—which often meant he had hours or maybe days to prepare for whatever they revealed—or slow, detailed clips, telling him he had months or longer to find a possible solution.

While the death of his mother no longer haunted him, he still begged for the opportunity to strike out and find her himself. Only he had no idea where to start. The Katori nation spent years searching with no luck. She may have been important to them at one time, but they had long since given up any hope of her recovery. Had this Keegan person taken her? A heavy burden weighed on his heart. Had he let her down again?

The wind tousled his hair and flipped the pages of his journal.

Kai smoothed the page and stared at the sketch of a strange armament that would someday strike down his friend. A piece from his vision. The nightmare of Drew's impending death now kept him awake. For more than a year, he had studied the scene around Drew's demise, preparing for the day he would race to save his friend. He only hoped that knowing the possible outcome meant he had the opportunity to change it. The fate of Drew hung in the balance.

Again, Kai's burden to bear.

In his lap, he flipped through the pages. A new handheld weapon was coming into the kingdom of Diu. One Kai did not understand. Drawn and redrawn, the device had a wooden handle and a silver barrel with a fluted end. None of the Diu men carried such a device. Everyone he asked had never seen anything like it before. But he had seen this weapon in a single brief moment after the return of his father two years ago. Kai's search of the armory had produced nothing.

This vision revealed a weapon that spat smoke, sparks, and shot a small iron ball across the sky, followed by a loud bang. His nightmare told him that Drew would be struck twice before he dropped to the ground dead. Kai needed to find this weapon, understand how it worked, and how to stop it.

Winter wind blew across his face, and the chill smelled of snow. Exhausted, he sighed at the thought of his coming day. Sleep had become a precious commodity. It was going to be another painfully long day with only a few hours of sleep.

Time for his morning training with Kempery-man Dresnor. Kai left his room, trying to remember if he'd completed his Bangloo essay for Professor Graydon. His education demanded the pursuit of academic knowledge, foreign languages, and world politics. Come nightfall his espionage lessons lay in the hands of Riome Timica—spy. Each day mimicked the next.

Kai took the spiraling staircase down the east spire to the old abandoned armory with Kempery-man Dresnor. The smell of musty dampness hung in the air. Spiders, rats, and bugs scurried away from the light. Dresnor carried a single lamp, lighting sconces on the wall along their way. Kai did his best to stifle a yawn. The air cooled as they descended. Their training room—an old, forgotten place—provided the anonymity they needed for his private lessons.

Kai looked at the back of Dresnor. The sides of his head trimmed to stubble and his long, pitch-black hair slicked back and tied with a cord. His usual scruffy beard now trimmed and brushed neat. Marabella's move from Town Hope to Diu two summers back had been a positive influence on Philip Dresnor. Kai was sure Dresnor would ask her to be his wife someday. She was the only good thing to come out of that terrible summer.

Something about today made Kai feel nostalgic. Dresnor reached the landing and led them down a short hallway and pushed open two wooden wrought iron doors. As he had done numerous times, Dresnor lit the sconces around the large stone room.

The white walls swept up into a high arched ceiling with exposed crisscrossed black wooden beams. The vast space was old, damp, and musty. Along the wall, Kai scanned the racks of weapons, various bits of beaten armor—padded and unpadded attack stands and targets.

Dresnor placed his lamp on a small table and turned to the armor. "Here, put this on," Dresnor handed Prince Kai a padded tunic and took one for himself. This tunic was considerably larger than the one he used in his first lessons. The latter now daggled unused on a hook.

Kai felt the thick batting quilted into the tunic and slid it over his head. The cotton fabric felt dry against his skin, but the sour smell flooded his nostrils. A full week of training had it past ripe.

Next, Dresnor handed him a silver shirt. The interlinking rings and overlapping miniature flat plates of the mail were surprisingly light considering it was metal. The combined weight, noticeable but not intolerable, distributed over his shoulders and biceps. Next Kai pulled a cuirass over his head and began to work the adjustable buckles; hard leather armor meant to protect his core. He synched the breastplate and backplate tight against his torso, adjusting until they felt snug, then he fine-tuned the spaulders attached to protect his shoulders.

Lastly, Dresnor gave him a pair of arm bracers, designed to protect his wrists and forearms. Kai knew the more armor his Kempery-man provided, the harder the lesson would be. He ran his fingers over the leather embellishments and straps. They were well worn and beaten. Marks in the leather told the story of battles long ago. His fingers grazed the wolf head pressed into the worn brown leather on his chest.

"Whose armor is this?" he asked, looking at the matching set his Kempery-man wore. "They are not what we usually wear."

"They once belonged to men under Adrian Cazier's father.

The Master General gave them to me since you have outgrown the other sets. Let the weight of them remind you of the responsibility of carrying a sword and the choices made wielding it."

After Hamrin, Kai struggled to find the balance between fighting, protecting, and taking a life. "I never knew you felt this way," Kai said, studying his friend and teacher. "I have watched you in battle. Your movements and blows are fearless—and unrelenting."

"You may never know the heart of another man. Consider your own soul. If we fight for another, I pray in the end l will be forgiven. Many argue the rights behind taking a life. It is an old argument and a timeless struggle. One you will have to answer for yourself." Dresnor picked up a sword and tested its balance.

"We won't bother with leg protection today. Although I promise you, a strike to the shins will put you on the ground quicker than you think." He held up a sheathed longsword to Kai. "Here. You can use this sword today."

Kai affixed the scabbard to his hip and unsheathed the sword. He held the black leather grip with both hands and held the sword up to inspect the fuller, or groove, that ran from the guard to the point of the blade. The edge was sharp and smooth.

While he warmed up his muscles with practice swings, Kai thought of his first morning learning to be aware of his surroundings—friend or foe. And the promise he made to Dresnor to never show off his skills or boast. Each swing was smooth yet deliberate. Side by side, they repeated choreographed cuts and thrusts—a series of overhand strikes down and across. Kai stepped into thrusts and jabs and retreated with blocks and dodges. Kai felt the weight of the blade with each methodical movement. His sword cut through the air, slicing imaginary foes.

Long swipes and short cuts, they were silent in their practice, quickening with each round. The sword's weight, once heavy and unnatural, was now smooth and fluid. Kai easily kept pace with his teacher. He felt the restraints of the armor, the weight of his sword—technique balanced by knowledge. "Remember," Dresnor instructed, "don't just use your hands, arms, and shoulders. Use your entire body."

Countless thoughts built up in Kai's mind. Going through the motions, his mind wandered. He was no longer focused on his lesson. His heart was not in his practice. Responsibility trumped his own desires to search for his mother. He cycled mechanically from one movement to the next. Memories slowed Kai's movements, and he fell behind.

Dresnor cleared his throat. "Are you training or daydreaming today?"

Kai snapped to attention. "I'm ready old man," he jested, thumping his fist against his chest.

"Now face me and attack." Dresnor motioned to Kai.

Swords and shields ready, the two men circle one another. Kai was no longer a boy. His height was now equal to Dresnor, and after years of training, so too was his build.

Dresnor made the first move. Kai parried and pushed back. Give and take, they crossed swords. One yielding ground, the other taking and then back again. Dresnor disarmed Kai. "Again," Dresnor insisted.

Kai shuffled his shoulders under the layers of protection and made the first move; swords rang out in the space once more. He kept his footwork close together, his elbows tight. With the next strike and block, Kai swept Dresnor's feet with a move Riome had taught him. Dresnor landed with a thud. Kai pressed a foot on Dresnor's wrist, which held his sword. With his sword at Dresnor's throat, he smiled.

"Again." Kai bowed and helped his teacher to his feet.

The pair continued for hours, one outmaneuvering the other and back again. Each now teaching, respectively. Selecting new moves, they challenged the mind of the other man to defend. Their styles became a mix of old and new techniques.

The shuffle of their feet was the only other sound. Over and over, Kai attacked, then blocked. Faster and faster they battled. Mid-motion, Dresnor egged him on. "Come on Kai, swing like you mean to cut me down. Is this how you fought Bevon? The monster of Hamrin."

The venom in Dresnor's words stung Kai, and he glared through their crossed swords. Dresnor pushed off and quickly sliced his sword at Kai, followed by more harsh remark. "You cannot defeat me, boy. I will cut you down," he said with a bit of a snarl.

The name Bevon fueled a rage within Kai. The man who'd tried to kill him during the battle for Hamrin. Heat welled in his chest. His mind twisted with anger, and Kai went harder, strike after strike he continued. Dresnor blocked and retreated, allowing Kai to push him back. Goading him more with each blow.

Bevon's face burned in Kai's mind—Dresnor became Bevon. Kai raged after his bitter memory. Improvising, he changed his attack, and Dresnor deflected each blow. Their pace was swift, each pounding strike elevated their breathing. Sweat rolled down their faces. Kai's jaw clamped tight, and his eyes glared.

The open space between them was closing. Dresnor parried later and later; Kai got closer with each challenge. Still, Kai launched attack after attack. Fury consumed his focus and blinded his thoughts. Dresnor rolled his sword on the next blow and disarmed Kai, his sword now pointed at Kai's chest.

"Be careful, my friend," Dresnor warned. "Never let someone goad you into a fight. Your emotions took over, and you missed my change in step, the angle of my sword. My shift in defense gave me the advantage you did not see coming. I allowed your blade to be caught further down my sword and closer to the tip of yours."

Kai stood there, speechless. His hand empty, his sword on the ground. "I'm sorry, Dresnor. I don't know what to say." He bent down and retrieved his sword.

"Don't apologize. That was all part of your lesson. Your opponent has more than his sword. He will try to get in your head. The better he knows you, the more he can use against you. In a real swordfight, the goal is to win. Half the battle gets fought here," he pointed to his temple, "in your mind." Dresnor clamped his hand on Kai's shoulder and gave him a nod. "Stir fear or plant doubt, and you may have the advantage."

The words of his teacher resonated truth. Kai needed to get a handle on his anger.

Exhausted, they placed their weapons back on the rack and removed their leather armor and mail. It felt good to be free of the confinement and weight. The padded tunic was now drenched in sweat and clung to Kai's body. His skin sticky and hot, he removed the tunic.

Dresnor changed into his shirt and looked at Kai. "If only we could take off the burdens of war like your tunic. Wash away the invisible scars." He took the tunic from Kai's hands.

Both tunics in hand, Dresnor snuffed the lights around the room. "I will see these laundered. Your father and Cazier are sending me on a mission. We must take a few days off. I have work to do with Kempery-man Farwick."

Kai nodded in agreement. He grabbed the lamp, and they climbed the stairwell of the east spire. The smell of fresh air greeted him at the top. He opened the door, and bright light spilled onto the landing. Squinting, he turned his head away from the brightness.

"You did well today. Enjoy the break and the upcoming Winter Festival." Dresnor waved and walked away.

Smoke sat waiting by the door. Together they made their way outside and down to the apple orchard. The bare trees bent and twisted in the wind, providing little shade in the midmorning sun. The day was surprisingly pleasant, given the nip in the air the night before. Kai found a dry spot in the center of the orchard and leaned against a tree.

While he waited, he let his mind wander around the palace grounds. He gleaned the bakery. Levi and Dori Kendrick, Rayna's parents, and their new assistant diligently worked the dough. He shifted his focus to their cottage—it was empty.

His mind wandered to the vegetable gardens, and there he finally found Rayna. Her hands in the dirt, tending plants. Around her, other gardeners turned the soil, removing dead plants and weeds, preparing the bed for spring planting. He marveled at her ability with plants, healthy and green, still producing fruit late into the winter season.

To see her with his own eyes, he moved near the edge of the orchard. In the gardens below, Rayna stood and dusted off her dirt-covered hands. She admired her handiwork and gathered the weeds she'd removed. He watched her drop the unwanted plants into the bin and walk in his direction.

A small smile bloomed in the corner of his mouth as he backed into the orchard. Caught in Rayna's honey-brown eyes, she smiled at him. Her long dark brown hair was woven into a tight braid behind her head. The front of her dress was a mix of flour and dirt. The two parts of her day.

His heart fluttered at the sight of her, and he ran his hand through his sandy brown hair. "Rayna," he said in a soft voice. He held his breath at the sight of her.

She batted her eyes in his direction. "Kai." Her smile was warm and subtle, her stride slow and graceful.

He stepped forward, closing the distance between them. Rayna's face was inches from his. Her creamy tan skin showed the slightest pink hue from the winter sun. He let his hand run down the side of her arm to touch the palm of her hand.

Rayna looked into his eyes and gasped. "Your eyes. I like it when you turn them green."

After his long morning, he was happy to have this moment, however fleeting. He dreamed about their future. "I am supposed to control the shift, but around you—I like the freedom."

She blushed and touched his cheek. "I like having our little secrets. I am glad we found each other. That you are teaching me what it means to be Katori."

His stomach fluttered at their closeness. "I came to tell you I won't be able to run with you for the next several nights. Riome has plans for me." He sighed at the thought of losing their time together.

"Can I still run with Smoke?" she asked. "It might be my only night, with your brothers' birthday in two days. There will be much to do in the bakehouse."

Rayna's presence hypnotized him. From the first day he met her, he was awestruck. "You may. I will search for you after dinner. If you're ready, I will send Smoke to you."

She looked towards her home. "I should go, I have chores, and you have class," she reminded him. Her hand slipped from his as she left.

CHAPTER 4

Keep the Faith

Head pounding, Kai leaned against the wall of the great hall. The marble was cool and smooth against his back. Even at the late hour, the Winter Festival was still in full swing. The room swarmed with Lords and Ladies, high-society people, and his extended family. Everyone danced, ate, and exchanged gifts. Blessed by Alenga for another year.

His cousin Alana buzzed in his ear, prattling on and on. Kai half-listened, his attention distracted by his departing brothers. Aaron and Seth headed to bed, too young to stay up through to the new year's hour. He envied their youth and lack of responsibility. It wasn't long ago that he went to bed at this hour.

Iver and his stepmother Nola bounced from guest to guest and then glided onto the dancefloor; a king and queen in the height of life. Kai had done his duty by dancing with Amelia, and he shuddered at the memory of everyone fawning over them. Kai didn't mind dancing; it was their future together that terrified him. The entire dance Amelia talked about Tolan as he daydreamed of Rayna.

Now Tolan and Amelia danced, and Alana chastised their choices. She was practical about letting duty dictate their lives. He shook his head in agreement, wishing she would stop talking. There was no use arguing with Alana. He didn't begrudge Amelia and Tolan their affections. He knew they would either find a way to change their fate or at least enjoy the last of their time with the ones they really loved.

"Alana, please forgive me, I need some air." Kai bowed and left the great hall. The evening was unusually warm for this time of year. He made his way to the small baker's home with two gifts; one wrapped in blue velvet and tied with a pink ribbon, the other a wooden box.

According to Kendra, he'd found the perfect gift. A must for any young Kodama. Kendra had explained that in Katori, people dedicated to plants and healing were called Kodama. Before he reached her home, Rayna stepped outside. Her dark hair framed her oval face, and her festive blue dress accentuated her maturing figure.

"Good evening, Kai. May Alenga bless you in the coming year." She took a seat on the small bench outside of their cottage and patted the spot next to her. She had a small, modestly wrapped gift in her hand.

He took the seat. "Good evening, Rayna. May Alenga bless you in the coming year." A playful smile curled his mouth. "I saw you at the Parade of Candles."

"I noticed," she blushed. "The Parade of Candles was, as always, amazing. We managed a much better spot this year. We went earlier to the Central City Gardens to see the winter-blooming plants and took a blanket to sit on the lawn. Mother didn't want to miss it. We left early to avoid the crowds swarming the streets. You would be surprised how early people go to get a good spot." She chuckled. "I guess the royal gazebo is reserved, so your view is guaranteed."

He nodded. "The parade was lovely, but I wish we could've sat together. I believe they are still playing music and dancing in the streets to this hour. If you listen, you can still hear the flutes and violins."

They sat in silence, listening to the faint music floating

over the wall. Kai watched two guards patrolling near the cottages. The men glanced in their direction but did not stop. He knew how they looked; the prince sitting with the baker's daughter in the middle of the night.

They spoke at the same time, excited to exchange gifts. "I brought you…" started Kai. "I hope it's alright…" started Rayna. Together they blushed. "You go first," she offered.

He hesitated, nervous about his gift. "Please, you go first," he insisted, setting her package on the bench at his side.

She laid a small package in his now empty lap. Wrapped in simple brown paper and tied with a blue ribbon, he felt the shape. He knew the form and feel of a book beneath the wrapper. Carefully he untied the ribbon and unwrapped the gift. Inside was a saddle-brown leather-bound journal, on the surface a two-tone embossed design of the tree of life. He ran his fingers over the design and the silver button secured with a leather tie. Along the bottom, he noticed his initials 'K.G.' embossed in black near the corner of the journal.

He recognized Abram Denholm's handiwork, and the publisher's stamp set inside the cover. The man was the best bookmaker in town. "Rayna, this is beautiful." He turned the journal over in his hands and marveled at the detail. His fingers traced the lines of the tree's roots. He didn't dare tell her she had spent too much. She must have saved all year to buy such a gift. "Thank you, I will cherish it always." Carefully he rewrapped the journal, set it aside, and passed her his two packages.

Her eyes widened at the weight he laid in her lap. She pulled the tie. The blue velvet fell to her lap. The top item was another beautiful journal created by Denholm publishing. A unique design made just for her.

Abram had helped him select a fanciful enchanted theme in vibrant hues of pink gold, moss, and sienna. The center held a heart-shaped emerald gemstone surrounded by intricate brass filigree, flowers, and eight matching oval cut emeralds. The bottom was embossed with her first name, Rayna, and the page edges dusted in stunning gold shimmer.

She released the gold clasp and flipped through the empty pages. "Kai, this is beautiful." She gently set the journal aside and briefly thumbed through the next three books.

"I bought those on my last trip to Port Anahita," he said. "I found a local apothecary who was willing to part with them. The books are filled with different plants from Nebea, Milnos, and Bangloo."

Rayna set the books aside. Kai started to fidget. "I hope you like this next one. The man at the shop swore it was a must for any serious apothecary or herbalist. It is not a fancy or delicate item." He worried its rough texture was less than beautiful. More practical than girly.

"Kendra told me to be a proper Kodama you must study herbs. The Kodama are highly revered for their ability to heal, at least that is what I understand." Kai nodded for her to open the package.

She opened the large wooden box. Inside was a white and gray granite mortar and pestle for grinding herbs. Excitedly she set the package on the ground at her feet. Before he knew what happened, she leaned over, hugged him, and kissed him square on the lips. A small peck, over before it happened.

Shocked by what she'd done, Rayna pressed her hand to her mouth and blushed shyly. She sat straight and looked towards the orchard. "Thank you, Kai. I love it," she said from behind her fingers.

Worried her parents might have seen them from the window, Kai sat frozen, afraid to move. "I, umm, I am happy you like it."

His stomach flipped with delight. Unsure what to do next, he rubbed his palms together. "Well, I love my journal. Thank you. I hate to dash off, but it is rather late," he said in a nervous tone.

She reassembled her wrappings. "It is late," she stood and collected her gifts. "I should check on my mother. Thank you again, Kai. Goodnight." She opened the door, glanced back, and smiled.

He waited for her to go inside; his new journal clutched tightly to his chest. Preoccupied, he meandered through the apple orchard. The night breeze blew through the trees. Ahead of him, he heard soft footfalls. Instinctively he reached out with his sight. At the same time, he heard a voice. "Kai, we need to talk."

Recognizing the voice, Kai saw Tolan walking in his direction. "Tolan. What is it? Is there something wrong?"

A mature young soldier, almost twenty years of age, Tolan's muscular build filled out his Fort Pohaku uniform. Tolan was taller and broader than Kai, even with his two years of training with Dresnor.

"Sorry for loitering in the orchard. I did not want to interrupt your moment. Not that your relationship with Rayna helps the four of us. I could not help but notice there is something between you two. I know you are aware of my affections for Amelia, which brings me to why I am standing in the middle of the orchard near midnight, on the eve of a new year."

Moonlight lit Tolan's face, leaving Kai's hidden partly in shadow. "I am aware of your feelings for Amelia. And I understand that my relationship with Rayna is no secret either. I believe we find ourselves in a rather unfortunate situation. Wanting what we cannot have. Or rather whom. Do you have a point?" Kai asked.

Tolan shifted his weight and crossed his arms. "I have no right to ask anything of a prince," he nodded. "Especially you."

"Are we not friends? I thought we made our peace years ago."

"You continue to amaze me. After the years of bullying, you are kind to me. You saved my service rank after Landon and I attacked you. Now I will be honest. I am in love with the girl you are meant to marry, and I am here hoping to have your blessing."

Kai wished he could give Tolan what he wanted, but it was beyond him.

"Tolan, if I could give you my blessing, I would. Amelia is a sister to me, and as you said, I have a connection with Rayna. Everyone tells me that our wishes are irrational. To even think we have a choice is foolish." Kai noticed the shift in Tolan's posture—head hung low, and his hands stuffed into his pockets.

"It is my duty to represent Diu." Kai stood up taller. "I hate it as much as you, the thought of going to Milnos haunts me. Everything I read tells me the city is nothing like Diu. They do not cherish art, culture, or science. I know from our history lessons Milnos has always hated Diu. Even before the war, Milnos meant to conquer this land. They wanted our entire continent under their rule, but Nebea fought back and held their own. Diu, however, struggled. We were not large enough. Our union with Nebea and the Katori saved Diu. But to this day, even without the support of Bangloo, Milnos is a massive war-hungry city."

"I don't need a history lesson, Kai."

"Maybe I do." Kai puffed up his chest. "I need to remind myself of the stakes. Without a marriage union between Diu and Milnos, the peace may not last. They could turn on us once more. Regent Maxwell could proclaim himself King and break the contract my father established all those years ago."

"So, what do we do?" Tolan asked. "I have been petitioning to get assigned near Milnos. I don't want to lose her, but if you marry her, I will not stand in the way. I will not have her live a lie, married to you and sneaking around with me. That would be wrong."

Kai nodded in agreement. "I would not wish a life of lies for anyone. None of us will live a lie or cheat in the shadows. I will do my duty if Alenga sets me on that path. But know this, I have no desire to marry Amelia. I don't know how to change our current path, but our fate is in the hands of Alenga. Trust me when I tell you, my destiny is with Rayna. I have seen it."

Tolan shook his head. "I pray you are right."

"Have faith but tell no one. We both need to do better hiding our feelings. Or at least hiding our motives. I believe your advancement could be the secret behind our freedom. Whatever you can do to raise your rank, it will help us. Your father must entrust you to run important missions, lead your own group of men. The rank of captain would set you apart. To be a captain, you must show them your aggressive side. You've always been a competitive person; show them you are committed. Lead by example and become the man your father expects."

Kai thought of Drew. Once just another guard on the wall, Drew took whatever assignment he could—and now he was a captain. "As I said, volunteer for whatever assignment raises your rank. Put in extra hours. Work with other captains. You must become a captain." He had no idea how long they had, but he knew they must be ready.

Tolan huffed. "Those assignments will keep me from Diu. I will not be able to see Amelia as often, and they will not put me in Milnos either. That would keep me in Fort Pohaku, which is exactly what my father wants. Me in his shadow."

Kai looked to the ground and shook his head. He could not help what he knew. His vision was clear. Tolan would be in a battle, and his rank was captain. Somehow he knew Tolan's status was critical. "Trust me, Tolan. I've seen your rank. You will be the youngest captain in history if things are to unfold as I have seen them." Kai gulped. Had he said too much? "I cannot tell you more, but you must become a captain. The cost of time now away from Amelia will seal our future and the rest of our lives." Convinced his visions were real, he pressed Tolan again. "Please, Tolan. I know this will not be easy, but it is the only way."

Tolan stroked his chin, trimmed into a short goatee. "I trust you. We seal our fate with your plan. You better be right." He extended his hand, and they locked arms.

"Have faith in Alenga. She will change our fates." Kai let Tolan's arm go, and they returned to the palace.

Overwhelmed and exhausted, Kai inched towards the exit.

He felt weariness creep through his bones. He hadn't slept soundly in weeks. Worrisome nights of contemplation and visions of the future left little time for sleep. Only sheer exhaustion eventually allowed Kai a few hours of slumber.

The next few weeks would be more of the same. Kai wished he could enjoy his night off, dance, and celebrate with his friends and family. Instead, he slunk along the wall and slipped out without saying goodnight.

CHAPTER 5

Snow Fall

Disinterested in attending dinner, Kai laid down on his bed to get a few hours rest before meeting Riome for his nightly training. He drifted off to sleep where his nightmares found him. The relentless vision around Tolan and Drew; the day in his aunt Helena's garden. His mind was full of frantic images, each coming faster and faster. His breathing quickened, and his heart pounded.

Ripped from his nightmare, he woke hot and covered in sweat. He slid his feet off the bed and went to lie on the rug beside Smoke. Lack of sleep was beginning to take its toll. He was near his breaking point, and it was just weeks from his sixteenth birthday.

His only solace was that his exhaustive pace made the days pass quickly. But the lack of meditation time had him bubbling with anxiety. "Seems my nightmares don't care that I've had no sleep." He ran his hand over his wolf's fur.

After another two hours' sleep, he awoke stiff on the floor next to his wolf. As much as he wanted to skip his training, Cazier insisted that he never miss a session. His cousin even came to some of Kai's lessons to see the improvement firsthand. He hoped this was not one of those nights.

He descended the east spire stairwell, his lamp flickering

downward. Riome never lit the sconces. She preferred the tower to be left dark and mysterious. He reached out with his sight. Bugs and critters scurried around the corner. He used his gift to venture down to the old chamber they used to train in private.

Illuminated with light, he saw Riome set down her lamp and select her weapons of choice for the evening. He entered and placed his lamp on the table. She offered him no padding, no armor. He had only his wits and his skill.

Like most nights, Riome said very little. Tonight, she started with throwing stars. She fired one after the other at a wooden target. Her aim was accurate, and she hit dead center with all five. Now it was Kai's turn. Only this time, she stood in front of the target and short sword in each hand. He knew better than to question her methods, so he tossed all five.

Her reaction time was wicked fast. Unusually fast, if Kai was honest with himself. With a twist and flick of her wrist, she deflected each star. They bounced off her swords and struck the ground. Kai knew what came next. His turn.

Surprisingly calm, he stood in front of the target, a blade in each hand. Riome would not take it easy on him; he needed his reactions to be instantaneous. When she raised her hand, he held his breath. He knew it was cheating, but he wanted to go unscathed just once.

In rapid succession, she tossed all five. The shiny metal stars flew in Kai's direction. He grabbed at the moment and time slowed. With ease he deflected the attack and let go of time. Riome was not pleased. "You must breathe, Kai. Do it again."

She collected the stars. "Center yourself. Focus on the lead star but watch my hand and where I aim."

Had he not done it already? There was no way she knew he cheated. Right? Still, he stood, swords up, and he focused on her hands. While he watched Riome release each star, her subtle flicks revealed their intended path. This time he did not cheat. Focused on her release, he knocked each star out of the air before they struck his body. This was the first time he got all five without so much as a scratch.

"Good," was all she said before changing weapons. Next Riome grabbed a set of battle batons, mid-range wooden staffs with a leather grip near the center. She tossed one to Kai and motioned for him to attack. With both hands on the staff, Kai pivoted his body and lunged. They started out slow. Strike, block, counterstrike, block, and retreat. Then Riome went.

They practiced over and over, faster and faster. Until he lost a step and Riome landed a strike on his thigh. Kai winced and fell to one knee. "What's wrong?" Riome questioned. "You never miss a block anymore."

Kai took a deep breath and collected himself. "I'm fine. Let's keep going."

"Hand me your staff," she insisted, placing hers on the table. "Change of plans." Riome moved back into position and shifted through an ancient Bangloo tradition; a graceful form of exercise. A series of movements performed in a slow, focused manner and accompanied by deep breathing. She taught him the various moves and how they worked.

Without questions, he found his place at her side and mirrored her choreographed movements, meant to align the body, mind, and soul energy. His breathing relaxed, his mind calmed. Their shadows bounced about the walls in the wavering light.

They moved in silence; each posture flowed into the next. Their constant motion lulled Kai's spirit and released tension. This was just what he needed. Her silence spoke volumes. She was a good teacher. He appreciated the change.

After they completed the movement, Riome turned and bowed to him. He bowed in return. Then she began her closing posture; he followed suit. Eyes closed once more; palms cupped facing up. He inhaled and drew his hands up to his chest, pulling his energy with his movement. On exhale, he rotated his hands and pressed downward, pushing his energy to the floor.

After several repetitions, Riome stopped. She bowed again and took a seat on a wooden bench. Her voice broke the evening's silence. "I have a new lesson to teach. It requires you to listen and consider," Riome announced. "I must teach you how to survive should you get discovered. We are spies, and the chances are high that at some point you will be captured."

Kai put up his hand to stop her. "I know you and Cazier think I am ready for this, but some days I feel like I will never be a good spy. I'm a prince, too recognizable. Now you want me to know what it's like to get captured?"

"It falls to me to teach you all I know. Some of these techniques you may never have cause to use. But you should be ready. I am planting a seed in your mind. One I pray you will never need to retrieve." She squinted at him as she often did when he would argue. "Yes, you are a prince, but not all know your face well. You can still be of value."

Unwilling to argue he relented. "Please continue."

Riome composed herself. "As a prince, your royal status will grant you access to any palace. I will teach you the art of disguise. With it, you can go anywhere. But if you're caught searching a room, reading correspondence, or eavesdropping on conversations, you need to know how to talk your way out. If you find it does not work, you need to know what to do next.

"When captured, most spies take poison to avoid interrogation and pain, while others will kick, claw, bite, even cut off a limb to escape. We are not animals. Your body is strong, yet easily broken. Your mind is stronger, yet easily confused. Your spirit is limitless. Remember who you are." Half her face was hidden in darkness, and her words felt eerie. "Fear kills the mind. Your suffering is temporary. Ignore the pain. You may feel trapped. Still, you must wait. Know your enemy. Establish a routine and let them see a broken man. Routine makes people complacent. Use that. Be submissive."

"Do you think this will matter? None of my missions have ever put me in any real danger. Right?"

"It matters," she insisted. "Stripped of my disguises, I was nobody. They had no leverage, and I eventually escaped." She gestured in his direction. "You are a prince. That will either hurt you or help you. Be prepared either way. When you see your chance, take it." She picked up her lamp and made for the door.

"Riome, why are you telling me this? Where are you going? You have a mission, and you are not telling me something."

"We do not know our future, Kai." She spun to face him. "I must prepare you for everything. Plant seeds in your mind. Ideas to keep you alive and strong even in your darkest hours. They are also words to remind me of the lessons I've learned. Mark my words—something is coming. I fear neither of us will be ready." She turned and charged to the door.

"But wait," he called at her back.

"That is enough for tonight. Remember my words. I will be away for the next few nights. Maybe longer. Get some rest, you look exhausted. Goodnight, Kai." She slipped into the dark hallway and did not look back.

There would be no use chasing her—spies never reveal anything. All too often she threw information at him like one of her throwing stars. They were meant to strike deep and leave a mark on his mind. Although her vulnerability was something new. She had never shown any fear before. Though faint, Kai sensed her concern. He let out a sigh and grabbed his lamp.

When he realized the time, he took the steps two at a time as he climbed the stairwell. His pace quickened. He turned out the lamp and left it on the hallway table. Without delay, he made for the breezeway near the orchard. Smoke was not there.

Kai closed his eyes and relaxed his breathing. Somewhere in the dark, Rayna ran. He needed her. Connected to Smoke, he found them passing the southern gatehouse. Eyes open, he hopped the breezeway railing and made his way down the stone stairs towards the garden.

The cold, crisp wind chilled his skin. His thin shirt was a poor choice, but he wasn't about to waste time changing. He had not seen Rayna face-to-face in over two months, since the Winter Festival. He ran towards the gardens to intercept her path. A guard leaning against a wall shuffled to attention when he saw Kai run in his direction.

Hoping for privacy, he ran away from the guard. He dashed beyond the garden sheds and waited. Rayna came from the right, fast and steady, Smoke at her side. Kai leaned around the shed to catch her attention.

Her eyes beamed as she slowed. Thrilled to see him, she wrapped her arms around his neck. Her cold cheek pressed against his and she squeezed him tight. He wrapped her in his arms and scooped her off the ground.

"This is the best birthday gift ever," she responded gleefully. "I've missed you."

His shoulders slumped, and he lowered her feet to the ground. "Oh, Rayna, I forgot. I'm so sorry. I missed your birthday. I meant to..." He stopped midsentence. "I have been so busy," he said, but his apology felt hollow. He hadn't planned anything. Between classes and training, he had merely forgotten. Embarrassed, he let her slip from his grasp.

"I understand." She stepped back.

Kai took a good look at her. Long pants and boots changed her figure. A look he was not sure he liked. Pants stole her delicate girl grace he was so fond of. Kai turned and walked along the wall, her hand in his. "Tell me. How does it feel to be sixteen?" he asked, desperate to make idle conversation.

"It should mean independence. My mother says I am a grown woman now." She laughed, squeezing his hand. "I think she expects me to find a man to marry. Both my parents expect me to be practical." She twisted her hair with her free hand.

"In less than a week, you will be sixteen, too. Someone forgot to shave again this morning." She teased, brushing her fingers across his stubble.

"Don't remind me, I hate shaving."

They walked along the wall hand-in-hand and Smoke followed. Months of pent up frustration melted away. "How are your herbalist studies coming?" he asked.

"I have read all the books you gave me. I am also researching some of the plants you suggested." She swung their clasped hands back and forth. "Professor Grayden was kind enough to lend me a few botany journals, and thanks to your recommendation, I've had a few classes with a local apothecary."

"Sounds great. I will have to get you new books this summer," he said without thinking.

He hated to contemplate leaving already. In a little over two months, he would travel to Albey, a new town far to the east around Baden Lake. Three months without her. His last summer trip before moving to Milnos.

"Right." Her mood mellowed. "Albey."

A group of guards was gathered near the Mryken kennels, so Kai turned them around. Their mood had already shifted, and he didn't want to make it any more awkward by weaving through a security guard change. Once they were close enough, he pulled her toward the apple orchard.

The sky darkened with heavy gray clouds. Winter wind whipped around them, leaving a few tiny snowflakes in its wake. Surprised, Kai stopped and looked up. "Did you see that?" The smallest snowflakes trickled down. Slowly more fell. With each passing flake, they grew larger. He looked down at Rayna, her outstretched palm catching snowflakes.

"Rayna, glean to see the energy within the snow. They look like tiny stars falling from the sky." He took a deep breath and felt the energy within his soul. Connected, he followed the power outward. His mind expanded, and he saw the world glow. Eyes open, Kai's gift of gleaning mixed with his natural view of the world. He saw Rayna's face in detail, outlined in a white glow.

Her eyes closed. Kai watched her soft, delicate features embellished by the light. Snow melted on her cheeks and eyelashes. When she opened her eyes, she smiled. "Of all the gifts we have, seeing the snow set aglow is my favorite," she said, looking into his eyes. "Well, that and being able to find you on your balcony when you can't sleep." She blushed.

He grinned at her comment. If they could not be side-by-side, it was nice to see her in his mind. The simplest gesture, just a wave from her, helped him get through his day. There was no denying the bond they shared. *If only this moment could last forever.*

Although he did not have forever, he could make the moment longer. The wind around them subsided. Snow fell softly, barely reaching the ground. Tiny star-like flakes floated down around them. He held his breath. His soul embraced the moment. Kai looked down. Caught in Rayna's eyes, his heart swelled with emotion. Time slowed, and snow hung midair. Magic buzzed in the air, tickling the hair on his bare arms.

He wrapped his arm around her waist and pulled her into his arms. Her beautiful face he cupped with his other hand. "May I kiss you," he asked softly.

She replied by pressing her lips to his. For a moment, the rest of the world stood still. Nothing else mattered but her. He felt his soul join with hers. Deep inside, he sensed a connection that would last a lifetime. Kai wished he could make that moment last longer, but as he held her in his arms, he felt time slowly resume. He could hold the moment no longer. The snow drifted downward, and the winter wind returned. They parted. He wanted to kiss her again. His heart pounded in his chest and heat warmed his face. As much as he hated it, he knew she needed to go.

"Rayna, you should go home before the storm gets worse or your parents come searching."

She blushed and ran her fingers over her lips and pressed her other hand over his heart. "Our first real kiss. I will cherish it."

He laid his hand on top of her hand. She was right; he knew no other moment would compare to this. He wanted to tell her he loved her, but he held his tongue and let her go.

CHAPTER 6

King's Day

It had been two months since Kai's sixteenth birthday. The city bells rang for his father just after sunrise. The hour of Iver's birth. Today was King's Day, the celebration of Iver's birthday. Everyone gathered in the great hall for an early breakfast to celebrate. Kai wished it had just been family, but Nola insisted on inviting dukes from around the land.

Any excuse to coordinate an event, Nola insisted on having lords and ladies at the palace. Cazier felt it was important to her to exercise her power as queen and build a reputation with the people, but Kai hated how she paraded Aaron and Seth, her twin boys, and little Cordelia around as the future of Diu. Even though he was destined to be king of Milnos, and Aaron, the first-born twin, would be the heir to the Diu thrown, it still felt forced. Today was no exception.

Throughout the morning, he heard her tell various guests Iver was grooming Aaron to be the future of Diu, his heir to the seat of power. Although being crowned king would only happen in the event of his father's death, and Aaron was only ten, Nola seemed determined to garner favor with the lords and ladies in Diu, instilling the idea of Aaron as their future king.

Typically, very celebratory, Iver was subdued and distant today. Since Kai's summer in Chenowith and Iver's return from his summer at sea, his father had not been the same. For weeks after, his father laid sick and unavailable. Nola hovered constantly. Sigry, the palace physician, would only say he was resting, exhausted from his trip abroad. Even now, Iver's color was muted. His eyes lacked their usual shine. Somber, Iver sat watching Nola flit around the room.

Today Kai felt set aside. Nola had placed his brothers on either side of Iver, leaving him to sit beside her. Nola sat on Aaron's left with her back turned slightly, blocking Kai's view of his father. Glass raised, she clinked the side to gather everyone's attention. "Thank you, lords and ladies of Diu, for joining my children and me in celebrating King Iver's blessed birthday. We give thanks to Alenga, the blessed earth mother for all she gave us. Long live the King of Diu." She lifted her glass and drank.

In unison, the group echoed in return, "Long live Iver, King of Diu. Long live the King."

Iver raised his hand, tamping down the air to calm the cheers and applause. "Thank you all for being here. Following the parade, please join us in the park later this afternoon for Linlou's newest performance in flower design as we again give Alenga thanks and welcome summer."

Then he rose to his feet and made his way to Helena, his twin sister. She rose and hugged him tightly. "Happy birthday, sister," he whispered. "I am happy you were able to travel from Port Anahita."

Kai watched them walk together. Their bond made him wonder what it felt like to have a twin. His twin brothers shared a similar bond; they had the unique ability to speak without words.

It was moments like this that made him miss his mother. In his heart, he remembered how close they were. As much as he loved his father, the bond with his mother was different. And now, Kai noticed a growing distance between him and his father. Only a few fleeting moments reminded him of their once-close relationship. He knew if his mother were here today, she would bring them together. They would be one happy family, instead of divided.

After the parade, everyone climbed the stone stairs leading up into the Diu Central City Gardens. The first thing Kai noticed was the addition of raised potted white flowers with large blue ribbons. Diu guards dotted the pathways throughout the park, each armor-clad man gleaming in the afternoon sunlight.

In the garden center, his immediate family took the white stone stairs leading to the left terrace, all except Iver and Nola. The lords and ladies of Diu went right to another raised garden; both lined with armored Kempery-men and additional guards. At the top of the garden, long white linen tables decorated with blue ribbons and fresh white flowers awaited them. Each table was littered with mixed fresh fruit, sweet and savory tarts, and teas.

While everyone relaxed and enjoyed the view from the raised gazebo, Iver and Nola selected flowers with Linlou. Kai watched their exchange. Linlou, with her sketchbook, took careful notes, as she continued trying to interact with Iver. At each section, Nola fervently interjected and pointed to different plants than Iver suggested. Still, Linlou took notes, looking at Iver as if she hoped he would countermand Nola.

Kai wondered how Linlou could create anything to please two people who couldn't be more opposite if they tried. When they finished, Linlou began to scratch her head. She looked at the plants and then referred to her notes. Iver had always made his suggestions alone. Nola's contradictive instructions would make this her most challenging design by far.

Kai watched Nola chaperone Iver around the group. It was the strangest sight to see her lead his father. There was indeed a new dynamic happening between them, a noticeable change in his father's demeanor. If only Kai could get a moment alone with him, but Nola never left his side.

The situation called for finesse. Kai waited for his opportunity. When Nola reached for a cup of tea, she let Iver's arm drop. His father stood frozen as if unable to leave her side. Kai took the opening. Silently he slipped between them, took his father's arm and ushered him away. Kai weaved Iver through the crowd of family and servants. He rushed his father down the steps, out of sight.

"Father, you should see the fabulous creation Linlou is creating." Kai gestured to the plants.

Iver acted lost. "Where is Nola? She should see this too." He tried to pull away, but Kai kept a firm grasp and marched his father around the gardeners, who were busily working to plant Linlou's design.

Kai hated being in their way, but this was the first time he and his father had been alone since last summer's end. "Father, I leave for Albey soon. Can we spend time alone before I go?"

Iver tugged again at Kai's arm. He acted like a small child wanting to sit after a long walk. Kai thought of Nola and how she treated his father. She hovered insistently. Without her, Iver's mind was lost in a fog. Kai needed to get through.

Rubbing the back of his father's hand, he felt Iver relax. Kai tapped Iver's hand lightly as he'd seen Nola do hundreds of times. "Don't worry father, I am here with you. Nola wanted me to show you the gardens," he said in a soothing tone.

Distance. We need to put distance between Nola and us. The farther he pulled his father away from the others, the more confident Kai felt. It was good to be alone with his father, even if it was but for a moment. Kai directed them to the opposite side of Linlou's workers, and he dared a look back.

A lump formed in Kai's throat when he spotted Nola. She stood at the top of the stone stairs. Kai was sure she was furious. She glared in their direction. He could tell she was eager to snatch his father away, but people continued to take her hand and chatter at her. While she played the dutiful queen, she kept a keen eye on them, never wandering away from the stairs.

"Father, are you still planning your trip abroad this year?" Kai asked. "I have not heard anything about where you are going. There are no signs of preparations for your departure."

"Son, are you leaving?" Iver asked, confused. "Is it summertime again already? My, how you've grown. You are as tall as me now. Nola believes I should stay home this summer. I did not fare well after my last trip. I might send Kempery-man Farwick without me. Or maybe Dante could go in my stead. He would do fine." Iver's voice lacked its usual confidence; his eyes were glassy and red.

This was news to Kai. Last summer his father had a successful journey—without Nola. Her absence was the key. When given enough time without her, his father improved. Only after Iver's return did he change. Clearly, she was not interested in Iver leaving without her this year.

Not wanting to press his luck or draw attention to monopolizing his father, Kai circled back towards the terrace. Seeing their return, Nola burst through the crowd and descended the stairs to grab Iver. Her face pursed with frustration. "Iver, darling, you shouldn't overexert yourself. Kai, you know better. Your father is unwell. He should not do so much walking in this heat." She pulled Iver halfway up the stairs.

Kai nodded in agreement. "Yes, Nola." He wanted to protest, but he knew everyone would only see what she wanted them to see. A weak man withering away, and a loving wife tending to his every need.

"My apologies Nola, I only wanted him to see the design up close. They are finishing now." He pointed to Linlou, who was approaching the stairs.

Linlou bowed and motioned towards the completed gardens. Everyone from above applauded and cheered. Curious, Kai turned and glanced over the design. While he had every faith in Linlou's ability, he knew their incompatible selections would provide a challenge. However, to his delight, she had created a magnificent display.

She used Nola's selection of small muted colors to create a blended backdrop for Iver's vibrant selections of taller plants. The design was a three-dimensional tiered masterpiece. The once-flat garden was now a rolling mound of flowers and sculpted ivy structures. On one side, she even installed an oval-shaped koi fishpond and a small bench.

In a rush, everyone hurried down the stairs to walk around the garden, each stopping at the small bench to marvel at the fish. Even though Kai wanted to enjoy his father's birthday, he felt terrible that he was leaving for the summer. He feared for his father.

All he could do was hope his cousin would notice upon his return. The Master General had been in Nebea since the Winter Festival. With Kai's emanant departure, they would most likely miss each other. Thoughts of telling Riome came to mind, but she had gone missing these past few days. She was most likely on a mission, and he was not told where she had gone.

Hands stuffed deep in his pockets; he followed the group for the rest of their outing until they rode back in the carriage to the palace.

With his family commitment done, Kai stood in the orchard watching the sky go from orange to purple, his cousin Gideon by his side. "I am glad we were able to say goodbye," Kai said. "I will certainly miss seeing you each day at the palace, cousin. I cannot believe we both leave in a few days. You are headed home to Port Anahita, and I am bound for Albey. Are you ready to move home permanently?"

Gideon stood proud, his shirt buttoned high on his neck, his hand grasping the side of his vest. "Yes and no. Moving now means I will be close to my parents. I am pleased to no longer travel back and forth. And I am excited to learn more about how to run the port warehouses." His face turned gloomy. "Completing my final year of education traveling with my father is exciting, but in turn, I leave behind Victoria. She has another few months left with the professor. We must wait until we are eighteen before I can ask her to marry me."

"Marriage, Gideon?" Kai questioned.

He knew they were close, but he had no idea Gideon was ready for marriage. Kai fell left behind by everyone's plans. *I have been too consumed with my training.* How could he have no idea what was happening around him?

"When you know, you know. What can I say? She is the one for me. Besides, she is a port city lady, and my prospects are limited. Every other family of note has sons. There is Trudy, but come on, you must admit, she is odd. Thick glasses, always spouting facts about history, and her squeaky little voice strikes my last nerve. Not to mention, she is two inches taller than I am. Awkward," Gideon declared. Then a delicate smile lit up Gideon's face. "Now, Victoria. Her angelic face and graceful nature... Well, I would be a lucky man if she will have me. We have so much in common, and we have talked about marriage. I had to be sure she felt the same."

"The two of you make a good pair, you are both fortunate," Kai added.

"I must thank you for the push," Gideon elbowed Kai. "Asking her to dance was the best thing for both of us. After the Winter Festival, two years back, our relationship changed. We are both rather shy, you know. All we needed was a moment together. We've talked nearly every day since."

Kai was happy for his cousin, and he slapped a hand on his shoulder. "Well, you let me know the day, and I will be there. Just remember, you have to ask her first." He chuckled at the thought.

"I will miss our talks, Kai," Gideon said. "I have no close friends in Port Anahita. You better come and visit me. A promise is a promise."

Gideon raised an eyebrow at Kai. "How can you let their

relationship go on?" He gestured towards the gardens below. "Amelia is meant to be your wife. Everyone talks about her and Tolan. You should put a stop to it."

Kai glanced down and saw Tolan and Amelia walking hand in hand through the gardens, her blonde hair blowing in the summer breeze. Tolan's fiery red hair was now shoulder-length. "Everyone?" Kai whispered. He was embarrassed they had done a poor job at hiding their relationship. "What can I do? I know our future, but I don't see her that way. I have no interest in marrying Amelia. At least Tolan loves her."

"Kai, you are a prince. You have no choices, only your duty. This is not about what you want. You will go to Milnos as your father wills you. You will marry Amelia and rule their country. We are lucky the peace has lasted this long. We need you, the Galloway bloodline, on their throne." Gideon's words took an assertive tone.

He knew his cousin was right. If he had not met Rayna, maybe he would feel different. Unwilling to argue, Kai watched darkness fall on Diu. He was relieved when the night sky lit up with fireworks. Bright shimmering streaks of white and gold expanded across the sky, followed by explosion sounds and crackles. Multiple blue and gold stars lit up the sky, crackling one after the other.

Cheers rang out through the city; music filled the air. King's Day was one of the most festive days of the year, behind the Winter Festival. "I wish this weren't the only time they set off fireworks," Gideon broke their silence. "My father buys them from Bangloo."

From their location, Kai could hear the faint *shloomp* sound from each firework launched off the inner walls of the castle. "I wish we had more," Kai added. "They only last about ten minutes, but it is a beautiful display of light."

With each wave of fireworks, they grew larger and louder. As the fireworks concluded, percussion sounds rolled out on the wind above the palace wall. Drummers beat their drums to complete the celebration, followed by rapid cannon fire around the outer wall of the city. Each cannon fired in succession to honor Kings Day, and then all fell silent.

"Goodnight and good luck, Prince Kai." Gideon bowed.

The emphasis on his title said it all. Duty-bound as the prince, Kai best get his head together, or he would be miserable for the rest of his life.

"Goodnight, Gideon. I promise I will visit. Safe travels." He shook his cousin's hand, and they parted ways.

The night before his departure, Kai slipped through the secret passageway to the Master General's tower and went into his cousin's office. Concerned for his father's wellbeing, he decided he should leave a note. Cazier had personally installed a secret compartment around his windowsill. If they needed to exchange messages, Kai put them in their secret spot. All he needed to do was keep the letter simple and imply just enough detail to inform him of his father's situation without saying too much.

Dear Cousin Adrian,

I trust your visit with your wife and children was pleasant and well spent. We all missed you dearly today, King's Day. It was a wonderful celebration.

My arrangements are made, and I leave tomorrow bound for Albey. Like my trip to Chenowith last year, I am sure it will be uneventful. Dante plans to send additional security per your instructions, and the guards depart on a ship across Baden Lake in the morning. They should arrive a full seven days ahead of us.

While I am away, please look in on my ailing father. He is most fortunate to have Nola tending to his every need. She is diligent in her care and rarely far from his side. Maybe she could use a break. I would be most interested in your opinion on his condition. Thank you for your attention to this matter.

Yours Truly,

Prince Kai Galloway

CHAPTER 7

Runaway Discovery

Over winter, a great distance grew between Kai and Kendra. While he tried in vain to use the ability to glean to search for his mother, he'd made no progress. Summer was upon him, and he felt the need to repair some of the damage his words had caused.

The hour was late when Kai welcomed Kendra into his room. He could see the delight in her eyes with the opportunity to mend their bond. They shared a few pleasantries, and Kai offered her a chair. "Kendra, I have missed our talks." She nodded in agreement, and he continued. "I wish you could see the damage secrets cause. You mean well, but the truth always comes to the surface. Please understand, I will not give up trying, but I know I need your help. Teach me how to search for my mother."

"I loved your mother, Kai. Her loss was very difficult."

The pain in Kendra's voice struck his heart. He had to remind himself that he was not the only person to love his mother and feel her loss. "Maybe in dragon form, she cannot be found," her expression turned to despair. "I just don't know."

The thought of losing his mother all over again pricked his heart. He had been haunted all his life by her loss, only to discover his nightmare had a different ending. His mother could still be alive, but where? Why had she not returned? His mind swelled with questions and hope.

Kendra stood and took hold of his wrists, pulling him to his feet and locking their arms together. Kai's heart elevated with anticipation. "Close your eyes. I know you're excited—use your adrenaline. Let everything else except your mother leave your mind. Memories are said to possess a power all their own. Concentrate on the energy her memory creates and add it to your own. I will push my energy to you, and all the light I can pull from our surroundings. I saw Haygan and your mother do this once when she searched for a lost ship at sea. Haygan's extra power allowed her to search farther." Kendra let go and began to move her arms. "Use your sight to see the power I collect."

He did as she instructed. Her cupped hands swirled through the air as she folded light and pushed it at Kai. The more he focused, the brighter the light became. Their two lights merged. Again, he heard Kendra: "Pull my energy inward. Connect the power to your desires and the spiritual power within you—to your soul. Press the raw power inward. Hold on to it as long as you can."

Mentally curling inward, he went beyond his sense of self. Waves of Kendra's collected magic flowed inward. His own soul felt limitless. He had never gone this deep inside himself before. The power became stronger, compounding on itself. He felt he could not hold it down much longer. The energy made him hot, and he had begun to sweat. His body shook with the intensity bubbling within.

Kendra locked her hands around his wrists and held him tight. Her whisper sounded distant. "Now, take all the magic you've gathered and push it into the world. Let it explode from your core. Follow the flow outward. Feel the energy of others and sense where they are, who they are. Focus on your connection with your mother. Call to Mariana."

Open-minded, he pushed outward—and an explosion of light rippled out from his core. He let his mind follow the wave. He felt everything, everyone. He noticed the essences of souls, small and dim (regular people), bright ones—Half-lights, and very bright spirits—Katori. The Katori souls spiked the wave onward. Focused on the memory of his mother, he called to her with his soul—*Mother*.

Vast oceans flowed beneath him. He felt pulled in all directions. Foreign lands spread before him. Clouds blew passed him, and starlight gave way to sunshine. His mind expanded; he was everywhere at once. Then he felt a massive wave of energy explode in the distance and push back through him. Focused on the pulse he heard but one word—*KAI*—and the light was gone.

The tremors stopped, and he opened his eyes. His heart pounded in his chest. Kendra placed a hand on his shoulder to steady him. "Remarkable, you did very well," she said, astounded. "I felt you push through me. You are very powerful. I had no idea anyone except your mother could physically collect energy and use it to glean. What did you feel?"

Kai was wide-eyed and overcome with emotion. He struggled to regain his composure. His knees felt weak. "Where do I start? I've never..." He paused to catch his breath. "I am not sure if this will make any sense, but collecting your energy felt natural. Like accepting a hug. Pushing energy usually feels heavy, resistant—believe me, I've tried. But holding it in—created pressure, it gained strength. The compounded light actually grew as it flowed outward. I don't know if this is right, but each Katori seemed to boost the flow."

With another deep breath, he contemplated what he felt, what he saw. There were so many images blooming in his mind at once. "At first, my mind was flying on a wave of energy or light. It rippled through..." He stopped to search for the right words. The hair on his arms and neck tingled with residual power. "The power poured through people, animals, plants, the oceans—the world. It was more intense than what I do here around the palace, sensing people close to me." He placed a hand to his head, feeling extremely drained.

She grabbed a glass of water from the table. "Here, drink." She offered Kai the cup. "It sounds disorienting, not at all like I've heard it described. Could you tell who those people were or where they are?" she squeezed his hand.

The water felt cool on his parched throat. The drain on his energy began to ease. "I could sense Haygan. I felt him, his essence. His spirit is strong, his soul very bright. You, I felt you. It was difficult to tell the difference between your light and mine. I felt Rayna. You know, it seemed to me each full Katori essence bolstered the wave. And Shane, although he is only a Half-Light, I felt a connection. There are other Katori and Half-Lights within the city and scattered around the outlying farms. There was a mass of energy coming from a distant place far to the east—Katori and the Mystic Islands. Odd... There was another Katori-filled land far away—Caroco, maybe." He paused to look at her, overwhelmed by the intensity.

She tilted her head. "I felt your wave pass through me; it was intense." Kendra looked away. "I hope this was not a mistake. Teaching you to light up the world. Neither of us knows what we are doing. Sounds like every Katori felt your magic, though they would not know who sent the energy, simply which direction it came from."

"Wait, if I am a Half-Light—half Katori, then how did I do it?"

"I don't know." A bewildered expression rattled Kendra. "Because you are not full Katori, Haygan and I held back. We assumed you'd show no gifts. We came to find out what Mariana might have told you about being Katori, what you knew about the day a dragon came to Diu—the day she supposedly died. There are only a few of us who refused to believe she died. You were our last hope. But then, you are no Half-Light. You can't be. This show of power could draw unwanted attention to you."

Her fears made sense; he had no idea who might come for him now that he'd exposed his ability to the world. Kendra's posture changed, and he could tell she contemplated her next words. "Since we are trying to be honest," Kendra said, looking him in the eye. "I must say that you look nothing like Iver. After this display of power, it could mean he is not your true father."

Kai squinted at her. "I don't believe you. Iver loves me. Of course he is my father. Why would my mother stay with him? Why would she lie to me? Lie to everyone."

"I am not sure," she responded. "Only your mother knows these answers."

An earlier memory slammed into Kai, and he gasped with surprise. "There is more, I remember! There was a large wave of energy. It exploded, and something or someone pushed back on me."

Kendra grabbed both of his shoulders, pulled his face close to hers. "Who was it, what did you feel? Tell me." Her eyes were half-wild, and tears welled in her eyes.

He pushed her away and laid his face in his hands. "I don't know for sure. It was so bright, so strong. The feeling was overwhelming. I am sure I imagined it, but I heard… I heard my name come back to me."

Kendra's mouth fell open. "Your mother! It must be. Do you remember anything, even the smallest detail? Did you see anything?"

The pressure to grab at any detail crushed him. He closed his eyes, sucked in a deep breath, and held it. He focused on the moment just before the light exploded and pushed him away. "Black sand. I saw black sand." Confused, he opened his eyes. "We don't have black sand in Diu. At least not that I've seen. Port Anahita has white sand."

"As does Katori," she added. "So does Nebea and Milnos. As far as I know, only Ahana has black sand. It's volcanic."

"I must go to her." Kai pushed around Kendra toward the door.

She grabbed his arm and spun him around. "You can't go unprepared. Besides, you leave for your summer trip within days," she reminded him.

"I am not going on my summer trip. Not now. I must go find my mother."

Millions of ideas flood his mind at once: pack, tell Dresnor, take Ember—RUN! He felt pulled in every direction at once. "You cannot hold me back. I am leaving with or without you."

He thought about how to leave the palace undetected. There was no time to convince Dresnor about his mission. A smile rolled across his face. "The secret passages," he whispered. Thinking of the one behind Gianfranca's portrait and its three exits: the tower, library, and kitchen."

Kai stepped to his bedroom door and opened it for Kendra. "You should look in on Cordelia and Nola. I am not waiting around for you or anyone to talk me out of this." Kai glanced at Smoke.

"Speak with Haygan," Kendra pleaded, "maybe he has an idea."

His room fell silent.

Now that he was alone, he wished he had more time to process everything, but he had to find his mother. There was no way he could tell anyone in Diu where he was going or why. From his armoire, he grabbed a satchel and packed the barest essentials. From a secret compartment within his desk, he took a leather pouch full of money.

Kai no longer took lamps into the secret passageways. He knew them by heart, and his ability to glean allowed him to navigate the darkness. The interlocking stone walls came to life and illuminated his path downstairs. With Smoke behind him, they waited in the dark behind the kitchen shelf. He paused to listen and glean. His sight spilled outward, and everything was set aglow.

In his mind, he searched the kitchen, the palace hallways, the courtyard, and beyond to the stables. Confident he was alone and knew where every guard patrolled, he released the latch securing the panel. With ease, he lifted the wooden cabinet off the ground and set it away from the wall. After he replaced the hutch, he and Smoke exited the palace.

Dressed in black, he slipped along the palace walls and peered across the courtyard toward the southern gatehouse. Shrouded in shadow, Kai reassessed the guards and their locations. Silently he and Smoke made their way around the yard, continuously using his sight to sense the area. At this time of night, several Mryken patrolled without guards. It only took a thought for the guard dogs to ignore his approach.

Keeping to the shadows, he matched the guards' pace to avoid detection, pausing where needed. He could not afford being noticed. In order to run away and search for his mother, he could not risk taking his security detail. This would be a solo mission. Standing within the arched doorway of the chapel, Kai waited for his moment to run through the gate.

When the opportunity came, Kai darted from his hiding place. Moonlight washed over his silhouette. Ten feet from the wall, Haygan rushed Kai, pulling him to a stop. "Hold on, Kai. We need to talk."

Not wanting to cause a scene, Kai followed Haygan back into the shadows. "You navigated the courtyard rather well. Where are you going exactly?" Haygan questioned.

"To find my mother. And you're not going to stop me." Kai tried to push around Haygan.

"Hold up, Kai. What are you talking about?" He shook his head, a combination of pride and concern showed in his eyes. "I know what you did. I'm fairly certain, based on the energy wave I felt pulse through me earlier, you've discovered something."

Kai pulled away and glance toward Smoke waiting near Shiva. "You've been keeping secrets, Haygan. Why?" He raised his hand to halt any response. "There is a lot I want to say." Anger welled anew, but he swallowed his feelings. His hands balled into fists. He opened and closed them over and over, venting his frustration. Torn between acquiring answers and lashing out, he released a deep breath.

"There are things I need to understand." Heat swarmed within Kai's head. "But you keep secrets from me. You could have been teaching me, but instead, you held me back." Now Kai couldn't hold back, his eyes turned a deep green. "How long were you going to keep her truth from me? You could have eased my suffering when you came here. Instead, you let me continue to believe my mother was gone. I know the truth now. My mother is the red dragon. She is alive."

Haygan's pursed his lips and nodded. "We wanted to tell you, Kendra and I. The elders felt it best to wait and see, but honestly, they gave up on searching for her years ago. They were not sure if the dragon seen that day flying away from Diu was your mother or someone sent to kill her. Given you are only half Katori, they saw no reason to bother with you and they told us to keep our distance. Kendra and I are out of bounds here, and the Chiefs and the Unie are barely tolerating our disobedience."

He felt Haygan's arm reach around his shoulders and pull him close. They stood side by side, looking out into the night sky. "There is something I need you to know. I am sorry we've kept so many secrets from you. If someone ever found out, we'd be put in cages and used as weapons. I believe that is what has happened to your mother. Someone has her trapped and is using her. I pray they do not know what they have, more importantly, who they have. I can only guess by staying in dragon form, your mother has protected our secret. All this time, she has sacrificed her life for us." Haygan's voice cracked under the emotion.

"We were alone in the garden that day. Nobody saw her change." A lump formed in Kai's throat when he thought of the guard who came to his rescue when he heard the commotion. "Well, one person did, but she took care of it before she flew away. The question is, why did she go and where?"

"I don't know Kai. I pray we find her, so you can ask."

"Me too." Kai agreed.

Relieved and lost by the same thought, Haygan faced Kai. "I need you to know I am very proud of you. It was difficult to stay away all those years. Mariana chose to live her life away from her people, and we respected her decision. I didn't understand it, but I respected her choice. It is our way." Caught in emotion, Haygan took a breath.

A tightness formed in Kai's chest as he listened to Haygan. "When she had a child, we assumed you would be a Half-Light. Katori children and Half-Lights emit a great deal of light until they come of age. Only then is their true light revealed—in their thirteenth year."

He stopped and took another deep breath before he continued. "News of Mariana's death shook the foundation of Katori life. We refused to believe it, and we searched for her, but nothing came of our search. We knew she was a red dragon, but the information did not help us find her. After years of searching, they gave up. It had just been too long. We had to accept that maybe she was killed by another red dragon. Ryker and I refused to believe it, but you were the only one with the answers. You were with her that day, but with no memory, we feared revealing anything until you were older."

Kai listened, welcoming the openness he felt. Haygan continued. "Unfortunately, we...I did not have the credentials to enter your life. None of us did. We had to build reputations and find a way to be invited into the Diu palace."

"I know this already, and I want to understand. Part of me is mad, but the rest of me understands the risks. Information is power, and Katori gifts would be a threat or a tool. I see how dedicated my mother is, giving up her life all these years."

"You're not alone anymore, Kai. You have a family. It is hard for me; I have never been one to share my feelings. These past three years with you have been a blessing and a curse."

With a brief look into the sky, Haygan continued. "Simone is my wife, and I left her to come to you. I changed my entire life for you. It is her I visit on my nature walks in the summer and for three months each winter. She was the dragon who helped us in Hamrin. They did not want me to tell you any of our secrets. They fear you. Which I barely understand, but that is the only truth I can find in their reluctance to teach you."

Kai interrupted. "Who is this they? Your leaders? I don't see them here now. No more secrets," he demanded.

The agony in Haygan's eyes, the fact he held his breath and clenched his jaw, told Kai he was torn between two choices.

"You're right," Haygan answered, "no more secrets. They will probably banish me for telling you against their wishes, but Mariana is my sister. I am your uncle. You're like a son to me now. I am sorry I didn't tell you sooner. Loyalty to my people has kept me silent."

A lump formed in Kai's throat. He considered the news. Overwhelmed, he hugged Haygan and felt Haygan's large arms pull him in tight. For the first time since he was young, he honestly felt connected to family, besides his father. His heart felt exhausted by the thought of his mother's trapped existence. Years of torturous nightmares had kept him withdrawn. Now he was free from the burden—he had not failed her.

Kai huffed and shook his head; he could not afford to be distracted. Choices rumbled inside of him. "Thank you for telling me, but I am not interested in wasting more time discussing this. Either help me or let me go, but I am going."

Haygan leaned against the chapel wall. "You are your mother's son. Stubborn and rebellious. Where exactly do you think she is?"

"Based on what I saw—black sand—Kendra believes her to be on Ahana." He studied Haygan's body language.

A glint of hope flickered in his uncle's eyes. Deep in thought, Haygan pondered in silence. His brow twitched in contemplation, then he bolted forward. "We need to get word to Ryker and Simone."

"Who is Ryker and why would he help us?" Kai interrupted.

"Ryker was in love with your mother. He refuses to believe she is gone. Over the years he has followed every sighting or rumor of a red dragon outside of Katori lands. He already checked Ahana a few years ago. It is a rather large country, but there are several caves near the southern shore, caverns big enough to hide a dragon. We must go now."

"You would take me with you?" Kai questioned, surprised by the offer.

"Yes, I will take you with me. I think it is time you saw for yourself." Haygan headed toward the northern gatehouse. Kai followed. Confused, he pulled on the stablemaster's arm. "What about Port Anahita? We're going the wrong way."

Haygan took a breath. "We are going to Eagles Peak. Only a dragon can fly fast enough and long enough to cross the ocean. Ryker and Simone must find her. Trust me Kai. I want to find her as much as you do.

"It will take a few hours, even at our speed, to reach Eagles Nest on the south face of Thade Mountain. We must be back in Diu before dawn—before someone misses you. Dresnor would not stand for you to be out at this hour without him, even with me."

Haygan led the way. "Stay as close as possible and keep to the shadows, just as you did earlier. Since I can come and go, and often do with Shiva and Smoke, I will distract the inner gatehouse guard. But you must avoid detection. Go, hide in the shadows."

Reaching the first gatehouse was easy. Getting through it, however, would take stealth. Kai silently watched the guards to study their patrol pattern. Haygan approached the guard within the archway. Kai waited for his chance. He observed the two patrolling guards: one on his side of the walls and one on the outside within the city. Kai stepped in line, a few feet behind the inner guard.

The guard passed the gatehouse and entered the archway, right behind the guard who spoke with Haygan. Smoke and Shiva wormed in front of Haygan, edging the two guards and causing them to step back and observe the wolves. When the exterior guard passed, Kai darted through the archway, across the street and into the shadow of a nearby building.

Haygan walked down several streets inside the city before Kai joined him. "We can easily make our way through the city in shadow to avoid patrols. The next gatehouse will not be easy. More men will be standing in the archway and on the towers above the gatehouse. Again, men will be walking the perimeter in regular rotation, inside and out."

They quickly made their way through Hightown Proper, dodging corner streetlamps and the occasional guard. High-society folk were not out at this late hour; the streets were empty. When they reached Midtown, in addition to the patrolling guards, there was the occasional resident stumbling home. Fewer streetlamps made their movements more direct. The rare unexpected vagrant forced them to crisscross side streets to avoid head-on interaction.

Given his training with Riome, Kai knew these streets well. She often took him to parties or pubs to study people's mannerisms and accents. Some nights she would select a person for him to emulate while other nights she had him track and report on their movements.

The only training he disliked was pickpocketing. At first, he feared getting caught, but Riome taught him the art of lifting any item. After extensive practice with her and palace staff, he was surprised he had a knack for the sleight of hand. He spent hours mingling through crowds, lifting things. His only solace was returning the items before the person reached their destination.

A skill he decided would finally come in handy. "Haygan," he whispered. "I have an idea for getting through the outer gatehouse. You can walk through with Smoke and Shiva, but it's as you said, if word gets back to Dresnor he will at the very least have questions. If we are not back in time, a search party could be sent to find me. We cannot risk it."

"What's your plan?"

"You create a distraction near the gatehouse. I will lift the key from the guard and unlock the door to the turret. All I need to do is climb down the wall away from the gatehouse. It's not that high." Kai tried to convince himself.

The look in Haygan's eyes pondered Kai's plan. "I think I can create a big enough distraction so you could slip out right behind them. If not, steal the key and hop the wall. For a Katori, it should be easy to scale down the wall and jump the remaining fifteen feet from the stone ridge along the walls. Climbing the wall upon our return will probably be your best option to get back inside. You will need the key."

Even at this late hour, Rimtown had people stumbling about the streets. Most leaving pubs or gambling establishments. They crossed street after street until Haygan stopped suddenly and turned down a side-street.

Kai heard men talking and stumbling down the street they had just left. Realizing where they were, he took hold of Haygan's arm. "We should not go this way. There is an alehouse on this street, favored by guards. Let's wait here, see if those men come down this street. If they do, we can let them pass and go back to the main street."

They crouched between two buildings and waited for the men to come near. At the corner, the men stumbled in the dim light a few paces and then stopped. "We can't go to the Black Bear, it's full of soldiers. We will stand out," one man said.

"But I like the barmaids at the Black Bear better," the other huffed.

The first man punched him in the shoulder, making him cringe and rub his arm. "Fine, fine," said the other man. "You're right. Let's go to the Drunken Dragon. Just one more drink before we call it a night." The other man's slurred speech trailed off as they turned away and headed out of sight.

"Good call. Let's go," Haygan said as he moved through the darkness of the Diu city streets.

At the outer gatehouse, Haygan stepped back and started walking parallel with the wall. Two streets down, he stopped. "Listen carefully, Kai. I'll go through the gatehouse with Shiva and Smoke. You wait before you double back to the gatehouse. Hide in the shadows and wait for your opportunity. You'll know it when it happens." Haygan called to Shiva and Smoke. "I will draw the guards just far enough from the gatehouse for you to exit. Run east along the wall. Stay in the shadows as long as you can, until you get close enough to the forest. I will meet you there. Search the trees for Shiva and Smoke." He placed a hand on Kai's shoulder. "Good luck."

Kai nodded. "I will be ready. If I don't get an opening, I will try my way."

"Agreed. See you on the other side."

He waited in the shadows as Haygan disappeared into the night. After a few moments, Kai ran and stood adjacent to the outer gatehouse and eavesdropped on the men patrolling near the wall. He heard their boots on the cobblestone streets and voices within the gatehouse and above on the wall. If he were discovered, the guards would most certainly question him. He could not risk explaining to Dresnor that he was searching for his dead mother. No, he needed to avoid any unnecessary delays.

Still, he waited. No sign from Haygan. Then he heard something. Howls came from the far side of the wall. The guards standing under the gatehouse archway began to chatter, and they stepped through to investigate. The various animal cries wavered in chorus; three different howls echoed in the night, each slightly from a different direction. He recognized Smoke's pitch.

Now is my chance. Kai stepped in the shadows inside the gatehouse to find he was less than five paces from the backs of two guards. "Did you hear that? Wolves," one guard said.

They don't usually come this close to the palace, do they?" the other asked. "Could be those two wolves that left with the Stablemaster?"

There, dangling on the man in front of him, was the key to the turret. With ease and craftiness, Kai pocketed the key. Either way, he'd need it to return through the gatehouse tower. One step back he hid in the shadows. Just then another guard passed right in front of him to join the others.

In the distance, Kai heard the howling again, and he saw it. They all saw the source. Two large silver eyes emerged from the dark. A beast approached. Moonlight and the torches along the road illuminated the wiry sheen of the creature's black fur. It stood as tall as a horse. He had seen this creature before at the battle of Hamrin.

The guard gasped. "A black Shuk." Each guard drew their swords and stepped towards the creature as it advanced, its menacing snarl and deep growl beckoned them. Fearless, the men advanced. The massive beast growled deeper, and the men froze in fear.

This was Kai's chance. He dashed out of the gatehouse, and ran as quickly as he could, staying within the shadows cast by the wall.

CHAPTER 8

Ever Faithful

The meadow was cast in moonlight. Kai moved as swiftly as his Katori feet could carry him. Within minutes he was safely hidden by the trees. Between two large oak trees, he waited. First came Shiva, and then he noticed Smoke. The two wolves circled around him. No sign of Haygan. *What could be keeping him?*

Frustrated, Kai paced back and forth. *What do I do if Haygan doesn't come?* He had no idea where to go or whom they sought. To center himself, he leaned against a tree and gleaned the area for surrounding dangers.

Through his sight, he sensed small creatures in the trees and others scurrying along the ground. He searched farther in the tall grasses, beyond the trees and the animals of the night. To his relief, there he saw the wisp of a man approaching. Haygan was running quickly in his direction. Kai smiled and stepped out as Haygan came through the trees. "Took you long enough," he joked.

"We need to run. There is no time to lose. Use all your senses, stay close. Be aware of everything. We will enter wolf and mountain lion territory up there. Shiva and Smoke will keep some animals away by their very presence. But don't be fooled, they might circle behind us." Haygan did not wait for a response. He turned, leaped over a downed tree, and started to run.

Kai caught up and weaved between trees, leaping over stumps and streams. Keeping his eyes and his senses sharp, he ran one step behind Haygan using his ability to glean the wave of energy emanating within and around every living thing. Tonight, as he ran, he also felt everything around him—a connection through all his senses.

He felt Smoke and Shiva about ten paces out, one on each side. He felt Haygan in front more than he could see his black clothing running through the darkness. It felt good to run. The air whipped through his hair and across his skin. He could now run great distances at great speeds without feeling winded.

Unable to talk to his uncle, he thought about the night's events. His mother was alive. His mind ran wild with theories. Joy and sorrow pulled at his heart. He speculated her long imprisonment, trapped in dragon-form all this time. Is that what it meant to be Katori? What one did to protect their secret? Or—could she not change back? Why did she transform into a dragon in the first place? Unfortunately, Kai had more questions than answers.

He desperately wanted to make sense of her absence. The only possibility he could accept—she was trapped. Unable to return to him. Who could hold a dragon? How were they controlling her? Could she not rip them apart and return? The thought made him shudder. Killing to gain her freedom would not be a simple choice, either.

Disrupting his thoughts, Haygan turned sharply uphill. Kai followed. Smoke ran at his side, and Shiva veered closer to Haygan. Kai continued to follow Haygan as he leaped over underbrush and weaved around trees. The dense forest started to slow them down. Still, Haygan climbed higher. Directly to their right, Kai heard rushing water. Moonlight shone through the thinning trees. They approached a small clearing. Large rocks and a downed tree lay across a deep ridge cut into the mountain by a roaring river.

Haygan stepped quickly across with Shiva two steps behind. Kai jumped onto the rocks. Below, the rushing water roared. He looked down into the blackness, gleaning the gap and the water below. Haygan motioned for him to make haste. Kai leaped onto the tree and made his way across. Smoke followed.

When Kai reached the other side, Haygan darted into the thicket. Pine needles and decaying leaves made their climb challenging. Several times they both slid a few feet backward. They finally stopped under a large overhanging rock. Haygan pointed. "We need to climb up there."

The trees were dense, and the incline continued to get steeper. Haygan showed him a technique of stepping on the base of the trees to advance up the embankment. Kai used the various trees like a ladder to scale the mountainside. Once they reached the rock overhang, Kai looked out over the trees. He saw the thick, black forest below. Moonlight danced across Baden Lake and a light spring breeze whipped through the mountain air. "What are we doing up here, exactly?" Kai asked.

Haygan sat down on the large stone outcropping. "You're about to call for help. I don't have time to explain everything you should have grown up learning. But should you ever need to do this again, alone, you need to know-how, and now is as good a time as any to learn. Sit."

He took a seat next to Haygan. "What do I do?" Kai asked.

Haygan pointed into the trees on the right. "Do you see those trees and the nests on top? Focus and find the largest eagle. Just like reaching out through your bond with Smoke. Share part of yourself. Give your intent and open your spirit. Call him to you. You will know which one. He will ignore you at first. You should sense wisdom and understanding in return. See who he is."

Kai closed his eyes. Connected to the energy within, he opened his mind. He reached into the darkness. Through his sight, he found two eagle pairs—their large nests were nearly five feet wide and four feet deep. *Astonishing.* Their peaceful nature cooed at his spirit, but that was all he felt.

Then he found a third nest, perched within a cluster of three treetops. Larger, deeper. Radiant energy emanated about the top. Another eagle. He sat alone, no mate. Its size was superior to the others. He was more than the eagle. His light was brighter than any animal. If he didn't know better, Kai would've said this spirit was a man.

Kai looked in more detail at the nest and shook his head at the image. *How can this be?* The possibility confused him. The three trees looked like they had grown together, massive live limbs interwoven with one another. Deep inside this enormous treetop structure was a home. He could hardly believe his senses. There were personal spaces with furniture—table, chairs, and a hammock.

Opening his soul to the eagle, he shared his intention, who he was and what he wanted. His soul and mind connected, he felt the eagle's wild nature—and something else. Wisdom. *Can he understand me?* Kai tilted his head at the thought.

While he felt silly to ask a bird for help, he reached out, and he sensed acceptance. *I need your help, come to me.* There was no reply. Only resistance. "I must be doing something wrong. I feel the wisdom within, but he refuses to acknowledge me." He looked at Haygan.

"Relax. Think of your mother, think of Kendra and Rayna. Ask again. Think of the people you love. Show him your truth and your soul."

The thought of the people he loved swelled his heart. Kai pushed those feelings to the eagle. He thought of his mother's face and Rayna's kindness. Their faces flashed through his mind. *I need your help. Come to me.* In return, he felt a sense of freedom come back from the eagle. He opened his eyes. In the distance, he saw the shadow of the great eagle fly out over the trees before circling back around to land in front of them.

His mouth agape, Kai stared at the eagle. From his seated position, the eagle towered over him. Sharp talons scraped at the stone, and a pale-yellow eye studied him. As it turned its massive head, Kai noticed a deformity. A deep scar was carved into its face. "He is amazing. Now what?"

"Watch," Haygan whispered.

The eagle's two massive wings expanded wide, blocking out the moonlight. Then the bird raised them high above its head and pointed upward. Kai watched in awe. Suddenly the bird dropped his wings, and they wrapped around the bird's body. In a puff of air and a glint of blue light, the eagle disappeared and revealed a tall man wearing black pants and a flowy white shirt.

The bright moon left the man's face shrouded in darkness. He stood proudly above them, his arms folded. Haygan stood and offered the man his hand. The stranger pulled Haygan into a one-armed hug and stepped to the side.

Kai hopped to his feet. Now illuminated by the moon, he saw the man's golden complexion and shoulder-length blond hair. The man had two huge scars on his right cheek; this explained the deformity on the eagle. He had one short cut through his eyebrow above his piercing blue eyes, and a much longer scar crept around the outline of his temple and cheekbone.

"Kai, I would like you to meet Sabastian. Sabastian, this is Kai. Mariana's son. I am sorry Kendra could not be here to meet you. I know she would have preferred to introduce you herself."

Stunned by what he had witnessed, Kai drew in a breath. Sabastian squinted his eyes together and clenched his jaw. "Why did you bring him here? Why have 'him' call for me?" Sabastian asked in a distrustful tone.

"He should know how. It seemed only right. He has news, news of Mariana. We know where to find her. This is the first real information we have had in years. Will you help us?"

Eyes fixed on Haygan, Sabastian asked. "You think you can trust this boy? This Half-Light raised by average humans. The ones who lost Mariana. If he is anything more, you know what that means for our people." He was not kind with his words. His eyes said it all. He loathed Kai. "If you had not been here, I would not have come to him."

The man's disdain shocked Kai. "I don't know who you are," Kai huffed, "but I do know this—you've watched me. I have seen your golden tipped wings in the sky over Baden Lake. I never thought to look beyond the giant eagle that blackened the sky. If you think so little of me, why bother?"

Sabastian scoffed, releasing his arms. "A favor for Kendra. And love for Mariana. She was a friend and I do not believe she was killed by a dragon."

Kai thought about the stranger's words. This Sabastian fellow's body language and tone changed when he said her name—Kendra. She obviously meant a great deal to him. Kai thought about what else he knew. Kendra took the occasional few days off. Maybe she spent her time here with this man.

He had no idea why the man seemed to loathe him. His comment about if Kai were anything more only provoked questions, which he was sure had no answers he would be privy to.

Kai focused his blue eyes on Sabastian's. He thought of his mother. "I am desperate. Right now, Haygan says to trust you. You are all I have. I trust Haygan and Kendra." As he spoke, he felt the passion for saving his mother fill his heart. "I am, as you call it, a Half-Light. Raised by ordinary people, but I am also Katori, and I mean to save my mother. Either you will help me, or I will find another way. You decide, but we are wasting time." His words were confident and firm.

He waited.

"Sabastian, you can trust him," Haygan assured him. "Kai is Mariana's son. He will keep our secrets. Surely you felt the energy in the air this evening. The wave of power came from him."

Unwilling to delay longer, Kai spoke up. "I am here for my mother. I have found her. Haygan believes you can go for help. I felt her energy push back on me. Please."

"The boy has power." Sabastian shook his head. "What Half-Light has magic? I suppose he has the gift of sight as well. Can the boy glean?" he continued to grill Haygan. "For that matter, what Half-Light can push their emotions to an animal. I felt great power tonight. None since Mariana's time have I felt such intensity." His tone softened, but he remained leery.

Kai focused his desires, letting his emotions build. He felt the change—his eyes turned green. Sabastian grasped at Haygan's shoulder. "Do you see that? How did you change the color of your eyes? This boy is NO Half-Light! You know what that means. Who he could be?" Sabastian's expression shifted from distrust to concern. "Haygan, this is dangerous. If our leaders knew, I cannot even imagine. What foolish person taught the boy how to light up the world. Now every Katori will know where he is, what he can do. I can think of one in particular. Keegan will come for him."

Kai knew Sabastian would not be happy to learn Kendra taught him how to collect and push energy. There was the name again, Keegan.

A concerned look crossed Haygan face. "I wonder myself the truth of his parentage, but that is a conversation for another time. Right now, we need you to find Simone and Ryker. We need their help. They are staying east of Chenowith. You know the spot. Send them back here to us."

"I will find them, my friend." Sabastian nodded. "We will talk about this further." In an instant, Sabastian took off at a run and leaped into the night. In a puff of air, he changed back into the great eagle and disappeared.

Kai had to believe they would find his mother. Although so much of his life was changing without warning, it did feel right. Haygan went and lay down in the grass near the trees. With his hands behind his head, he closed his eyes. "Now we wait. Try to get some sleep. The wolves will keep watch. Katori eagles are fast, but it will still take several hours for Simone to arrive."

Kai had learned over the years during their summer camping trips that small naps were often a necessity when traveling. This night seemed to be raising as many questions as it provided answers. Now it appeared this Sabastian feared him as much as loathed him.

Haygan rested. Frustrated, Kai watched a small cloud drift in front of the moon. As the last tiny sliver of light winked out of sight, he huffed in protest. Even the moon was hiding. Reluctantly Kai followed suit, finding a soft spot in the grass a few feet away. Surprisingly, he too drifted off to sleep despite his active mind.

He woke hours later to a small nudge from Haygan. "You won't want to miss this," Haygan said, pointing to the massive overhanging rock in front of them.

Kai stared into the night sky. The clouds had cleared, leaving bright stars twinkling against the blue-black heavens. A large shadow loomed across the sky, blocking out the stars. He could barely hear the flap of its wings as it swooped up and dropped with a thud on the rock in front of them.

Torn between fear and excitement, Kai held his breath. Long sharp claws scraped at the rock as it shifted its weight back and forth. Its near-black scales glimmered with hints of blue in the moonlight, and its amber eyes pierced Kai's soul. Its massive size was unbelievable. The fierce nature of its appearance was terrifying, yet he sensed peace. He had seen this creature before. This was the dragon from the battle at Hamrin, two summers ago.

Still afraid, Kai stepped back and bumped into Haygan. He watched in awe. The massive horns about its head and the almost palpable heat emanating from within was intense. From its back, slid a man dressed in all black—Ryker. Before Kai could react, the dragon raised its wings above its head and wrapped them around its body. With a burst of air and a small blue light, the dragon collapsed inward and disappeared, leaving behind a woman with short-cropped black hair, olive complexion, and dark almond eyes. She wore a blue shirt and black pants with gold crisscrossing chains around her bodice.

Around her neck, she wore a long necklace with a blue triangle-shaped crystal pendant. Kai felt astonished by the mystery he'd just witnessed. She was a dragon—a Beastmaster. Haygan stepped forward and greeted them. "Ryker. Simone."

Simone stepped forward. Her hand tenderly touched Haygan's chest. Kai could see the affection they shared as Haygan pulled her into his arms. Letting her go seemed difficult, but Haygan offered his hand to Ryker.

Meanwhile, Simone took Kai's hands in hers. She studied his face. "This is Mariana's boy. I can see her in your eyes and smile. I am guessing it is you I felt this night, pushing your soul out into the world. Dangerous move, young man. But as I understand, you have information about Mariana's whereabouts."

She let him go, but Kai could tell she yearned to wrap him in a hug. Kai watched Haygan's eyes, the depth of their connection was evident. "It was me," Kai responded.

"Sabastian was breathless when he found us and did not explain. He only mentioned there was news about Mariana and to come to you."

Haygan reached his hand to touch her arm. "We need you both to go to Ahana. We believe Mariana is there."

Ryker interrupted. "I searched the island of Ahana—two years ago. She was not there. I have followed every clue. Any news about a red dragon. The only thing that makes any sense is she is a prisoner, and they move her around. I've come close a few times over the years. News of a dragon defending a ship."

"You are a good friend," Haygan nodded to Ryker. "Thank you for continuing to believe in my sister."

It struck Kai's heart to feel such loyalty for his mother.

"I have searched abandoned beach campsites, still smoldering." Ryker continued. "They're a large group, soldiers, I think. They march in formation. Pitch tents in rows. Always near the shore. They must have access to a fleet. I am speculating, of course, but I am trying."

The passion Ryker had for his mother made Kai wonder about their relationship. If this man loved his mother, did she once love him back? Why else would he continue to search?

"Well, she is there now," Haygan insisted. "We must act now before they move her again. She is in dragon form, which would explain why we have been unable to find her. I know of no other Katori who can search for her as Kai did tonight. We cannot lose her again."

Ryker's intense look softened when it landed on Kai. "Your mother is a strong woman. I hate to make promises I cannot keep but mark my words I will bring Mariana home. No matter what, I will never give up on her."

Simone let go of Haygan's hand and approached Kai. "We all care deeply for your mother. I am sorry the burden of finding her fell to you. "We will depart immediately," Simone walked away, a burst of blue light and black smoke surrounded her, and she turned back into the black dragon.

Ryker looked to Kai. "I will save your mother, I promise." Then he climbed up the dragon's back. In an instant, they were gone.

Kai's mouth fell open. He wanted to say something, anything, but he didn't know where to start. In one night, he had learned his mother was alive, Haygan was his uncle, Katori Beastmasters could turn into animals, and he could push his energy out and sense the world.

He thought of his father and his anguish over her loss. There was no way Kai could explain what he knew. People would think he was crazy. Not to mention, it would reveal a Katori secret—one his mother gave up her life to protect. A secret he would now protect with his own.

CHAPTER 9

Old Anger

It was a warm summer morning just before dawn. Everyone had packed their gear and saddled their horses. Prince Kai and his group prepared to depart, and he was far from excited about visiting the small town of Albey located at the base of the Katori Mountains, south of the Conha River, which is the primary source of Baden Lake. What he wanted was news about his mother, but Ryker and Simone had only been gone a day.

As the sun rose, he climbed onto Ember's saddle. From the stables, he watched the sun's rays glisten across the stone of the Master General's tower, and he gave one last look toward the bakery. Rayna pressed her hands to her lips and blew him a kiss. He gave her a nod and urged Ember into motion following his group.

Kai craned his neck to see his massive group head down the dirt road. Leading his group were four scouts—men he knew well, selected last summer by Dresnor. Kempery-man Redmon rode ahead of Shane and his father, Hunter Micha Marduk. Riding on either side of Kai were Haygan and Kempery-man Dresnor, both focused on scanning their surroundings. Kai glanced over his shoulder to see Finlee's delighted smiling face. Three pack horses, two with carts, followed.

Kempery-man Albey and the newly promoted Captain Drew brought up the rear with four other soldiers. This was the largest group he'd traveled with so far. Kai was both surprised and disappointed to see so many carts traveling with his group this year. The additional burden on the horses meant additional stops and a slower pace.

The first scout crossed the bridge over Stone River, and they were officially underway on Kai's third and final mission around Baden Lake. Provided everything went as planned, it would be at least seven long days in the saddle, two days longer than usual. All in preparation for his journey to become the King of Milnos.

Behind them, in the Diu harbor, a Diu ship was preparing to set sail across Baden Lake with Captain Wallis and thirty guards, also bound for Albey. After Kai's trip two summers back to Hamrin turned into a battle for their lives, Cazier and the Grand Duke now sent men to secure the city before the prince's arrival. Kai thought about how easy taking the ship would be. He knew Wallis and his men would be in Albey around dinner tonight. Meanwhile, Kai would travel by land around the water's edge for almost a week. Along the way, he would collect taxes and make a royal show of his father's support for his people.

The billowing white sails expanded as the ship cut across the lake. The idea of sailing intrigued Kai. He'd heard tell of thirteen-foot waves on the lake, and he'd always wanted to see them for himself. At this time of the morning, however, the lake was calm—smooth as glass. The sun tossed its bright reflection across the water and pulled Kai into a memory.

He recalled walking hand-in-hand with Rayna beside Baden Lake last autumn. The sun had been shining on the lake that day, too, and he remembered the feel of her hand in his. Her long hair, full of flowers she'd collected along their walk, blew gently in the breeze. Her small wicker basket was filled with wild herbs.

"Must be a pleasant memory," Haygan muttered, interrupting Kai's daydream.

"I was thinking of Rayna," Kai admitted. "I must find a special gift for her for the new year's Winter Festival. Any ideas?"

"I know she is rather special to you," Haygan cocked his head to the side. "Given your betrothal to Amelia, is it wise? I know you talk to Kendra about these things, and I try not to tell you what to do. What do you know about her or about her real parents?"

Sadness over the awkwardness between him and Kendra made him wonder if he'd been too hard on her. "Rayna said her parents found her as a baby tucked in a crate mixed within their supplies on the docks. While they took her in, they had always expected someday someone would come to reclaim her, but they never have. They wanted her to know they were blessed by her, being unable to have children of their own."

"Admirable of them to be honest with her," Haygan said.

"They didn't want her to find out from someone else. If her long-lost parents did return, Rayna might feel Levi and Dori had lied to her."

"Never in my life have I ever known of a Katori to give up a child. I cannot imagine being so desperate I would willingly give away my child." Haygan focused on the road ahead. "Does she have a spice box yet? I am sure she could always use bottles. If you want to surprise her, consider colored glass bottles. We will be in Chenowith for a night. If you'll remember, there is a glassmaker in the village who specializes in colored glass. He created the stained-glass windows in the Diu chapel."

Kai's eyes lit up. "That's perfect. I could have several pieces reserved when we reach Chenowith and pick them up on our way back through. I can have a spice box commissioned in Diu, custom-designed to hold the various bottles. Thanks, Haygan." Pleased with his plan, they rode on in silence toward their first campsite, south of Town Hope.

Later that evening, they rode into a camp hoping to find the area already established by the Master General Cazier and his men. The grounds were pitch-black. No campfires burned. No men told stories to pass the time. Everything was quiet. His cousin and his men were nowhere in sight.

Just as well, Kai thought, all the better to settle into road life without distraction. His men set to establishing the camp. Kai left Ember in the horse corral and climbed the steps of the newly renovated hunting lodge. Inside the rustic lodge, his men gathered around the large table, eating beef stew and telling stories. It was a pleasant sight.

"Your Highness," Drew extended his hand, "may I take your pack upstairs?"

"Thank you, Drew. Meet us in the study when you are finished."

Drew accepted several packs from the other Kempery-men and darted upstairs.

Across the large common room, the lodge boasted a large study. The structure had come a long way since his first summer. His Kempery-men followed him into the study. Over the mantle on the large stone fireplace was an eight-point buck's head. "The old place has certainly come a long way since our first summer. Why didn't we stop here last summer?" Kai asked.

"Hunters." Dresnor raised one eyebrow. "They were already here, and you refused to kick them out. Admirable to a point, but you are a prince, soon to be a king. Your subjects should accommodate you, not the other way around."

Not wanting to argue, Kai waved his hand. "I will not debate with you, Dresnor. We must agree to disagree, or better yet skip the discussion."

Changing the subject, Kai made a proposal. "Any thoughts on skipping our time in Town Hope?"

Dresnor watched Drew enter and take a spot near the window. "We have all summer. Why push the men?"

Kai knew his man was right, but he felt anxious and sitting

idle in Town Hope for two days playing the prince was the last thing he wanted to do. "Each trip was meant to prepare me for the long ride to Milnos—a ten days ride in open and possibly unfriendly territory. My men also need to be ready. This is easy living here at the lodge, and within the estates along our route. It will only take us—what, six, maybe seven straight days to reach Albey? With one or two overnights at each stop, it will be ten days to Albey."

"Your Highness, I will not argue against your command." Dresnor glanced around the room. "But you have obligations along our route. Expectations of the prince to greet the people. Your visits each summer remind them Diu still cares. Lest I remind you what happened in Hamrin only two years ago. There must be constant connections with these western communities."

Kai did not need reminding of the evil they faced and the battle they fought. "How about a compromise? A few hours in Town Hope and one overnight in Chenowith."

Dresnor's pursed lips told Kai he wanted to argue but held his tongue.

"Your Highness," Kempery-man Albey interrupted their staring contest. "If we arrive several days early to Albey, Captain Wallis and his men could remain, giving the men several days in a row to recover."

Silence fell over the group. "Excellent, it's settled," Kai clasped his hands together. "We leave at first light, spend a few hours in Town Hope and one overnight in Chenowith. Any other news we need to discuss?"

Before anyone could respond, the Master General strolled into the room. "Your Highness, you are looking well." Cazier bowed and extended a hand to Dresnor. "Dresnor, good to see you. I hope I am not interrupting."

"Master General," Dresnor nodded. "We are all finished, please excuse us." Dresnor bowed to Kai. "Your Highness, I will inform the men of our change in plans."

Kai's men departed.

Cazier collapsed into the sofa. "Everything alright?"

"Yes, yes." Kai settled into a large chair. "I was surprised we beat you here. Any trouble on the road?"

"We had a little skirmish south of here, but nothing my men couldn't handle. Raiders attacking a small settlement."

Chatter from an influx of men echoed into the study. Kai eyed the men in the next room. Finlee approached with a tray of food and a bottle of wine. "Thank you, Finlee."

"Your Highness." Finlee exited with a bow.

"I am glad we have this time to talk." Kai took a handful of grapes. "There is something we need to discuss. I left a letter for you in your Diu office, in case we didn't get this chance. While you've been away, my father's health has declined. One day we spoke about his plans for his summer trip abroad. The next day, he was taken ill and laid up in bed. This year he has no interest in sailing. He plans to send Dante and Farwick in his stead."

Cazier took a sip of wine. "True, Iver is not one to miss going out to sea, but if he is unwell, I suppose it makes sense he sends others to collect tributes and affirm Diu connections to foreign lands."

"Wrong," Kai said, raising his voice. "None of this is right. Father is not right. He is distracted and lost. Some days he is short-tempered. The next, he falls silent and looks to Nola to speak for him. My father has never missed a trip in my lifetime. My mother died the year he extended his trip and stayed abroad. Maybe if he had been home, she would still be with us." Anger welled in his eyes, and he slammed his fist down on the arm of his chair.

"Sounds like you blame your father for her death." Cazier leaned forward. "Maybe you needed to say it. But you know it's not true. Even if Iver had been there, he would not have saved her. We were lucky you were not killed."

Knowing his mother was alive didn't change his deepest sorrow. His mother was gone, and he had blamed his father's absence on her death. The more he thought about the lies around his mother, the angrier he felt, but the Master General was not the person to help him cope. "I suppose I have blamed him. But right now, I am concerned about Nola. She is not as she seems—I know it, only I still cannot prove it. And Riome is too busy chasing Andrew's rumors to help me investigate."

Cazier shook his head. "We need to get to the bottom of Nola's duplicity, but whenever I inquire, everyone reports her as the dutiful queen. Your word is not enough Kai, even as a prince. I need multiple witnesses or tangible proof she is harming Iver. Sigry, the physician, cannot explain what is causing Iver's condition. I promise to investigate this when I return. Trust me with this matter and enjoy your summer. Albey is a sleepy little mountain town, you should have no worries."

No worries. His cousin had no idea. Kai had concerns aplenty, only not the ones he could tell the Master General of Diu. "I am sure you're right."

Cazier leaned forward. "Our friendship goes beyond my duty to protect you. You're more than my prince, you know that, right?"

"I do." Kai refilled their cups.

"How are your pickpocketing and lockpicking skills coming along?" Cazier laughed. "Riome is the best of all my spies. Her natural ability to become another person is almost uncanny." He said with pride.

It was difficult to deny Riome's ability. Kai had watched her fight two men twice her size and hardly break a sweat. "She has taught me more than I thought possible," Kai added.

"She said you are really coming along in your fighting skills. I know she pushes you, but it is for the best. Trust me."

"A compliment from her is high praise," Kia smirked. "Wish Riome would tell me how I am doing. You know she is relentless, right? Some nights I can't tell if she is training me or trying to kill me. Did you know she put me in a dress?" Kai said with a huff.

Chills ran down his arms as he remembered the night. "Seriously, a dress, shoes, wig. The works." He crossed his arms in front of himself.

Nearly choking on his food, Cazier laughed so hard he began to cry. "I would have paid good money to see you in a dress. Although, you do have the legs for it," Cazier added, wiping a tear running down his cheek.

"Very funny. Riome said someday it could save my life to change genders in a crowd while trying to avoid being found." Pondering the idea, Kai softened to it. He hated it when she was right.

Cazier finished his wine. "She is correct, you know. It could save your life if you ever needed to hide. As a woman, you'd be passed over without a real look. It could be the advantage you need to escape capture. Watch out for your shoes, they often give you away if you can't manage a change."

"Well, enough talk of me dressing as a girl." Kai stifled a yawn. "We both have early starts, come dawn. Goodnight, cousin."

Cazier stood and shook Kai's hand. "Goodnight, cousin."

CHAPTER 10

Watery Mistakes

Transitioning from palace life to the country living always took Kai a night or two. The hustle and bustle of the city and the noises of others were replaced with the rhythmic hoofbeat of his horse, the sound of the cart's wheels rolling along the dirt road and wild noises of nature. The campsite was quiet. The silence was almost deafening. Most of the men were bedded down in bedrolls for the night. Haygan sat poking the fire and a newly placed log. "Walk with me to the water," Kai whispered to him, nodding at the lake.

Haygan stood, and Kai spotted Shiva in the distance. The wolf rose to follow them. Over his shoulder, he caught Smoke flanking them on the opposite side. Pushing out his senses towards the water, Kai checked for danger and other guards in the area. Finding the area clear, he approached the water's edge and knelt to wash his hands.

The lapping lake water was cool on his skin, and he relished the thought of going for a swim. "Any chance we can take an early shift tonight?" Kai asked. "I sense six guards awake patrolling the outskirts. I'd prefer taking the next shift or the morning shift. I hate waking in the middle."

Haygan nodded. "I am well aware of your lack of enthusiasm for the midnight shift. However, you drew the short straw tonight—or rather, I drew it for you. Get some rest. I will wake you when it's our turn."

Upstairs, inside the lodge, Kai found his pack sitting on a narrow bed. The small room provided a bed and a single chair; his home away from home. He laid down and gazed at the stars through the small window. Smoke slept near the door.

Thoughts of his past and future battled in his mind. The foundation of his life was built on a lie. Everything he thought he wanted for his life had changed. His betrothal required him to marry Amelia and move to Milnos. But his heart belonged to Rayna and he wanted to go to Katori. More importantly, he needed to reconcile his future and come to terms with the truth of his fate, he may not have a choice in the matter. Fighting his responsibility would only cause heartache.

After years of being angry at his father for the loss of his mother, he knew she was alive. For one brief moment, he had felt his mother's spirit. There had to be a way to save her. He didn't know how or when, but he would save her. Finding her and bringing her home would set his world right. He would never give up on her again.

Although he knew he should let his anger towards his father go, it seemed impossible. If Iver had been there that day instead of away at sea, Kai was sure the outcome would have been different.

Heavyhearted, Kai yearned to chase the clue to find his mother. He should be the one to rescue her. Instead, he was traveling to a small town to collect taxes and put on a royal display for the locals.

A yawn surprised him.

Hands folded over his chest, Kai tried to relax. A rush of adrenaline raised the hair on his arms. Over the years he'd learned the cues that preceding an impending vision. Something was coming.

It had taken practice to prepare his mind for receiving and remembering the finer details of a vision. Slowing his breathing and closing his eyes was a good start. What worked the best was an open mind. Not easy when you spend most of your day angry and frustrated. Always reaching for answers with no help.

When he finally dozed off to sleep, something called to him. A knowing sense pricked at the front of his mind.

The dream unfolded outward in front of him. Rolling hills bathed in moonlight rose and fell before him. Kai felt the wind on his face—not his face. Adrenaline pounded in his heart—not his heart. He was running—not as a man, but a horse. Kai felt a connection to the rider. The man pleaded for more. The horse surged. Kai sensed exhaustion. Each hoof pounded into the ground. The steed was near its breaking point.

Whisked skyward, Kai felt a lift in his soul. The gallop of the horse was replaced with the rhythm of wings. Massive black wings folded up and down at his sides. The energy within the dragon was unlike anything he'd ever experienced. The presence of another soul echoed in Kai's mind—Simone. Desperation pounded in her heart.

Below, a man in black rode a horse across the countryside. The man dismounted, and without skipping a beat, he disappeared into the trees.

Aimed towards the thick forest, the dragon followed. A carpet of green treetops covered the ground. Her dragon eyes scanned for glimpses of the man through the thinning canopy. Caught in the moonlight, the man glanced skyward—Ryker.

Drawn into Ryker, Kai felt the man's steady heartbeat. The terrain whizzed by in a blur. Ryker moved swiftly, but Kai felt he was conserving his energy. Kai had the feeling Ryker was preparing for some inevitable fight. Moonlight splashed through the treetops. Standing near a rocky ledge, men pointed and shouted, their argument unclear. Ryker motioned Simone forward.

Drawn back into the dragon, Simone circled the area. She

scanned the ground for a lay of the land and the size of the camp. On the next pass, Kai watched Ryker take advantage of the men's distraction. Ryker converged on the group with two battle axes. Precision and speed were his greatest advantage. The warrior swept through the area, slicing down every man before they had time to react.

Again, Ryker glanced skyward and motioned for Simone to advance. Pulled back into Ryker, Kai saw the black dragon, Simone, fly ahead. Ryker hopped boulder to boulder as he traversed down a steep cliff. Below, more men quarreled on the beach. Kai could smell the salty air. A loud thud shook the earth. Rocks tumbled down the slope.

Kai heard a man yell, "The beast is no longer under our control, it has gone mad!"

Men ran from a cave.

The identifiable screech of a dragon bellowed from the cave entrance followed by fire and smoke. Soldiers scattered. What Kai could only imagine were claws feverishly scratching on stone pierced his ears. The beast was trapped and desperate to escape. It rammed the boulder blocking its freedom. More rubble tumbled down the cliffs.

Moonlight glinted off the blades of Ryker's axes. Fire belched out holes above the cave and around the entrance. Ryker shielded his face. Fleeing men stopped when they saw Ryker and drew their swords. Kai felt Ryker clench his jaw.

The group clashed; metal clanged against metal. Bodies slumped to the ground at the end of Ryker's fury. As the last man fell, Kai saw the Galloway crest on the dead man's uniform. Again, the ground trembled. Rubble exploded from the mouth of the cave. The shock wave knocked Ryker to the ground.

Back on his feet, Ryker ran to the cave. A dust cloud made Ryker cough and cover his eyes. Dead men lay near the entrance, burned alive. Inside, moonlight beamed through three holes above. Black soot covered the walls, and claw marks gouged the surface. The cave was empty. Ryker ran outside.

In the distance, a set of small shacks and boats blazed in the night. Men ran screaming in terror. The black dragon, Simone, bathed the beach in fire, and men burned where they fell.

Ryker glanced in the opposite direction; he saw a woman stumble towards the surf. She wore the remnants of a tattered blue dress. Shouting over the wind and waves, Ryker pursued and called to her. "Mariana, wait."

She did not stop. She walked into the surf and sunk beneath the waves. Gone.

Overwhelming grief ricocheted through Kai's soul from Ryker.

Pulled back into Simone's black dragon, he felt residual heat in his throat. Across the sand, Kai saw an arrow strike Ryker in the back, and he fell flat on the sandy beach. Back in the sky, Simone flew. Anger, followed by an unusual burning, swelled in Kai's throat. The dragon shot a blast of fire across the line of remaining men, archers hidden on the hilltop above the cave entrance.

Alone, Ryker lay bleeding in the sand. Fires burned across the night sky. The dragon circled above the cliffs, searching for survivors. When all was silent, Simone landed near Ryker's motionless form. Kai saw a faint blue light briefly illuminate the sand.

"I lost her," Ryker moaned, rolling onto his side. "Mariana, I'm sorry."

Simone knelt and touched the arrow in Ryker's shoulder. "This is going to hurt," she said.

In the far reaches of his mind, Kai heard a voice call out. "Wake up, Kai." Something pushed on his shoulder. Kai moaned. "Wake up. Kai, it's your turn at guard duty."

Jostled again, Kai awoke. "Alright, already, I'm up." He opened his bleary eyes.

Haygan knelt beside him.

Heart pounding from the dream, Kai sat up and swung his feet to the floor. "Haygan, we need to talk." He looked out the window behind him. "What time is it? Seems near dawn."

"It is," Haygan agreed. "Dresnor took your shift so you could take the last one. We'll have work to do in an hour to ensure we are ready to break camp when the others wake."

Desperate to explain what he'd learned, Kai led them down to the lake, clear of the others. Mist lingered above the surface of the water. Kai waited to be sure they were alone. In a whisper, he leaned toward Haygan. "I've had a vision of Ryker and Simone. The last thing I remember is Ryker in trouble. There was a great battle, Ryker against many others. Simone sprayed dragon fire over the beach. Men were screaming—Galloway men. Why are my father's men guarding a dragon—my mother? In the end, an arrow struck Ryker in the back. He could be dying. My mother, she was there, and now she's gone, gone into the sea." In a panic to get it all out, Kai made little sense.

"Relax," Haygan placed a hand on Kai's shoulder. "Your mother had visions. You prove to be more like her every day. Slow down."

"But we must help them. Help my mother—Ryker!" Kai insisted.

"There is little we can do right now. Slow down and begin again. Tell me everything."

After slowly retelling what he saw, Kai slumped onto a rock near the shoreline. "What now? My mother's gone. Tell me how she could be gone. She can't possibly swim across the ocean. I have no idea where she thought she was going. Why were there Galloway men there? Does that mean my own father is to blame?"

Haygan pushed his hands into his pockets and turned his back to the lake to gaze around the camp. "I keep forgetting you know so very little about our world, and your mother. She was very powerful. She is one of the few Katori who can turn into multiple animals. Manta rays and dolphins live in the ocean. She knows their forms well." Haygan paused, chewing on his lip. "Her mind must be a jumble after years in captivity. If she stayed in dragon form all these years, her spirit is confused between the animal spirits within her and the human she wants to be. We Katori are warned before making the change. There are some Beastmasters who, once they connect the thread of an animal to their own, choose to give up their humanity and remain as animals. They become wild."

The news shocked Kai. He stood there stunned in the revelation his mother was once again lost. The reality caused his stomach to twist. Energy swelled in his chest. "How can we help any of them? How do I save my mother?"

"When we reach Albey, I will go to Katori," Haygan assured him. "Trust me, Ryker and Simone will be fine. It will take more than one arrow to end Ryker. Simone will protect him. If they did indeed eliminate all the Galloway soldiers, our secret is still safe. Finding your mother is another story. But there may be a backlash from your father learning his men were killed, and his dragon is gone."

Nothing made sense—how would his father have a dragon? Why were his men keeping it locked away? His mother was a prisoner. "Are you not worried? Galloway men were holding my mother."

"I am worried. What would you have me do? Ask them politely why? Has Iver ever mentioned he had a dragon?"

Kai thought about the many conversations he'd had with his father. "A few years ago, he mentioned a dragon. He spoke of wanting to kill it, but Sigry convinced him controlling the beast for their own purposes was better."

"Good," Haygan bobbed his head. "Hopefully, Iver had no idea the dragon was Mariana. If he did, I will kill him myself."

"So, now what? I want to go after her." Kai demanded.

"No, I will get word home. A ship to Ahana would take weeks; by then Ryker and Simone will be home, and Mariana is still long gone. Let the Chiefs and the Unie decide what to do. The sooner we get to Albey, the better. I am glad we are skipping the extra days in Town Hope and Chenowith." Haygan turned back towards camp.

"Go, wake Finlee," Haygan motioned. "We need to begin saddling all the horses."

Kai did as Haygan suggested, but he hated feeling so powerless. There had to be something he could do. Maybe he could find other Katori. People who would help. His mother, after all, was the daughter of a Chief and apparently very powerful. Now that he knew she was alive, they would have to help her.

Dawn pushed against the black sky. All over the camp, men began to rise from their slumber. Everyone hustled, collecting bedrolls and dousing water over campfires.

While Kai packed his saddlebag and considered the ability to push power outward. A gift he experienced only once when he searched the world for his mother a few days ago. If he could repeat the experience, maybe he could find other Katori nearby. The question was: could he control the wave? Could he draw someone to him with this power? And would they help him?

Both groups broke camp. Cazier's group head home to Diu. Kai's group rode to Town Hope. Between Dresnor and Drew, Kai practiced reaching out. Each time the energy built, but he was unable to push the wave outward. It resisted. It fought against him.

Clearly, he needed to do something different. Without Kendra to push him extra energy, the power built too slowly. He tried so many times he got a headache.

By the time they reached the center of Town Hope, Kai felt drained. He was no closer to finding his mother or drawing another Katori to his side. Duke Eugene Sknash was pleased to see him, as was his wife, Heidi. Familiar faces gathered around to shake Kai's hand, each delighted to see him return. Hands reached for him, and a few young children touched Smoke's thick fur.

The town was prosperous and healthy. Lord Sknash had turned the community around. Real joy and affection flowed from person to person.

"Lord Sknash," Kai extended his hand.

"Your Highness, Prince Kai." Lord Sknash bowed in respect. "Wonderful to see you. Your lead scout was just telling us you are not staying the night. I can understand your desire to make haste to your destination. I have requested some food be brought from the university kitchen to serve you and your men."

"You are too kind, Gene. How is the construction coming along? Last summer, you started building a dormitory. Or was it a library?"

Gene laughed. "Well, both actually. We completed the dormitory this spring. I am afraid we were a bit too ambitious. The library will take considerably more time. I hope the structure will be finished before winter. The interior, well, I want to make it rather engaging for both teachers and students, and that takes time. Educating the masses is a priority."

"Sounds wonderful." Kai grinned from ear to ear, hearing the pride in Gene's voice.

Year after year, the once poverty-ridden town expanded. The signs of slavery and fear were gone. While the duke and his wife continued to share their plans, the back of Kai's mind was focused on the realization his mother was once again lost to him, and he needed Katori help to find her.

Torn with the idea of staying to learn more and reaching Albey, Kai and his group said their goodbyes. It was going to be a hard two days ride straight to Chenowith.

Along the way, he continued to practice pushing his power into the world. This time he held onto the light and pressed it inward. He felt the pressure build and build until it pushed back. Kai focused on the hillside and pushed the pulse into the woods with one thought attached—*Hello, is anyone out there? Help me.* He had no idea if anyone was there or if they would answer his call.

His mind followed the wave. High on the mountainside, four lights—Katori—radiated like beacons back to him. Unfortunately, he did not have control of the flow, and his message also washed over his small group. One bright light beamed ahead of him—Haygan, and one dimmer Half-Light behind him—Shane. He heard Shane speak to his father. "Dad, did you feel that? Something... someone... I heard a voice in my head. How odd, I noticed something like it a few nights ago."

Kai knew what Shane felt—his searching. Seems even Half-Lights heard him. Ahead on the road, he saw Haygan bolt out of line and gallop in his direction. His stern look told Kai that he was in trouble. "Dresnor, Drew, do you mind if I ride with Kai for the next bit?" Haygan asked.

His men nodded and dispersed amongst the group. Haygan and Kai rode in silence for a few minutes. Kai could only imagine Haygan was formulating how to chastise him without drawing too much attention to their conversation. The agony of waiting blossomed into a fist-sized rock in his stomach.

"Kai, what are you doing?" Haygan scolded. "Don't answer that. Better yet, how far did you send your little message? And to whom?"

Feeling guilty, Kai cocked his head east toward the mountains. "Far enough. Though I have no idea if they will come."

"Oh, they will come. If only to see who you are. Foolish, bloody foolish mistake. I am warning you, Kai, you must stop this before the wrong people take notice."

Haygan never said another word, but Kai could see the turmoil rolling around in his uncle's head.

An hour later, the sky let loose. Torrential rain fell from dark clouds, soaking them in seconds. The blinding rain forced them off the road. They took shelter under a cluster of trees.

Huddled together, they waited. When the rain eased, they ventured out into the drizzle.

They needed to keep going. It was a messy wet trot. Mud splashed on the horses' legs. Water dripped into Kai's eyelashes, and he wiped his face. The wind shook the trees. The rain continued to pour from the sky in buckets. Thunder rolled through the clouds and lightning cracked the sky. As the rain resumed its full wrath, they were again forced from the road to wait out the weather.

Their feet swam in growing puddles. Water collected around them faster than it could soak into the soil. Haygan nudged Dresnor. "Do you hear that?" he asked.

"Besides the rain and wind?" Drensor's eyebrows knit together with worry. "I don't hear anything else. What do you hear?"

"Water. Debris, runoff from above. I can hear it. There is a creek northeast of here, it comes down the hill and runs under the road up ahead. There, through the trees, you can see it. The stream is starting to swell. If it overflows, it will flood this area and the road ahead of us. We need to move and get back on the road before it gets washed out."

"Agreed," Dresnor nodded. "We need to find higher ground. Everyone back to the road. Move quickly. Go north—to higher elevations. Then we'll find a new place to take shelter until the storm passes."

Everyone started moving. Rain beat on Kai's head and shoulders. Each footfall sank in the over-saturated soil. He used Ember to steady his stride. Water filled the ditch near the road—a foot deep. The compacted gravel road made for faster travel, but it was a muddy mess.

Using his sight, Kai gleaned the hillside. Haygan was right; the creek was beginning to overflow. Water pushed up its banks. Debris-filled water would soon rush in their direction. "We need to move faster," he called out.

Through the thunder and rain, nobody heard his words. He urged Ember faster, up next to Marduk and Shane. Marduk managed two horses, his white mare and a packhorse, which pulled a small cart. "Marduk, you need to go faster," Kai urged. "Everyone needs to move faster, or we won't make it."

Marduk popped his horse's rump and forced him into a trot, along with his packhorse. Shane kept pace, quickly putting distance between them and the rest of the group. Drew shouted to the scouts, and they charged ahead with Marduk.

As the group divided, Kai looked between the two groups—the men pulling packhorses and carts were falling behind. Kai turned toward the stragglers, but Dresnor pulled at his arm. "No, Kai. We need to keep riding."

"I need to help the others," Kai insisted. "They aren't going to make it. Here, take Ember ahead." He forced Ember's reins into Dresnor's hand and slid from the saddle. *Ember, GO!* Kai instructed his horse to make for the hilltop, pulling Dresnor with him.

Kai raced to the lingering group. His uncle, Haygan, joined him, shouting through the wind and rain. "Do you seem them?" Haygan pointed into the hills. You brought them here. I warned you to stop."

Confused, Kai searched the mountains. High on a rocky ledge, four people stood. Their hand motions seemed familiar. Each pulled energy from their surroundings and rolled it in their hands and tossing it skyward. "What are they doing?" he yelled, but Haygan moved to help the others.

Guards tugged at the packhorses and those pulling carts. The cart's wheels sank into the muddy road. Panic emanated from each horse. They reared and refused to budge. Kai ran to help; he sensed their fear. Standing between them, Kai laid his hands on two horses to connect to their spirits. Calm, peaceful thoughts flowed from his soul.

The men pulled the reins. Kai took a step, and the horses inched forward, but the carts pulled them back. The cart's wheels did not budge—they were gripped by mud. Again, they tried. The wagon jerked, but the wheels held fast. Kai ran behind one cart, and Haygan took the other. They pushed the sinking carts free. Kai and Haygan both encouraged the horses forward. Free from the mud, they crept along.

Yelling for the guards to go faster, Kai motioned for the guards to dart ahead. "Ride on," Kai instructed. "Take the packhorses. We've got the carts."

The guards darted ahead, each dragging a packhorse behind their own horses. Kai and Haygan ran between the horses. With each step, they moved a little faster. The cart's wheels moved easier. Random gravel spots supported their weight. Haygan's team moved ahead until his cart's wheel sank in a muddy sinkhole.

Kai ran to his uncle's aid, hefting the cart out of the mud. With them moving again, he returned to his horse and steered them around the muddy sinkhole. Confidence flowed through his touch to the horse, and they quickly gained momentum. They trotted through the rain. Thunder and lightning cracked the sky, but the horse was not afraid.

The others waited up the hill. The water washed over the road, and Haygan crossed in ankle-deep water. Through the trees, more water raged. Kai kept running. He could see a debris-filled wave was coming. When his team reached the overflowed creek-bed, now a raging river, Kai encouraged the horse to run into the now knee-deep flow.

Deeper and deeper, the water rose, eroding the path in front of them. The horse hesitated. The small creek that had once run under the road now flowed freely over a fifteen-foot-wide swath. Kai urged the horse to continue. With each step, the water gushed around him. He felt the ground beneath him begin to wash away. *Keep moving,* he urged the horse.

Haygan ran to his aid, pushing at the back of the cart. Muddy water pushed against Kai's legs. Each step was harder than the last. Working together, they plodded through the rising water, threatening to wash them away. Everyone else watched from the opposite side. Kai gleaned the hills for the four Katori strangers—their movements increased with intensity.

He wasn't sure how, but they were causing this storm. And if he didn't know better, he'd swear they were forcing the surge of water in his direction. There was no time to figure out why. For now, they needed to survive. His heart quickened, and the horse jerked backward and stopped. "This is no time to panic, Kai!" Haygan shouted, holding on to the cart so it did not wash them all away.

Fears calmed, Kai stepped forward. The horse advanced. A small tree branch rushed by, but still, they continued onward. Bits of debris rushed around Kai's legs, and he stumbled. Another limb caught in the cart's wheel, and Haygan pulled it free, throwing the brush aside. "Keep going!" Haygan yelled through the rain.

Kai knew why Haygan yelled. Dead trees rolled down the hill toward their location; the spear-like projectiles would rip them apart. All he could do was hold on to the horse, keep calm, and pick up the pace. Haygan pushed on the cart to keep it from pulling the horse away with the current.

Quickening his steps, the horse moved faster. His footing was precarious, but Kai kept moving, barely touching the ground. He hopped through the muddy, waist-deep water.

Just a few feet more, he thought. Mid-hop, a small branch knocked Kai's leg, and he lost his footing. Feet first, he slid under the horse. Gasping and flailing through the water, he reached for a dangling leather strap. His fingers gripped it tight. Water pushed against his side, threatening to tear him away.

Unable to regain his footing, Kai held on with all his might. He dangled by one arm. Tossed about by the water, he held his breath and pulled. His head rose above the muddy water. Focused, he asked the horses to advance, dragging him along. Through the splashes, he saw Haygan point and yell. His words were obscured by the noise of the river.

Again, he gleaned the hillside, and the downed trees headed in their direction. No longer able to see, he continued to hold on. *We have to be close,* he thought. A few steps further, he felt a hand reach out and grab him. Then another hand. He let go of the strap, and Drew and Dresnor pulled him to safety.

Back on his feet, he watched fallen trees wash behind his uncle.

Relieved they were across the river, they traveled north to higher ground. Kai gripped Ember's reins with wrinkled hands. Exhausted, they trudged through the downpour to the next ridge. Drew directed them to a dilapidated barn that struggled against encroaching vines.

Inside, they made a small fire. The warmth felt good against the chilled mountain water in which Kai had nearly drowned. Kai was thankful that with everyone huddled together in the small space, Haygan was unable to lecture him about his mistake. Unfortunately, he was also unable to ask any questions about what had happened. Or how the Katori strangers were able to manipulate the weather.

CHAPTER 11

Chenowith

Two days later, they arrived in Chenowith soaking wet. Albert Chenowith, son of Lord Oliver, greeted them at the gates. His blond hair was considerably longer than last summer. Pleased to see his friend, Kai dismounted Ember and locked arms with Albert. "Albert, it is good to see you. I was disappointed you missed the Winter Festival, bringing in the new year without you was not the same. Your father mentioned you were unwell. How are you feeling?"

"Prince Kai, good to see you." Albert rubbed his chest. "It was a harsh winter for me. Our physician had concerns I would not recover. Mother feared I might die—she never left my side. I was bedridden for weeks with severe fever and difficulty breathing. My cough still lingers."

Kai knew it was serious enough to keep Albert from the Winter Festival, but he'd had no idea his friend was at risk of dying. "Your father did not elaborate. I should have come to visit."

"I feel fine," Albert wheezed, "but mother still won't let me do anything. Mothers. You know how they can be."

The words pierced Kai's heart. He wished he knew how mothers were. He didn't dare remind Albert. "Lady Clair is a good mother," Kai nodded. "Good of you to meet us. I hope you've not been waiting long. Maybe we should stay in town."

"Nonsense—we've been ready for days. When your scout arrived, announcing you were coming early, I clamored to meet you. I am lucky the rain stopped, or I would not be out here." Albert's bright blue eyes sparkled with joy. "Come, let's make haste, they are holding lunch for you."

A small lump formed in Kai's throat. "Albert. Are you sure we are not imposing? We plan to leave come dawn. I don't want to inconvenience your parents for a few hours' sleep."

Albert mounted his black stallion. "You know my mother." A sly grin bubbled into a small chuckle. "You can tell her you're staying in town, but I'm not about to show up without you." He raised an eyebrow and sidestepped his horse to the gatehouse.

After a moment, Kai raised his hands and relented. Lady Clair was a persistent woman. He was not about to challenge her wishes. "Lead the way. Show off." Kai hopped back into the saddle and followed Albert. He had always been impressed with all three Chenowith brothers. Their equestrian training skills were outstanding. He had never seen horses prance until he came to Chenowith last summer.

Chenowith was a beautiful city nestled amongst the small foothills above Baden Lake. Together they passed through the gatehouse. Kai eyed the large interlocked gray blocks of the city walls. While the walls were not as tall as those in Diu, they were well maintained and had multiple lookout points with soldiers patrolling between the watchtowers.

"Albert," he said, motioning to his friend to slow down. "I need to make a stop in town. I hate to ask since they are expecting us, but it is important."

Haygan rode forward and pointed in the direction of the glassmaker's shop. "Albert, he needs to visit Pinellas Glass Wonders."

"Certainly." Albert led the way, dismounting outside the charming shop.

The glass shop was sweltering. Kai entered with Albert,

Haygan, and Kempery-man Dresnor. Sweat dripped down the face of an old leathery bald man. He pulled a glowing ball of molten glass from a furnace and rolled it back and forth. A young apprentice blew into the long tube guided by the old man.

Kai wished he had more time to watch the men work, but he had to find a gift.

All around the shop were shelves filled with glass vases, bottles, and small beads. Around the ceiling hung various decorative glass panels. Their beautiful array of colors catching the light that bounced around the shop. "There is so much," Kai whispered to Haygan. "This man should live in Diu; he'd make a fortune."

Fingering several glass beads in a bowl, he wondered if Rayna would like something decorative. "Haygan, do you think Rayna would like some glass beads strung on a bracelet?"

Haygan cut his eyes at Kai and raised one eyebrow. "Jewelry is a very personal gift. Only give it to the girl who holds your heart."

"When did you give Simone jewelry?" Kai said with a grin.

Haygan's expression softened, and a sense of pride puffed up his chest. "Simone is the love of my life." He slapped Kai on the back of his shoulder. "I would stick to the bottles. Your relationship might not be ready for jewelry. Let's hurry up, we all need rest. Dresnor and I will wait outside."

Albert watched them leave and approached Kai. "What are you searching for?"

Embarrassed, Kai pursed his lips. "I need glass bottles made by the end of summer. We will stop back through at summer's end to collect them on our return trip."

Albert took him to a large shelf. "Here, pick the style you like from this shelf. Tell them the colors you want. I will see that they are ready when you return." A sly grin crossed his mouth. "Are they for a girl?" He nudged Kai's arm.

"Umm, they're...I...yes they are," he stammered, selecting

a few bottles and approaching the counter. Not wanting to keep everyone waiting, Kai placed his order with the old man's assistant.

Back outside, he glanced around at the unique buildings of Chenowith, remounting his horse. The large gabled eaves were supported by scrolling decorative braces and massive wooden beams, and the weatherboarding was painted in an assortment of colors. Like last summer, their front windows were pushed open to catch the breeze blustering through the hillside.

At the center of town, they rode through a large open plaza. The cobblestone was a variety of white, gray, and black stone. The design swooped and swirled around a large marble fountain. Kai's favorite part about the town was the fountain centerpiece. One large chunk of marble, an architectural marvel.

The base remained jagged and natural with three small waterfalls and three giant wolves carved around it. The top was cut into a man and wolf. The pair stood together in harmony, gazing into the distance.

Townspeople gathered around the bubbling fountain, talking and enjoying a pleasant rain-free day. Kai let his eyes wander around the meandering crowd. Studying the people, he quickly remembered that nearly everyone had various shades of blonde hair, from pale-sunshine to golden-straw. Their clothing was also different from Diu. Everyone wore festive colors with embroidered flowers and vines.

Beyond the square, Dresnor stopped at a sizeable cream-colored inn. The Linwood House took up the entire block. Four guards stood with the innkeeper; their silver armor gleamed in the sunshine. Dismounting, Kai watched his soldiers reposition as he followed Dresnor inside.

Up two flights of stairs, Dresnor escorted Kai to a large corner room overlooking the square. "Kai, I thought you might want to freshen from the long ride. Three days in the mud and rain did little for your regal appearance."

"Well, if we are being honest, Philip, you've looked and... phew... smelled better," he bantered in return. "It couldn't hurt for you to splash the mud off your beard and change your uniform."

Dresnor looked down at his shirt and tugged at his mud-splattered beard. "Agreed. It would be better if I didn't look or smell like a barn animal." He laughed.

"I wanted to ask your opinion of the Chenowith family," Kai said. "In all of Diu's towns, there could not be a more loyal household. Would you agree?"

"If you're asking should you someday consider one of the Chenowith boys for your council in Milnos, I would agree. Albert especially has bigger ambitions than horse breeding and winemaking. He would be a true asset. You will need someone on your side to advise you and keep you informed of what is happening here in Diu."

Milnos was on Kai's mind. Dresnor was right; he would need people he could trust. "I was thinking about someone who could look in on my father when I move away. I would want someone I trusted to send word."

"Consider Albert. I am sure he will welcome the opportunity when the times comes."

Refreshed, they remounted and continued through the streets of the town with Albert. Their journey led them high into the hills with fewer and fewer buildings. When they reached the Chenowith Estate, he was still astonished to find that no wall separated the estate from its people. The sprawling grounds out front were open and lush. Its only barrier was a rolling evergreen hedge, interspersed with clusters of towering pine trees and mounds of red rose bushes.

High in the distance, jagged white peaks scraped against the sky. The snowy summits were barely visible against the pale-blue sky. Kai was back in the lower part of the Katori Mountains and happy to see them once more. The sketches in books never did them justice.

Once again, the Chenowith home took his breath away.

The massive wooden mansion was unlike anything he had ever seen before. Like in town, gabled roofs gave way to wide eaves and exposed beams, supported by decoratively carved brackets over large, open balconies. Decorative carvings and moldings accented oversized windows and a thick stone foundation.

Four of his guards, who had ridden ahead to announce his arrival, stood out front. A row of groomsmen waited nearby, poised to assist with the horses. On the front steps stood two rows of servants, beaming with pride.

Lord Oliver, Lady Clair, and their two other sons, William and Noah, stood in front of the large double doors. All three sons were the spitting image of their father. Tall, broad shoulders, narrow waists, and shoulder-length straw-blond hair with hazel green eyes. Lady Clair's statuesque frame was equal to her husband's. Her golden locks, braided into long coils, swooped about her head. Their elegant clothes made Kai thankful he had stopped in town to freshen from the long ride.

Dresnor approached the Duke. "Duke Chenowith, I am pleased to formally announce His Royal Highness Prince Kai Galloway of Diu, son of King Iver and Mariana Galloway."

The Chenowith men gave a deep bow while Clair curtsied. "Your Highness, Prince Galloway, it is an honor to have you here with us again. Please come in." Oliver glanced lovingly at his wife and turned to swing both doors wide. He gestured into the grand foyer.

Kai stepped forward into the grand entrance. He'd spent last summer in Chenowith. Something about the place made him feel like he was home. Being this close to the mountains moved him. He had no idea how much he'd missed the estate until now.

The interior was beautiful. The flooring design was a mix of diamond-and-square-shaped interlocking pieces of wood. Each piece was stained red, black, or neutral to create a flower pattern across the floor. There was an expansive wrap-around staircase decorated with tapestries, stained glass windows, and large paintings.

"You have a magnificent home," Kai said, nodding to Lord Oliver. "Thank you for hosting my group. It is gracious of you to open your home, given our early arrival and quick departure. I hope we are not intruding."

"It is our pleasure, Prince Kai." Lord Oliver bowed deeply. "We are honored by your visit, even for one night."

Taking the lead, Oliver motioned. "If you will follow me. We have prepared a small meal for you and your men in the banquet hall. I would imagine you are all tired from the journey. Since you plan to leave come dawn, I have taken the liberty to request supplies for the next part of your journey."

Kai ushered his men forward. "I am humbled by your generosity, Lord Oliver. Bless you."

"After refreshments," Oliver motioned, "you can retire to your rooms. Like last summer, there is room in the house for you, four of your men, your hunter and his son. A few can stay in the servants' house; my steward tells me he can accommodate only three tonight. The rest can stay in the stable loft rooms. My groomsman will see to their needs."

"Thank you, Lord Oliver." Inside the banquet hall, there were three long tables, covered in food and flowers. How he loved this room, with its multicolored inlaid wood that decorated the floors, walls, and ceiling.

Oliver held Clair's hand until he reached the head of the table. "There is room for all of your companions. Please, everyone, take a seat." Oliver insisted, pulling out Clair's chair.

Dresnor held back, instructing two Chenowith guards, while everyone else took a seat around one of the tables. Kai looked around, thankful for his friends. Over the past two years, he and his men had become very close.

Everyone smiled and chattered with the Chenowiths as if no time had passed since last year. It was good to feel at home. Kai couldn't help but watch Albert. His illness had thinned his face, and his mother could not help fawning over her youngest.

The warm meal filled Kai. He wiped his mouth with the floral napkin. "Lord Oliver, while we are staying the summer in Albey, is there a chance you all could come to visit?"

Oliver took a drink to clear his throat. "I doubt I could make the trip, but I could send the boys for a week. William and Noah have traveled to Albey many times. Albert's illness has taken a lot out of him, however, so I am not sure he is strong enough. Let's see how summer goes."

"Dad, please, I can make it," Albert insisted. "Mother, please, don't make me stay behind." He coughed ever so softly.

"If your cough is completely gone, I will consider sending you." Oliver's tone was stern. The Duke turned back to Kai. "Thank you for thinking of my boys. End of summer just before early harvest, I will send a bird and let you know whom to expect. Your Kempery-man shared news about your troubles on the road. Men are already looking into repairing the washed away section. When the rains let up, we need to build a bridge over the creek. That road washes out too often."

"The weather took us by surprise," Kai nodded. "I had no idea that much rain could fall at once. Good to hear you are putting in a bridge." He pushed back his plate. Rubbing his chin, he felt embarrassed that he'd not shaved in days.

After the polite conversation, everyone adjourned to their private quarters. Everything looked the same. The small writing desk was bathed in sunlight near the tall wall of windows. Its surface was inlaid with different shades of stained wood, and the thick ornately carved edges coiled down into each leg.

His fingers floated over the intricately carved desk chair as he looked at the wooden armoire. Like everything else, it was hand-cut and stained to bring out the design—flowers, vines, and trees. The carved headboard and four-post bed frame was a welcome sight to his weary body.

Outside on the large balcony, Kai enjoyed his view of the gardens and the clear view of the Katori Mountains. Even though it was good to be back, he wished he was elsewhere.

Ryker's failed attempt to save his mother weighed on him, and there was nothing he could do to help.

Leaving the doors open, he changed and lay down across his bed. He could hardly believe how good it felt to lay in a bed after two miserable days in the mud and rain. The fresh air blew through the open balcony doors, bringing with it the smell of pine and wet earth. Between the soft bed and fresh air, he was asleep in no time.

CHAPTER 12

Conhaspriga

Kai awoke to a dark room. Through the open balcony doors, he felt a light cool breeze brush against his face. The sun's rays clawed at the jagged peaks of the Katori Mountains. He watched the sky became a mix of warm orange and yellow, pushing against the dark sky.

Smoke lay on the balcony between two chairs, looking out into the forest behind the Chenowith estate gardens. Joining him, Kai took a seat outside to watch the sunrise. Restless and unable to go back to sleep, Kai ventured out for a stroll through the gardens. He loved this place. Last summer was a blessing. No battles. No bad men. The town of Chenowith was on a good path. They welcomed him, and he savored their loyalty.

With the freedom to enjoy the countryside and time alone, Kai went exploring the hillside. Shiva and Smoke joined him in the woods, and together they ran around the estate. Enormous pine trees and tall aspens grew densely along the perimeter, and their alignment made it impossible to run. He zigzagged through the trees, moving deeper into the thick forest. The smell of pine mixed with moss and dirt hung in the air.

Connected to his sight, he ventured deeper into the wood. The wolves sniffed the terrain. Deeper into the forest the sounds of birds and a small brook came to his senses. Above him in the hills, Kai's sight revealed a small clearing.

The dense pine gave way to large pin oaks and bits of blue sky. Through the trees, Kai sensed a presence. He closed his eyes and reached out. Her nature was calm yet alert. Kind yet protective. A doe and her fawn. The pair stood near the brook.

His breathing calm, he pushed Smoke and Shiva away. Gently he reached out with his spirit to the deer. Her head perked up, and she stared through the trees in his direction. He held still, waiting for her approval. Motionless, she stared fixed on his location.

Unable to move, Kai waited. The smallest twitch might spook the doe. He needed to get the doe to approach him. In his mind, he called to the deer; she took a step across the brook, then another. Her baby fawn ran and jumped through the water to keep up. The fawn's tiny white spots were speckled across its back—a sharp contrast to its brown hair.

Confident that the doe was comfortable, Kai took a few steps in their direction. She continued her approach. Five feet away, he stopped and let her close the gap. He held out his hand, and the doe sniffed it. The pair was content in his presence, and he ran his hands down the mother's neck, while the young fawn pranced around the tall grasses and wildflowers.

Peace and tranquility filled Kai's heart. He did not understand how people could hunt these beautiful creatures.

A large brook bubbled out of the base of several large rocks. The gurgle echoed around the clearing and trickled away into the surrounding trees. The warm morning sun shone overhead, and Kai knelt and took a sip of the fresh, clear water. The taste was refreshing and cold. Pleased to be in their company, he sat on a large rock and watched the pair snack on leaves and vines.

Their delicate, graceful nature was a joy to behold. The doe nuzzled her baby fawn and then looked into the trees. Kai pivoted and glared in the same direction. He saw nothing with his eyes. He felt for Smoke and Shiva. It was not their presence that startled her—they were behind him on the hillside. He gleaned deep into the trees.

His sight set the trees alive with light. Deep within the woods, a wolf glared down into the clearing. Seven more joined the leader. Quickly Kai connected to the wolves, one after the other. The eldest wolves acknowledged him. The two youngest in the pack felt anxious. Their wild nature bounced with the urge to run. Concerned for the deer, his pulse quickened. He needed to warn them. They must run now.

Kai stood and pushed his senses to the deer. "Run," he told her.

She bolted for the trees in the opposite direction, her baby fawn shadowing quickly behind.

The secret to balancing a wild pack this size was to remain calm. Kai placed his hand over his heart and calmed his breathing. His senses told him they were not hungry or savage. Their spirits were open to him, and he smiled. He knew them. He called the lead wolf.

As they approached, Kai again searched for Shiva and Smoke. They were returning to him. They too had picked up on the wild pack and were flanking their approach. The pack had been following him since the old lodge. The same location they'd found him his first and second summer.

Knowing the distance between Town Hope and Chenowith was nearly eighty miles made Kai wonder how vast their territory was, and how far they were willing to follow him. In Diu, he had researched wolves. Most of the books agreed they usually hunt within a region, which can range from fifty to over a thousand square miles. Given the size of their growing pack, their territory was probably vast.

Shiva and Smoke reached the clearing first—one on either side of the lead wolf. There he stood—the alpha and his pack. His gray and white fur ruffled in the breeze. The pack was now eight wolves strong.

Both Nebean black wolves ran to Kai. Positioned in front

of him, they faced the alpha. Smoke growled, and Shiva remained quiet. Kai pushed his thoughts to Smoke, urging him to stay calm. The younger wolves in the pack growled back. If Kai didn't intervene, there would be a fight. Any sudden movement would set things in motion.

The two young wolves twitched with the urge to charge. They were the larger group, but Smoke and Shiva were over twice their size. Clear-minded, Kai sat in the tall grass. Sunlight reflected off the babbling brook between him and the pack. He shifted his focus to the younger wolves; they needed to yield first. To his surprise, the alpha matched his posture and sat. The others stopped growling but stood their ground.

Shiva, Smoke, heel, he instructed while pushing his calm nature. Accepting his instruction, all the wolves relaxed and sat in the grass. For the longest time, they watched each other, none of them willing to move.

When Kai rose to his feet and crossed the water, he did so with confidence exuding from his aura. He moved from stone to stone until his foot landed on the other side. Smoke and Shiva followed. The pack stood, but the alpha did not. The clearing was quiet except for the brook and the occasional chirping bird.

Kai knelt on his knees and faced the alpha. His heart pounded heavily in his chest. The alpha stood and approached. He mentally balanced the pack and his two black wolves. They all remained calm.

The alpha stared into Kai's eyes. Locked in the moment, Kai felt a strong bond deep within his soul. He passed the feeling to Shiva and Smoke. Relieved, he saw them sit at his side.

The alpha stepped forward and licked him across the face. A smile spread across Kai's face, and the wolf continued his display of affection. Reassured, he fell on his side in the grass, and the wolf relaxed with him.

He laid in the grass next to the gray wolf. His hand on the alpha, he looked into its golden-yellow eyes. *I have missed you, my friend,* Kai thought with his heart more than his mind.

In return, he heard—*Protect.* And he felt a sense of loyalty.

"Old friend," Kai said aloud. "I think of you often."

His mind went back to the night he had laid outside their den—exhausted, his eyes drifting from one cloud to the next. What an excellent spot and a beautiful day. He secretly wished all days could be like this, living one with nature. Together they all lay in the grass. The fresh breeze brushed against them, and the sun warmed his skin.

Shiva perked up and sniffed the air. Her senses told him something or someone was near. Smoke raised his head. Through the trees, Kai sensed a young man approaching. His spirit was bright and intense. The alpha and his pack remained calm, unperturbed by his approach. Shiva and Smoke, however, both stood and stepped toward the trees.

Kai stood. The alpha and his pack surrounded him. They did not growl but took a defensive posture.

The young man stopped at the edge of the clearing. His rugged features, ink-black hair, and dark-blue eyes told Kai he was not native to Chenowith. His dark clothing again suggested he was not a local. Kai put his hands in his pockets. This young man had approached him and a pack of wolves without fear. No average person would do that. A quick glean solidified his theory. "You are Katori."

The young man smiled. "Yes. My name is Liam."

"My name is Kai. What brings you to Chenowith?"

"Same as you, I suppose. Spending my time in the outside world, before the Conhaspriga. Before I must make my choice: stay out here or return home." Liam tilted his head and nit his brow together, analyzing Kai.

Hesitant to reveal himself, Kai held his tongue. He knew the Katori protected their secrets. How could he learn something without giving away his lack of knowledge? "Where are you staying?" he asked, trying to sound confident.

"In the woods. I only have two weeks left before I turn seventeen. I am already feeling the pull to return. It is time for my Conhaspriga. How about you? You look, what, nearly sixteen? You must be at the beginning of your year."

"I am sixteen," he responded. Kai watched the alpha and his pack depart. They kept just inside the tree line for a moment before darting away into the hills.

"Impressive," Liam said, watching them go. "I have never seen someone so at ease with wild wolves. The black wolves, I gather they are with you."

"Shiva and Smoke are with me." He carefully considered his next question. "Where do you call home?"

"I live on the Mystic Islands. Have you ever been there?" Liam took a seat on a large rock near the brook.

Kai joined him. "I have not."

"They are beautiful jewel islands." Liam plucked a blade of grass. "Protruding high above the blue-green Caprizian Sea. You will have to visit me there someday. There is nothing like my home. We live amongst the trees, like you on the mainland. Behemoth bodhima trees and the cosmos vines create one connected canopy."

Listening to Liam, Kai could tell the young man was homesick. Katori and the Mystic Islands sounded beautiful. Given Kai's recent encounter with four Katori who tried to wipe him off the hillside, he was unsure he would be welcome. His prospects did not look good.

"Are you nervous?" Kai asked.

"About the Conhaspriga?" Liam rolled his eyes. "Yes and no. My father is rather disappointed I will not be a Beastmaster. Everyone in my family has the same gift. Instead, it seems I have an affinity for the earth. Want to see?"

Not wanting to seem overly excited, Kai casually tossed up his shoulder. "Sure. What can you do?"

Liam wiggled his hand into the earth of the riverbank. The stones and dirt surrounding the young man's hand began to wobble and shake. Slowly Liam raised his hand, and the rocks and mud converged. He swirled his hand slowly in an outward circle. Below his palm, Kai could see the collection of soil and stone was creating a twisted spiral sculpture.

"Impressive." Kai gulped at the realization he had no idea that was possible.

"Not really." Liam lifted his hand, and the form held its shape. "I have much to learn. After the Conhaspriga, I will be able to harness my full potential and create great structures, move boulders, and help shift mountains." Liam smashed his hand to the ground, crushing his creation and scattering the pebbles as if he'd never been there.

"You should be proud of your gift." Kai stood to look at Liam. "Alenga blesses us all. We should not take for granted if we are directed to serve differently."

"Wise words. I will try to remember that when my brothers harass me for being a Stoneking and not a Beast-master."

Stoneking. Kai had never heard that term. How many gifts were there? Beastmasters and Kodama were the only two Haygan had mentioned before. Not wanting to tip his hand, Kai held his excitement from reaching his face. "So, you've made your choice? You are going home."

"Life in Katori is simple. We live in paradise. My father says adventure strikes at the heart of only a few Katori. I am sure you can relate. Plus, if you wish to become a guardian on the mountain, you must see the world around us to know why we protect our simple way of life. A few Katori find this world fascinating. They want a faster pace and advancements. Although, between you and me, I believe they later regret the choice and wish to return to Katori. They live in the woods outside of Albey." The thought of them brought a small smile to Liam's eyes.

"Why do they not return? There are plenty who come and go from Katori freely." He thought of Haygan. "My uncle Haygan..." he stopped short, worried he should not mention Haygan's name.

"Pride," Liam answered. "Haygan. Hmmm, I have heard the name. I might know him. Anyway, admitting they chose wrong is not easy, and sadly most are shunned by family if they try to return. The rare few, like your uncle, that cross between both worlds. They only do so to keep us informed. We must not lose sight of the rest of the world."

Liam stood and glanced over his shoulder across the brook. "Well, Kai, it has been a pleasure meeting you. Find me if you decide to return. I look forward to showing you the Mystic Islands. This land is not for me. I am bound for Albey to complete the Conhaspriga, my rite of passage. If you do decide to stay here, consider north of Albey a fine place to live. My father told me they welcome all Katori strays into their hilltop community."

Kai didn't want Liam to go. It was too soon. He had more questions. "Any tips? Tips your father might have shared with you." He asked in a rushed tone at Liam's back.

"Kai, the way will be difficult, but my father said as a full Katori we need to learn to navigate and trust our gut. Their challenges will distract you, the terrain will change. Your ability to glean will be stripped from you. At least that is what he told me. Follow your soul. They will not make it easy. Guardians must be strong. If you wanted it to be easy, you should have chosen a year of meditation at home."

"Right, that's what I was told, so nothing new." He let his voice trail off, feeling bad that he'd just lied.

Liam turned and extended his hand. "Well, remember you only have until you turn seventeen. Do not delay, or you will pay the price. I hear the sickness and fever are unbearable. Farewell, Kai. I must run if I am to make it to Albey by nightfall. I want to be close when my time comes."

A fever? What fever? Kai didn't know anything about a sickness. With the warning about turning seventeen, Kai wished he could ask for details, but that would prove he did not know what he should. He took Liam's offered hand. "It was good to meet you too. Good luck, Liam. I hope to see you again." He watched the young man dart off into the trees, gone in an instant.

Dreading the time, Kai himself darted through the trees

and returned to the Chenowith estate. His time with Liam would be his secret—the Conhaspriga, the Katori rite of passage. Kai wondered if he would be called when he turned seventeen. Would Rayna? She was full Katori. He was only a Half-Light. Given their birthdays were less than two weeks apart, it would stand to reason they would be called around the same time.

Kai wanted to know what it would feel like to be drawn to a place. There were still so many questions. Why had Kendra and Haygan kept this from him? Unless Half-Lights did not feel the calling...his stomach twisted in knots over the desire to belong.

Collecting his things, Kai made for the stables to join the others gearing up for their departure. Albert and Oliver approached the stables through the morning fog. It was going to be two long days in the saddle before they reached Albey.

CHAPTER 13

Albey Honey

By the time they neared Albey, Kai was saddle sore and anxious for news from home. From the moment Kai left Diu, his father's wellbeing was not far from his mind. He hoped Captain Wallis had a report or a letter from the Master General. Anything would be better than no update. Not to mention, he knew a lecture of some kind was coming from Haygan about his stunt on the hillside between Town Hope and Chenowith. Sending his magic into the world was bringing unwanted attention to him, and so far, the Katori people were not receptive.

He glanced backward and surveyed his men. Although they were accomplished and trained to endure long rides on little sleep, he could tell they were near the end of their respective ropes. Hopefully arriving a full three days early meant Captain Wallis's men would take the lion's share of guard duty.

Their path was a narrow road pressed into the earth between the rocky hillside and Baden Lake. Through the trees, Kai caught a glimpse of a stone guardhouse built into the side of the mountain. There were no walls, no guard towers, only the guardhouse. The only way into town was this narrow road. Although given the rocky terrain, maybe they didn't need conventional protection.

Four guards occupied the gatehouse—if you could even call them guards. One sat whittling wood while the others threw axes at a nearby tree. Kai's group passed with little more than a wave. Strange. Maybe they dismissed his group because Wallis had informed them of their imminent arrival. Yes, that had to be the reason nobody stopped them. Diu uniforms commanded respect and instilled confidence in the people.

Dresnor slowed their pace along the narrow road at the sight of Wallis's men approaching. After a word, Dresnor allowed them to continue toward the gatehouse, and he sent two scouts ahead to announce their approach to Captain Wallis.

Around the bend, the town came into view. Kempery-man Albey rode to Kai's left. "Beautiful. Wouldn't you agree? Although from here, you can only see a small portion. As we ride around the next bend, the mountains divide. The small valley is filled with shops and homes. My father's home, the Albey Estate, sits in that valley. I, however, have a small house built on the side of this mountain. It was my great aunts' home. While we are here, I will stay at the estate with you. If you wish, I can show you around the cliffside homes."

An instant kinship to Albey struck Kai. This picturesque town was built on the edge of Baden Lake, pressed into the valley below the expansive Katori Mountains. Homes engulfed in greenery; their reflections rippled across the glassy water below. Two ships sat in the harbor with a few men scurrying about.

"Kempery-man Albey, your town is charming. I look forward to spending the summer here."

"Prince Kai, call me Zayne, if you please. I believe we've known each other long enough." He grinned. "Not to mention, my mother may find it too formal."

The name 'Zayne' felt strange on Kai's tongue. "In private, you may call me Kai. For your mother, I am happy to keep things informal. Titles do not make the man."

Together, Kai and Albey continued. They watched Captain

Wallis and his men scramble to meet them. Scattered about the town, Kai watched the Diu soldiers interview villagers. They were preparing for his visit as they had done last summer in Chenowith, after his first trip to Hamrin and the battle for his life, they took no chances.

Both groups gathered in the town square.

Kai admired a detailed carving. From a distance he had thought it was a tree. However, upon closer inspection, he realized the trunk had the face of a woman carved into the base, eyes closed with a demure smile. Taking another look, he decided the design made the branches look like hair caught in the wind.

Surrounded by his own men and joined by Captain Wallis's group, they were a sizable force. Kai peered around the square. He was relieved to see clean cobblestone streets, filled with happy, healthy people and the occasional horse-drawn cart. The buildings were large, with black roofs and faded yellow or pink weatherboarding. A few others were built of gray stone.

Listening to Kempery-man Dresnor receive the report from Captain Wallis, Kai brought his eyes down to street level. Bystanders gawked at their group and whispered. Three young ladies giggled and waved at him. An old man sipped tea; a dog sat at his feet.

Having come by ship straight from Diu City to ensure no secrets lay in wait for the prince and his entourage, Wallis and his men dominated the town. Their silver armor gleamed in the afternoon sun, a welcome sight for everyone in his group. Fresh able men ready to protect the prince.

Before they entered the Albey Estate, Dresnor pulled everyone aside. "I advise everyone to take advantage of the next few days to rest. Wallis's men are willing to stay ten full days before returning to Diu. Make the most of this extra time to recover. We are all road-weary, and I need you sharp. Spend some of your time learning the streets and meeting people. Speak to Wallis's men to learn what you can before they depart." Excitement lit up the faces of the men. This was good news. Free time was more than they expected.

Dresnor shifted his weight to one side. "Captain Wallis will secure the grounds and patrol the town. Relish these next few days, but I need not tell you how to conduct yourselves." He fired a stern glare at his men.

"Albey, Drew, and Redmond, once Wallis and his men depart, you three have the estate unless Kai goes into town. We have fifteen men this trip, not counting Haygan and Marduk. This trip should prove uneventful and pleasant; however, keep your wits about you. I don't want any surprises." His tone remained firm, his eyes serious.

"Prince Kai, should you wish to leave the estate grounds at any time, you're with one of us. I trust Wallis and his men, but you are in my care, not his. Clear?" Dresnor raised his eyebrow. "I suppose Shiva and Smoke count if you take a run," he added.

"Crystal clear, Dresnor," Kai acknowledged.

His group rode through the gates of the estate. Their surprise arrival meant nobody waited outside to greet the prince. Kai preferred the simple entry. Dresnor and Drew hung back to speak with Captain Wallis. Everyone else entered the estate grounds following Kempery-man Albey to the stables. Leaving the horses with the groomsman, they made their way to the main house.

The Albey Estate was made of gray stone with some sections painted white. Like everything else in the town, white seemed to be the prominent color. The overall structure was reminiscent of an old castle, only smaller. One end had a tall castle tower, and the other a structure built entirely of glass. Nearly half of the building was covered in green vines.

After a formal greeting with the family, Kai and his group had the opportunity to freshen their attire before joining the Albey family for dinner in the banquet hall. Another room painted entirely white. *Do they not have any other colors?* He wanted to ask but feared it would be rude.

Duke Lars Albey was an older, heavyset man, and his wife, Lady Emma, was noticeably younger. Her light brown hair had only the faintest hints of gray, and her eyes were a unique ice-blue. Kai learned that their eldest, Kinnon, was traveling and was expected back soon. Their other two children, Brianna and Kempery-man Zayne, were both the spitting image of their father. They had black curly hair and green eyes, although the Duke's hair was streaked with gray, revealing his seniority.

The old man seemed kind enough, but Kai got a sense of laziness on the old man's part. When it came to helping the town grow, he had no real interest. Kai listened to Lars say, "I've done enough work in my life. It is time to enjoy my golden years. Besides, the townspeople need to make way for themselves. When Kinnon, my son, returns, I want him to start managing the town."

"How long have you been the duke of Albey, Lord Lars?" Kai asked.

"Ten years, this winter, after my father passed away. He lived an unusually long life. I was humbly honored to accept the position, but it was never my ambition to govern. They really do not need my leadership. The town seems more than capable of running itself."

Being a duke was an honor, yet Lars was disinterested. This news surprised Kai. Outside of security, Lars let everything run as his father, the previous duke, had arranged. Kai was thankful to hear Lars maintained a hand in ensuring that the city guards kept the peace, but it was disappointing to discover the rest.

The best Kai could tell, Lars had no real knowledge about the inner workings of the town. Nor did he care to learn. Like Dresnor had once said, if they pay the taxes to the kingdom, they were left to run themselves.

Conversations continued late into the night. The more he learned, the less he wished to know. There were many challenges left unaddressed about town. Clearly, Kai had his work cut out for him on this trip. While he liked the small-town feel, it sounded more like a fading, dying town. This was not what he wanted to do. He was beginning to resent his duty as a prince.

It was near midnight when Kai climbed into the bed at the Albey Estate. He looked around at the simple yet elegant furnishings of his room. Smoke slept peacefully near the door on an oval rug; his massive body overflowed onto the wide plank black walnut flooring that matched the ceiling's exposed beams. Three walls were stark white, while the exterior wall was made of multi-colored stone.

After a good night's rest, Kai hopped out of bed and looked around his room. Behind the desk, he marveled at the red velvet paisley covered window seat below the diamond-shaped windowpanes. While appealing, the metal dividers and the wavy glass made it difficult to get a clear view. He opened three of the large windows and caught a fresh morning breeze blowing through the hills.

His view was simple: rows and rows of apple trees. White, sun-kissed blossoms coiled around the branches like clumps of cotton. The apple trees made him think of Rayna and their many walks through the Diu palace orchard. At this hour, he knew she would be awake, busy making bread in the bakehouse. It had only been a little over a week, and he missed her dearly.

Disinterested in his obligations, Kai pondered how he would manage an entire summer trapped here. Nothing about this trip was what Kai wanted. His mission was to connect with his people and report back on the condition of their lives and help make improvements where he could. How could he not help his people?

Like it or not, he would do his duty. The place to start— get to know the servants. He needed to learn about the men and women who worked in the estate. Then he could venture around the town and any surrounding farms. Their stories would tell him more than those in charge.

The backbone of every home was the kitchen. Gossip and rumors would spring from the kitchen and the laundry. He would need to start there.

Circling down the spiral stairwell, he entered a long hallway. Past the dining hall, Kai found the kitchen. Although it was early, the kitchen smelled of freshly baked bread. From the doorway, he watched the hustle and bustle of the servants.

Quickly identifying the woman in charge, he studied her. His sight told him she was part-Katori, as were several people he'd seen through the estate and town. Prin, as they called her, was a quiet woman compared to Lizzie. In fact, she said very little as she stepped from station to station, tasting or inspecting their work. All the ladies had their hair pulled back into a neat bun and wore pale-yellow dresses with white aprons tied at the waist.

The older woman's hair was snow-white and much like any good cook, according to Lizzie; she was a bit lumpy in the middle. *Never trust a cook that won't eat her own food,* Lizzie would say. Seemingly satisfied with their progress, Prin crossed the kitchen to greet him. Smiling, she gestured toward the long table at the center.

In the softest voice imaginable, she said, "Have a seat, Your Highness. My name is Prin. You honor me with your visit to the kitchen. How may I serve you today?" She squinted slightly, studying him.

Kai nodded to her and took a seat, wondering what she hoped to discern. "Thank you. It's a pleasure to meet you, Prin. I wanted to see the backbone of the Albey Estate. The nature of the staff tells me more about the estate than its Lord and Lady. I look forward to meeting people in the village later today."

She smiled at him and then glanced over to a girl separating freshly baked bread rolls. With a nod, the girl stopped, found a plate, cut a roll in half and smeared one side with a dark purple preserve and light orange jam on the other. She smiled and passed the plate to the next girl who placed two slices of thick roasted ham on the plate, before handing it to Prin.

Prin stepped forward and offered Kai the plate. "I would be happy if you tried our blackberry and orange preserves. They are both made right here at the estate by my girls." She bowed her head ever so slightly.

Her gentle smile set Kai at ease. "Thank you, it would be my pleasure, Prin." He accepted the plate. "I am sure it will be difficult to choose a favorite." As he bit into the roll smeared with the orange preserve, he was delighted. *Nothing could be better,* he thought. Then he tried the blackberry preserve. His eyes lit up, and he smiled more and more with each bite. "I guess I was wrong. The orange was wonderful, but the blackberry was divine. Thank you."

She grinned and nodded. A tall old man entered the back of the kitchen, approached her, and slid his hand around her back. "Good morning, my dear. Have you taken in a new boy?" he asked, hugging her softly.

Before she could answer, Kempery-man Albey entered the kitchen. "Good morning, Prin, Leo. I see Prince Kai has found his way to you. You're in good hands here, Kai. Prin makes the best preserves. Her secret is the sweetener. She makes them from the honey Leo harvests from the hives along the back of the estate."

Kempery-man Albey pulled up a chair next to Kai just as Prin offered Kai a plate of eggs and bacon. Albey's plate had his rolls smeared with blackberry preserves.

Leo bowed in embarrassment. "My apologies, Your Highness. I had no idea I was addressing…"

Kai raised his hand to stop the kind man. "Please. I am a man like any other." He rubbed at the stubble across his chin. "I know Diu etiquette requires formality, but then we are not in Diu, are we? Please, call me Kai." He pulled out the seat next to him. "Sit, eat with us."

Leo nodded and took the offered chair. "Well…Kai, it is a pleasure to have you with us. Any friend of Zayne's is a friend of mine." Prin handed her husband a plate and turned back to her assistants.

"Zayne, I see you clearly have a well-known favorite." Kai noticed both pieces of Kempery-man Albey's bread were slathered with blackberry preserves. "Prin, you should ship your preserves to Diu. I know they would be famous. The honey, too. We don't get much honey." He took another bite and savored the fruity flavor.

Prin blushed at his comments and continued her work. Leo, equally reserved, tilted his head to the side. "You really think they would buy our honey? In the big city of Diu? I would think they have everything in your city."

"We certainly have access to a great many things, but local honey is not currently on our list. It is shipped in from Nebea from time to time. If you were to ship it across the lake, I could certainly see a benefit to both of us."

This was the first time in three years where he had spent actual alone time with Kempery-man Albey. The man always kept to himself. A quiet soul. Albey laughed. Only ten years his senior, Zayne Albey was one of the youngest Kempery-man in the history of the King's Champions. Kai had been his first charge.

Curly black hair mopped about his head, and his short stubbly beard gave him a rugged yet mature look. "Kai, you are always working the angles to help someone," Albey observed. "You are a good man. You will make a fine king someday. I am most fortunate to be in your service."

"Kind of you to say, Zayne. I find it easy to help people. Besides, more honey in Diu means more honey for me," he joked, hoping to lighten the mood.

CHAPTER 14

Haygan's Warning

"**S**orry I am late. Breakfast with Kempery-man Albey ran long." Kai called through the trees to Haygan. Smoke sprang from the underbrush to greet Kai with a playful jump.

"I did not mind waiting," Haygan answered. "I knew you'd be here when you were able. We have much to discuss before I leave. Hike with me along the Conha River. I will guide you to the first of three great waterfalls and the edge of the Zabranen Forest. From there you will need to return to Albey on your own. I must get word home about Ryker and Simone. I can only hope the news about your mother will stir the elders into action."

"Wait. No. I want to go with you. Mariana is my mother." Kai demanded.

"I will not argue with you, Kai. You know they will not let me bring you across. It is bad enough I must also hunt down these four rogue Katori who tried to wipe you off the hillside. I have no idea who they were. You know the storm and water surge was not natural."

Part of Kai was thankful his uncle would get news home, and part of him resented his own inability to travel to Katori. Kai followed his uncle, grumbling under his breath. The terrain started out simple–short grasses and a few scraggly trees. The farther they walked, however, the thicker the brush became. In their silence, Kai listened to the rush of the water flowing from the Katori Mountains down the Conha River. On the ground, he noticed animal tracks large and small from creatures seeking water and food from the river.

Half-listening to Haygan lecture him about the mistake of sending his magic into the hills and drawing unwanted attention, he thought of Liam. The young man would have reached Albey three days earlier. He imagined the young man had faced his challenges and completed his Conhaspriga, his rite of passage. Surely, Liam must have traveled along this very river. Kai wondered what the rites of passage entailed and what it meant to have a gift. Three gifts came to mind: Beastmaster, Kodama, Stoneking, and some ability to affect the weather. Were there other gifts? He knew his mother and Simone could both turn into dragons, and Sabastian was an eagle.

Kendra and Haygan kept too many secrets. How different his life would be if his mother were with him. She would have told him everything, he was sure of it. While they walked, he fantasized about his mother taking him home to Katori. How they would be welcomed. Details Kendra had shared painted a magnificent picture of their marble city amongst mammoth bodhima trees he'd only seen in sketches. The endless natural rivers and pools threaded throughout the city.

"Haygan. Can I ask you about...?" He hesitated, stepping around a bent tree limb.

Afraid to say the words, Kai bit his lip. He feared being rejected—or lied to. Would his newly christened uncle answer all his questions now? He swallowed hard and took a chance. "The name of this river—Conha. What does it have to do with the Conhaspriga?"

Haygan cocked his head around to glance at Kai. A small smirk bloomed out of the corner of his mouth. "Clever boy. Where did you learn about the Katori rite of passage?"

"A friend."

Before Haygan could respond, Kai asked more. "If my mother were here with me, would she keep secrets? Or would she have taught me about the Conhaspriga?"

There in the middle of the forest, Kai saw something he could have only hoped for: his uncle's expression showed agreement. "She would have been training you, Half-Light or not. How in Alenga's name did you learn about Conhaspriga?"

"A boy I met three days ago before we left Chenowith. I was in the forest with the alpha pack. A young man named Liam came upon us. He was bound for Albey, returning after his year abroad visiting the outside world. He was about to complete his Conhaspriga. For all I know, he is in the hills here right now."

The ground shook beneath their feet. A low rumble. Haygan smiled. "Maybe."

Kai was confused by the sound but waited for his uncle's response.

"Correct," Haygan continued, "the rite of passage got its name from the river. Youth are given a choice. When they turn sixteen, they may leave Katori and travel the world. Most choose to stay and meditate in silence for a year. When they reach seventeen, the mountain calls all Katori. It is different for everyone. Some feel a gentle pull at their soul, while others get sick with a fever. I believe the harder the mountain grabs at your spirit, the stronger the power within you."

"Liam mentioned a fever," Kai stared at Haygan, thrilled he was willing to share more information. "He did not appear sick. Did you travel the world?"

"I most certainly did. I left for two years—to my father, your grandfather's, dismay. I left at fifteen. Mariana left on her journey one year after me. She actually found me in Nebea. The city, with its dense forests and animal life, fascinated me. I am not fond of ships and the ocean like her. We traveled together a while."

Not wanting to get off-topic, Kai interrupted. "So, you obviously returned. What is it like, the rite of passage?"

Haygan stopped. They had walked for hours. They stood near the first of a three-tiered waterfall. The massive wall of water towered over twenty feet above them. Its majestic nature roared overhead and crashed into an enormous mist-covered pool.

"Someday, you will return here without me. Remember to follow the river. The three waterfalls are your guide into Katori." Haygan turned to him. "You are family. My leaders may not like me saying it, but I believe you should be able to come home. I believe you will be called. We shall see soon enough."

"How do you know what gift you will have?" Kai looked to Smoke drinking from the splash pool. "What are the gifts?" He added.

"Mariana would tell you—I know she would." Haygan searched the trees before continuing. "If you choose to develop your magic, you need to do so before the gift burns out. At seventeen, you must go through the rite of passage. Since you are not in Katori, you must travel up the Katori Mountains." Haygan pointed to the waterfall "you will need to be granted access. A Stoneking will need to open the mountain for you."

"To answer your other question. There are many gifts. A Beastmaster can communicate with animals, and a few can turn into animals. There are Kodama, who are healers and tree spirits. They have a natural way with plants. Rayna is most likely Kodama. A rare few women can turn into trees and manipulate plant movement. No male has ever managed the change, nor are they able to influence the plants to move. Men become great healers.

"There are Weathervanes," Haygan continued. "They have limited influence over the weather. Like the four strangers you drew down on us a few days ago. They can only create huge storms if there are enough of them gathered together. Normally they create misty rain, fog, isolated winds, or localized temperature shifts," Haygan continued, revealing more Katori secrets.

"There are Lumens. Not sure how to explain what they do. There are so few. They bring the energy we see through gleaning to the surface for all to see. They enhance the power found in nature and illuminate the area. I have heard some can pull power from anything and manipulate it for their own purpose. They can light up a stone, and it will stay lit until they release the light and let it fade. Know this—they can also hide the light we see." Haygan locked eyes with Kai. "Heed my warning on this point, Kai. When you return, you will be tested by the Guardians of the mountain.

Kai's eyes widened. "Liam mentioned the Guardians."

"Part of your test involves traveling without your ability to glean. A gift all Katori youth seem to rely on too much. The Lumens will block your gift. You will be unable to track others or see beyond your immediate surroundings. Even your connection to Smoke will be tested."

All the details felt like information overload. Years' worth of knowledge was being dumped onto his shoulders. Overwhelmed, Kai felt his head swim with excitement and his stomach flutter with anxiety.

"I take it, Liam told you about Stonekings?" Haygan asked.

"Yes. Liam will become a Stoneking. He showed me how he was able to manipulate stone to build a small structure, then he smashed it into nothing with the ease of crushing a sandcastle."

"Stonekings are masters of the earth. A large enough group can raise mountains. They can take a precious stone and turn it over in their hands to reveal its desired shape. They form our crystals. Like the one I wear." Haygan pulled a blue and white hexagonal stone from deep within his shirt. It dangled on a long silver chain. "Your mother had a stone. I am guessing whoever has it was controlling her all these years."

"Wait, what?" Kai blurted out. "The stones control you? Kendra never told me!" he barked.

"Well, they are linked to your soul. Part of your light will go into the crystal. It is rumored a crystal can call the owner. If the person who has it is stressed, in danger, or even angry, they pass those feelings through the stone and affect the owner. If the holder concentrates, they can summon you—call you to their aid. One Katori to another, or so I've been told." Haygan's eyebrows knit together.

"Sigry and my father. They have a necklace. I have held it many times. Ocean blue crystal, silver chain. Sigry keeps asking me if I feel anything when I hold it. Kendra said it was my mother's necklace. It even felt warm in my hand. I didn't want to share that with Sigry, so I lied."

"Oh Kai, blessed be Alenga! You need to get her necklace. It may find your mother. This is why keeping secrets is a waste of time. They've been so afraid to share anything with you and Kendra, and I have been reluctant to tell them everything we know about you. We could have found her three years ago if I had been able to speak freely."

Angry, Haygan clenched his fists.

"Does everyone get a stone?" questioned Kai.

"Yes, everyone gets a stone. The stone does not determine your gift, your spirit does. Alenga does. Although, we all show signs between the ages of thirteen and seventeen. There is rarely any mystery about which gift you will have."

Kai shook his head. He had held in his hand the very tool that could have brought his mother home. Then Haygan's previous comment smacked him on the head. His mother's stone. "Do you mean to tell me," Kai begged, "all this time, my father might be to blame for taking my mother away from me? Or at the very least, he had the stone to call her home and didn't know it." Frustrated, Kai tossed his hands in the air. "His Galloway soldiers were guarding her. My father's men. My own father has kept her a prisoner."

It was impossible to wrap his mind around the idea. All these years, Kai blamed the red dragon for her death and his father for being away at sea. He remembered his father wept in heartache for months after he returned to find her dead and gone. Kai reeled. "What can I do?"

"Nothing," Haygan said. "Well, except steal her necklace. I don't understand how this happened, but I do know we need the necklace. My father, Lucca, will want it."

"I have a pretty good idea where they keep it. Sigry has me hold her necklace every autumn. Like clockwork." His heart quickened at the thought. A clue to finding his mother would be in his hands soon.

There was an easiness to Haygan Kai had never known before. His uncle seemed to breathe easier. As if telling Kai all their secrets were a burden lifted off his soul. "Uncle, what can you tell me about the actual Conhaspriga? It is not the adventure abroad or the year of meditation, right?" Kai asked.

"Correct. The rite of passage involves you carving out a hunk of white crystal from the mountain. A Stoneking will mold it into a shape befitting your soul. Inside the Agora, our spiritual temple, you will enter the sacred spirit pool. The rest is up to Alenga."

"But I am on this side," Kai noted.

"This side comes with challenges. Meant to test your mettle. Men and women who wish to be warriors travel to this side. I can't tell you what you will face. It depends on who is in charge. Each challenge is meant to test you, even prevent you from returning."

"How many will challenge me?"

"I don't know. Ten—fifteen? Remember, Lumens will hide the light. You will not be able to glean. Stonekings and Kodama will change the very landscape around you. Weathervanes can bring mist to disorient your sense of direction. Blocking out the sun with clouds. Finally, the Beastmasters will test your fears. They will stalk you and fight you. They are the guardians of the mountain."

The fear on Kai's face must have told Haygan he'd said enough. "You can do this, Kai. I have faith in you. What I can tell you is to follow the river. Keep the sound of the water to your left. I warn you not to leave the river. Behind the third waterfall, there will be a symbol. One that is carved into the

Agora. Every Katori grows up seeing it."

Haygan bent down and ran his finger through the sandy riverbank. "See here. It will not be easy to find, but it is three interlocking loops with no end. If you pass their tests, survive and find this marker, they must let you in."

Thunderous water roared behind them. Confused, Kai looked deep into the woods. "Are you going in there?" Kai jutted his chin forward. "I thought the Zabranen Forest was dangerous and the Katori Mountain range impassable. Not to mention the Shuk live in there. Along with many other vicious creatures."

Haygan laughed and clapped a hand on Kai's shoulder. "Boy, haven't you figured it out? I am a Shuk. I do not fear the wild ones, and they do not fear me. And I am going home. I can only hope Simone and Ryker make it home soon."

The realization stunned Kai. "That was you that night, outside the palace gates. I knew it was my chance to run. I don't know why I didn't consider it was you. I was too afraid to consider anything."

"You can't be afraid. Out here, it is survival of the fittest. Choose to survive or choose to surrender. Your life will be determined by your strength of spirit, and you have a strong spirit—trust it. As far as getting over the mountain, the pass I will take is protected, hidden. A maze manipulated by the Stonekings. Mine is different than the one you will take.

Eyes skyward, Kai took in the enormous waterfall above him. "What about Rayna? Can I tell her all this?"

"Tell her everything I've told you. I think she deserves to know. One more thing: remember to look for the three sisters. Three oak trees near the base of this waterfall." Haygan pointed. "At that point, you enter the Zabranen Forest. Your test begins there. The steep incline around the base will force you to venture away from the river's edge. You must find a way up to the second level. Follow the riverbed to the next waterfall. Again, the cliffs will force you back into the woods to climb higher and reach the third level. Stay as near the river as you can."

Kai's mouth fell open. "Why are you telling me all this now? Are you not coming back?" His heart sank.

"I plan to return," Haygan looked around, "but given that your search for your mother lit up the world, all Katori will be focused on Diu. They know about you now. Then there is your stunt on the Chenowith hillside, calling those Katori. I need to find out who they are. In case I do not return, I felt I must warn you about your gifts and turning seventeen. Head my warning Kai, do not wait too long." Haygan pulled Kai into a hug. "I am proud of you. If I have not told you enough, I am."

With his back turned to the woods, Haygan looked west toward Albey. As he took a deep breath, he held it and watched. "Now, I must leave. Follow the river back to Baden Lake and travel north of Albey, across the river rocks. There you will find a small community of Katori people. Talk to them. They are Katori people who did not return. Learn what you can. It may help you make your choice. Take Shiva with you and Smoke."

Haygan stepped into the shadows cast by the tree canopy. His uncle grabbed the stone hanging around his neck. A blue light beamed through Haygan's hand. Slowly he rolled his neck and shoulders. Then he dropped to all fours. In an instant, his uncle's body morphed into a black Shuk. He was a beast near seven feet tall, as wide as a bear with silver eyes and wiry black fur.

It was the most fantastic sight Kai had ever seen. As he'd done with Sabastian, Kai reached out to Haygan with one thought—*thank you, uncle.*

Through their connection, Kai heard his uncle—*be careful.* Without another word, Haygan disappeared into the woods and was consumed by a strange mountain mist.

CHAPTER 15

Hidden Community

The walk back was riddled with random thoughts—everything Haygan had shared: the dangers of the Zabranen Forest, wild beasts roaming the woods. People claimed the land shook, animals disappeared, and trees moved. Now he knew the truth. The guardians used their gifts to feed the fears of the people. To keep them away from Katori lands.

As his uncle recommended, Kai followed the river back to the lake. There he crossed the large river rocks to the northern side, even though it led him away from Albey. Curious about whom he was to meet, Kai gleaned the area. He pushed hard against the limits of his sight. A small cluster of shelters came into the edges of his mind. Excited, Kai walked in their direction. Smoke and Shiva stayed close, sniffing the ground and air.

Hidden by the trees, he watched. People worked the land, sat by fires making food, and cleaned animal skins. The first three homes were built in a semicircle around a central fire. Each house perched on numerous posts over a foot off the ground. The roofline was unlike anything he had ever seen. Steeply angled sides began near the foundation line and met at the top, making the house look like a triangle.

The people had no idea he was there, but four dogs barked.

The people stood and faced his direction. His only choices were to back away or meet them. Unafraid, he stepped through the trees, Shiva and Smoke at his side. When he reached the edge of the clearing, he stopped and let the sight of him, and his wolves, sink into the Katori settlers.

"Hello," Kai called out.

One man whistled, and all four dogs stopped barking and ran back to the group. The man motioned for Kai to approach. Clearly, the sight of him did not frighten them. Cautious, Kai kept a little distance between him and the others. Unsure what to say, he waited for them to start, but the silence lingered.

Liam's words rang in his ears. *Albey is a good place to settle. Should you choose to stay in this world.* If this is what it means to live off the land, this was not too bad. Kai wondered what his uncle hoped to tell him through these Katori people.

He noticed the older man glanced at his two wolves. Although he was not afraid, he did not approach. Kai instructed Shiva and Smoke to stay, and he took two steps forward. "Hello, my name is Kai." He offered his hand.

The older man approached. His long, free-flowing gray hair showed his years, but his skin looked youthful and smooth. Kai noticed the hesitant glances amongst the group, but the man offered his hand. "My name is Davi, and this is my wife, Naia." Davi's grip was firm, and he stood a few inches taller than Kai.

Naia offered a wide smile, and she embraced Kai with the enthusiasm one would greet an old friend. "Welcome to our community, Kai. Are you out on your adventure before completing your Conhaspriga?" she whispered.

Surprised by her question, he stepped out of her arms and noticed the rest of the group walk in his direction. "I am," he answered.

Davi continued the introductions. "This is Gabe and his wife, Kaila." Davi paused for them to shake hands. Gabe and Kaila were an odd couple. Gabe's bear-like appearance dwarfed Kaila's delicate features. He shook their hands and nodded hello.

Davi motioned to the last man, who seemed wary. "This is Hale. His mate Jada is resting. She is due to give birth any day." Hale waved, keeping his distance.

Naia studied Kai and continued to eye his wolves. "Do you wish to join our group?" she asked, then corrected herself. "No, you are at the start of your adventure. Your eyes are fresh, and you have no fever. Do you wish to learn about our choice? You are most welcome here, as are all Katori. We do not judge or harbor ill will." Kindness sparkled through her eyes.

The others stared at him, waiting for a response. Kai needed to play this right if he hoped to learn more Katori secrets. He was indeed sixteen, the age in which most Katori left for their year abroad. They were Katori who chose not to return. Their power was diminished by their choice. He wondered what had they given up by not completing the Conhaspriga.

He decided honest omission would be better than outright lying. "Thank you for welcoming me into your community. If I may ask, what made you choose this life?" He gestured to the landscape.

Naia visibly waited for Davi's approval. With his nod, she responded. "Everyone leaves for their own reasons. The journey before Conhaspriga is for the curious. Surely you chose to see what was hidden on the other side of the great Katori Mountains. You left your sheltered view of the world to explore. You have a strong spirit." She pointed up to the massive looming peaks. "You will see when you leave this mountain. The town of Albey is small and peaceful. It was once a mix of Katori, Half-Lights, and ordinary people. More ordinary, nowadays. But then, their ancestors made their choice." She motioned for everyone to sit around the fire.

"They were cut off is more like it," Davi interjected under his breath.

Kai sat on a stump, but he stayed on guard. He called Smoke

to sit at his back. Shiva kept her distance and remained closer to the trees.

Naia continued her story. "The world beyond is vast and not always kind. Their advancements—timekeepers, printing press, and other machines—replace people. They squabble over land and money. There is more to see than you have time, but you needn't travel too far to discover their nature. Greed drives this world to be selfish. Before you make your choice, be sure what you give up. Either way. I am guessing that is why you visit us."

Curious about Davi's statement, Kai studied the man's change in posture. His peaceful nature turned hard. *Cut off. What had Davi meant?* Kai waited for more details. "My uncle sent me to learn. I guess he wanted me to understand your choice."

"Choice! They call this a choice!" Davi said bitterly. "The chiefs ordered the Stonekings, every last one, to raise the Katori Mountain range. They left the Katori on this side behind. Sure, they were given a choice. But Albey was their home. Diu was their home. All these small towns were cut off. We once mingled freely, keeping our secrets, of course, but our ancestors were free." He waved his hands in dismissal. "The year abroad was only offered to appease the curious minds of the young centuries after. The fight to return was established to test the determination and fortitude of their future warriors —their so-called Guardians. Mark my words, there is only one choice—return."

Kai swallowed hard, shocked by the news. They had raised the mountain. Liam was right—the Stonekings were very powerful. "There are ways to cross if you know how," Kai said sheepishly. "My uncle travels back and forth."

"Davi, don't yell at the boy." Naia let her hand rest on Kai's knee. "It wasn't his choice to hide behind the mountain. The longer people were away, the more they forgot our ways. Their children and their grandchildren never saw our homeland— lessons were lost over the generations. Katori from this side stopped crossing over. Their children stopped trying. Separated, the young lost their gifts. Each burned out and faded away." She bit her lip.

This was surprising news to Kai. He had no idea Diu and Katori were once one nation. They had fought together in the war, but this was astounding to learn.

Naia continued. "Davi and I left in peaceful protest. Youthful children, hopeful that unity could heal the world and the rift. We wanted to remind the lost generations where they came from. Welcome back any who wanted to come home. Our leaders refused to welcome home their lost children. Let me tell you, those who venture too far lose everything. We had no idea what it meant—our choice. Not really."

The sadness behind her eyes struck Kai's heart. "Losing my sight made the world dull and dark." Naia's voice wavered. "I still care deeply for plants, but my gift to make them flourish by my touch is gone. All we have left is our strength and speed, which will fade with each generation after us."

Hale spoke for the first time. "Gabe is a wandering spirit; he never cared about the gifts. He just wanted to live secluded with nature."

Gabe nodded in agreement. "It's true. I am happy to live free, where I choose. But honestly, it was their rules—the chiefs now dictate who can travel and when. And Naia is right. This world is dark, without the ability to glean. I had not yet manifested a gift as a young man. Some believed I would be Lumen, but I don't know. There are some who have no real talent outside of being able to glean. Though seeing you walk with beasts, well... happy to meet you, Beastmaster."

Hale pointed towards his home. "Jada and I left because we were told we couldn't go. Our parents forbade us the rights of the journey. In protest, we ran away. We boarded a ship in Port Anahita and sailed to a place called Bangloo. When we ran out of money, we were trapped in Bangloo. By the time we were able to return..." His head hung low in disappointment. "We were simply gone too long. When we sailed home, we were shunned by our families. Now we live here. Our child will be a Half-Light with no power. Within a few generations, the light within each child will fade. Future generations will be weak, like ordinary folk."

Stunned by their willingness to share and their bitterness about their choice, Kai cupped his chin. "Forgive me for the asking, but is everyone who doesn't return bitter?" He winced, waiting for their response.

Davi snorted. "I suppose we sound angry. Naia and I left seventy years ago. We've had time to come to terms with our choice. Kaila is our daughter. She has no gifts beyond speed and strength. We are lucky Gabe chose to stay with us. They are a good match. To answer your question, many are very happy on this side, though every now and then pangs for home prick at our hearts. I doubt there is one of us who wouldn't return, given a choice."

"This certainly sheds new light on my choice," Kai said. "What of the child? Will you share Katori secrets, like you have with Kaila?"

Hale shook his head. "No, we will keep our regrets and the Katori secrets, as we were raised. They never need to know what we gave up or why."

Davi stood and motioned around the clearing. "You should meet the others. All around us are nearby settlements. Let me introduce you to your future neighbors should you consider staying on this side of the Katori Mountains."

Kai accepted the invitation. It made him happy to find many who were very happy with living away from Katori. He was grateful Davi and Naia's group was willing to share. Although he wasn't sure if they were encouraging him to return to Katori or live with them.

Realizing the day was getting late, Kai said his goodbyes.

On the long hike back to Albey, he thought about the Katori secrets he'd learned.

The more Kai knew, the more powerful the Katori people became. For him, Davi and Naia's wisdom was needed to serve a purpose. When his time came to choose, he would have to be sure what he wanted and what he was willing to give up. He did not want to live in regret, either way. Rayna would need to be given the same choice.

Crossing the enormous river rocks in the Conha River, Kai thought about the risks his uncle Haygan took in sharing secrets, and that frightened him. What would they do if they knew how much his uncle had shared? Maybe they would banish him, or perhaps they would keep him in Katori.

Shiva and Smoke ran to his side. They sniffed the air. Kai's own sight told him a pack of wolves approached. The Nebean wolves relaxed. The gray wolf pack ran out of the deep woods. They approached Kai and trotted in line with the two black wolves to create one large group. His heart lifted at the sight of them. Smoke placed himself between the alpha and Kai. Kai chuckled at the thought Smoke was jealous. *You are my forever bond, Smoke.*

Smoke cocked his head. *Companion.*

Content, Kai shifted into a run as the trees cleared enough to make bolder moves.

He and his pack ran through the trees. Their path kept them at a reasonable distance from town. His own wolves made people a little nervous, but he knew the wild wolves would not be welcome. He stopped in a clearing just outside of town and sat with his pack in the tall grass. It was good to run with them.

The warm sun rose overhead, a cool breeze rustled the trees, and the sounds of birds chirping bounced through the glade. This was the life. He could spend hours outdoors. The forest felt natural. He did not belong in the city, in a palace. Before he could stand, the alpha's ears perked up, and Kai sensed a man walking in their direction. It was Dresnor. The pack reared and darted off into the trees.

"Kai, were you lying with a pack of wolves?" Dresnor asked, his expression surprised and confused. "A *wild* pack of gray wolves?"

Kai wasn't sure how to answer. Was this a secret he needed to keep? If only he knew all their rules. He nervously ran his hand through his hair. "Well, I...um. They were just..." He stumbled through his response and avoided eye contact, hoping Dresnor would not press for an answer.

"You are incredible. What I wouldn't give to be at ease with wild animals." Dresnor raised the back of his hand to Smoke's nose. Smoke sniffed him and stepped forward. He let his hand softly sink into the thick black fur on the wolf's back. "Smoke and Shiva are the only wild animals I've ever been near. Shiva still won't let me pet her. She will sniff my hand, but then she moves away."

"Don't be offended, Philip. She is very wild. She acts civilized, but she would rather be in the woods. She is not one for strangers." Although Kai could pet her freely, he knew her heart. The woods called to her, and she missed Haygan when he left her behind.

The walk into Albey was pleasant. Kai and Dresnor walked down several small streets and peered into the windows of a few closed-up shops. Some were boarded up, others just abandoned. One shop's little wooden sign read *Apothecary*. Cupping his hands around his eyes, Kai pressed his face to the glass. The place was in shambles. "How could they let this shop go neglected?" he asked Dresnor.

Behind them, Kai heard a voice. "Hello, Your Highness. Would you like to go inside?" The man offered a small bow in greeting. "I am Kinnon Albey, Zayne's brother. I just returned this morning. I was hoping to find you in town."

Kinnon was tall and lean. Like Zayne Albey, he had black curly hair and a short stubbly beard. "I'd love to go inside," Kai nodded. "Pleasure to meet you, Kinnon. This is my Kemperyman, Dresnor." He watched as the two men sized each other up before shaking hands.

"Why is this shop empty?" Kai asked, following Kinnon inside. He noticed a small hitch in the man's stride.

"The old man died about ten years ago," Kinnon replied, wiping away a cobweb.

The small shop looked like someone had walked out one day and never returned. Dried herbs hung from the rafters, and dead plants sat in pots near the window. Dust and cobwebs covered everything. The shop smelled stale like a forgotten place.

On the center table, a mortar and pestle still held the remnants of one last concoction. Along the back wall were two small chairs, a desk, a long bookshelf, and a spiral staircase. Kai tilted his head upward. "What, may I ask, is upstairs?"

"The living quarters." Kinnon followed Kai's gaze. "For an apprentice. Near the end, the old man moved in. Said traveling across town to his home was too much of a bother. The house also sits empty. His apprentice left the following year." Kinnon ran his fingers down the length of the table, leaving a trail in the dust.

"We've had a few others come for a season here or there, but they are not interested in staying in a village. We have a few midwives in town. They know a thing or two about herbs, but little about setting bones. We've never had a physician." Kinnon rubbed his hip.

Kai listened and continued to inspect the books on the shelf, pulling out a few. "Would you mind if I take a few of these with me?" He eyed two books: one on local herbs, their preparation and use, and the other on blending oils with herbs and creating healing ointments.

"They are yours," Kinnon answered.

"If you ever want them back, let me know, and I can have copies made and return the originals," Kai added, laying them down to climb the spiral staircase. "I hope you don't mind, me going upstairs. I find this place fascinating."

Upstairs was a spacious loft, equal to the downstairs space. Simply decorated with a double-wide bed, an armoire, two chairs, a square table, and a corner desk. Like downstairs, everything was covered in dust.

Kai's solo footprints displaced the dust, proof the place had sat empty for years. The loft's double-window overlooked the street below with tattered curtains hanging on each side. A brown and tan braided coil-rope rug covered the floor. On one wall hung a set of crudely sketched plant diagrams. *Rayna would love this place,* he thought.

Kinnon's voice echoed up the stairwell. "The old man had no family. You are welcome to take whatever you wish. The books and tools are of little use to us without a healer."

Kai came downstairs. Books in hand, he dusted off the bottoms. "Dresnor, what do you think of this place?" he asked.

"You plan on moving in, do you?" Dresnor jested.

Kai chuckled. "You know, if I thought I could, I would. But Rayna might like this place. She is studying herbs and plants in Diu."

Kinnon opened the door and walked out into the fresh air. "Well, I have a few tasks to complete before the day wastes away. We can talk more at dinner tonight. My sister Brianna and her family will be there; she is expecting her second child this winter. I would be pleased to introduce you to Petra, my wife-to-be. We will be getting married in a few weeks. We were pleased to hear Zayne would be home for the wedding."

"We look forward to meeting Petra," Kai nodded. "See you at dinner."

After dinner, Kai approached the old duke. They sat across from each other in large leather chairs. "Lord Lars, I've been looking around the town, meeting the locals. Everyone loves the town and those working at the estate are very loyal, proud, and kind people." With a nod, he raised his glass to the man.

Lars raised his eyes. "We treat them like family, not servants."

"I also noticed that there are several empty homes and empty shops. Kinnon tells me your apothecary died a decade ago and nobody has taken his place. I heard his only real skill was plants and herbs. You've never had a physician. Is that true?"

"Yes, it's true. Kinnon broke his hip. He fell from a horse when he was young—it was never reset properly and healed wrong, not that it ever stopped him. We are proud of both of our sons. They've accomplished so much in different ways."

Kai studied the old man. Lars seemed like a good man; only he had no ambition. "I will write several letters tonight. We will send word to Nebea, the other estates and to Diu city. Surely we can find someone by summer's end. You may have to offer the shop space and land to get them to move. Winter is no time to be without, considering you have a baby on the way. He nodded to Brianna.

"Empty space is of no value to me. A physician willing to move here could restore faith in our city. Now, your other ideas... I am not sure we have it in the town treasury to build a warehouse and a factory, but I will set Kinnon to explore bringing people here to process our wool intro thread and ship it abroad. We had people when my father was alive, but they left several years back."

The old man tossed up his shoulder at the idea. He acted ambivalently to the idea that his town would fail if he didn't show an interest.

"Financially speaking," Kai tilted his head, "we should look over the town's books. If money is a concern, use two of the empty shops. One for storage, the other for processing. I can investigate loaning you the equipment. Start small. There are ways to grow with minimal cost."

"I suppose," Lars scowled. "Shipping our honey and preserves, but I don't know if we can spare them. Kinnon? Son. Are you getting all of this? You'll have your work cut out for you now that you are back from Port Anahita. No more travel. We should send someone else for supplies." The old man sat back in his chair, pleased there was a plan in place, and someone else was responsible for the outcome.

Kinnon finished the last of his tea, set his glass down on the small table, and stood. "I will see to the changes father. Now, please excuse me, everyone, I need to walk Petra home. I look forward to working with you, Prince Kai. Thank you for your ideas. Goodnight, everyone."

Kai set his cup down to shake Kinnon's hand. "Thank you for listening. I look forward to helping you. I should also retire for the evening. I have several letters to compose and send on the morning ship to Diu." One letter, in particular, needed to recommend Kinnon to become the next duke.

CHAPTER 16

Summer's End

Nothing about this summer had gone as Kai had hoped. He wanted to travel to Katori. His uncle had said no. He wanted answers about his mother—there were none to be found. With one week left in Albey, Haygan had yet to return. Was this the price for helping Kai? Would the elders forbid Haygan to return?

Soft sheets and a comfortable bed cradled him after a long day. His long day weighed on his tired mind. A sensation raised the hair on Kai's arms. The air around him felt thick and powerful. Whispers floated into his mind and beckoned for attention. Magic surged up his spine. Even with the electricity coursing through his body, his heavy eyelids struggled to stay awake.

He felt the influence of someone manipulating his awareness. A powerful presence drew Kai into a vision.

A pitch-black forest, specks of moonlight trickled through the trees. The smell of pine lingered in the night air. Unbearable heat welled in Kai's chest. His body was consumed by fever. The pain in his head crippled his focus.

His shirt was drenched in sweat as he marched along a narrow ledge. Rayna led the way at a quick pace. The snap of a twig behind them caused Kai to swivel around.

He lost his footing.

Kai tumbled down a large embankment covered in a strange, flowery vine. A plume of pollen filled the air.

Darkness clouded his vision. When he opened his eyes, his skin burned. Large red welts covered his hands, arms, and face. His lungs burned, making it difficult to breathe.

Rayna's voice sounded distant and echoey. Hands trembling, he reached for her. His vision waned again. Two large hands wrapped in black cloth reached under Kai's armpits. Someone was dragging him through the tall grass.

Freezing water splashed his legs and back. His hot body tensed as it was engulfed in the cold water. A rushing river enveloped him. He began to wheeze. Rayna's face came into view, towering over him. She offered him something to drink.

Her hand was wrapped in black cloth, and she wiped cool water across his sore skin. "Dragon's Breath is a dangerous flower," Rayna said.

Kai's airway opened and he gulped in air. She set her bare hand on his chest. She pushed him under the water and held him in place. He could feel the heat pulse through her hand into his chest.

Her face blurred, and he woke gasping for air.

Sweat drenched his nightclothes.

"What was that?" he said. His voice sounded too loud, and he covered his ears. Not fully awake, he looked to Smoke and joined him on the floor. Smoke's calm, relaxed heartbeat soothed Kai's restless spirit. Back to back, they lay in silence.

Early, just before dawn, a crowd gathered at the Albey Estate for Kinnon and Petra's wedding. The garden path was lined with tall posts, topped with white paper cones that were illuminated by small white candles. Their warm glow made a delicate trail through the gardens. Kai walked behind Haygan.

Near the back of the garden, everyone assembled under a tall banyark tree, surrounded by rows and rows of small white paper lanterns, lit with tiny candles. The chaplain addressed the crowd. Kinnon and Petra held hands.

Watching the couple stand together and commit their lives to one another, Kai couldn't help but think of Rayna. He wondered if the fates would bring them together or pull them apart. Given that he still had no idea how to convince his father to call off his betrothal, he was bound to Amelia and Milnos.

Lost in thought, Kai watched dawn's early light splash into the garden as the crowd focused on the happy couple. Hands raised above the couple, the chaplain spoke, "Now by the power entrusted to me by the blessed Alenga, I now pronounce you husband and wife. You may seal your promise with a kiss."

Kinnon gently cupped the side of Petra's face. He paused to look into her eyes. "I love you, my dear, you've made me the happiest man in the world." Then he gently kissed her lips.

With the ceremony concluded, each person took a lantern from under the tree and followed the couple through town. They then released them out onto the lake, spreading the joy of their union.

Kai stood at the water's edge, watching the cluster of lights scattered across the lake in the morning mist.

"Beautiful, isn't it?" a voice whispered.

"Yes, it is." Kai turned to see Haygan standing beside him.

"It was a beautiful ceremony. I doubt anyone knows, but the ceremony was similar to our Katori weddings. Albey was originally Katori land before we all moved behind the mountains. People would be surprised if they really knew where all their traditions started."

"When did you get back?" Kai asked. "Tell me, how was your trip? You were gone all summer. I've been busy with the changes in Albey, but that did not keep me from worrying about you. I thought maybe they would not let you return."

Haygan faced the water, his hands tucked into his pockets. "It was good to be home and difficult to leave Simone. Ryker is alive and well. It's all good news."

Kai asked with a clenched jaw. "How is this good news? What about my mother? Knowing she's alive and now missing, I can't go a day without thinking of her. How do we find her now?" Regretting his tone, Kai pressed his lips together. "I know you were worried about Simone and Ryker. I don't mean to discount their contribution…"

Haygan faced Kai. "Ryker is very disappointed in his failure, but I promise you, he will not give up. Mariana will be difficult to find in an animal form, but manta rays migrate and stay near the coastline near the Mystic Islands."

"And how exactly do they know what animal form she has taken? Sounds like a guess."

"I only know what they told me. I do know it was one of the forms your mother practiced. But I suppose it could be a guess. Lucca—my father, your grandfather—said he sent people to watch the coast around the Mystic Islands. But if you want to help, we need her necklace. You will have to find a way to steal it." Haygan eyed a passerby.

"Steal from my father?" Kai shook his head. "There is no way he will part with it, and stealing it will be nearly impossible. He keeps it in a lockbox in his study. That is when he isn't carrying it around in his vest pocket."

"I never said it would be easy." A smirk curled Haygan's mouth. "Although, it's the perfect test for all those skills Riome has been teaching you. We need her crystal. Consider it. I will accept your decision." Haygan raised an eyebrow.

Kai pondered his uncle's words. In truth, he knew stealing the necklace would be easy. Sneaking into his father's study in the dead of night would be simple. Not only did he know where his father kept the key; he could pick the lock in seconds. Even if he had to lift it out of his father's pocket, he was not worried.

"It's not about the challenge getting it. It's about stealing from my father. Taking something so precious. You think giving it to Lucca would matter? I need to think about this." Kai shook his head. Hurting his father to save his mother seemed counterintuitive, but he was more than willing to do anything for her. Giving it over to Lucca, now that was another matter.

Haygan took a breath. "I understand. Either way, it will work out. We know more now than we ever did. Now I think we should join the others. I don't know about you, but I would like some cake." Haygan smirked, pulling Kai along.

The more Kai considered the request, the more he wanted to keep the necklace himself. Why let them have it? He pondered the possibility of searching and rescuing her. No, he did not trust the Katori people. They certainly did not trust him. No, he would need to do this himself.

The next afternoon turned out to be swelteringly hot. Kai and Shane sat on the shore of Baden Lake in the midday sun. Glancing at Shane, he asked. "What do you say? One more race to see who can swim the farthest?"

They both had incredible speed and stamina on land and in the water. Testing each other seemed almost pointless. But it gave them something to do. "Sure," Shane agreed. "I almost beat you last time. I'm going to miss this when we get home."

The two boys waded into the water, then dove under. Shane rose up first. Kai came to the surface a few seconds later. They swam with exceptional speed. Bodies straight, legs extended, briskly kicking. They pulled through the water with curved elbows high.

The real question was not who would tire, but who would want to turn back first. Who wanted to win more? On a vast lake that took eight-to-ten hours to cross by sailboat, they had room to challenge each other.

Kai kept his breathing relaxed. He took a deep breath

through his nose between strokes. At the same time, he gleaned Shane's location. He knew they were evenly matched. For now, he kept pace with his friend. Palms turned downward, he pulled rhythmically through the water.

Stroke after stroke, he imagined himself pulling ahead. Still, Shane kept even. He focused on his technique, making each movement count. Inch by inch, Kai kicked a little bit harder.

Focused on the far side of the lake, Kai took short, quick breaths. He pulled his arms through the water faster. Slowly he pulled into the lead. With the extra distance, he slowed his movements and held his pace. Just a few more strokes, he told himself. He knew how far Shane was willing to swim.

It wasn't long after, he heard Shane. "Kai, stop. We've gone too far. We should turn back."

Kai stopped. The water ahead of them offered no view of the other shore. Behind them, Albey was a burry distant stretch of shoreline. He heard echoes of children laughing and playing on the beach. Kai turned around and they both began the long swim back. Keeping an eye on Shane, they made easy work of the return trip.

Panting, they both crawled up onshore and lay in the grass. "How?" Shane asked, between breaths. "How do you always beat me? We stay together most of the way, then you pull out ahead, and I can never catch you."

Relaxing, Kai looked up at the clear blue sky. "You really want to know?"

"Of course."

"My only chance is to swim like I am aiming for the other side. I have no intention of turning back. I have often thought of swimming all the way across. For no more than a few strokes I push and stretch a little more, and I pull ahead of you. Then I can relax into a normal stroke. Swim at the same tempo. By pulling ahead of you and staying there, I get into your head. From that moment on you begin to question and doubt. Wondering if I am better. Then you think about the swim back. You wonder if we have gone too far this time. That is why I win. You are trying to beat me; I am trying to beat the lake." He sat up and looked down the shore at Smoke splashing along the beach.

"Hmmm," Shane replied. "I never thought of it like that."

Wrapping up the summer could not happen fast enough. While he was well-received by the people, all he could do was fret over where he'd rather be. The morning of their departure, Kai was a buddle of adrenaline. He led his group through the countryside at a wicked pace. Each stop felt like an eternity. Although everyone else was anxious to get home, he could tell they were set on edge by his constant prodding.

Near the Chenowith gatehouse, Albert stood with arms crossed, talking with two women. One of them turned in their direction. Kai instantly recognized Riome. Her long hair flowed freely down her back, and she was wearing a brown leather vest over a white shirt and olive-colored pants.

Well, at least she's not wearing black, he thought—a pleasant change. The other woman's features were similar to Riome's. If he didn't already know Riome's history, one would mistake them for sisters. The woman's eyes carried depth and wisdom, but her appearance was deceiving. Kai could not help himself, and he gleaned her spirit. The light betrayed her—she was Katori.

He slid from his saddle, and Dresnor and Drew quickly joined him. "Albert, good to see you again. Looks like we will not be staying the night in Chenowith" The two friends clasped hands.

"Riome," Kai nodded. "What are you doing here?" He studied her face.

Composed, she held her chin high and offered a bow. "Your Highness, I come with news." From her pocket, she pulled a letter and handed it to Dresnor. "We sailed all night. I was told to deliver this letter to Dresnor and escort you across the lake. I have Diu soldiers waiting on the Grand Duke's ship. We need to depart immediately."

Dresnor cracked the Master General's seal and read the letter. "Drew, Redmon, Albey, Haygan, Shane and Marduk, you are with the Prince and me on the first boat. The rest of you will stay behind with the horses; you will return to Diu on the next ship. Cazier wants us home quickly." He pointed toward the pier.

Once they were underway crossing Baden Lake, Kai approached Riome and the older woman. "Riome, will you introduce me to your..." he hesitated. "Your mother? I am guessing, of course, but you are the spitting image of each other. One would say, maybe an older sister, but then you have no sister—that I know of."

Riome smiled and nodded. "Mother, this is Prince Kai, Mariana's son. Kai, this is Yulia, my mother." She softly touched her mother's arm.

Yulia shared her daughter's dark green eyes and auburn hair. She had not one gray strand to be found. Her long thick hair was braided into three sections and tied at the bottom, halfway down her back. Her navy leather vest crisscrossed in front and hung about her hips. A braided black leather belt was synched around her waist with various pouches, a dagger, and a short blade. Her white blouse billowed around her arms and her black pants were tucked into rugged black boots. The most important thing Kai noticed was a silver necklace with a teardrop crystal with a swirl of deep purple mixed with lavender.

Yulia bowed. "Your Highness, it is a pleasure to meet you. I have heard so much about you from my daughter. She speaks very highly of you. Let us hope you live up to the reputation. Please excuse me, I have matters to attend to." After another short bow, she stepped to the stern of the ship.

"So, Cazier sent you to collect me?" Kai eyed Riome. "Why the rush? We would have been home in a week."

While he waited for her reply, he glanced at Yulia. Riome's mother took a meditative state at the stern. Eyes closed, she pressed her hands together at her chest and bowed forward. Eyes open, she reached down and pulled at invisible air about her feet. She rolled it about her chest in a ball, then she threw the air upward.

Kai felt the wind stir and toss his hair about. He turned away from Riome to study Yulia's movements. They reminded him of Riome's meditation movements. Next, she pulled the air from one side, rolled the wind in her hands and pushed it towards the sails. Momentarily, he closed his eyes and accessed his sight. Yulia's wispy spirit energy floated on the stern of the ship. Flowing power gathered around her. Waves of magic rolled in her direction. Then he opened his eyes and saw her natural form. Her spirit's energy and physical form overlapped.

Yulia's hands collected elements of life energy. Rolled within her hands they became wind, which she directed at the sails. He noticed the wind stir and the sails billowed. Suddenly he felt the ship's speed increase. All the signs were there —Yulia was a Weathervane.

"Things must be serious if Cazier sent you and your mother. Can you explain to me how she is...out in the open in front of everyone?" He nodded to Yulia and then up to the sails.

Riome looked at her mother. "The others only see her meditation. The wind stirs about the entire ship. They think nothing of her exercises. Yet, you see her purpose. Interesting." She squinted her eyes, studying him.

Concern struck him. He had said too much. Did Riome know about his gifts? He had to think quickly. "Isn't it obvious? Her moments coincided with the wind's velocity. My mother was Katori, you know. They have many secrets, and

I know a few. Seems she is doing the same mediation movements you taught me. I am guessing she was your teacher." Sailors walked by them, eyeing Riome with the prince.

Kai stepped away from the railing. He was desperate to learn why she had been sent, so he changed the subject. "What was in the letter from Cazier? Why are you both here?"

"My mother came to Cazier," Riome whispered. "She warned of ships spotted north of the Mystic Islands. She saw them."

"Who are they and what do they want?" Kai questioned.

"They are Caroco ships, not seen here in these parts in many years. In all my travels I have never been to Caroco. Caroco is on the far side of the world. Mother said we will know them by their flag, a black star on a field of red."

As the words escaped her mouth, he instantly linked his dream to these mysterious ships. The red flag he knew, but the black symbol in the middle was obstructed. *Surely they are one and the same*, he thought. His face went pale, and his heart quickened at the news. Kai wondered how long he had before he would find himself in the water beside two Caroco ships. Not to mention, he had no idea why he would be there.

"What is it, Kai? What's wrong?" Riome grabbed his arm and delicately pressed two fingers into his wrist. "Your heart is racing. What do you know?" She turned to look at her mother, still about her work, hastening their travels. "She said they are men we should fear, but she won't tell me who they are or why we should be afraid. She spoke privately with Cazier."

Nothing could have prepared him for this news. The Katori were concerned about the Caroco people. They did not fear anything, yet it would seem they did. *Why?* Kai shook his head in disbelief.

Putting distance between them, Kai slowly pulled his hand away. "It's nothing, just something I saw in a dream. Or at least I thought I saw them. Two ships. It doesn't matter. It was only a flash of the flag, nothing more." He stepped away from her. This could only mean his dream was real. Whatever they wanted could not be good. If they were spotted sailing around the Mystic Islands, they were close—and coming soon. Worry filled his eyes, and he looked back at her.

Pensive, Riome returned the look but did not question him further. The rest of the trip she sat near her mother with her eyes closed. Kai imagined Cazier's letter told very little, and Dresnor would know little more than the story Riome had shared. He would need to speak with his father or the Master General.

When his group reached the Diu pier, horses were waiting. They mounted up quickly, all but Riome and Yulia, who walked away in the opposite direction. *More secrets,* Kai thought. His group rode hard through the city, and the Diu city bells rang in celebration as they came through the gatehouse. Prince Galloway had returned.

There was something about coming home. The smells of the city, the bright white palace high in the distance, the interlaced gardens throughout the city, the familiar faces within the palace grounds. And the people he cared about most. It had taken only six hours to cross the lake with Yulia's assistance. Two hours less than usual.

Once everyone settled in, he tried to find out more details about the mysterious ships. All Cazier and his father would tell him was that these warships had not been seen in these parts for over a decade. Their arrival might mean nothing, but they did not want to take any chances. Katori had sent the warning, and their word was more than good enough for Iver. If nothing comes of it over the next few weeks, security would go back to normal. He knew they were keeping something from him; he just didn't know what.

The more important thing keeping Kai guessing was why Yulia has such influence over his cousin? Who was she to him, that she would warn Diu or that he would consider her information worthy of his attention?

He hated not knowing more, but there was nothing more to tell. He had to wait until his vision played itself out. Since they were back early, he desperately wanted to find Rayna. Even though everyone in the city knew he was back, he needed to tell her. He wanted to see her.

Gleaning, he searched the grounds for Rayna. First the bakehouse, then the gardens and even the laundry. She was not with her parents or Julia. *Where could she be?* he wondered. That is, until he saw Rayna walking across the courtyard. She approached him with a shy smile on her face and an open hand. He took her hand, and they silently stood in the early evening light. "I can't stay outside," she said, glancing over her shoulder towards her parent's home. "They are waiting for me."

"I know, but at least I got to see you. Maybe I can see you again tomorrow. Security is strict right now, but they hope things will relax in a few weeks."

"Is there cause for concern?"

"No, everything is fine. Just precautionary. Foreign ships spotted northeast of here." He assured her.

"I look forward to seeing you tomorrow if you're free." She squeezed his hand and bumped her shoulder into his. "Goodnight, Kai."

"Goodnight, Rayna." He clung to her hand as she slowly walked away until their arms were outstretched, and she pulled her hand through his fingertips. Once she ducked inside her home, he returned to the palace.

CHAPTER 17

Rayna's Persistence

Kai had been planning this day for weeks. Concern over the foreign ships had faded. He was finally free to leave the city and get some alone time with Rayna. And it looked like the perfect day. The sun was shining, there was a warm breeze coming from the south, and Lizzie had prepared them a basket lunch to take to the lake.

Smoke and Shiva both lay in the shade nearby, and three guards stood at a respectful distance. While they ate, he kept the conversation light. He thought about the words of advice from his uncle. Haygan believed she should know all the secrets he'd share with Kai in Albey. She would need to make her choice, same as Kai.

Kai opened his eyes. "I sometimes wonder what my life would be like if my mother were still with me. Without my mother to guide me I have had to learn in other ways." He cleared his throat.

Haygan told him so much over the summer. He had no idea where to start. There was no question he trusted Rayna, but it was a heavy burden to keep all their secrets. But if she was to make her choice, she needed to know everything, including what Davi told him about giving up their gifts.

"I must confess you mean the world to me, Rayna." Kai

touched the back of her hand.

"I know you too well, Kai. You're choosing your words too carefully. I trust you, and you can trust me. If our relationship is to grow, we cannot have secrets."

"I agree, there should be no secrets between us. Although we may need to ease into what I know." He let that thought float around them to see if she would grasp his meaning.

"I'm ready," she insisted.

Over the next hour, he told her everything Haygan told him about the Lumens, Weathervanes, Stonekings, and Kodama. Even with Haygan's advice to guide him, it was still on him to craft the conversation. Then he shared with her the story of meeting Liam and the fact that their seventeenth birthday would come with a choice. It was a lot of details to cover and a lot for her to consider.

He struggled with telling her that she would very soon have to make a choice. Stay here in Diu or travel to Katori, through a gauntlet of guardians aimed to keep them out. When he was finished, he was pleasantly surprised at how well she took the news.

"So, what your saying is, when we turn seventeen, we might get sick and need to travel to Katori or risk losing our abilities. Abilities you insist I have, because we are Katori?" she asked doubtfully.

"Not might get sick. *Will* get sick."

Again, she seemed to wander through her own mind looking for answers. "Is this something you know for sure? How do you know I am a Kodama?"

He gulped at her question and pondered his reply. "Your abilities fit what Haygan told me this summer. The fact we can glean proves we are special."

She glared back at him and sighed. "You didn't answer my questions."

"I will answer one of your questions today. The hour is late and our time here is about up. I know for sure you are Katori—and a Kodama. The how will require time and privacy; privacy we don't have right now, the guards are coming. Has gleaning and sensing others not given you pause? What about how you healed Snowflake?"

Rayna sat there in silence with her eyes wide. "I simply enjoyed the gifts. It connected us. I was not about to question how or why. Being abandoned as a baby left my ancestry an unknown. As for Snowflake, I believe she got better on her own. When can you tell me more?"

"I have somewhere to go tonight for Cazier. Find a morning you can sneak out of your house and leave the rest to me. You will also need to promise to never tell what I share with you with anyone. *Ever.* If you can commit to keeping a secret from your parents, then I will answer all your questions."

Early the next morning, Kai walked through the palace courtyard with Smoke. Dresnor was busy with other tasks, so he had no morning training session. As was his practice, he reached out with his senses to study his surroundings. Rayna stood hidden in the fog, waiting for him. "You said pick a time. How does this morning work? Can we talk now?" she pleaded. "The new girl my parents hired is covering my work this morning. I am free for a little while."

Kai took a deep breath and slowly released it. "Well, I have to give you credit, you are persistent. We will have to glean for any guards we pass, but we should be able to discuss a few things."

Excited, Rayna took his hand. "Let's go then."

For a moment, Kai cherished the quiet nature of this hour of the morning. Only a few workers and guards were awake at dawn, and fewer still were out walking the grounds around the palace. "I think we will find the most privacy in the gardens. At this hour, nobody should be there, and the guards usually stay outside the perimeter." He assured her, motioning towards the apple orchard.

"We can cut through the apple orchard down to the palace gardens." He took the lead down the black stone stairs leading to the royal gardens.

He continued to ensure they were alone, surveying the area, gleaning their surroundings. As they walked into the gardens, he once again remembered the peace of walking these beautiful grounds with his mother. Now he walked with another woman who meant the world to him, and he wanted her to know, but he was afraid his words would fail him.

He slowly pushed open the arched wrought-iron gate. Careful not to make too much noise, Kai closed the gate behind them and continued down the pebble path through the topiary garden. Fantastic living art—decorative hedges sculpted into spirals, cones, and other geometric shapes—towered over them, interspersed with blooming plants and other green foliage.

Through the dense fog, he could hear the splashing sounds of the various fountains. Having checked the entire garden, he was pleased they were alone.

Their shoulders briefly touched as they entered the maze and he felt the warmth of her. At the next turn, he glanced over his shoulder. Rayna smiled. Kai led her around the hedges, zigzagging through the labyrinth. Her warm hand in his made him flutter inside. Turn by turn, they neared the center of the maze and the great banyark tree.

Once they reached the center, they stood in front of the giant tree, which was shrouded in white fog. Its finger-like branches reached up to the sky, covered in fall-colored leaves. Standing beside each other, she leaned into his shoulder.

Breaking the silence, Rayna asked. "Is it really alright being here? I know we've talked about your mother, and I know what happened that day. More importantly, *where* it happened." She ran her hand down his arm and turned to face him. "Should we go somewhere else?"

Kai looked deep into her eyes. She was always thinking of him. Still holding her one hand, he scooped up the other, his heart pounding in his chest. Her beautiful brown eyes looking back at him made it difficult to think. His pulse quickened. They hadn't had much private time alone. Family, friends, and guards made getting close tricky. Not to mention he had her reputation to consider. This was a rare opportunity, and he was so nervous that he felt his temperature rise.

A deep breath calmed his nerves. "Rayna, you mean the world to me. I want to share something with you because I trust you. What I am about to say must remain a secret, even from your parents. Can you do that?"

She leaned into him. "I have not shared the ability to glean and sense others around me, or my ability to nurture plants to grow faster and healthier with my care. I thought about what you said, that I might have the ability to heal. When I think about Snowflake's eyes, how she had Moon Blindness and was unable to see. I want to believe. I promise to keep these secrets between us. Even the Katori secrets from yesterday."

Kai looked up at the banyark tree. Golden autumn leaves fell delicately to the ground. He released her one hand and pulled her with the other towards the bench below. "You asked about this place and what it might mean to me. The world indeed believes my mother died in this place, and now very few people come here because of it. My father would have cut the tree down if it had not been planted by his great, great grandmother."

"I stand here today because it is the perfect place to tell you the truth. My mother did not die in this place; my mother did not die that day. She is alive. Missing, but alive." He paused to let her consider his words.

Silently Rayna placed her free hand on her heart and squeezed his hand with the other. "How is that possible?"

Kai nodded in agreement. "People believe she was killed by a dragon, a red dragon. I was there, but the event was so traumatic at my young age, I had locked it away," he said with a bittersweet tone. "The red dragon was here, but it did not kill my mother… because they are one and the same. My mother became the red dragon—she is a Beastmaster. The person who died here that day was a guard, presumed missing days later and forgotten over time. Remnants of her dress and blood were all the evidence they needed. My night terrors convinced them I was traumatized and incapable of telling them any different."

With a sigh of relief, he relaxed into the bench and leaned into her. "What a relief to be able to tell you. I only learned the truth recently. I am sorry I did not tell you sooner," he said, his voice torn between sadness and joy. He was beginning to understand the burden of keeping secrets.

Rayna rested her head on his shoulder. "It is a beautiful place; I am glad it no longer pains you." She paused and took a breath. "But the story you told me yesterday. I am not sure I can believe..."

"It is hard to believe," Kai agreed. "But it is all true, I have seen it with my own eyes. Well, most of it."

"But you are asking me to believe people can change into dragons?"

"Not just dragons, but other animals too."

"Does that mean you can do that too?" Rayna looked shocked.

Before he answered, he looked up at the pale blue sky emerging from the dispersing fog. Again, he paused to sense the area and felt it was clear to continue. "I don't know." He shook his head at the thought and ran his hand over his mouth. Their time was coming soon. "There is one more secret that Haygan told me. He and Liam both said that if we choose to develop our gifts, we need to do so before the gift burns out with age. Around our seventeenth birthday."

Kai's mood shifted. He glared out at the gardens as if he was blaming them for the secrets they held. "I get the feeling that was not something they meant for us to know."

"Who is this *they* you often speak of? I am not sure I am interested in meeting them." She said matter-of-factly, crinkling up her nose as if she'd smelled something foul.

"The Chiefs and the Unie of Katori. I am not sure why, but they do not seem interested in bringing either of us home. If it were not for my mother, I would probably not care. I believe they are the only ones capable of helping me find her, and for now they seem interested in her recovery."

Kai stood up. "We need to go. People in the palace are starting to wake and move around. When the fog clears, we will be visible from above. I'd prefer to keep this little moment, and my changed feelings about this place, private."

She stood beside him. "I understand."

He took her hand. "Come with me," he said, leading her back through the maze. Turn by turn, faster and faster through the maze he went, constantly sensing their surroundings until he abruptly stopped.

Caught off guard, Rayna ran into him. "What's wrong?" she asked. "I don't sense anyone around us."

Heart pounding, Kai stood frozen in place. Three long breaths gave him courage. He wanted to tell her how he felt, at the same time he wanted to run away. Her hand still in his, he turned. Their eyes met. He pulled her waist into his. "Would you mind if I..." he stammered. Looking in her eyes, he leaned in close, his mouth near hers.

"I don't mind," she finished for him. Rayna met him halfway and pressed her lips to his. For the briefest moment, time seemed to stop for them. Caught on the precipice of emotion, Kai felt if they were not careful, they would inevitably fall and be lost forever. They were not meant to be. Still, he wanted to spend a lifetime with her.

When they parted, he looked again into her eyes. She smiled and touched his face. "I love you, Kai," she said, then she stepped around him, exited the garden maze, and ran for the stone stairs. She paused briefly when he clinked the gate closed. They stared at each other, and Kai felt the pain of wanting something he should not have.

Deep down, he wanted to chase after her, tell her he felt the same. But no, how could he pursue her knowing she could never be his? Duty commanded he belong to another, and he saw no way clear of that fate. His heart felt like it was breaking into a thousand pieces.

Frustration burned within Kai, and now he needed a run more than ever. With all his strength and speed, he set out towards the wall. He wanted his legs to burn, his lungs and his body to burn to match the fury in his heart. How could he find the other half of his soul only to give her up? He'd known better than to get close to her, but he could not deny what he felt. His soul had connected with another. They belonged together.

He began to run faster and faster with each step around the wall. Still, his breathing did not labor. He needed to push harder, run faster. With his sight wide open, he gleaned and made his way avoiding guards as he passed. Still, he accelerated. His feet punched at the ground. Tears streamed across his face, but he would not stop. He wanted to run until his feet could not carry him.

When he finally did his third lap around the wall, he caught a glimpse of Haygan ahead of him, leaning against the stones. He knew what that meant. Time to stop. At that point, he wasn't sure he could. His heart pounded in his chest as he neared his uncle. By the time he slowed, he was out of breath and fell to his knees. He panted and waited for his mind to stop pushing and his heart to stop pulling.

"Need a hand?" Haygan asked. "You've caused quite the stir with your run this morning. If you have the energy to burn, you should find Dresnor or Riome. I am sure either of them would love to help you extinguish what ails you." His uncle offered him a hand up. "You know I am not one to pry, but you seem particularly overwhelmed. If you need to talk, I know a thing or two about…life."

"I appreciate the offer," Kai said, "but I am not sure how you can help me. I want what I cannot have, and I knew that going into it. Every moment I spend with Rayna is beyond words. I don't know how you live without Simone." Kai hated bringing her up because he now understood what it meant to care for someone you could not be with. At least he got to see Rayna every day.

"I made a choice to be here with you," Haygan said, "and I will see this through. Simone knows I love her, and when I can, I will return. For now, we settle for moments. She comes here more often than you think," Haygan said with a soft look in his eyes. "Now for your situation, trust in the blessings of the universe. Trust Alenga will find a way. I doubt she would show you your soulmate only to keep her from you. Let her guide you. If it is meant to be, it will be. Now, no more speed-running in broad daylight. Off with you. Don't you have a class or something else to do today?"

Kai nodded. It felt better to talk, but it didn't change his situation. "Thank you for understanding and not judging." He ran towards the palace, where the smell of Lizzie's almond cakes welcomed him inside.

CHAPTER 18

Riome's Beginnings

Riome sat at her desk, staring into her mirror. "I have a mission for you today. I am going to disguise you as an old man. Simple mission. Observe and report." She continued applying freckles and wrinkle lines to her hands and face. With each stroke, her face aged. Her final touch, a dusting of white powder through her hair.

Her skills as a spy amazed him. The ability to become someone else and convince others her identity was real was second to none. So many of Riome's disguises were often young boys, old women, or dirt-covered beggars. While she worked, she reminded him, "Attractive people garner too much attention. Our work requires anonymity. People dismiss the elderly and the young, especially if they appear poor. If you want to make an impression, do it with a scar or a tattoo. Something you can wash off quickly. People focus on the disfigurement and the ink, remembering little else."

She finished with her own disguise and turned to him. "Sit here. I need to work on your face. Tonight, you will walk alone to the Drunken Dragon and order ale and stew. Choose your seat wisely. You want to be close enough to listen to the bartender." She pressed a wet sponge against his face, followed by powder.

Surprised, he sat up straight and let her do her work. "You're sending me on a mission? I have been back for months now without so much as a word from you since you brought me home from Chenowith."

Ignoring his response, she continued. "The bartender is meeting with someone today, and I need to know who that is and what their purpose is. I will get there before you and sit just inside the door."

In the mirror, his face changed. With each brown makeup line and pat of her sponge, he aged. She left little time for idle chit-chat. When she was finished, he wore an oversized ratty brown shirt that smelled of old ale. His face had dark lines and age spots, in addition to dirt and grime. In the mirror, his face and hands looked unrecognizable.

She tucked a few small layered pads under this shirt, over his shoulders, and around his back to create a small hump. She gave him a thick black vest and a large cloak. To finish the look, she put the same white dust in his hair. "Now you just need a cane and these old boots." She smiled, pleased with her handiwork.

Kai went down through the tunnels and exited the metal gate into the warehouse section of Hightown Proper. With a pebble in his boot, Kai hobbled down the street toward the Drunken Dragon. Early winter wind nipped at his face. There had been no snow yet, but the air had a definite bite. Grateful for the layers, he kept his hands inside his cloak.

Outside the pub, men lingered. Before he could enter, a group of men brushed him aside. They were loud and obnoxious, and the entire place turned to look at them. Their disruption gave him the opportunity to study the room and slip in unnoticed.

On one wall a roaring fire heated the pub. The place reeked of sweat and ale, which matched the clothes Riome had given him. Patrons noisily conversed around the large tables, leaving the bar empty. On the opposite wall was a single table adjacent to the backroom door, yet still close to the bar. A perfect spot. Kai slid up to the table.

Facing the door, he had a great view. That's when he saw her, the little old woman eating a slice of pie. If he'd not seen her get ready, he'd have never known this old woman was the young, vibrant woman Riome. Her disguise was flawless. Even the quiver in her hand as she ate made you believe she was frail.

A barmaid approached, and before she could ask, Kai barked. "Ale and stew, missy, I don't have all night." He used his cane to tap the edge of the table, sending her scurrying away. He wanted to laugh, but he knew better. He thought of an old man he'd studied as inspiration for his voice and gestures.

When the barmaid returned with his request, she slopped down the cup and a bit of ale splashed the sleeve of his ratty brown shirt. "Come on missy, mind my shirt." He grabbed the mug of ale and took a sip. He was glad he'd taken a small sip; the sour taste was unpleasant compared to the wine served at the palace.

Thankfully the stew was more to his liking, and he slowly ate while he watched the door.

The next patron to enter scanned the room before taking a seat at the end of the bar. He was a shifty middle-aged man with frazzled unkempt hair with a grayish-white streak in the front. He was dressed in dark gray pants, a white shirt, and a green vest. Strapped to his side was a reddish-brown leather satchel with golden embossed corner tips.

The barkeep approached the man with wary eyes. "You look thirsty. Can I offer you a drink?" he asked as he leaned in close.

"Just a room upstairs, please," said the shifty man.

Kai took another sip of ale and glanced over his mug. In the dim light, he noticed the barkeep slip the shifty man a slip of paper and a key. Kai was not close enough to see what it said. Unsure what to do, he watched the two men exchanged glances.

Moments later, a well-dressed man entered the establishment with a small book gripped in his hand. He also initially scanned the room and took a seat at the bar, one down from the shifty man. They eyed one another but said nothing.

He had an air of wealth, just enough to suggest a merchant of means. He was a stout man with a faint bald spot on the back of his head and a curly black mustache. His clothes were all neatly pressed and well made. Not the typical person who frequented the Drunken Dragon. He was clearly out of place and nervous.

"Sir, can I offer you some ale, or maybe a slice of freshly baked pie?" the barkeep offered.

"Ale please," the merchant requested.

As the barkeep served him a mug, Kai caught sight of another slip of paper pass between the barkeep and the merchant. In return, the merchant slid a white envelope to the barkeep.

Riome approached the far end of the bar. Kai watched her speak to the barkeep, offering him coins. Then she departed, leaving the pub. He knew the rest was on him, so he listened to their quiet conversation. His young ears focused on the two men, the merchant and the shifty man, at his end of the bar.

"Can you make it? If I get you the formula—can you make it?" the merchant asked.

"I am sure," insisted the shifty man. "I can make anything. I might even be able to make it better. Get me the formula. I will get you a list of the ingredients once I have tested a small batch. Then I will make you as much as you want. You could blow the place sky high if you wish."

"Not so loud, fool!" the merchant protested. "You've no idea who could be in here."

"Get me that formula and get me my money," the shifty man demanded as he slid off his stool. He grabbed his case and took the stairs leading to the rooms above the pub. A black iron key twirled between his fingers. Kai kept his eyes low as the man passed.

The merchant remained behind, scrawling something in his small leather book. Kai needed to get a look at that book. As the merchant twisted in his seat, he knew this was the time. The merchant was about to leave.

Kai tossed a few coins on the table to cover his meal and hobbled towards the bar. As the merchant went to slide off his seat, Kai collided with the man, knocking the book from the merchant's grip.

As it struck the ground, it opened, and Kai read the first few lines. Slowly he bent down as any old man might. He reached down, reading several more lines before he closed the book and read the cover. Then he jabbed it in the merchant's gut. "Watch where you're going, mister."

Not waiting for a response, Kai hobbled out the door. Outside he shuffled across the street into the shadows of a pottery store. From there, he watched and waited for the merchant to leave while he removed his cloak, vest, and the ratty brown shirt, which he used to rub the smudges from his prematurely aged face.

The padding fell to the ground as he used his hands to shake the white dust from his hair. He put on the black leather vest over his light gray undershirt. As he collected his disguise and tucked it under his arm, the door to the tavern opened and the merchant emerged.

Kai gave the man a few moments before he ducked out to follow. He followed several paces behind, moving down several winding streets until the man entered Willow Auctioneers. The man turned and locked the door behind him. That was good enough for Kai. The ledger said Willow Auctioneers and the merchant had a key to the place. They were connected. Now he needed to deliver this news to Riome. She would want to know what he learned.

Before he even took a step, a frail old woman came up to his side carrying a basket of bread and fruit. "You look like a strong young man. Mind helping me with my basket?" she asked.

He looked at the crinkled skin and gray hair. Half of her face was cast in shadow by the cowl of the cloak she wore. Even up close, her disguise was believable.

Before he could respond, she handed him the basket and patted his hand. "You did well," Riome whispered, no longer sounding like an old woman. "Walk with me. Tell me what you learned and why you were standing outside Willow Auctioneers."

After he conveyed his tale of the merchant and the shifty man's conversation, she stroked her chin. "It is good you chose to follow him. I can keep an eye on the merchant, find out what he deals in. I will continue to watch the shifty man staying at the tavern." She insisted. "Is there anything else you remember?"

"I am afraid there was nothing else. What are you searching for?"

"Everything at this point is rumor. Our spies in Milnos heard hints about an ancient substance being developed here in Diu. Highly flammable stuff. Some kind of oil. We can't have something like that in the wrong hands or here in Diu."

He was pleased she was willing to share the details. "Do you want me to ask around?"

"No need. Thank you, Kai." Riome waved him off, grabbed her basket, and turned back the way they'd come. She disappeared into the evening crowd, and he walked home alone.

A few weeks later, Kai closed his balcony doors to a wicked winter storm. It had been another long day. He needed a rest. Hopeful for a moment's rest, he laid down before going to dinner. His eyes felt heavy and they closed slightly. He willed them back open, but they started to close again. Finally, he gave in. If he could only close them for a moment. The second he let his eyes shut, he fell asleep.

Smoke's growl startled Kai. He bolted upright. As the sleep cleared from his eyes, he saw the Master General kneeling to soothe Smoke in front of the open hidden passageway. "Good evening, Your Highness. Retiring early tonight? You missed dinner. But it looks as though Kendra has brought you a tray. Here, come and eat while we talk." Cazier took a seat. "You know there are times I wish I were a young boy again sleeping in this room—dear old dad a tunnel away in his tower."

"That's right, this was your room." Kai hopped off the bed and grabbed the plate of food from the tray. "Sorry, I only closed my eyes for a moment. It was a long day. Between Professor Grayden's classes and Riome's training with daggers, ciphers and poisoning lessons, I was exhausted. Then Riome sent me on another mission. After the same two men from the other week. She had me running all over the city chasing clues, stealing a ledger, and other trinkets. This time she had me drug the merchant and this shifty man. Then I had to carry them both like a sack of potatoes two blocks to some storage house. Since when do I kidnap people?"

"Sounds like a very productive day," his cousin teased. "I am quite pleased with your progress. Nobody can know I have trained you in the art of deception and stealth. I need you to be able to discern the truth, intimidate and evade. You need to know more than everyone else in the room. More importantly, you need to know the intention of others and when you're being manipulated."

"Is all of this in preparation for me going to Milnos? You know I don't want to marry Amelia, right?"

"Cousin, I understand, I truly feel for all four of you. Tolan knew better; he should have never let Amelia get so close. Not to mention, who chases a girl betrothed to a prince? I warned you about your relationship with Rayna, and I am sure I am not the only one. I see no way out of this. Your father needs someone he can trust ruling Milnos. Who better than his own son?"

With a whine, Kai responded, "Tolan is better suited to go to Milnos. Maybe he should marry Amelia. He does love her, after all. He has years of fighting experience in the military."

Cazier laughed. "Who are you trying to convince? I'd lay money on you over Tolan. He may be taller, with a longer reach, but I have every faith he is no match for your speed and cunning with a short sword or a dagger. Has Riome given you one of her throwing stars yet?"

Kai conceded the argument. He knew Milnos was his responsibility. "Riome has provided me with four of her metal stars. Impressive little weapons."

"Strength will come with time," Cazier noted, "but size doesn't matter. Look at Riome, she is rather small compared to others, yet she can take on anyone. Her speed is unmatched; I'm sure you've noticed. And I seem to recall a young man not so many years ago putting Tolan in his place. Landon too." Cazier leaned back, pride lifting the corner of his mouth.

"You heard about that? That was years ago now. Tolan and I have mended our relationship."

The rest of Cazier's comments caught up with him. There were several things Kai had started to notice of late, besides the fact that Riome's mother Yulia was a Weathervane and a woman Cazier trusted with Diu security. Yes, he knew a great deal.

One more thing he knew: there was a connection between Riome and the Master General, something secret. Did he test their friendship and reveal what he knew? Information was power, and he did not have all the information, not yet. But could he weed it out? What did Cazier know about the Katori —about Yulia?

Kai looked to the painting covering the hidden passage. "Are we alone?"

"Whatever do you mean?" Cazier cocked his head to the side.

"Listening to others can tell you a great deal." Kai sensed Riome in the passage. "Come in, Riome. I know you're there," he called. He heard a barely audible click, and the panel slowly opened to reveal Riome. The painting blocked most of the light from illuminating her face, but he saw her silhouette. "Have a seat, if you're going to listen. You might as well have a front-row seat." Kai gestured to the sofa.

She stepped from behind the painting and closed the panel. "Took you long enough," she said, taking a defensive stance near the balcony door to watch the winter storm.

Cazier raised his hands. "Hold on now. I did not set her to spy on you," he said adamantly.

Taking his time, Kai thought out his next move. They trusted him. "Here's what I know. The shifty man you had me kidnap, with the frazzled blond hair and a white streak in the front, is a chemist. He smelled of chemicals, unlike what Sigry uses medically. He had serious burns on his hands, face, and neck. Those are new from the last time I saw him in the Drunken Dragon. Our shifty man carried black powder, metal fragments, and some handheld weapon. I kept those, by the way."

Since his vision of Drew's death, Kai had been searching the palace for this new weapon, and now he had one to study. He was not about to give it up. "Although I've seen the weapon before, or something like it, I intend to study it for now." He said with a smirk. "You mean to question the merchant, not about the ledger, but the shipping manifest hidden within the cover. I found that too. He deals in ammunition, black powder, foreign chemicals, and secrets, though he plays at being a humble auctioneer. How am I doing so far?" Kai questioned with confidence.

Cazier looked over his shoulder at Riome and nodded toward the empty chair. Without question, she crossed the room and joined them near the fire. "You're doing very well," Cazier nodded. "Good to know you're not just blindly following orders. You were paying attention. Don't stop now. What else do you know?"

Kai heard the pride in his cousin's voice, but hesitation still lingered in his eyes. "Are we really laying it all out tonight?" He questioned. "No more secrets? Are you willing to reveal the secret between you and Riome?" Kai let the silence linger about the room, hoping one of them would speak first.

All the information Kai needed was in this room, he was sure of it. Cazier trusted Riome with the life of a prince and with the secrets of the kingdom. Trust like that cannot be bought; loyalty and duty only go so far. Spies are natural-born liars. And she was the best. No, their connection was personal, but not intimate. He thought back over the years, through several interactions he'd witnessed between them. Yulia came to mind. Who was she to warrant a private consultation with the Master General of Diu, unless they already knew each other? He smirked at the revelation. It suddenly became clear.

Riome smiled and tossed a look at Cazier. "Looks like he's figured it out, or at least he thinks so. Let's have it Kai, what do you think you know?"

Still doing the math in his head, he looked to the Master General, his cousin, mentor, and friend. "Cousin Adrian, I believe, before you married Ella, you had another relationship. You were, what, nineteen maybe?" Pausing, he studied his cousin's reaction. Although his cousin was good at controlling his emotions, this memory was strong, and Kai knew he was right. "I believe that relationship resulted in a child, to be more specific—Riome. She is your daughter. Her mother is Katori—Yulia." Now that Kai looked hard enough, he saw the similarities.

Cazier bobbed his head. "Well done—I was eighteen. It is true. In my younger years, I had hoped to be excused from all this responsibility. You may not know this, but I had two older brothers. My brother Adam was in line to follow Dad as Master General. However, when Adam died in a riding accident, it left me to one day be commanded to serve. I would follow my dad as Master General here in Diu." He cleared his throat. "Nebea is not the same as Diu. We must not marry below our station. Society and court demanded I marry a lady of nobility, and as you know, I do my duty. Years after I married Ella, Yulia came forward and told me about my daughter. Riome was curious about the world and staying in Katori was no longer an option. Yulia would not explain, and I did not press her. I was happy to learn I had a daughter. She wanted to meet her father."

Cazier sighed in regret. "Unable to publicly recognize her as my own, Riome asked to be sent abroad. It pained me to send her away. She was so young, ten or twelve, but I was happy to provide her with anything she desired. It was in Bangloo she discovered their spymaster school. She has become a loyal asset to Diu, to your father. And I like having her here. Nobody else knows her true identity."

Kai studied them as they spoke. Their body language told him they were relieved he knew. But he wondered how much Riome had told her father. How long had she lived in Katori? Did she know more than she should as a Half-Light?

"While we're being open, you know I have long since suspected a duplicitous nature in Nola. I still don't have solid proof, just my childhood memory and the hearsay of a person loyal to my mother."

He looked at them both, fishing for a reaction. They seemed to believe his idea had merit, nodding their heads in agreement. "This summer is the first year my father has ever missed traveling abroad. Just before my father was to depart, he took ill, became dependent on Nola, and lost a ton of weight. While his weight has recovered this winter, his moods still fluctuate between confident and depressed. He was just feeling better a few days ago, and now I think he is back to being confused."

Riome responded first. "I am sorry, Kai. I am preoccupied with my search for Andrew and now this chemist and his flammable oil being produced right under our nose. Which I have yet to find. Not to mention I have been following leads on Regent Maxwell's travels. I want to help you. What do we know about Nola? Where did she come from?" she asked rapidly.

"Those are all great questions," Kai acknowledged, rubbing the back of his knuckles. "What I am about to propose, I know from anyone else, would sound like treason. In all seriousness, we need to question Nola. Riome, one of your truth serums could help. We may also need to poison her. Nothing deadly, just something that will keep her bedbound for a few weeks. We need to keep my father and Nola apart long enough for her effects to wear off." He stared at them, waiting for a response.

A sly grin came over Riome as she leaned across towards Kai. "I agree. If she is responsible for your father's poor health, we need to be sure she does not suspect she has been poisoned. I will concoct something, but it will take over a month to get the ingredients. I could have everything I need just after the Winter Festival."

"What about Sigry?" Kai questioned. "Do we need to worry about him discovering what we've done?"

"No. It will leave no aftertaste or symptoms of poisoning. I am basically giving her a cold to weaken her system. Once she is sick, the physicians will sequester her into a private room. Sigry would not risk Iver's weakened state or young Cordelia getting sick. She will have symptoms like a headache, stomach pains, and fever." Riome shook her head, pleased with the plan.

Cazier raised an eyebrow. "Will she actually be contagious?"

"She will not. I will give her herbs to create each symptom. And while I'm at it, I will administer a truth serum and question her. I can continue to administer my concoctions within the physician's treatments. They will give her daily doses to help with her suffering. She'll have no idea. Meanwhile, we can observe the King."

Cazier held his chin. "I wish I didn't know what you two were planning. Deniability would make this easier. I will do my part, maybe arrange for Hunter Marduk to take the king hunting. Iver will not say no. This will allow you to administer your concoction."

"Agreed, cousin, excellent idea." Kai felt relieved for the first time in years. Knowing the truth about Nola and his father's moods would finally be put to rest. "Well, we have our plan. After the Winter Festival, in the new year, we will set our plan in motion. Get our proof."

Who poisons a queen? Kai thought as Cazier and Riome departed back through the hidden passage.

CHAPTER 19

Winter Betrayal

Before the Winter Festival chapel service, Kai met with Shane to exchange gifts. Shane loved the new saddle Kai gave him. In fact, he made quite the fuss, like it was the best gift he'd ever received. Oddly, Shane offered no gift in return. Kai didn't dare ask where his gift was, as that would be rude, but Kai was nevertheless confused. They left the stables together and went to the chapel.

After service, the guests departed for the Central City Gardens to watch the Parade of Candles. The Winter Festival celebration was an evening of thankfulness and blessings. Everyone came together to welcome in the new year. Next, the dukes, lords, and ladies of the land would come to the palace to offer gifts and bend the knee to King Iver Galloway.

If Kai was going to exchange gifts with Rayna, it had to be now before going to the gardens. As he entered the bakehouse, he found Levi and Dori chatting about tomorrow's needs. Their tasks were done early so they could enjoy the entire Winter Festival. They had delivered the bread, pies, and cakes well before noon.

"Mister Kendrick, Dori. I wish you many blessings for the coming new year. Is Rayna available? I have a gift for her." Although he knew she was in the cottage loft, he wanted them to know he was entering their home.

Levi bowed. "Your Highness, Prince Kai, she is in the cottage next door. You may go and see her. We will be right behind…"

Dori interrupted him. "Go ahead, Prince Kai. We will be there, …shortly."

"Thank you," Kai bowed back. "I will not take long. I know you are planning to attend the Parade of Candles." With a smile, he ducked outside. He held the large wrapped gift under one arm and knocked on the cottage door. As Rayna opened it, he began to get butterflies in his stomach.

"Kai, blessings to you for the coming year," Rayna beamed. "Come in. I just finished cleaning up from dinner." She pulled him inside and closed the door.

"Blessings to you for the coming year, Rayna." He smiled at her. "I spoke to your parents; they will be home shortly." He could hardly stand the wait. He had collected things all summer.

On the small table lay a wrapped gift. Taking a seat on the sofa beside of Rayna, he placed his own package on the table in front of her. Before he could speak, she handed him the box. "I get to go first," Rayna demanded. "I know it's not much, but Shane helped me."

Slowly, Kai pulled the blue ribbon and folded back the white cloth. There sat a wooden box with a pattern of alternating inlays of white birch and dark ebony wood squares. Curiously he released the golden latch and lifted the lid to reveal two sets of chessmen, one in red mahogany and the other in dark ebony. They were intricately carved and stained to perfection.

"It's a chess set." Rayna patted his hand. "I know you are learning to play, and now you have a travel set."

Graciously he accepted and touched the back of her hand. "Thank you, Rayna. It is magnificent. I will have to start playing more often."

The rosy blush on her cheeks told him she was very excited. "As I said, Shane helped me. We bought it together, so this is from both of us. He was gracious enough to let me present it alone."

"That explains the odd looks. When I gave Shane his gift, he gushed over the saddle and then just said thank you. Anyway, now it's my turn. I hope you like everything, although two items are on loan. If you like them, and they are different enough from your growing collection, I will have copies made."

With much anticipation, she pulled the pink ribbon, and the blue cloth fell into a puddle on the table. Her eyes went wide, and she stifled a gasp with the palm of her hand. She took the two leather-bound books in her hands and stroked the covers and flipped through the pages. "I will study them thoroughly." Placing them on the sofa, she stared at the large wooden box on the table.

"It is an apothecary box," Kai explained.

The box was made of beautiful flame mahogany, with a flush-fitting brass carrying handle on top. Rayna gently ran her fingers over the lock on the double doors. "With a lock," she said mysteriously.

Kai produced a key from his pocket and handed it to her. As she opened the double doors, she found three jars on the inside of each. There was a mix of clear, green, and brown bottles. In the center were four more bottles, all in blue, above two fitted drawers. She removed each bottle, rolled them in her palm, and replaced them.

Then Kai spun the box around and he let her stare in confusion at the back for a few moments. He slid the back panel to one side to reveal a concealed compartment holding four more bottles, all in red. "Oh, Kai, this is amazing. Thank you so much." After giving him a big hug and a kiss on the cheek, she began inspecting the engravings around the outside.

"I am so pleased you like it." Kai arched his back to get a look out the front window. "Given your desire to become an apothecary, I spoke with your father. He approved, so this also comes with formal training by way of apprenticeship. You know so much already, but formal training would allow you to practice and set up your own shop someday. I have arranged daily lessons over the next few weeks with a Mister Embly here in the city. He is a friend to Yulia, Riome's mother. He is from Katori and he is willing to teach another Katori his skills."

"Really? Thank you, Kai." Rayna leaned in again and hugged him.

"Oh, and do me a favor, look through your book collection. Find anything you can on a plant called Dragon's Breath."

With a look to the door, she kissed him on the cheek, then sat up sharply. "My parents are almost here. You should get going."

He winked ever so slightly at her. "You are delightful," he said, gently touching the top of her hand, which was still on his knee.

The door to the small cottage opened, and Rayna's parents entered. "Thank you again, Rayna, for the chess set." He whispered, wrapping it in the cloth she'd provided. Kai stood and crossed the room, extending his hand. "Mister Kendrick, Dori. I really should join my family before I am missed. Many blessings to you in the new year."

Rayna quickly ran behind to see him to the door. "Many blessings to you Kai for the coming new year."

As he left, he saw through the window as Rayna hugged both her parents. He knew how much this meant to her, and he was happy they were willing to let her pursue her dream. What would they do if she chose to leave one day? Would they be open to allowing her to go? He knew that day was coming sooner than everyone realized. She would be seventeen in a little over two months, and his birthday was only a few days later.

Late into the evening, Kai stood talking with Tolan, watching the crowd dance. He was pleased their relationship had outgrown their childish rivalry. The skills Tolan had developed, and the rank he'd earned at Fort Pohaku, had matured him. Tolan was now the youngest captain in the history of Diu, and he had truly earned his rank.

Kai was most pleased to see the new uniform. "The last time we spoke, what a year ago, I suggested you pursue the rank of captain. I see you followed my advice. Have you decided where you want to be stationed?"

"You know I want to go to Milnos," Tolan responded. "Let us just say, I am still negotiating. Obviously, I'd prefer to be stationed at the Milnos fortress rather than a Diu fort or down south with my father. Diu's navel fort is the farthest point from Milnos, which is where my father proposes I continue my service. I can only guess to follow in his footsteps. Either way, I am not standing in his shadow. All my hard work abroad would be lost if I stayed under him in Fort Pohaku." Tolan's voice trailed off as his gaze shifted around the room. "I may not be able to be with Amelia, but I will see to her safety."

Kai noticed Tolan's face soften. Across the room, he saw Amelia's eyes connect with Tolan. Continuing around the room, his eyes locked onto an older but familiar face stepping through the archway of the great hall. "Look who decided to show his face." Kai jutted his chin. "I didn't know Landon was coming tonight. It's been years since I've seen him." Interrupting the moment, Kai nudged Tolan. "He must have come with the Maxwells. Did you know?"

Tolan glared at Landon. "We've lost touch. He came to Fort Pohaku with me years ago, but while I flourished in the environment, he seemed to turn bitter and angry. He left within six months after a skirmish in the field. He never took the oath. I've not seen him since."

Tolan took a few steps away from the wall. Kai noted the stern look growing in his eyes. "Do you think he is here to take the oath and pledge fealty to my father?" Kai asked, watching

Landon greet a few lords, hovering near the entrance. "Are you going to go say hello?"

"I doubt he is here to bend the knee to your father," Tolan replied. "That was never his nature. I guess I should find out what he is doing here."

Tolan crossed the crowded room, and Kai noticed a man appear at Landon's side. From the side, Kai initially thought it was Kempery-man Marcone; however, something did not feel right. The man silently stood near Landon with his hands behind his back. Between the low lighting and all the people, it was difficult to get a good look.

The air was thick with energy. Kai needed a better view. He took a step, forward crashing into Seth and Aaron. His stepbrothers blocked his path. "Goodnight, Kai," Seth sighed. "Mother says even at ten we are too young to stay up till the new year. I think she is worried because people start getting out of hand with all the wine." Seth pointed across the hall at Nola walking hand-in-hand with Cordelia towards the doors. "There they go. We need to catch up, Aaron."

My little sunshine, my little Cordelia. Kai smiled at her cuteness. He had grown rather fond of his little sister. The sight of her warmed his heart. As she stopped to curtsy to Grand Duke Dante, Kai caught a glimpse of her dimples. Her curly blonde hair bounced as she skipped away.

Nola and Cordelia neared the archway, and Kempery-man Marcone stepped forward, blocking their path. Bending over to address Cordelia, Marcone took her little hand in his and whispered something in her ear. As he did, a necklace fell from inside his shirt. Dangling from his neck was a black hexagonal crystal on a silver chain. Kai felt a bristle of energy rake across his senses. *This is not right...*

After Nola and Cordelia departed, Kai saw Marcone reach inside a small leather pouch cinched to his waist. He withdrew several silver balls and handed a few to Landon, who hid them in his pocket as Aaron and Seth burst between them. A brief snarl crossed Landon's mouth as he watched the boys exit.

Tolan came up behind Landon and clasped a hand on his old friend's shoulder. Kai wished he was close enough to hear what they were saying. The two men shook hands, but Landon's face did not match the gesture. While they spoke, Landon occasionally stepped back towards the archway, his manner implying his desire to leave. To Kai, he seemed almost put out that Tolan was interrupting him.

Meanwhile, Marcone held his ground, his head down, and his arms behind his back. From time to time he glanced back at Landon, almost as if he were waiting for something. Abruptly, Landon ended the conversation and left. Frustrated, Tolan waved off the discussion and made his way toward Amelia, letting his smile return.

Still concerned with Marcone's behavior, Kai shifted his location to gaze at the man as his expression seem to change. Or rather, Marcone himself appeared to be changing, right in front of Kai's eyes. *Does anyone else see this?* Kai looked around the room. Connected to his sight, he sensed the room, and he saw the truth. The man was not Marcone; Kai could see the intense light emanating from this man's soul. He was Katori.

Slowly, the man raked his hand over his head and revealed a different person. The man had an olive complexion, blue-green eyes, and a shaved head except for a long braid of sandy brown hair running down the center of his scalp, ending just below his shoulders.

Before Kai could react, the man pulled a thick black cover over his nose and mouth. Abruptly he lifted his hands over his head and threw two silver balls at the ground on either side of himself. A bright flash lit up the room, followed by a loud bang and a cloud of foul smoke. Everyone around the man dropped to the floor as the rest of the room screamed and panicked.

The smoke dispersed in seconds.

The man eased the mask down to his neck. The Kempery-men converged on the king's throne, surrounding Iver with swords drawn. Other than the Diu soldiers, everyone was disarmed at the palace entrance. Yet this man pulled out two swords that had been concealed at his side. They were black blades with a slight curve, broader near the tip and at least two feet in length.

"Don't be too hasty, boys," the stranger suggested. "Nobody needs to get hurt. At least not tonight." He sneered at Iver.

The air thickened as Kai stared at the stranger. A moment of dread welled in the pit of his stomach. He needed to act, but what could he do?

"I've come for compensation. Iver, you took something from me many years ago. I want restitution. I came to collect her, as she was my prize. Although, it would seem death separates us now. Still, I was sure she was here, but my spies tell me I now seek another. But you know, I need you to suffer. You will know my pain tenfold, so I will take your precious little sunshine and whatever else I please." The man's eyes shifted about the room in Kai's direction. "Yes, I do believe you have something else that belongs to me."

Panic pricked at Kai's heart. *Who was this man?* How could he walk in undetected? How could he change his face? That was not a gift Haygan had ever mentioned. Who was his prize? Did the stranger mean his mother, Mariana? Did he expect to take Kai instead?

"Stop this man," Iver demanded, gesturing to his men.

Five Kempery-men released arrows in his direction. The man moved lightning fast, swinging his two swords in a swirling motion, blocking all five shots. His swords were back in their place as quickly as he'd wielded them. Other Kempery-men took a few steps forward, swords at the ready.

The man withdrew two more silver balls, rolling them around his fingers. "I wouldn't if I were you, unless you want to join the others slumbering on the floor. With nobody left to defend your king, I could wreak all sorts of havoc." The man laughed at them. "No, you will stand your ground while I deal with Iver."

Kai backed away from the scene until he felt the stone wall

hit his back as the riddle unfolded. This man must mean to take Cordelia. She was Iver's little sunshine. How did this man know that? What if Landon is helping him? Is that why they were together? Fear struck Kai's heart. Hurriedly, he slid along the wall to the last painting at the back of the great hall. Using his forefinger, he released the hook holding the framed panel in place.

Everyone focused on the stranger. Blocked by a stone pillar and a crowd of people, Kai opened the passage and slipped behind the painting. Hook secured, he quickly made his way up the stairs of the secret passage, gleaning all the while to ensure that his father's study was empty. Inside the study, he reset the painting back into place. Out in the hallway, he heard a commotion. He smelled the hint of the same foul smoke. Thuds of bodies dropping confirmed Kai's suspicions. Someone, possibly Landon, was upstairs in the royal hallway.

The door to the study was slightly ajar, allowing Kai to hide behind the door. Gleaning the hallway, he saw one person hastily approaching. In his wake, two soldiers lay on the floor with the Mryken dogs, all knocked out. Not wanting to reveal his position, Kai waited. Through the crack behind the door, he saw Landon across the hall. He opened the nursery door.

Kai remembered this moment. He needed to wait. In his vision, he'd passed out in the hallway. *Not this time,* he thought. *I must wait.*

Nola's voice rang out. "Landon. What are you doing here? Don't do this. Put down the knife. I'm your..." Bang. Kai heard the pop of a silver ball, followed by the foul-smelling smoke. Instinctively Kai held his breath, covered his face with his shirt, and waited for the smoke to clear the hallway.

Leaving his hiding place, Kai saw directly into the nursery. On the floor lay Kendra, Nola, and all three children. Landon waved his dagger over them, a wicked look in his eye. "Keegan wants this little blonde brat alive. Instead, I think I should kill you all, bring an end to the Galloway family's future."

Kai knew this was his chance. With a burst of energy and

speed, he rushed the room. Landon's dagger flew across the room and his body sprawled out. His head struck the edge of the sofa table before hitting the floor. Slowly Landon rolled over. Blood oozed from his head down the corner of his face.

Through glazed eyes, Landon glared at Kai. Propped up on his elbow, he pressed a hand to his head. He winced in pain and looked at his blood-soaked hand. "You little bastard. I will have my revenge. I will kill you and your family." Landon wobbled as he struggled to stand.

Before Landon could recover, Kai pounced. He pushed him back to the ground. They landed in a heap, shoving the sofa out of place. Landon jabbed Kai in the jaw. Kai punched Landon in the kidney and rolled him onto his stomach.

Kai was no longer the little boy he'd been the first time Landon tried to push him around. Kai pressed his knee into Landon's spine and pulled his arms behind his back. Set at an awkward angle, Landon cried out in pain. Kai knew he needed to subdue him before he regained his senses. Pinning Landon with his body weight, he swiftly removed his belt. After he secured Landon's hands, he gagged him with a piece of quilting cloth that was lying on the sofa.

Even though he seemed restrained, Kai was unsure how much time he had. Would the man from downstairs, this Keegan, be next through the door, swinging his two black swords? Gently he rolled over Nola and Cordelia; they were alive but unconscious. No cuts or bruises. Beside them lay Kendra. He removed her apron and tied Landon's legs. Satisfied, he checked on Aaron and Seth. They were asleep. No injuries.

From the hall, he heard loud voices and boots rapidly stomping up the stairwell, then came the sound of dogs barking. Mryken burst into the room followed by Cazier, Dresnor, and two guards, all with swords drawn. Then Iver entered. Kai stood over Landon's bound and gagged body. Iver crouched down to Nola and Cordelia, relief welling in his eyes. "Bless you, Kai. Are you alright?"

"I am fine," Kai answered. "Landon used a silver ball and

knocked them out. I was able to take him by surprise. He is still breathing, but he hit his head hard on the table when he went down. He is bleeding pretty badly."

Still in shock, Iver looked over the scene. "I'm proud of you, son. How did you get here so fast?"

Kai ran his thumb around the corner of his chin and glanced at the Master General. Cazier's stern look told him he needed to keep it simple. "I came upstairs to check on Smoke when I heard a commotion in the hallway. When I peeked down the hall, I saw Landon toss a silver ball at the ground. There was a flash, a loud bang, and a plume of smoke. Then all the guards fell to the floor, along with the Mryken. Landon ran to the nursery and I heard the same loud bang, and smoke rolled out into the hallway." Kai placed a hand on his heart and continued. "I ran to the nursery and found Landon standing over Cordelia with a dagger. He mentioned a man's name—he said Keegan wanted him to take Cordelia. He didn't know I was there, so I slammed into the back of him. Fortunately, he clipped the table with his head, nearly knocking him out. The dagger landed somewhere over there."

Kai stepped to the window seat and picked up the dagger. It had a twisted metal blade and a black leather handle.

Cazier stepped around Iver and retrieved the knife. "Dresnor, have one of your men escort Landon to the tower cells. I will question him later."

Confused, Kai shook his head. He could not believe what just happened. "Father, what's going on? Why would Landon do this? I've known him all my life; he grew up here. Sure, he is not the nicest person, but why would he do this? Who is this Keegan?"

Iver placed a hand on his son's shoulder. "We all have questions. Let's take care of our family and then we can talk." Iver lifted Cordelia and gently placed her on the bed. "Son, I will carry Seth. Please bring Aaron. We can take them to their room. Cazier, please put Kendra in her bed, there in the corner. Once you've secured the floor, meet us in my study. Dresnor, see to the guests. Double the guards on every floor. Question everyone before you send them away. Finally, instruct Dante to pull extra men back to the palace."

Dresnor bowed, "As you command, Your Royal Highness."

CHAPTER 20

Mariana's Secret

The tension in the king's study left Kai on edge. He sat on the sofa, staring into the fireplace, his father in a chair to his right. Lost in thought, he nervously waited for the Master General. *How could this be happening? Nothing makes sense.*

Cazier entered and took the vacant chair. "They found Marcone, under the stone walkway leading up to the palace entrance. He'd been stripped of his uniform, bound and gagged. It took him several moments to speak. Most of what he said was gibberish. We will get nothing of use from him tonight. We took him to Sigry." The Master General shook his head in bewilderment. "I've never seen anyone so incoherent from what appeared to be nothing more than a minor head wound."

"What of the palace?" Iver questioned. "The Maxwells, have they been secured?"

"Dante is seeing to all guests," Cazier acknowledged. "We are getting them accommodations outside of the palace grounds. Those asleep are under armed guard in the great hall. The Maxwells are in their room, with armed guards securing the hall. I will see to questioning them myself once we are finished here."

Iver nodded to Cazier and turned to Kai. "Son, we need to

talk." Iver looked to Cazier. "I have a story to tell my son, and you need to learn it too."

Kai looked from his father to his cousin and back again. "What happened downstairs? As I left the great hall, I saw Landon arrive with someone. Was that Keegan, the one Landon spoke of? Why does Landon hate us?"

The look of anguish washed over the king's face. "It's a long story," Iver began. "The Diu kingdom has a long history with the Milnos kingdom. The Bangloo empire once ruled Milnos. They tried to take Diu in a great war. King Nicholas Galloway made an alliance with Nebea by marrying his daughter Eden to Brandon Cazier. But they were still not enough to stop the iron city of Milnos. Bangloo supplied so many men. They wanted to devour our entire continent, piece by piece. Diu was simply an easy target."

"My great grandmother Gianfranca called on the Katori to come to our aid. The Katori sent dragons to Bangloo. King Nicholas tricked Milnos and struck directly at the heart of Bangloo. He moved the war to a new front. Bangloo was not prepared to fight on two fronts. Over half of their warriors were here attacking us. They retreated home back across the sea to defend their homeland. The second wave of dragons finished the battle here in Diu. We drove Milnos back. Our palace burned to the ground, but we won that day."

"I had no idea," Kai astounded. "Our history books never go into this much detail."

"In every story, various parts get lost or changed." Iver agreed. "Details are forgotten. Anyway, the Penier family were once kings that ruled Milnos for generations, serving the king of Bangloo. When my King Nicholas Galloway made peace with Bangloo, Milnos surrendered the war. The Penier family pledged peace. They could no longer afford to fight.

"In exchange, they could keep their kingdom. Nebea and Diu remained close allies. When Bannon Penier, Landon's father, became king, the relationship between Diu and Milnos changed. I remember my father saying the conversations between him and Bannon were awkward one minute and friendly the next.”

Taken back in time, Iver paused. The weight of the world seemed heavy on his shoulders.

“Wait—Landon is a Penier? Not a Maxwell?” Confused, Kai looked to Cazier.

“Yes, Kai,” Cazier responded. “Landon is a Panier, adopted by Regent Maxwell.”

“Years later, my father,” Iver drew them back on topic, “King Everett Galloway, and Master General Aerin Cazier, Adrian’s father, traveled through Nebea to meet with King Trenton Cazier. They were hunting at the southern end of Lake Eden, near the border between Nebea and Milnos, when they received word about an uproar in the city. King Bannon called for my father’s help to establish peace. King Cazier sent word to Nebea for more men, but he and my father continued onward to answer the call for help.”

“With two small armies, they went to Milnos offering assistance. King Bannon Penier welcomed us in with open arms. He assured my father the riots had stopped, and the city was secure. King Bannon was pleasant and welcomed both kings into the fortress.”

The more Kai listened, the less he wanted to hear. It was hard to hear firsthand how your ancestors lived and died. Somehow coming from Professor Greydon it seemed fictional and distant. Still, he listened, hoping to learn something, not in his history books.

“After a meal, they adjourned to King Penier’s study, as they had done many times before. Master General Aerin Cazier told us that King Bannon ran my father through the heart with a dagger from behind. In the fight, Trenton sustained only one wound, a shallow cut across the chest. Trenton managed to kill King Bannon before succumbing to a poisoned blade. Master General Aerin was wounded but survived.

“Reinforcements came from Nebea and Diu over the following days. They captured the fortress, Aerin at the helm of both armies. As the next in line as King of Diu, I traveled to Nebea. As my first act, I sent an emissary to Bangloo for answers. Their young King Seibur said he had no knowledge of King Bannon Penier's actions, nor did he have an interest in a war with Diu or Nebea."

Most of this was not news to Kai. He knew his history well. Milnos was a massive city, five times the size of Diu. Nebea was its only equal. Still hearing it firsthand from his father wrenched his heart. The pain of retelling it showed on his father.

Taking a breath, Iver raked his hand across his face. He looked exhausted reliving the loss of his father. "Are you alright, father?" Kai asked.

"Yes," Iver responded. "As you can imagine, we were all devastated by the treachery—the loss of two kings in one day, King Trenton Cazier of Nebea and my father, King Everett Galloway. My own mother, Bellamay, died of a broken heart—the loss of her husband was more than she could bear. King Trenton had no children, so the crown fell to Andrew Cazier, Aerin's eldest son. He became King of Nebea, while Aerin Cazier remained at my side as Master General.

"At the time, King Bannon Penier's wife was pregnant." Iver looked away, unable to look at Kai or Cazier. "Unfortunately, she was found complicit in her husband's plan to kill my father. Killing Trenton had not initially been part of their plan, but they were just as content to take his life. They all but relished in their accomplishment while in prison. She gave birth to Landon, and after his birth, she was put to death.

"Lucas Maxwell, a high-ranking Duke in Milnos, assumed the role as regent by local recommendations. We did our best to influence that decision given the outrage in Diu and Nebea —many people wanted us to divide the country and take its spoils, but Milnos is massive and we did not want another war or civil unrest with such a large country."

"So, Landon was raised in Milnos," Kai interrupted, "until he was five and then brought here for guidance and formal education.

"Correct," Cazier acknowledged. "Duke Raebun reported Landon missing two years ago. I have no idea where he has been all this time or when he turned against us. After a skirmish near Fort Pohaku, Landon quit and left the naval base. One can understand his desire for revenge, even though he has lived here for most of his life."

Kai was astonished, and he sat there, mulling over everything he'd just learned. "That explains Landon's hatred. But what of this other man, Keegan? Who is he and why was he after Cordelia? What did you take from him?"

"Keegan is Katori," Iver answered. "He said he wanted compensation for something he feels I took from him. I never took your mother. She ran away from him. Said she feared his ruthless nature."

Kai's eyes bulged. "Keegan knew my mother?"

Iver covered his chest with his hands. "I promised your mother her secret would never be told unless she told it. But I guess it's time. Since she is not here to tell you, I will have to tell it for her. She would want you to know." Leaning to one side, Iver rubbed his forehead with his hand. "This part Cazier does not know but needs to learn." Iver's voice faltered.

The room fell silent, except for Kai's heart pounding in his ears. His stomach twisted into a knot. The seconds felt like hours while he watched his father struggle to assemble the words that were stuck in his throat.

Iver's eyes welled with emotion. "Kai, I am not your blood father. Three years after I became king, I began to travel the world seeking alliances and establishing trade. On one such trip, I met and fell in love with Mariana, from the first day I found her lying on a beach, covered in seaweed and sand. Her ship was destroyed, and she washed up on the Bangloo shore after running from Keegan."

"I never knew how you and my mother met," Kai interrupted.

"Yes, well, according to your mother, Keegan wanted to

rule Katori. Maybe even the world. She said her elders banished Keegan from Katori after he attacked a sacred gathering place. Weeks later he came in disguise and tricked your mother. To him, she was some sort of prize. She was someone important to their community. Mariana said they were friends once, but he became violent. She rebuffed his advances, but he would not take no for an answer. He pushed himself on her." Iver recoiled at the thought and yet he relaxed in the unburdening of his soul.

The world swam in Kai's head. This could not be true. None of this could be real. "But you are my father," Kai insisted.

"In every way that matters, I am." Iver shifted in his chair and resumed his story. "We spent time getting to know each other while exploring the world. After sailing around the Caprizian Sea, Mariana began to show her pregnancy. I hid her from the crew until we landed off Ahana. On their sandy shores, I promised to love her forever. I promised to be a father to her unborn child if she'd have me. We were wed that afternoon, and we returned to Diu. The Diu people were happy to see I'd finally taken a bride, and nobody ever questioned if the baby was mine. Everyone who met your mother loved her instantly."

Kai sat there overwhelmed by the story his father had just shared. *What does this mean? If Iver is not my father, who am I now?*

Iver looked at Adrian. "I shared this with you so that Kai is not alone with this news, and because we are family. There is trust between us. There is trust between the two of you." He looked at Kai. "You are still my son—I chose to be your father. Nothing changes. I love you, son. This man Keegan is bad. Your mother feared him. Now he has his sights set on us. On you. I believe he has come to take you away from me."

"This is all too much to believe," Kai whispered to himself. So many thoughts ran through Kai's mind. Keegan was his father. Which meant Kai was full Katori, not a Half-Light. This explained all his power. They sat in silence for a few moments.

None willing to utter a word. It was almost too much to believe.

Quietly Iver stood and pulled a chain from his pocket. "Here, son, I want you to have this." Iver dangled a necklace in front of Kai. "This was your mother's necklace. She gave it to me when we first met. I've always kept it close to me. It will protect you as it has me."

Kai accepted the chain. The crescent moon and stone dangled in front of him. He was surprised his father was willing to part with such a treasure. "Thank you, father. I will keep it safe."

"Father, what happened with Keegan downstairs?"

"The long and short of it—Keegan escaped. He called young Amelia to his side. Tolan tried to pull her back, but Keegan tossed a blade at her dress. She was not hurt, but the dagger tore the hem of her gown. He threatened the next would strike her heart. Out of fear, she complied."

Kai gasped. "Where is she? Is she alright?" Fear welled in his heart.

"She is fine," Iver patted his son's shoulder. "The party-goers outside had no clue there was any chaos happening inside the palace. Seems Kempery-man Decklar saw her and wrapped her in a hug as they exited. Keegan released her hand and disappeared within the crowd. We are most fortunate that Decklar is a hugger, and Amelia looks like his daughter. She is with her parents now."

Iver's study filled with Kempery-men, followed by the Grand Duke. Iver turned to speak with Dante, and everyone left for the king's council chamber.

Overwhelmed by the news, Kai retreated to his room. He needed to think. His mother's necklace felt warm in his hand. He slipped the long chain around his head and tucked it under his shirt for safekeeping.

CHAPTER 21

For days and days after the attack on the palace, security around Diu remained intense, and Iver was constantly in his council chamber. Kai spent any time he could attending and listening. He wanted to gather any useful information he could. There had to be more to Landon. More to Keegan. Yet everything he learned was basically useless. They knew no more than he did. Spy reports mentioned Caroco ships near the Mystic Islands, but Keegan was a ghost in the wind.

The Winter Festival events concerned Kai: Landon's betrayal, Keegan's ability to look like Marcone, and the worst possible outcome...Keegan was his father. With this failed attempt to make Iver pay, would he come at them again? Who would he look like the next time?

Then there was Nola's incomplete sentence—*I'm your*—it festered in Kai's stomach. Who was Landon to her? Kai needed to know. This was not something he could ask her straight out. He would need Riome. Maybe she could uncover the queen's secret.

Locked away in a dark cell, Landon was interrogated by Cazier repeatedly. Landon refused to divulge any accomplices. He offered no clues and insisted that he did not know

Keegan, nor did he have any knowledge of Keegan's plans. All indications led Kai to believe Landon would rot in prison. The last of his lineage. And he feared Keegan would return in force.

Master General Cazier requested extra men come from Fort Pohaku to secure Diu. It seemed to Kai like a short-term fix. They would not stay forever. At some point, the influx of men would go home. Every spy at Cazier's disposal was set to search for Keegan or news of his whereabouts and plans.

New faces reported daily to Dante and Cazier. Spy networks from Diu and Nebea came to provide any news they could discover. While no news was not necessarily bad, it was not necessarily good either. All reports came back empty; the man was gone. There was not so much as a rumor of how he came into the city or where he went.

It boggled the mind to wonder how Keegan had managed to look like Marcone. Kai knew it was unnatural to change your face, yet when questioned, nobody else saw him change. They all remembered Marcone in the great hall, but they were unclear about how this stranger came to be wearing the Kempery-man's uniform.

Sadly, Marcone was now little more than a vegetable. He had no memory of what happened, and his verbal skills were reduced to that of a young child. Regrettably, he was their only witness, and his memories were lost forever.

The king's council chamber continued to be a hive of activity. Iver walked with authority, back to his usual self. Nola, shaken by the events, had withdrawn with her children. She kept to the family floor, rarely going outside. She even took meals in her room or the nursery. As far as Kai could tell, she only ventured down if Iver insisted she stand at his side.

The discovery Iver was not his real father whirled around in Kai's mind. So many secrets. He was his mother's deepest secret. Was every part of his life a lie? His mother was alive, his father was not his father, and he was full Katori. Did this man Keegan, his real father, mean to hunt him down? He shuddered at the thought. Anger welled in his heart for a man he had never met.

If I am full Katori, he thought, *then I can find this man Keegan. No more holding back.*

Dwelling on the man who hurt his mother, Kai turned anger into rage. Methodically, he gleaned the city, searching for any Katori he could find. Building after building—warehouse, shop, and home. Each stoked the anger in his heart. *How dare this man treat my mother like a dog. How dare he come in my home and attack my family.*

By the time he'd searched the entire city, he could barely see straight. If Keegan was no longer in the city, Kai figured he'd retreated to Port Anahita. The Katori feared this man. Maybe he was part of the Caroco fleet seen around the Mystic Islands. Kai had to find him.

Determined to track Keegan himself, Kai collected his men and they met in private near the snow-dusted Mryken kennels. Everyone pressed their hands under their arms to keep warm. "Kempery-man Dresnor," Kai addressed him formally. "I want you to put a group together. We are traveling to Port Anahita."

Dresnor shook his head in disagreement. "That is unwise, Your Highness. With Keegan at large, we should remain here. You don't mean to hunt this man yourself, do you?"

"Certainly not," Kai lied. "If this man means to hurt my family, would his next move not be to hurt Iver's sister, Helena? I simply mean to see she is safe. Everyone is focused on finding him here, hidden within the city. Keegan is long gone from Diu, but we should focus on securing Helena. With a small group, we could sweep into Port Anahita and back out again before anyone was the wiser."

"I don't like it," Dresnor grumbled. "We should bring in Cazier, Dante and my captain, Kempery-man Farwick. At least inform them of our plan."

"We cannot afford to wait." Kai insisted. "Moving en masse will draw attention to our arrival. I fear we will spook Keegan if he sees an army."

"The prince is right," Drew countered. "If we wait, Helena could be killed. Everyone is distracted with the search for Keegan, but we need to focus on Keegan's next move—and King Iver's sister would be a worthy prize."

Dresnor pondered over their argument. "Fine. Redmon, gather five men from your unit. Albey, you do the same, but be discreet. Tell them it is a training mission. We will only be gone for a few days. We travel light to Port Anahita and back. Drew, pick a few scouts. I want them riding point to ensure the route is clear."

Satisfied his men would be suitability busy securing Helena and her family, Kai would be able to search the port city for Katori stragglers. If Keegan still lingered in the area, he would find him and stop him. This man must be found before he learned Mariana was still alive. The idea Keegan might hurt his mother forced him into action. The only thing Kai knew— Keegan would never touch his mother again.

His men readied for departure in secret. This would be his first trip without Haygan, Shane, and Marduk. Haygan was still in Katori, and Shane and his father were hunting in the hills. Dresnor alone made the arrangements.

The thought of leaving his father without word felt like a rock in Kai's stomach, but they still needed to follow his plan.

Not my father. Kai pondered the thought.

Did that matter? Why should it matter? No, he chastised himself. *Iver loves me, and I him,* he assured himself.

One thing he had noticed, however—without Nola's hovering, Iver's mind and appetite had returned. Iver basked in the strategy sessions and took to the training yard a few hours each day. His strength continued to recover.

Ready to leave, Kai mounted Ember, and his group departed for his Aunt Helena's home in Port Anahita. Their departure was set to coincide with the changing of the guard. In addition, Kai wore a scout's uniform, all in the hope of putting distance between them and Diu before anyone knew the prince was gone.

His plan to find Keegan hinged on his team believing they were to rescue Helena.

The ride to Port Anahita was chilly but quick. They rode fast and stopped less. As always, his favorite part of the ride was cresting the hill above Port Anahita. The ocean town was beautiful with all the brightly colored stone buildings—a mix of pinks, yellow, and white. When they reached the edge of town, Dresnor sent one scout ahead to announce their arrival and ensure all was well at the Avar Estate. Slowly the rest of the group meandered around the outskirts of town, winding up the hill to his aunt Helena's home.

Set high on a hill, their stunning blush-pink stone estate overlooked the southern part of the town and vast harbor. Large stone and wrought-iron walls surrounded the private gardens with two small ponds and several large-canopied trees.

As Kai's group approached, he saw Gideon hop to his feet. He anxiously awaited Kai's arrival near the decorative gate. When Kai hopped off Ember, he embraced his cousin. "Gideon! Good to see you, cousin. See, I told you I would visit."

Behind Gideon, something caught Kai's attention: wrought iron twists in the gate. A sense of déjà vu pressed against his memory. He removed his glove and ran his hand down the twists as he had done many times before on his visits. There was something eerily familiar about those bars.

Gideon ushered Kai through the gate. "Come. Come. I am anxious to see you after what happened at the Winter Festival. We were all rushed into our rooms, then mother insisted we return home the following morning. We didn't even tell uncle Iver we were leaving. Mother insisted King Iver's security restrictions not trap us in Diu. Still, I want to hear any news you bring. How are you here this evening?" his cousin rambled, pulling Kai around the estate.

"I am a prince. I go where I wish if I apply the right pressure." He smiled, trying to dissuade his cousin.

Kai had always enjoyed visiting his aunt and uncle. Helena loved the ocean and his uncle Kaeco would do anything to please her. As Duke of Port Anahita, and harbormaster, Kaeco established new trade routes and nearly tripled the size of the once-small port. His influence had made Iver and himself extremely wealthy over the years.

Walking the estate with his cousin, Kai wondered how things might change if the world knew he was not truly a prince?

The Avar estate bustled with people coming and going. Kai watched his aunt Helena in the gardens teaching a painting class to local ladies and young girls. He noted her attire—while she had to be formal in Diu, here she was modest and earthy. The winter wind made her cheeks pink and her nose red. She winked at Kai as she spoke to her students.

"I wish we'd known you were coming, Kai." Gideon waved to his mother as they skirted around the group toward the house. "My father is fishing down at the pier with the young boys' club. He should be home any moment."

"You must be kidding," Kai chuckled. "Uncle Kaeco is fishing?" Although Kai teased, he knew his uncle was content to support youth activities, even if he wasn't very good at the outing they chose.

"He is." Gideon grinned back.

Before they reached the house, his Aunt Helena caught up with them. "My dear Kai, I am so happy to see you." She wrapped her arms around him. "Welcome. What brings you here? Is my brother alright?" Her expression turned to worry.

"Father is fine, Aunt Helena." Kai glanced at Dresnor as his group followed his aunt inside.

Kai knew convincing his aunt Helena to leave her home would be no simple task. She was stubborn and not one to cower from a fight. "Aunt Helena, we came to escort you all back to Diu. It might not be safe here. We have not found Keegan, the man who attacked the palace at the Winter Festival. I would feel better if you returned with us to the palace."

"Kai, honey," Helena soothed. "I appreciate your concern for us, but I am not leaving my home. We have guards here on the estate. Thirty men, strong and loyal. The city also has soldiers. We are safe here. Safe as anywhere—even Diu. Given your recent events at the palace..." She jutted her chin.

Duke Kaeco crossed the room. "Your Highness, welcome to my home." His uncle extended a hand and offered a polite bow.

"Uncle Kaeco." Kai stood and shook his uncle's hand. "My apologies for the unannounced arrival. With this madman on the loose, I feared for your safety. If only you could see reason. We have no idea what this man's next move could be."

"We respect your authority," Kaeco said, "and we appreciate your concern, but I must agree with my wife. We are safe here. You are welcome to stay a few days if that might put your mind at ease. Search the town. However, I cannot see any real reason to leave."

A few extra days. Kai liked the sound of that, but he had work to do. Searching the city, even gleaning, would take time. "It would ease my mind if my men could search the town. Twenty-five extra men could go a long way in securing the estate. I will send word back to Diu tomorrow that we are staying the week."

Dresnor's displeasure in this delay was evident behind the glare he gave the prince, yet he clamped his jaw shut and said nothing—although Kai was certain he'd have a few choice words at some point.

The pace of life on the Avar Estate was slower and, in most ways, more enjoyable. Helena and Kaeco were a happy couple. Kai watched them wander the estate gardens hand-in-hand. It made it easy to see where Gideon got his gentle nature.

On the far side of the gardens, Gideon sat with Victoria enjoying a quiet moment by a small outdoor fireplace. It was sweet to see these two quiet souls chatter away. To think all it took was one dance to seal their relationship. Knowing one day they would marry and be together forever, made Kai a little jealous.

Being a port city, Anahita had a large city guard and the occasional influx of Diu servicemen boarding ships bound for Fort Pohaku. This should have made it easier on his guards, but Dresnor was ever vigilant about hovering over Kai. Either Dresnor, Drew, Redmon or Albey were always at his side whenever he ventured into town, always lingering on the periphery.

The next day Kai spent hours listening to his cousin Gideon ramble about working with his father on bookkeeping and shipping manifests.

How a person could find warehouse inventory fun, Kai would never understand. But he enjoyed his cousin's company, and he was able to divide his attention and search the docks for the wanted man Keegan. However, much to his frustration, his real father was not there.

What Kai needed was quiet reflection. No disruptions. Gleaning had produced no results, and he needed to search beyond the city.

Retiring to his room for the afternoon, Kai meditated. To search beyond the city, he needed to push his power outward. It was a gift he could not yet control, but it was the only way to search the sea. It was risky to use his energy to bounce off others, because that power would resonate like a beacon, revealing his location. But it was his best bet to draw the man out of hiding.

The question was, could he control the wave, focus on one

person? Recently his success was rather broad. Kai wanted Keegan. If he was to rescue his mother, he must first deal with this man. He felt it was worth the risk exposing his power to bring this man to face him.

Without Kendra adding to his energy, however, he feared he wouldn't be able to search far enough. And, unless he learned to focus on one person, his wave would light up the world.

No, this time needed to be different. Kai could not alert the world—he needed to find just one man—Keegan.

As Kai had done over the summer, he held onto the light and pressed it inward. He felt the power build and build until it pushed back. With his mind, he pulled at his surroundings. He collected more and more energy. From the stone and wood of the estate, he drew strength. From the very fire that warmed his room, he found more. He even took magic from the trees outside his window.

His head began to pound.

Kai focused on the memory of Keegan's face. His eyes. His essence. He thought only of him. A knowing welled in his soul.

His body shook.

Unable to hold the magic back any longer, he pushed the pulse out, with one man in mind and one thought attached—*come to me.*

A spear of light bolted from Kai's mind, over the city, and across the ocean. Ripples of waves flowed beneath him. His mind traveled in one direction. Wanting to extend his range, he pushed every ounce of power he had.

A singular focused beam crashed into the mind of Keegan. Kai saw the man's face smirk, and one thought returned—*already on my way, my boy!*

Drained of all his power, Kai collapsed on the floor. He lay helpless beside Smoke.

When he awoke, he was lying on top of his bed, and Dresnor sat near the window. "How long have I been asleep?" Kai asked, rubbing his face.

"Since last yesterday," Dresnor acknowledged. "Any idea what happened?"

While Kai knew precisely what happened, he could not tell Dresnor he'd overextended his energy searching for Keegan. "Not exactly. I felt dizzy, and my head began to swim. I sat down next to Smoke…and that's the last thing I remember."

"Well, when you did not come down for dinner last night, we searched for you. Drew found you here on the floor and placed you on the bed. Helena sent for a physician. He believes you were dehydrated."

Dresnor offered Kai water, and it felt good on his throat. "Maybe you're right." Kai swung his legs off the bed and stood. "I feel much better, but still very thirsty." Kai finished the entire pitcher of water.

For the next two days, everyone coddled him. His Aunt Helena continuously poured water into him. Dresnor watched him like a hawk. Whenever possible, he sat with his cousin in a shaded part of the garden playing chess. Gideon was an exceptional player. *Finally, a worthy opponent.* Kai smiled at his first loss.

Each time Kai managed to escape the estate; it wasn't long before Dresnor caught up with him. "Where do you think you're going?" Dresnor demanded.

"Come on, already." Kai slumped his shoulders. "Am I a prisoner now? I need some space. Some peace and quiet. I am fine, really. These past few days loafing around the estate has me stir-crazy. Come with me if you want, but please, no more banter. I can't possibly take any more racket."

They walked in silence. It felt good to stretch his legs. Even Smoke seemed happy to escape the confines of their luxurious prison. Down at the docks, the salty air assaulted their faces. People chattered, and seagulls squawked. "So much for peace and quiet," Kai joked.

"What are we doing here, Kai?" Dresnor asked, staring out at the setting sun.

"Taking in the view," Kai responded.

"No, why are we still here at your aunt's home? Clearly, she will not leave with us, and this is no longer a rescue mission. So why are we still here? Or maybe I should ask, why are we *really* here?"

Not wanting the onlookers to overhear, Kai walked away from the crowds. Down near the beach, he leaned against an upturned boat. Over his shoulder, Kai caught sight of more of his men following them. "Never far behind, are they? Redmon, Drew, and Albey."

Dresnor eyed them. "It's our job, and we take it very seriously, even if you don't. You never make it easy on us, I must say. But we are lucky the Avar Estate is perched on a hill. There's no getting into town without one of us spotting you."

"We came for my aunt, honestly." Kai held his expression.

"You're a good liar, Kai. No disrespect. I almost believe you. Only I know better. Redmon is a good man, loyal to a fault, he did not rat you out. But you used his men to question citizens about this man Keegan. Really? Did you think I wouldn't find out? I am good at my job Kai."

"Someone had to have seen him. Where could he possibly be? If he came in by ship, this is the most logical place. You cannot convince me that he just *left*. Yes, I came here to find him." Kai raised his tone.

"Are you insane? This man attacked us in our own city. ONE MAN!" Dresnor thundered. "He walked in under our noses and back out without a trace. The man's a ghost. One who openly threatened your little sister Cordelia, your father, and you."

Anger welled in Kai's chest. "And I am telling you—Keegan is not done with us. And I meant it when I said I thought he would strike at Helena next. I will stop him. He is coming. I know it."

Half out of his mind, Kai blurted out more than he intended.

Dresnor shook his head in frustration. "I will be lucky if I don't get dishonorably discharged from my station after this."

Too angry to listen to reason, Kai balled up his fists. "I will put him down. He must pay for what he has done."

Dresnor stepped in close. "Who is the man to you, Kai?" he whispered.

There was no taking his words back. And he didn't even care who knew. "This man hurt my mother, and now he's come for me. It must be me who stops him."

With a firm hand, Dresnor pulled Kai away from the crowds. "Come, let's get back to the estate."

CHAPTER 22

Twist of Fate

I f ever there was a morning to sneak out, this was it. Kai hoped he had risen early enough to get out and back before anyone was the wiser. Time by himself had been non-existent these past few days. He needed this.

Smoke ran by his side as they cut through the estate and slipped out the back. Dense fog engulfed the port city as Kai set out towards Anahita Park. There he dropped off his black cloak and lapped the park several times before running through the empty streets of the town.

This was his favorite time—predawn. He had the town all to himself. Everything was silent. In the distance, he could hear the faint sound of the ocean. Each pounding wave a drumbeat. He felt pulled by its rhythmic movements. The salt air washed over the town. An unforgettable scent. Drawn by the waves, he turned down the next street.

His destination was the beach. The salty air and crashing waves brought a smile to his face. The first day he had met Rayna, they had come to this beach. Kai stood on the sand, listening to the waves crash on the shore through the fog. In the distance, he could see the lighthouse's rotating beacon.

He knew Dresnor would be furious if he awoke and found Kai missing from the estate—again. He wanted to heed his

Kempery-man's warning, but he needed time alone. Time to think. Time to let all the changes in his life settle.

The thought of Keegan coming for him, terrified and thrilled him. With this man still on the rampage, Kai was in danger. And yet he had basically told the man where he was and offered himself as bait to lure him out of hiding.

Ready to head back, he set a quick pace towards the Anahita city center. There he slowed to marvel at his uncle Kaeco's newest acquisition. His uncle had bought and demolished four old buildings, which had doubled the size of the city park. In their place, he had erected an ornate white marble lotus fountain, his aunt Helena's favorite flower.

Lush gardens surrounded the new fountain, and walkways and hedges blended into the older part of the park. Kai dipped his hands into the water and stared at the bottom of the pool and noticed the decorative blue and yellow tiles. How he wished to be able to express his feelings for Rayna in a grand manner.

On his walk back through town, he picked up the black cloak he'd left lying across a park bench before his morning run. Turning the wrap over in his hands, he inspected the lining and was pleased that it was still dry. With the cloak draped around his shoulders, he lifted the cowl to cover his sandy blond hair.

To avoid being detected returning to the estate, Kai walked toward the city stables. There he could take backstreets up to the Avar Estate. At this hour, only a few locals and the occasional city guard with Mryken attack dogs walked the streets.

As he passed, most civilians avoided getting close to Smoke. Only a few dared to walk on the same side of the street.

As Kai neared the stables, he saw lights in the windows through the fog. Quietly he stepped near an open window. He heard men talking inside. *Who could be coming in at this early hour?* His heart skipped a beat.

Around back, he found a few barrels and crates stacked high enough to allow him to reach the loft window. Once inside, he walked across a broad beam to get a better view and listen to the conversations below. From his vantage point, he saw the back of a broad-shouldered man with fiery red hair handing money to the stablemaster. "Yes, that will do nicely, thank you. We will be back around midday. Have my cart ready."

The corner of Kai's mouth turned up. *I know that voice. Tolan, what brings you to Port Anahita at this hour, and why is your stay so short?*

"Sir, yes sir, the cart and your horses will be ready," said the stablemaster.

As Tolan and his men left the stables, Kai climbed out and up onto the rooftop. He leaped across to the next building's balcony. Scaling the wall to the roof, he was able to walk across the flat edge of the building around to the front to get a view of the men on the street. In his mind, he held Smoke back a street out of sight.

Wrapped in the black cloak, he crouched down. From this distance, he could not hear what Tolan told his men. One man stayed behind, returning to stand guard at the stables, while the others walked with Tolan down the street. The thought of hopping down to surprise Tolan crossed his mind—but then he thought of Riome. She would consider this the perfect opportunity to practice his skills.

The rising sun began to burn off the fog. His view improved, and he could see farther down the street. Citizens started opening shops and setting out their wares for the day. To keep up, he leaped across a small alleyway between two buildings. Four buildings later, Tolan stopped, gestured toward the shopkeepers, and gave instructions to another man. Leaving the man behind, Tolan and his men continued toward some unknown destination.

"Where are you going, Tolan?" Kai whispered to himself.

The fog continued to lift, and his improved view revealed he was approaching a major cross street. The expanse would be too wide to jump. His only choice—run ahead and climb down. He made his way along the rooftops, each footfall precisely placed along the narrow ledge. At the end, he shimmied down the side of the building, still shrouded in darkness. His thoughts brought Smoke in his direction, still ensuring he would not be seen by Tolan or his men.

Unsure of their destination, Kai took a risk by going ahead of them. On the street a little farther forward, he saw a woman setting out crates of fruit. The oranges and apples glistened like bright orbs in the morning sun burning through the fog. Her stand would be an excellent place to let Tolan pass. Kai slowed his pace as he crossed the street to the fruit stand. While he sniffed a few apples, the woman placed one last crate on the end of the table.

"Morning, sir. How can I help you this fine day?" the woman asked.

"Good morning," Kai replied, as he cut his eyes over his shoulder to see Tolan and his men pass behind him. "I'll take one yellow apple, please." Apple in hand, he dropped the adequate coin in her hand and took a bite. The juicy fruit filled his mouth, and he bowed kindly to the woman as he walked away after Tolan.

Tolan and his men were still making their way straight through the center of town. They seemed to be on a mission, heading straight towards the harbor. With that idea in mind, Kai decided to take another chance and dart down a side street to run ahead. He chucked the apple core and slipped into the shadows of a narrow road. Winding through the streets, he neared the harbor.

On an old familiar street, two blocks from his uncle Kaeco's warehouse, Kai found himself in front of the old bakery Rayna's family once owned. The smell of freshly baked bread still filled the air, bringing the memory of that day back to him. He peered into the shop. Little had changed besides the owners.

Since he was so far ahead of the others, he removed his cloak, folded it neatly, and laid it on the bench outside before taking a seat. Next to him, the bakery shop door opened, and a young boy stepped out. "Good morning, sir. Can I offer you some freshly baked bread? Perhaps a muffin or fruit shell pie?"

Kai chuckled at the "sir." He rubbed his knuckles along his stubbly chin. Was he really a sir now? "Yes, a fruit shell pie, thank you, but only if you have apple." Like his mother, apple was his favorite kind of pie.

The boy hurried back inside, returning with a seashell-shaped apple pie on a white plate. "Here you are, sir. Anything else?"

Accepting the plate, he dropped three coins into the boy's outstretched hand. "Thank you. Keep the change."

With wide eyes, the boy smiled happily. "Thank you, sir. I will come back for the plate shortly."

The street continued to come alive with people as Kai finished the last bite. Not as good as Lizzie's pie, he thought, but still good. He stood in time to see Tolan and his men pass on the main street to his left.

Behind him, the bakery door opened, and without turning, he held out the small plate for the boy. "Tell your mother that was wonderful. Also, would you mind holding onto my cloak until I return?" he asked, dropping two more coins on the plate the boy now held.

"Happy to, sir." Then the young boy ducked back inside, grabbing the door blown wide by the ocean breeze.

CHAPTER 23

Wrought Iron

Back on the main street, Kai caught a glimpse of Tolan and his men heading down to the harbor where a small crowd had gathered. Several people pointed at several ships out on the ocean, which were advancing fast toward the port at full mast. Kai silently folded into the crowd to hear the news. In the distance, he saw them. Their pennant was barely visible as it whipped backward by the wind, a sliver of red.

A city guard stepped up to Tolan and glanced at Tolan's shoulder. His rank of captain was clearly indicated on his Fort Pohaku uniform. "Sir, shortly after the fog lifted, those four ships appeared on the horizon. Two have now rounded the corner of the bay and are closing on the harbor. Best we can tell they are from Caroco, based on the flag: a black star on a field of red. We have orders not to let them anchor in the port. We've sent one of our ships, the Intrepid, to intercept them."

Everyone stood anxiously anticipating the arrival of the foreign ships. The Intrepid flew the silver wolf on a field of blue. It moved quickly in the heavy breeze, angling around to block the lead ship's path. One of the Caroco ships cut sharply toward the stern of the Intrepid. The crowd held their breath. A plume of orange, yellow, and white blasted out the end of the cannon. A single shot fired. The Galloway men on the Intrepid sent a warning shot at the other ship.

Again, everyone waited.

The Caroco ship did not heed the warning. They continued advancing towards the harbor.

Aware the Caroco ship had no intention of yielding for inspection, the Intrepid began its turn. The intense ocean breeze aided their maneuvers and intensified their speed. Once alongside, the Caroco ship fired on the Intrepid. Two cannons shot at once, and both cannonballs ripped through the port side of the Diu vessel. One struck below the railing. Lethal wooden splinters littered the air. The second was a direct hit on the side, near a cannon port. Still moving, the Intrepid returned fire with four cannon shots in rapid succession.

The blasts echoed across the water. Despite being one cannon down, the Intrepid was making short work of the lead Caroco ship. The mast from the enemy ship split in half, and the vessel now listed to its starboard side. Sails burned. Men scurried for longboats. Part of the crowd gasped in fear while others cheered on the Intrepid.

"Look!" one man called out. "The Intrepid means to ram them broadside!"

Set on a collision course, the Intrepid fired two bow chaser shots. Both shots penetrated the hull of the Caroco ship, and water gushed into the enemy's gun deck.

Not giving up, the Caroco men fired one last shot. They missed the stern of the Intrepid by mere feet. The Intrepid was still on the move. It veered away, circling around to engage the oncoming ships.

Coastal defenses near the lighthouse opened fire on the three enemy ships coming around the point. The Caroco ships returned fire, and several shots ripped through the rock walls of the lighthouse. Rubble tumbled into the ocean, but the structure held fast. Multiple wall cannons fired on the advancing enemy ships. One lucky shot ripped through the ship, striking their cannon port. The Caroco vessel exploded, sending debris and smoke billowing into the air. Caroco sailors scampered to longboats, while their ship started to sink. Still, it lumbered toward the bay.

Kai watched in awe. He wondered if Keegan was aboard any of these Caroco ships. He gleaned the ships. Only a few Katori were aboard. And in his mind, he did not see Keegan's essence. Then Kai wondered if he should be doing something to help. Not wanting to wait any longer, he stepped up alongside Tolan. Smoke was on his other side. "I could be wrong, but I doubt the Intrepid can take on all three ships. Even if one is limping along." Kai nudged Tolan's arm.

"They've sent out the Reaper to join in the fight." Tolan jutted his chin to another Diu ship.

Kai crossed his arms, waiting for Tolan to notice him.

Suddenly realizing who he was speaking to, Tolan turned. "Kai? How did you get here? Are you here alone?" He looked back at the battle. "Never mind, of course you are. Even after all these years, you are still ditching your guards. And no, Smoke does not count as an escort."

Kai squinted at the view. "If I am not mistaken, looks like two more ships are coming in behind them. What can we do?"

Tolan ordered the city guard: "Sound the alarm, get every guard in the city to the harbor. If they land, we need to be ready."

"Sir, yes, sir. But we do not have many men. Many are in Diu since the recent attack." The guard responded.

"Sound the alarm," Tolan barked. "Gather all the men you can and send them here to the harbor to fight. Send one rider to Diu for reinforcements. We've wasted too much time. They won't wait for us to be ready. Now GO."

"You five with me," Tolan waved his hand. "Kai, you too."

Tolan broke through the crowd and made his way to Kaeco's warehouse. Outside, Duke Kaeco stood with Kempery-men Dresnor, Albey, and five other guards. "Inside, all of you," Tolan ordered.

Dresnor gave Kai a stern glare. "Where have you been?"

Ignoring the comment, Kai kept close to Tolan, eager to

help protect Port Anahita.

Inside the warehouse, windows illuminated the long row of crates and barrels. Workers collected containers and carried them outside, while others stacked newly received items on shelves. Tolan gathered everyone off to one side. "Kaeco, where is it? Where do you have it stored? Is it here yet?" Tolan demanded in a heavy tone, his sentences clipped short.

Fear welled in Kaeco's eyes. "What are you talking about? What is happening in the harbor?"

Frustrated, Tolan grabbed Kaeco's arm. "We don't have time for this. I know it's here. Some time ago, Cazier's spies discovered a chemist in Diu and a merchant planning to sell a chemical. I am here to collect something called Arkin Oil. My father sent me to intercept the lot of it here. Did you not receive his letter? He informed you I was coming." From his pocket, Tolan pulled a letter and another sheet of paper. "I have my orders here."

"I might have," Kaeco searched the satchel over his shoulder. "With Kai's visit, I did not read all my correspondence last night."

Shaken, Kaeco read Duke Roark's letter, then reviewed Tolan's document. Shocked, he pushed through the group to a small desk. He riffled through a stack of papers and matched it to the sheet from Tolan.

Kai recognized the shipping manifest he had last seen and taken from the merchant. *Spies indeed.* He had given that very sheet to Riome less than a month ago. Not that he knew anything about this Arkin Oil or any of the other items. She had been searching for each of the items on the list. The shifty man, with the frazzled blond hair and white streak, must have made this before they caught him.

"If I am reading this correctly," Kaeco pointed, "it's sitting on dock number four, to be loaded on a ship called the Hsiu, bound for Milnos. What is this stuff, Arkin Oil? I've never heard of it before." he asked.

Tolan ignored his question. "Show me," he motioned to the

door.

Frantically, Kaeco led the group outside. The city bells rang out. The harbor was now in utter chaos. People ran from the shops, bells rang out, and cannon fire assaulted the once-tranquil port. Guards gathered on the docks while others ran for the shoreline. Cannons exchanged fire between land and sea.

Tolan and Kaeco quickly looked through the cargo stacked up on the pier and then boarded the Hsiu. Kai and Dresnor took in the developing battle in the bay. Ships set ablaze, longboats floating on the waves.

Three Caroco ships slowly sank; the Intrepid was listing to one side with a fourth Caroco ship along its starboard side. The glint of steel and the faint sounds of metal clanging against each other now added to the scene. Interspersed in the chaos, Kai heard a foreign bang from time to time and the screams of men calling out in pain.

The Reaper fired cannons in rapid succession at the next ship. Thud and creaks groaned across the water as the two vessels collided. Men swung across, engaged in battle. Fainter sounds. Strange minor explosions assaulted his ears.

Far in the distance, one ship drifted on the waves alone, watching. It made no movements to aid in the battle or flee in defeat.

Kai reached out with his sight. The ship bloomed with Katori light. He could sense they were the main cause of the increased wind. Energy oozed from the decks. Gusts of wind blew across the ocean toward the battle in port. Two more wind-enhanced ships advanced. They splashed through the outer defensive cannons with minimal damage.

Afraid to push his sight, there was no way to tell if Keegan was among them. But if he was, this was all Kai's fault. He'd tempted Keegan, and now others would pay for his mistake.

He shook his head and gazed west across the harbor. "Dresnor, look." He pointed. "Those two other ships are headed for the western shore. If they drop anchor and lower longboats, a hundred men could pour out of those ships. That beach leads up the Avar Estate. Aunt Helena, who is with her?"

Not waiting for an answer, he found Tolan stacking several small barrels and three crates filled with small clay jars. "Tolan, I trust you know what you're doing here, but we have several longboats from the downed ships coming in." Kai grabbed a crate and chased after Tolan.

"Are you listening? Can you not see what is going on behind us? We are under attack, and you are sorting crates. TOLAN!" Kai thundered.

"I see well enough, Kai. Help me get the last of these crates." Tolan grabbed another crate.

"Why are you getting this stuff? We need to do something."

"I am doing something," Tolan shouted back.

Kai looked to the harbor battle. The Sun Raider warship was now in the battle. Its massive size made it slower, but its multitude of cannons made it a massive blockade blasting in the bay. "Tolan, please. The Reaper is the only ship left chasing the enemy. I can see two new ships about to anchor offshore below the Avar Estate. Tell me you are planning something?" Kai asked, a little frustrated.

Tolan put up his hand to block the sun from his eyes. He watched the chaos in the harbor. He looked west at the new Caroco ships approaching, and he did not appear thrilled with their options.

Tolan's continued silence worried Kai, but Tolan had over four years of military experience. It had taken him less than a year to become a captain over his own squad. Strategy had always been Tolan's strength, and he was fiercely competitive. The battle raged in the distance, and they waited for Tolan to formulate a plan.

"We have to split up," Tolan instructed. "Hurry everyone, grab a barrel or a crate, but be extremely careful. Whatever you do, don't drop it. Follow me." Tolan grabbed two small barrels and marched down the boardwalk.

As they reached the sandy shore, Tolan gently lowered his barrels into a small rowboat floating abandoned along the coast. In the distance, the two Caroco ships continued to approach. Everyone knew they were running out of time, but they followed his orders.

"Put only the barrels in the boat. Now, we split into three groups. One group will cross through town and make for the Avar Estate. The second group will take the crates with the clay jars through the harbor to the east beach. Grab a torch along the way. Once the Caroco longboats are within range, light the fuse and quickly toss them at the boats just before they hit the sandy beach. Toss them at soldiers as they come into shore."

Dresnor interrupted. "What is this stuff? What will it do?" His brow knit together in concern.

"Arkin oil. All I know is, you don't want to get this stuff on you or get it anywhere near fire. I've not seen it used myself, but the information Cazier sent said it burns white-hot. Now the third group—someone must drag this boat out through the surf. Before you do, pull the cork on one barrel. Don't hack at the barrel with your blade, a spark could cause it to explode. Spread the contents of the oil over the other barrels." Tolan looked at their cargo.

Kai could see the worry on Tolan's face. Everyone knew they all fought to save Port Anahita.

Tolan glanced around at the chaos. "Again, I cannot stress enough—don't get this on you. One person will swim through the abandoned fishing boats floating in the harbor towards the two incoming ships. Secure this boat alongside the ships once they drop anchor. Someone from shore will need to shoot a flaming arrow and hit the barrels. As I understand, this Arkin Oil is very volatile. I am hoping it will explode and sink both ships and their men right along with them."

Kai's vision of the two ships came to mind. This was his mission. He needed to be the one to swim. "I will do it," he said. "I am a fast swimmer. I am the best option."

Tolan shook his head. "No, that's insane. It's probably a one-way mission. When this stuff explodes, it will spread across the water. If what my dad says is true, nothing can extinguish it. It will continue to burn." He shook his head again. "It can't be you."

Dresnor placed a hand on Tolan's arm. "Your plan is sound, but we don't have time to argue about who is best for this. Take five men with you to the Avar Estate. Drew and Redmon are already there with the rest of our men. Gather any men you see along the way. Albey, take the rest of the men and the crates and help the city guard defend the beach. Kai and I will take care of this. I've seen him swim, and there isn't one of us who could swim the distance in this current. Trust me—he can do it. Now go!"

It was clear Tolan wanted to protest, but he closed his mouth without rebuttal. Kai knew Dresnor was right; there was no time to argue. Taking a moment, Kai pushed his thoughts to Smoke. *Go with Tolan, help save Helena.*

Smoke followed Tolan.

As they separated, Tolan gave one last look over his shoulder before disappearing into the city crowd.

Dresnor turned to Kai. "Now, remove anything that will slow you down—boots and weapons—and place them on the back of the boat."

Kai complied without question. Dresnor ran off, and returned moments later with two oil lamps, cloth, and striking sticks.

Placing everything together in the boat, he pointed. "Together we'll push the boat along the shore. Then, before the end, I will run up the beach and around the point to those trees. You will swim out into the water, maneuvering the boat between the abandoned fishing boats. Tie it onto the anchor rope between the two warships and swim away as fast as you can. You won't have much time. I dare not delay much before firing off a shot."

Kai thought about what Dresnor proposed. It was true that his speed and his tolerance for cold water made him the best suited for this mission, but the waves would make it difficult.

Exposed to the cold water, it would not take long before his muscles locked up and his core temperature dropped. He knew the risks. He only wished he knew how this would end.

Together they pushed the small boat out into the water just far enough that it began to float. Running through the shallow water, the boat skimmed the tiny waves. Filled with Tolan's Arkin Oil, they ran along the coastline toward the point. Meanwhile, Kai tried to think warm thoughts. His core temperature began to rise, and even in bare feet, the cold icy water did not bother him.

Anxious to get this done Kai, pushed harder and harder. The movements warmed him further, and he began to sweat. His speed increased faster and faster. He had so much more to give, but Dresnor struggled to keep pace.

"You really are fast." Dresnor let his words fade as they neared their destination. "We should stop here."

While Kai stripped down to his undershorts, Dresnor tossed Kai's weapons and boots into the tall grasses along the beach. Then he took one Arkin Oil barrel and set it aside. Slowly he dowsed the boat with the oil from one of the lamps. "Just in case," he smiled. "A little extra oil can't hurt."

Cautiously Dresnor popped the cork out of the extra barrel. Oily brown syrupy liquid splashed over the other barrels, coating the wood. Small metal fragments plinked out of the hole. "Hmmm, it looks like they are meant to shoot shrapnel bits when they explode." Gently, he laid the empty barrel in the boat.

Kai turned his nose away from the awful smell. Worried, he touched the shoulder of his champion, his friend. "Philip, if I don't..." He stopped midsentence. He didn't want to finish. There was no choice. It was up to him. If he focused, he could do this.

Dresnor gave him a nod and took the other lamp. They separated without another word. No need to wish each other luck; they would do what needed to be done whether Kai came back or not.

Focused on his core temperature, Kai began to pull the boat through the small waves out into open water. Before long, the cold water felt like needles on his skin. His abs clenched as the water reached his stomach. Not wanting to belabor the moment or get spotted, he sank into the water up to his neck.

Keeping his head dry, he pulled the boat around in front of him. The water was shallow, but with each step, it began to get deeper. His movements helped him feel warmer. His body was even warm enough to create a little steam in the water's surface. From behind the small boat, he began weaving it between the larger fishing boats. He could no longer touch the ground.

As he swam, he heard loud explosions, followed by smaller bangs and screams coming from the other beach. The sounds of battle floated over the waves in his direction, again reminding him of his vision.

He feared what he could not see onshore behind him. Caught off guard, a wave slapped him in the face, bringing him back to his task. Squinting, he pressed the saltwater from his eyes. He coughed a few times and took a deep breath. Hidden by the boat, he glanced at the shore.

To his dismay, he saw six longboats rowing onto the shore. Caroco men poured out of the boats as they hit the west beach. They wasted no time. Bound for the outskirts of town, they ran toward the Avar Estate. Did they know where they were going? Were they really after Helena? Or was this all his fault for reaching out to Keegan.

Kai pushed the questions away and continued to swim, forcing the boat through the water. The waves continued to persist, and he took a few more splashes to the face. But he was getting closer to the large warships. Their looming presence weighed on his memory. Closer to the anchored ships, he began to hear sounds of men shouting. He hoped they would not notice his small boat drifting in their direction.

He kept his head low in the water, close to the boat. Water splashed up his nose. He coughed, but then he covered his nose and mouth. *Did they hear me?* He hoped not. The two ships were side-by-side, blocking out the sun above. Once in position, he used the rope from the rowboat to tie it to the anchor line between the two ships. His boat knocked on the other ships.

In a hurry, Kai swam away from the small boat, and the red flag came into view. As with his vision, he could not make out the black symbol, but now he knew it was a black star. This moment had consumed his sleepless nights for too long. Today it would be finished, one way or another. He swam hard. The tide pulled against each stroke.

Back on the shore, he saw Dresnor standing at the ready. He nocked an arrow in his bow, barely noticeable in the tall grass. He lit the lamp at his feet. Desperate, Kai swam, fighting against the strong tide threatening to pull him back towards the ships. He struggled but made little advancement. Panic crept inside his mind. Cold seeped into his bones. His muscles were feeling stiff. He looked to shore, then back at the ships.

Frustrated by the rip current, he changed direction. He swam parallel with the shore to get through the undertow and away from the ships. Finally, he made progress. Still, the cold stung his skin. He swam and tried to refocus on feeling warm, but he'd been in the water too long. Panic consumed his heat, and he felt colder by the second.

Between strokes, he saw Dresnor raise his bow and let the first flaming arrow fly. Kai watched it fall short of the small boat. He swam a few strokes and saw another arrow. It overshot the rowboat, sticking into the side of the ship. Not waiting for the third arrow to land, he dove below the water and began to swim with all he had. Under the water he heard a loud explosion, and he felt a shockwave push him through the water.

The blast pushed him deeper, and he saw bright flames scatter across the water above. Bits of wooden debris struck the water all around him. Metal fragments grazed his leg. Frightened, he pulled and kicked through the water. Behind him, under the water, he could hear the crackling of wood and more debris falling into the water. Chunks of the ship sank beneath the waves. Men thrashed, screaming. Dying. It all echoed around him.

White and yellow flames floated on the water's surface. He needed to go faster. There was no edge to the fire. His thoughts went to the summer on Baden Lake with Shane. Beat the lake, he thought. In his mind, he focused on the shore. He began to kick. *Swim faster,* he thought. *Faster than you ever have before.* He pushed himself harder.

How he wished he could turn into a fish and swim away like his mother. Sadly, he did not know how. Focused on the dark blue water, he swam. His lungs screamed for air. Still, he kicked. His movements slowed as he grew lightheaded. He was out of breath. His eyes closed.

The world went black. Kai felt an eerie peace pull him down. He sank into the deep, but one last time he willed his eyes open. The surface was fading from view. Particles of energy, tiny lights, pooled in front of his eyes. The lights formed a woman's face. *Wake up, KAI!* echoed through his mind.

A burst of air filled his lungs. The same air pushed him toward the surface. He kicked and pulled. Clear sun-filled water gleamed overhead. He broke the surface with a gasp. Cold winter air swept across his face. He'd made it. *Thank you, Alenga,* he thought, making his way through the onslaught of waves.

Over his shoulder, he saw both ships ablaze. Flames gnawed away at large holes blown in the side of both sinking ships. Screaming men jumped into the water, only to burn in the Arkin Oil floating on the surface.

Exhausted and cold, Kai swam back through the fishing boats drifting along the shore.

Dresnor ran out waist-deep into the waves. "Are you alright? I thought... I thought you were dead. Blessed Alenga. She saved you." Dresnor dragged Kai to shore.

"I thought I was dead myself." Kai coughed and wiped the salty water from his face. He had never been so tired after a swim. Unable to grasp what he saw under the waves; he calmed his racing heart. Tossing a wish into the sea, he silently spoke to his mother. *I will find you, mother. I will make them help me. Alenga, thank you for saving me.*

"We're not done yet, Kai. Get dressed," Dresnor directed. "It appears that the east beach has been contained, but we've sustained heavy losses. They have some type of weapon that can cut a man down from a distance. A hand-cannon of sorts. Thankfully it seems to only be good for one shot, and we are overwhelming them by sheer numbers. But some have made it into the city."

While Kai dressed, Dresnor continued his report. "They sent several more longboats in with men. The Reaper sunk a second Caroco ship and is assisting the survivors of the Intrepid. The land defenses and the Sun Raider took out the remaining ships. The harbor cannons took heavy damage, as did the lighthouse. Best I can tell, the Sun Raider took minimal damage." Then he pointed up the hill. "There are several buildings on fire in town, all in a line leading up to the Avar Estate. We must reach Helena. Tolan will need our help."

Kai looked at the smoke-filled sky as he finished getting dressed. Buildings burned. People burned. Death hung in the air. He clenched his teeth as he thought of Keegan, his would-be father. Guilt weighed on his heart. His call brought the man here.

Sounds of short bangs disrupted his thoughts. That sound. It resonated with his soul. He had heard it before today. His vision. The hand-cannons. The weapon from his nightmares.

Dresnor handed him the last of his weapons, and they ran toward town. They took the most direct route towards the estate. Men dressed in black with an embossed star on their chest armor fought Galloway soldiers and civilians alike. Caroco men—Keegan's men.

People ran through the streets, screaming for help. This would be Kai's first real fight. No armor, no holding back. These men meant to kill him or anyone they came across.

There would be no quarter.

Against two men at once, he defended a young woman cowering in the street. His movements were swift, his sword precise. The woman thanked him and ran.

On each street, they found another group of men attacking locals and setting fires. They attacked men, women, and children without care. Bodies littered the smoky streets. The images burned in his memory. Cruel men—with a general disregard for all life—were all they were.

Cutting down one or two here only led to two or three more on the next street. The city was infested with the invaders. There were way too many to have come from the boats. Some of them must have hidden outside of the town.

Each corner had another group to contend with. At this rate, they would never make it up the hill. Still, they pressed on. Kai moved at great speed, taking down each assailant he could. Dresnor fought at his side, protecting the Prince.

"We're outnumbered, Kai!" Dresnor called out as a horde overwhelmed them. "Run, I can hold them off. Get away."

Undaunted, Kai pulled the silver throwing stars from his waist. With the flick of his wrists, he dropped four men. Dresnor's mouth gaped open. One last star dropped a fifth man. "Where were you hiding those?"

Together they moved as one double-edged fighting machine. Their blades blocked and sliced men at every turn. The remaining men now lay dead in the street. Kai collected his stars and rubbed his ribs. Both he and Dresnor had multiple minor cuts to their arms and midsections. From where they stood, he saw the street leading to Aunt Helena's home. They were finally free to run for the estate.

Wasting no time, they ran up the hill. Kai bolted ahead only to hear Dresnor shout, "Don't you dare run ahead without me! I belong at your side. Slow down, Kai. KAI!"

Reluctantly, he slowed to allow his Kempery-man to keep pace.

When they neared the top of the hill, Kai heard more bangs

and men screaming. At the main gate to the estate, they found two men cutting down a Diu soldier. Dresnor dispatched the first man, and Kai took the second.

The Diu soldier clung to life but urged them onward. "Go, they need more help!"

Out of the corner of his eye, Kai caught a glimpse of the black wrought iron and stone fence. The twisted metal.

DREW.

He knew this moment, too. He'd had this vision so many times. This was his chance to save Drew. But unlike his vision, he would not hesitate today.

Inside the grounds, they found more men dead or dying. Most were Caroco men, dressed in black with shaved heads. Each had a strange scar: a star branded on the side of their neck. Beyond them lay a line of Avar estate guards, all dead and riddled with strange holes. Blood-splattered bodies collapsed in a heap.

Black swords and strange metal weapons littered the ground. He knew that sword. Keegan carried the same swords the night he invaded the palace. These were Caroco men, come to attack their city. Rage welled in Kai's heart. He hated this man—his father. A man he'd never met. A man his mother ran from all those years ago, then lied to the world to hide Kai's true parentage.

Identical to his vision, battle sounds echoed on the wind. Swords clashed. Metal against metal. He pulled at his memories. Fires raged in the distance. Smoke billowed in the sky. He needed to focus.

The smell of burned wood and flesh filled his nostrils, making him cringe. He ran through the grounds. The garden fence was too high to jump; he made for the side gate. Sweat rolled down his face. Helena's garden was a battlefield. Men in black lay dead on the ground. Estate guards grasped at gushing wounds.

Kai could not let fear control him. Instead, determination drove him to run faster. His nightmares never let him forget.

This was Drew's moment.

He stepped over the bodies. Through the hedges, he saw Drew slice down a man in black. Drew's sword dripped with blood. Kai held his breath. He knew what came next. Bang. There it was. The same foreign sound he dreaded. Drew twisted in pain, struck in the shoulder. "No!" Kai yelled out. He was still too far away, separated by Helena's water garden and rose bushes.

It cannot end like this.

In the distance, he saw them. Two men in black, each reloading silver weapons. Hand cannons, as Dresnor had called them. Kai reached for his belt and Riome's metal stars, secured within the leather. He focused and slowed his breathing. He pulled at the energy of the moment. He needed more time.

The first Caroco soldier raised his arm. Kai focused harder, pulling the surrounding energy inward, holding it with his breath. He felt time slow to a crawl. While leaping across three steppingstones, he released two stars with the flick of his wrist, one after the other. Jagged metal teeth sliced through the air. End over end, they raced against time.

Bang! The first weapon fired. Still, he ran toward Drew. The scene blurred in his mind. His movements felt thick, slowed by time's resistance. By his magic.

Sparks ignited and smoke plumed in slow motion. Debris sliced through the air. He pushed through the massive rose bushes.

Bang! The second weapon fired. Spark, smoke, and debris. Both shots cut across the sky, aimed for Drew. Kai took a breath and time gave way. The first star struck the round ball bound for Drew's chest. Metal bits ricocheted into the trees. The second star struck the metal weapon one Caroco man held.

Kai struck Drew with such force that they both flew into a bush, one massive heap tangled in the shrubbery. The second shot struck the Alenga statue where Drew once stood, punching a hole in the stone.

Dresnor spotted the two men attempting to reload their one remaining weapon. With extreme accuracy, he shot two arrows with one pull of his bow, dropping both men. Several yards behind Kai, he called, "You two alright?"

Kai climbed out of the destroyed rose bush and pulled Drew to his feet. Thorns stuck in his shirt as he pulled free. From the trees, he pulled both stars out of the craggy bark and returned them to his belt. "I am fine. Drew, are you alright?" he asked, relieved that his friend still breathed.

"I am not sure what hurt worse, the metal ball in my shoulder, or you crushing me into that bush." Drew pressed at the bloody hole in his shoulder.

Kai pulled a thorn from Drew's arm.

Drew rolled his eyes. "Where in the world did you come from?" He took a deep breath and glanced at the Alenga sculpture. The iron ball protruded out of the cracked cavity in her chest. "Thanks, by the way." Drew nodded.

Kai motioned for them to follow. "Come. The rest are on the other side of the gardens. I am sure they could use the help."

Worried about Smoke, Kai searched for his animal companion. Sensing Smoke was alright, he relaxed and led the way. "This way," Kai pointed. "They are here."

Around the west wall of the estate, they accessed another part of the gardens.

Tolan fought with brute force. He punched one man in the face with the pommel of his sword, dropping the man to his knees. Then he crossed blades with another man. Drew charged the man on the ground while Tolan deflected the next attack. Anger surged in his eyes, and he raged at the Caroco man, beating the man's sword repeatedly until the man's arm could no longer hold his sword.

As the man slumped to the ground, Helena ran from her hiding place to where her husband Kaeco knelt wounded in a flowerbed. She helped him to his feet and clasped his tan, sweaty face. Blood trickled down his cheek from a small cut, and a gash in his sword arm dripped with blood. From the estate, two of Tolan's men, Kempery-man Redmon, two of Kai's scouts, and three estate guards burst into the gardens. They were all that remained.

Kai wondered about the other men. Kempery-man Albey battled on the beach. Were they still alive? They were skilled men, but against this new weapon, no one stood a chance. These hand cannons shifted the balance. It gave the enemy the upper hand. Kai looked at their small, battered group.

Tolan seemed relieved to see everyone, but he remained focused. His shoulder was soaked in blood, his arms had several gashes, and his shirt was cut across his chest. Thick blood ran down the side of his face. "We've cleared the estate. We should sweep the town, ensure nobody got away. We also need to start collecting these new weapons. They cut through our ranks like a knife through butter. Kai, Dresnor, how are things on the beach?" His tone carried authority. Everyone focused on Tolan.

Dresnor leaned in and addressed the group. "The east beach was hit hard. Some made it past our men, and I can only guess they also had men already onshore. There were too many already in town. They all made quick work of killing our men with these new weapons. Kai and I fought our way here. I believe you are right—we need to search the city for any stragglers." He nocked his bow in preparation.

Kai chimed in. "There are no Caroco ships left. Between the Intrepid, the Reaper, and the Sun Raider, they've sunk all the Caroco ships that came into the harbor, and the Reaper is assisting the survivors of the Intrepid. Last we saw, the Sun Raider was positioned near the point close to the lighthouse. There was one Caroco ship watching on the horizon, but it never advanced. It left when Dresnor and I managed to destroy the other two ships anchored off the west beach. There appeared to be no survivors that made it to shore after both ships caught fire and sank."

Dresnor nodded. "They sent six longboats filled with men

before we could reach them. There is a long string of fires leading all the way to the estate. I'm guessing they were the ones you killed here within the grounds." He added, "I'm just glad to find you all in one piece. This new weapon shoots a small ball and takes a man down in an instant. I've never seen the like. Like Kai said, the last we saw, the one remaining ship turned tail out to open sea."

Tolan breathed a small sigh of relief. "We need to get those fires out and search the town. Have the townsmen help. Dresnor, I want more men here at the estate. Find a physician in town to see to the wounded. Drew, take two of my men and secure the grounds. Make sure there are no enemies left in hiding." He turned to the duke. "Kaeco, we need to send word to Diu and Fort Pohaku. Kai, go with your uncle and get birds in the air right away. We need help to arrive before nightfall in case the Caroco ships return in force. The rest of us will check the wounded and sort the dead. Secure any prisoners."

Kai nodded. "Certainly, Tolan." Escorting his aunt and uncle, Kai headed for the house. For his own peace of mind, he gleaned the grounds. *All clear. Good,* he thought. No ambushes lay in wait. He let out a breath he hadn't realized he was holding. It was over. He was relieved his vision had come to pass, and that Tolan's experience had saved them. Saved his family. And thankfully, Kai's own training and determination had saved Drew.

CHAPTER 24

Aftermath

It took hours to clear the lost souls. Bodies were sorted by allegiance. Loyal Diu and Port Anahita men and women were buried with honors—returned to the soil from whence they came, back to Alenga's loving spirit. They hauled away the Caroco soldiers to the poor man's burial field. People were honored in death, even if they were not honorable in life.

Kai walked the estate. Everything smelled of earth and blood. There was no place outside to get away from the death lingering in the air. Too many had been lost this day. The surviving servants worked to wash away blood-drenched walkways. Guards collected the discarded weapons.

A city physician helped the wounded. His children worked at his side. One son managed triage, sending those with critical wounds to his father and those with minor injuries to his two older brothers. Surprisingly, even the man's young daughter helped. She poured water, cleaned tools, and stitched small cuts.

Helena insisted on bringing fresh water and linens to help in any way she could—although Kai was sure she was simply trying to stay busy, avoiding the reality of the day.

Exhausted, Kai entered the estate house in search of his uncle. Fortunately, the majority of the interior was free from signs of battle. Only the foyer and back breezeway had seen action. Regretfully, he realized everyone, himself included, tracked the chilling events of the day in on their boots.

He continued to his uncle's study.

Left with nothing more to do, his Aunt Helena rubbed her arms with her hands as if she could not get warm. Uncle Kaeco stared helplessly at his pen, frozen in his hand.

"Uncle," Kai said. "Your letters are on their way. Your birds are in the air, and we've dispatched a rider as a backup to Diu. Riders were dispatched to Nebea and Port Pohaku. Uncle, can you hear me?" No response. They were in shock. Both lost in what had occurred.

Concerned, he escorted his aunt to the sofa. No sooner did she sit than Gideon and Victoria burst into the room. Victoria went to Helena, and sobs passed between them. His aunt grasped the girl as if she might be lost if she let go. Gideon held himself under control.

"We hid in the pantry with a few of the servants," Gideon announced. "Cowardly, I know, but I know little of swordplay. A decision I now deeply regret. Father! You're bleeding." He rushed to his father's side, and the pair hugged.

Tears welled in their eyes. Quiet sadness and relief passed between them. Kaeco searched his son for unseen wounds and hugged him again. "Bless Alenga for keeping you both safe. You were right to hide. You kept Victoria safe." Kaeco glanced at Helena with affection.

"Sorry to interrupt, cousin," Kai offered a hand, "but we need to get your father to the physician. Someone should see to his wounds. Stay with your mother. She needs you more. I will see to it that Kaeco is cleaned up and returned to you shortly." Kai took his uncle by the arm and escorted him outside to the makeshift medical area.

Kaeco stumbled, still half-dazed, Kai righted him, and they continued down the hallway. "Thank you, Kai." Kaeco patted Kai's arm. "I am so glad you are here. You've helped me keep my focus. Not sure I could have written a single note without your guidance. Alenga surely blessed us, sending Tolan to our aid. We would have perished had he not arrived when he did."

Kaeco stumbled to the floor. "Sorry." He grabbed his dizzy head. "I don't know what's wrong with me. I feel so overwhelmed by everything. How are you doing? How is Tolan?"

"We are both fine, uncle. Let me help you." Kai found a chair and pulled it closer. "Here. Sit. I will find someone to look at your head and arm. Both are still bleeding. The cloth I tied around your arm is soaked through. Wait here."

Kai returned with one of the doctor's sons who was capable of stitching his uncle's wounds. Shortly after, the young girl came with a damp cloth and freshwater. "My name is Kirin. Here, you need to drink. I will find you some bread to eat. It will help you regain your strength."

Her gray apron was marked by the work she'd performed. She couldn't be any older than fourteen. Her kind yet overly mature eyes told him she had seen more than a girl her age should. But he was thankful she was there.

While her brother tended his uncle, Kirin turned to him. "Your turn." Her strong hand tugged at his arm. "Sit. I will stitch up your cuts. They are not too large. I can manage." Kirin cut away his shirt sleeve and washed away the blood and dirt. Tiny tweezers in hand, she removed bits of debris from the gash. While she continued to clean and mend his wounds, he looked around at the other men. He was pleased to see more men survived than he initially thought. Most had been shot and left for dead as the Caroco men raided the estate. Four women also sat cradling injuries of one form or another.

Behind him, he heard Drew's voice. "Several fires still rage. Ships smolder in the shallows of the bay. They burn with what I hear is Tolan's Arkin Oil. Sticky syrupy oil that floats. It seems the fire won't go out. They caught one pier on fire and several small fishing boats. Albey said the fires in town are being dowsed, and the people are coming out of hiding. Two other doctors in town are helping citizens."

"How's your shoulder?" Kai asked, glancing at Drew. His

movements frustrated Kirin.

"Sit still. Only one more cut to go." She pressed his shoulder back into position. "I'll need to cut away more of your shirt to clear the gash over your shoulder." Scissors in hand, she went to work.

Drew gave a heavy sigh. "I am fine. The physician took out the ball. He said it would be sore, but I will still be able to wield a blade. I was lucky you showed up when you did. Thank you, my brother."

They nodded in silent understanding. There was a bond between them.

Drew offered Kai water. "Those metal stars, I've never seen the like. Where did you get them?"

"They were a gift." Kai grinned, unable to tell Drew that Riome, Cazier's spy-daughter, gave them to him.

"Well, either way, thank you." Drew sat in the grass, pawing his newly repaired shoulder. "You best go find Tolan. Your little healer could have a field day on him. He's rather cut up, and I doubt he will come here unless forced." Drew chuckled.

Pleased she was finished with him, Kai stood up. "Thank you, Kirin."

"Your Highness," she nodded and helped the next person.

"I will look for Tolan. I am sure he is bleeding all over the place, giving orders and helping others."

It did not take long before Kai found Tolan pacing around the entrance to the estate. "Tolan. There you are. Why are you out here?"

"You did well today, Kai," Tolan responded, ignoring Kai's question, "as did your wolf. He's wicked fast and fierce. He ran straight for the gardens, straight to Helena, taking down two Caroco men along the way. We were lucky to have him on our side."

Kai wondered how much his magic rushed Keegan's plan to

attack. How different things might have been if Tolan had not been sent to intercept the Arkin Oil, and if Kai himself had not come to Port Anahita with his men. Would Keegan have taken the city? Would Helena, Kaeco, and Gideon still be alive?

Keegan. The very thought of the man set fire to Kai's soul. Revenge raged in his heart. He had never felt pain this deep before. This man was striking at the heart of Diu. Something told him Keegan was not finished. He would return. They had not seen the last of these branded Caroco warriors.

He shook away the darkness growing within. "It was a long day," Kai sighed, desperate to ignore his true feelings. "How's your arm? I am guessing you are fortunate the shot only grazed you. Although I don't think Amelia is going to like that you were cut across the face," he joked.

Tolan smiled at the sound of her name. "I am thankful she was not here. I had planned to invite her to join me. I so desperately wanted to see her on my visit, but my father pressed me to make haste. I was to collect the supplies and return to him immediately. Father will be disappointed I wasted the lot. If I had lost Amelia…" His words faded, and he concealed his face.

"Well, everything worked out for the best." Kai looked at his feet. "What are the chances I can get you to see a friend of mine? Kirin is a healer. A bit pushy if you don't sit still, but she does good work."

"If you insist." Tolan approached the other men standing guard. "Let me know immediately when reinforcements arrive."

Tolan turned to follow Kai.

Hours later, a clear starry sky promised a peaceful evening. Both Kai and Tolan laughed and swapped stories about their summers abroad. Anything to move beyond the devastation around them. Grateful the battle was over, Kai thought of Dresnor and Riome's training. How his three years of hard work had saved the lives of many today.

The events left him with a heavy heart. All the lessons in the world could not have prepared him for the choices of war. He felt the invisible scars collected on his soul, burdened by the faces of the men he had fought hanging in the periphery of his mind. Each a decision he would have to live with.

Like Dresnor once said—*If only we could take the burdens of war off like a tunic. Wash away the invisible scars.* Not that he would change any choice he had made, but he hated taking a life. And he blamed Keegan for forcing his hand. He could only hope Dresnor was right; Alenga would forgive him.

Tired, they let the conversation lull, and they sat on the steps in silence, waiting for support. Although according to Dresnor, all the fires were extinguished, Port Anahita lights blazed against the darkness. Nearly every light in town pushed against the night.

Voice echoed around the estate. Tolan tapped the ground with his foot as they sat in protest of going inside. They both refused to leave their posts. "It seems like they will never arrive." Tolan sighed.

With heavy eyes, they gazed down the hill. "They will make it," Kai insisted. "Not long now, I am sure of it."

Smoke lay on the ground between them. Tolan's hand rested casually on the wolf's back, and thick black fur sprouted around his fingers. "I think Smoke and I have bonded, or at least put our past behind us. He seems at ease with me for the first time since the day he growled at me, protecting you."

"Battle has a way of binding spirits." Kai closed his tired eyes. "We've all matured over the years. Smoke knows your true nature. I trust you, so Smoke trusts you. He can sense my ease around you."

Wind swept through the trees.

Echoing up the stone steps, Kai heard a methodical thump—thump—thump. He sat up. "Do you hear marching?"

Tolan tilted his head to the side and held his breath. It wasn't long before he too heard the telltale thunder of men marching up the street towards the estate. At the lead was Kempery-man Decklar and Kempery-man Henley, Drew's uncle, followed by a long line of men, lined up four abreast.

"Thank Alenga. They are finally here." Tolan hopped to his feet to greet them. "Blessed be, how many are you?" He asked, extending a hand to Decklar.

"We are lucky you made it." Kai shook Decklar's hand next. "Did you get our bird, or did the scout reach you first?"

"Your Highness. The bird came first," Decklar responded. "He was in Diu city within two hours after you sent him. The scout arrived an hour later. In your father's absence, Grand Duke Dante commanded five hundred march your way. My group is one hundred strong, fifty to secure the estate. Another fifty are securing the surrounding houses. I have instructed each captain to divide the other four hundred men as they come in and secure the city and the outlying farms. Men are marching around the outskirts of the city and down to the harbor as we speak."

"Thank you for getting here." Tolan eased back on his heels. "I am sure you've had a long afternoon organizing and a hard ride to get here." Tolan nodded to Decklar. "We will keep watch on the coast for ships from my father. We sent a bird to him as well, though it will take considerably longer to reach Fort Pohaku."

"Thank you, but no, Tolan," Decklar refused. "By the look of you, you can hardly stand. You've fought a battle today, you need rest. We'll stand watch. I am guessing your father's ships won't arrive until the day after next. Word has been sent to Nebea to watch their shores. Men march to bring King Iver back from his hunting trip. Other men have been sent to every outpost around the countryside. They will keep a watchful eye out for these Caroco invaders."

Hesitation swelled in Tolan's eyes. Kai knew all too well his friend wanted to avoid being alone. Silence and solitude offered no comfort, only flashes of horror. Kai put his hand on Tolan's shoulder. "It's been a long day. Let's get some food." He attempted to distract his friend's mind.

They reached the stairwell, and Tolan stopped. "I can tell you from experience; it will not be a good sleep for either of us this night. Professor Greydon made us read a book once. Do you remember? The author said that in war, there are no victors, only survivors. I can't remember the exact quote, but he went on to say something about guilt, slowly killing those who remain. All the battles I have fought are permanent marks on my soul."

"You did what you had to do," Kai said. "None of us asked for this fight. We fought to protect our own." Although his words were meant for Tolan, Kai needed to remind himself. "A friend once told me if you stand for another, in the end, it will be forgiven. Alenga knows your truth."

They stood in silence until Dresnor approached. "You both look horrible. Get some food or get some rest. There will be much to do come in the morning." He motioned to the second floor.

Voices echoed down the hall. In silent agreement, Tolan and Kai both opted to skip the crowd and went straight to their rooms.

It was all Kai could do to remove his clothes and cleaned his skin with a scrub brush. Emotions ran deep and swelled in his chest. When he looked down, he'd scrubbed his skin near raw, trying to remove the stench of battle from his body. Finished, he collapsed into his bed and drifted off to sleep.

Two mornings later, Kai stood in the warehouse district with Dresnor and Tolan surveying the harbor. Delicate fog lingered around the bay and warm sunlight worked to burn it away. Uncle Kaeco delegated tasks in the background. Kai could tell it helped his uncle to keep busy. It also helped to have Gideon close by. The pair worked in tandem, reassuring the other they were still alright.

Kaeco instructed his workers to organize supplies, and stonemasons and carpenters were sent to shore up the lighthouse. He sent various groups to remove burned debris from the water's edge, while others cleared rubble near the port's defensive cannons. A throng of blue and silver guards worked to clear the remaining dead and retrieve any remaining weapons of war.

Kai, Tolan, Dresnor, and Decklar ventured down the beach and were all pleased to see the Intrepid resting in the shallow waves. Men worked to salvage cannons, sails, and supplies, while others were taking measurements to make repairs. They may have been hit hard, but they were resilient. Not one man appeared broken. Each stood firm to help repair the damage.

Near the outskirts of town, tents sprang up like weeds. The additional guards created a second city around the port. "Do they mean to stay here, to establish a permanent base?" Kai asked Kempery-man Decklar, noticing they were clearing land.

"Dante has instructed barracks and housing to be established outside of town." Decklar nodded. "The first wave of men will stay. Port Anahita needs a stronger army presence. Not sure who will be put in charge, but I believe Kempery-man Henley is interested in the post. He has the seniority. I see no reason Grand Duke Dante would choose another."

Kai agreed. He knew Henley was a good man. Considering his nephew, Drew, nearly lost his life in the battle, he understood the man's desire to secure their borders. "Henley is a good leader."

They continued their survey of the town. While the damage was immense, many repairs were already underway. "If you have no need of us," Dresnor interrupted, "I mean to escort the prince back to Diu."

"Agreed." Decklar bowed to the prince. "As I understand it, Duke Raebun intends to go with you. Tolan's father arrived this morning with a fleet of ships. They made excellent time up the coast. In addition to more soldiers, he brought carpenters and stonemasons to aid in recovery and restoration. This fair city has been shaken to its knees. Blinded by peace, we have let our guard down."

"I hate to say I agree with you, Decklar," Kai interjected, "but you are right. We need to change. Two strategic attacks. This cannot go unanswered."

"Well, time will tell what they want and if they are done testing our mettle. After the battle, I hope they know we mean business and will not go down easy. We hurt them—six ships are no laughing matter. I am sure they have more, but we lost one, and the Intrepid is repairable." Decklar puffed up his chest. "Anyway, there are two relays set between here and Diu. You are meant to switch horses and make haste. No lingering on the road. Your personal horses can follow later with one of the many groups patrolling the route." Decklar bowed. "Your Highness, Prince Kai. Safe travels to you."

"Thank you, Kempery-man Decklar." Kai shook the man's hand.

Decklar shook hands with Dresnor. "Safe travels, my friend."

They parted ways, and Kai and his men made for the estate to plan for their departure. Kai hated leaving, but he was anxious to return home. He was hopeful Riome would have learned something in her time with Nola, and he hoped to spend some time with his father.

CHAPTER 25

Heroes

Two days later, Kai and his party made for Diu and the safety of the city. His city. Tolan and Drew were bandaged but stable, and they rode by his side. He quietly gave thanks to Alenga that they were both still alive.

While they rode, Kai kept a keen eye on Smoke, happy to see he was not feeling the strain of their pace as much as Ember, his horse.

All along the road, they passed men marching between the two cities. Halfway into their ride, they met a large contingent of men from Diu—a security checkpoint. Never in Kai's lifetime had he seen so many soldiers amassed in one place. Led by his scouts, the Diu troops parted to let him pass.

Tasked with securing the road, their camp was equipped with a temporary horse corral prepped and ready for their exchange. Within mere moments they were off and running with fresh horses. Kai hated leaving Ember behind, but he understood the risks. The distance between the two cities was too far, and he would not risk Ember's wellbeing. Nor were his men about to take chances considering the threat that could be lurking.

Among their group, Admiral Roark Raebun, a proud and powerful man, rode with them to petition the king. Over the last two days, Kai listened to the Admiral discuss the need for additional ships, men, and battlements. The speech the admiral gave was sound. The expense for a larger fleet would be another matter. Like Fort Pohaku, he would ensure Port Anahita would be a secure city. All their coasts needed to be protected. If there was a new threat on the horizon, they needed to be prepared. And according to him, these Caroco people would need to be put in their place if he had anything to say in the matter.

They arrived in Diu a few hours behind the king. Kai learned Dante had sent word to the Master General and the king the moment he heard about the attack. Iver was swept back to Diu with haste, his four-day ride reduced to two arduous nonstop days in the saddle. They were not taking any chances with the king. While their hunting party had been closer to the Nebea's fortress, Iver belonged in Diu.

Kai noticed right away that security was on high alert. Every checkpoint had double the guards. The closer he came to the palace, the more guards and Mryken dogs he saw on patrol. Inside the palace, his father was swarmed by his council, neighboring lords, and Kempery-men. Kai couldn't even get near his father's council chamber. Resigned to the idea of not speaking to him, he went to his room.

Over the coming days, he attempted to see his father. Soldiers and Mryken guarded every corner and patrolled every hallway. The palace felt stifling. Again, he did not speak with his father. There was no chance of talking to Iver, especially not alone. The few times Kai found his father in his study, he was surrounded by Cazier, Dante, and Kempery-man Farwick. Frustrated, Kai went to the stables, hoping Haygan had returned. Guards stalked him everywhere he went, always keeping within a pace or two.

He couldn't even brush Ember without feeling crowded.

Anytime anyone approached him, a guard stepped to his side.

Outside the palace, each step he took was monitored. Weeks passed and he desperately wanted to speak with Rayna, but they would have no privacy. Even at night, he was forbidden to run. He was losing his mind. The only room where he had any privacy was his own.

For the first time in weeks, he entered his father's council chamber to find a smaller group. He listened to the ministry of treasury. While Diu was a wealthy city, the man argued, they could not afford everything everyone wanted. When he delivered the list of approved city repairs everyone nodded.

It was good news to hear the lighthouse damage was being repaired. Although the lighthouse had been a beacon of light for ships, it needed to be a symbol of hope. Upon Grand Duke Carmello's suggestion, the king had requisitioned multiple blacksmiths to fashion a series of bells. They would be installed in the lighthouse and throughout Port Anahita.

When the man listed the approved expenses for military port cannons, new ships, men, and forts on his list, several men balked. Especially Admiral Roark Raebun. He was the loudest. Kai knew the man had passion but to see him debate in person impressed Kai. Much like his father, Roark commanded the room. By the time he was finished, Iver had approved two more ships and the support needed to recruit two thousand more men.

Grand Duke Dante reviewed previous orders and provided progress updates. Kai was pleased to learn crews worked around the clock to make repairs in Port Anahita. They were rebuilding quickly. Every builder in the land had been summoned to work on the project. Cazier confirmed men from Nebea also volunteered to help.

Kai thumbed the parchment papers on the table: multiple maps, a supply requisition, and several sketches for the new fort in Port Anahita. This was his first look at the architectural plans. The fort would be massive. From the drawings, it seemed to Kai the fort would nearly be its own city. The name at the top was Fort Kahu.

While he had managed to get close, his father hadn't even noticed his presence. Kai realized there would be no speaking with him today. It was good to see his father in his element. Still, disappointed, he caught his cousin's attention.

With a few subtle hand gestures, Cazier sent him a message. *Soon. We will speak soon.*

He left wondering what "soon" meant. It had been weeks. He was tired of waiting. Short of a hug, a handshake, and a hero's medal, he'd had no time with his father. Still, he had no choice. He went back to his room and sat on the balcony. This was the only outdoor experience he could have without a guard present.

Days later, he stood outside of Cazier's office. After nearly an hour of waiting, Jarrod and Brannon, Diu spies, filed out. They gave him a nod but said nothing. Riome and Cazier waited inside.

"We need to talk," Kai huffed. "Or more importantly, I wish to speak with my father. He's barely said two words to me. That and I need to get out of the palace. Security is ridiculous. If I set foot outside, they stalk me like prey. Dante needs to ease off. There is little room to breathe as it is inside the palace, with guards in every hallway. I wouldn't be too surprised to find them in my bathroom next."

"I am in agreement," Cazier said. "Give them a few more days. Given that this man Keegan came into these very walls, Dante is being overly cautious. I promise Dante will come to see reason. Now, what did you really come to ask? I know there is something bothering you. You come to see your father multiple times a day. What's on your mind? Maybe I can help."

"Cousin, I wish you could help. To put it bluntly, I mean to ask my father to release me from my betrothal with Amelia." Kai crossed his arms. "Matter of fact, I mean to ask him tomorrow."

"I don't mean to give you false hope, Kai," Cazier stood, motioning to the door, "but I would wait to ask him. Fresh after a battle, emotions run high. He is of no mind to hear you right now. Riome, can you give us the room?"

Riome rolled her eyes and left. The door closed behind her, and Cazier sat on the edge of his desk. "If you think you can get out of this because you are not his son, that will not be enough. He needs you in Milnos. We all do. Iver means to send you this fall. If not sooner. Spring is but a few weeks off. Arrangements have yet to be made, but you must prepare. After your birthday, you may end up sailing back with the Maxwells. I don't know yet."

Kai thought about what he'd just heard. Not yet. He wasn't ready. This couldn't be right. Everything he believed told him he belonged with Rayna. He was meant to travel to Katori, not Milnos. His dreams promised it to be so. "No, you are wrong. I can't let that happen. I won't go."

Cazier chuckled. "Won't you? You think you have a choice? Don't act like a petulant child. You will do as your father commands. You will serve your country. Sacrifices must be made." His cousin's tone changed. "Happiness is an illusion. Believe me. None of us live the life we want; we serve. You will serve."

Kai felt his muscles tense. "I disagree. Happiness is a choice. My father must see reason. There must be another way."

"Well, you better choose to be happy with marrying Amelia, because you are going. You have until your birthday to get right with the idea."

Matching the changing tone of the discussion, Kai fought back. "Cousin, I am sorry they pushed you to marry Ella. Seeing Yulia must be difficult. Working side-by-side with Riome must be a small consolation. Wondering what your life might have been under different circumstances. I cannot imagine."

After the words came out, he regretted saying them so harshly. "Adrian, I...I didn't mean..."

"Make no apologies. I made my choices and I stand by them. I was meant to be the man I am. Allow Alenga to lead you but stand by your choice. Live your life but remember there is more to life than your desires."

Cazier's words cut deep. King and country struck Kai's heart. He loved Diu. But there had to be a way to have it all.

To save his mother he needed his gifts, which meant going to Katori, while he still had the chance. His mother was still his biggest desire. "Do you think my father would consider Tolan? He already loves her, and he was honored as a hero of Port Anahita."

"Like I said when you came in, now is not the time. Tensions are still very high. Dukes from all over the land are pressing your father for additional security. They fear being attacked. You've heard enough of their petitions to know Iver is under enormous pressure."

"Fine, I will wait a few more days." Kai stood and approached the door. "I appreciate your advice. It means a lot."

Back in his room, Kai felt pensive as he slipped into bed. He wanted to sleep, but something told him he would find no rest this night. He felt the well of energy overflow his soul. The air became thick. A surge of power tapped his spine. Like it or not, a vision was coming. Resigned, he closed his eyes and let the night take him.

The vision hit him hard. Everything felt enhanced. The golden light of early dawn burned across Baden Lake. Rayna held his hand. Her skin was hot. Yulia stood with them, her keen eyes focused on the horizon. He felt the electricity lift the hair on his neck.

A huge wave splashed his face. He blinked. Their ship was in the middle of a storm. Gale-force winds created twenty-foot swells. Wave after wave smacked against them. Beaten by rain and hail, a flash of lightning blinded him momentarily.

Their ship made landfall north of Albey. Light rain danced on their shoulders. Soaked to the bone, he helped Rayna into a small rowboat. Dresnor, Drew, and Albey climbed in beside him, and they rowed towards a small cove below the Katori Mountains. They rowed to the northern side of the Conha River, and Kai pointed. "We should get out there. That clearing will make a suitable campsite."

His vision continued to reveal a path, unmarked by signs of man. A feeling guided him into the Zabranen Forest. Giant oaks blocked out the sun. They were engulfed in an eerie, fog-shrouded forest. When he stepped through the trees, he found a roaring waterfall. The thundering water crashed down beside him and a cool mist sprayed his face.

His head ached and he closed his eyes. When he opened them, he found his hands on a white and gray marble wall. The stone's surface was jagged and rough. Kai's finger caught on something. Haygan's crude drawing cut into the stone wall. Three interlocking loops with no end. Pain ached in his trembling hand as he ran his finger over the design. Rayna's hand touched his.

Kai awoke drenched in sweat, tangled in his sheets. His head throbbing, he sat on the edge of his bed.

Awake before dawn, he walked the halls of the palace. He felt like a caged animal. Waiting for Dante to relax the security within the inner walls was taking longer than he could bear. He couldn't even sit in the library without a guard standing guard in the corner. Even Professor Greydon was getting unhappy with the disruption.

Still, day after day he walked the palace halls, or sat in the corner of the king's council chamber, listening. Each day felt like a waste of time. He slogged through his classes. Two or three guards even followed him when he walked Smoke. Any hour of the day or night, they were there. Waiting.

Kai splashed water across his face. Stubble raked across his palms. In the mirror, he looked at his reflection. His little boy face was long gone. He was a man now. Tonight, he would try again to connect with his father.

Next to his water basin sat a large wooden box containing his straight razor and shaving powder. He hadn't shaved in days, but today was important. He wanted to confront Iver about his future.

Clean-shaven, he pulled on a fresh white shirt. Feeling a little too warm, he opened his balcony doors and let in the cool spring air. Below he watched the guards patrol the grounds. Kai noticed a difference. Where there were four men yesterday, now only two stood guard. *Finally,* he thought.

Outside his room, he scanned the hall. No guard waited to shadow him. The palace was back to normal, men did not loiter around every doorway.

Before he could close his door again, he heard Kendra. As he buttoned his shirt cuff, he turned to address her. "You wanted to talk the other night, but Cordelia was unwell. How is she, by the way? Better, I hope." He'd heard the rumor she had the same illness Nola had. He very much doubted that, since Nola was deliberately given a sickness. Riome wouldn't dare risk his sister's life to cover her tracks. *Would she?*

"She is considerably better. Her fever is gone, and her cough is much better. But I did not come to talk about your sister. I came to talk about your future. Have you made a decision?"

Kai fastened his cufflink. "I need to speak to my father first."

"I think you should travel to Katori. Not because you will suffer greatly if you don't. The pain will pass. Not because you will lose your gifts. Plenty of Katori people live without special gifts. I think you are *meant* to go. It is something I cannot explain, but I felt guided, almost pressured to encourage you this morning. I don't believe..." her voice trailed off and she looked away.

"Kendra, we agreed—no more secrets." Kai lowered his head to find her eyes.

"I do not believe you are meant to destroy our world but change it." She cupped her hand over her mouth. "I should not have said that."

"What do you mean? Who says I am meant to destroy your world?" His face twisted with concern. "Kendra."

Taken aback, she tilted her head. "Sabastian told me I should not return to Katori. The elders are angry with me. I have helped you too much. I believe they are keeping Haygan in Katori. They do not want him helping you anymore."

Kai watched doubt change her expression. "I am full Katori," he placed a hand on her shoulder, "we know that now. I am not a Half-Light. I have every right to go to Katori. And let's be fair, most of what I learned I did on my own. Yes, you helped me search for my mother. And it was probably a mistake to light up the world. But what's done is done."

"Every Katori felt your power that night. With the arrival of the Caroco ships and Keegan, I am sure the Chiefs and the Uni came to the same conclusion—you are no Half-Light. Kai, your future is not set in stone. Be your own man. Let Alenga guide your soul."

"Kendra, what are you not saying?"

"I have so much to lose, Kai. I want to go home. Katori is my home. I want to raise a family there. My children must know their homeland."

"I will not force you to tell me, but I would be better equipped if I knew what you do."

"That's just it, Kai. I cannot be certain. They cannot be certain. Everyone fears change. The loss of control. Legend speaks of a story depicted on the walls of Alenga's lost Agora. Literally carved in stone. Two warriors stand against one man. A man whose soul is as black as night. Our chiefs believe they will destroy our way of life. Lucca is certain the symbols point to war among our people. I believe you may be one of those warriors, but again I can only guess. The carving also shows two maidens—young Lumens—who will change Katori. Perhaps your children." She paused to let him absorb her words. "If the chiefs can prevent you from completing the Conhaspriga, they may avoid a horrible future."

"Let me guess. Keegan, my father, is the man with the black soul. I saw his crystal—solid black. Who is the other warrior?"

"You know Kai, I was as shocked as you to learn your mother's secret, but it makes sense to me now—why she did not return. Katori would have been the first place Keegan would have searched when she fled. Being pregnant with Keegan's child she probably feared the elders might shun her. Chief Lucca being her father would have made no difference.

"I knew Keegan," Kendra stared at her hands, "when I was young. He lost his way years ago, when he attacked Agora. If there is anyone whose soul has turned black, it's his. As for the other man. There is one man who could fit the story. I believe your grandfather—Keegan's own father, is the other warrior. Most believe Benmar is dead, or at the very least halfcrazy. The last anyone heard, he was living on top of the Katori Mountains. Nobody sees him anymore. But I have seen him. Spoken with him in this very room. Years ago. He left you his book. It sits there on your shelf: *The Invisible Thief*. I am sure you recall finding it on your desk the day you moved into this room."

Kai peered at his bookshelf. "I remember the book. How could he get into the palace?"

"Your grandfather has a very special gift. He can turn invisible. Even if you gleaned to search for him, he remains hidden. It is this magic Keegan sought, but could not attain. Drove him crazy trying."

"But..." Kai stared at her and then the book, "that was a work of fiction."

Suddenly unsure, he stepped to retrieve the book. The leather binding was weathered, the individual pages stitched together. Handmade. He had known the book did not come from the library. It felt and looked old. He had simply assumed it was left behind by cousin Cazier during his childhood. "You mean to tell me the story is true?"

"I have not read the book," Kendra admitted. "I have no idea if the story is true. I just know your grandfather left it for you. He said it was a way to get to know him. His cunning nature. His sense of humor, his courage. Even see his rebellious choices. Like I said, I never read the book. I simply put it on your desk as he instructed and let you read it."

His head swam with information. Invisible warriors—Lumens—his own children. More curious than ever, he had a thousand questions.

Before he could ask, Kendra interrupted his thoughts. "Look, what matters first is making your decision. I cannot speak for your mother, but as someone who cares deeply for your future, I believe you should go. I have watched Rayna over the years, her Katori light shines bright. Talk to her. She needs to understand. She needs to tell her parents she may never return."

"You think Rayna will leave with me?" Kai asked.

"I have no doubt Rayna will follow. She may be torn about leaving them, but she will go with you. I would lay my life on it. She learned to glean to be closer to you. Everything she has done: the nightly running, even the minor hand-to-hand combat you've taught her. She has endured it all to be closer to you."

He thought about what to say. The decision would need to be Rayna's. His words could not sway her into leaving. "Thank you for the advice. I will speak to her again."

Kendra walked to the door. "Don't wait too long. You should leave within a few days of your birthday. I believe your father is dining in his room tonight. I saw maid Mary carry in a tray before I came to speak with you." Her lips pursed in a straight line. Graciously she nodded and left.

Kai was irritated by the news. Tonight would be another wasted night. Disappointed, he made his way down to the kitchen to dine with Lizzie and Dean. Happy to have him, they made a place at the table. Although it was highly irregular for a prince to eat with the servants, Kai didn't care. He cared for them deeply. They were every bit his family. Shared laughter warmed his soul. He would genuinely miss them when he left.

On his way out, Julia stopped him. "Kai, have you spoken with Shane? You should find him. Not sure it is my place to tell you, but he is making plans to move to Albey. I plan to join him." She smiled bashfully.

"I will speak to him. Thank you, Julia," he nodded in response. "Shane mentioned he'd sailed back to Albey twice in the past two months."

Julia shook her head. "The new year did not start well."

Kai rolled his eyes. "The Winter Festival is meant to celebrate the new year; instead this man Keegan turned it into a night of fear. Then with the battle in Port Anahita a few days later, security has surrounded me. Shane and I have not spoken since."

Parting ways, Kai walked outside. The evening air felt thin and cold. After a few warm evenings, tonight's shift surprised him. After another failed attempt to speak with his father, he felt the need to find Rayna. He watched her from afar as she left the bakehouse. She pressed one hand to the side of her temple, and each step seemed to be agonizing. Unable to go any further, she sat in the grass outside. Knees up, she held her head. She rubbed her temples.

He wanted to go to her. Like him, she suffered from the effects of their delay in performing the Conhaspriga. Near the edge of the orchard, he waited for her to see him, he leaned against the stone wall that surrounded the orchard. Her pain worried him. Still, he gave her time to calm her mind, release the tension.

Feeling better, Rayna looked up. He waved. Quick to her feet, she joined him in the orchard. Once hidden within the trees, she wrapped her arms around his neck. She kissed him without warning, and he let her. After everything, this was the first time he'd been alone with her since new year's night.

Rayna held him tight. "I've missed you so much. It has been torture not being able to speak with you since you returned. I can hardly enter the kitchen or the laundry without being questioned. What do they think I might do?" Her tone was sassy but light.

"Don't worry about the guards. They are keeping order. Dante is not willing to make another mistake. Landon's betrayal hurt Dante. Landon lived here for years. We thought he was one of us. Anyway. We have more important things to discuss." Kai gleaned their surroundings for guards. "Are your headaches getting worse? How is your fever?"

"No fever today, but my head hurts. It helps to sit and rub my temples. Meditation helps release the tension, but the headaches only return. Thank Alenga for Charlotte. She is a blessing to my parents, a blessing to our family. Did you hear that Charlotte married the blacksmith's apprentice? She will be a permanent addition now."

"I had heard. Speaking of Charlotte helping your parents, have you told them you may be leaving?" he asked delicately.

She looked away. "I have not. I am not sure I can leave my parents, but I want to go with you. Honestly, I am not sure what to do. How can I leave them? They would never understand."

"They *will* understand," Kai assured her. "Charlotte was hired to ensure the bakery ran smoothly. Your father knows you were planning to move to Albey. It was all you talked about last fall. Why change your mind now?"

She twisted her hair between her fingers. "I am not going to Albey. I am going to Katori. They would never understand. How would they visit me? We both know they could not come to see me. There is no way to know if I will ever come back. Ever see them again."

He understood her hesitation. It would not be an easy decision. "You need to make a choice. Either way, your parents will understand. Be as honest as you can about where you are going. Tell them you are searching for your birth parents. Tell them we are leaving to see where my mother was born. Tell them whatever you wish—aside from the actual truth." He ran his hand down her forearm.

She looked away. "I need more time. Please don't make me choose today."

"I would never make you choose. Follow your own path. Talk to your parents. You do not have to make your decision alone. Let them help you. I promise they will listen. They are more observant than you may believe." Along the orchard's periphery, he sensed guards pacing. "I must go." Kai kissed her cheek, and they parted ways.

CHAPTER 26

Clarity

Head pounding, Kai buttoned his shirt. He'd been having headaches for days. Thankfully his body had not yet spiked with fever; still, he did not feel right. An urge nagged at him to leave Diu. It was apparent, he should have left weeks ago for Katori, but nothing was going as he'd hoped. Now the rite of passage was upon him, and if he did not leave soon, his power would burn out.

If only he could ask his uncle what he should do. Stay or go. Unfortunately, Haygan had not returned from his winter trip to Katori. Kai wondered if it was his fault his uncle was detained. Kendra believed the Katori elders must be keeping him.

Kendra provided no new information. Unfortunately, his young sister Cordelia was four, and she loved repeating phrases. It was impossible to speak privately, as she needed more attention. He dared not take a chance Cordelia might repeat something they discussed.

Kai originally thought being called to Katori would feel exciting, but he knew better now. The closer it got to his seventeen birthday, the more uncomfortable he felt. The question was what should he do? Should he make the journey and finish the Conhaspriga? Or let his gifts burn out? He knew he had already made his decision, but he wanted to be sure. These were not questions he would solve today. Today was about another matter. Overwhelmed with anticipation, he left his room.

Taking a deep breath, Kai knocked on the open door to his father's study. He had built up the courage to talk about his future. Speech prepared, he planned to tell his father about how he felt for Amelia. He needed to convince him they were a poor match, he loved her like a sister. He needed to convince the king there was another option.

"Father, may I speak with you?" Without waiting for a reply, he continued. "I turn seventeen tomorrow, and I am aware you have plans for my future. The security of Diu and its peaceful connection to Milnos depends on uniting our two countries. I know this summer I am to travel to their city and spend the year before the wedding preparing to be king." His heart ached at the idea.

Iver silently offered Kai a seat while he stoked the fire. The chilly mornings still had a chill in the air, and the fire's warmth felt like a cozy blanket. His father tossed a new log on the fire and knowingly took in his son's nervous demeanor. "I am listening."

Anxious, Kai watched the flames pop and crack around the newly placed wood. No matter how many times he had rehearsed this moment, he knew it might not change anything. He took another breath and let his hands fall to his lap. Posture open, he looked seriously at his father. "I know duty commands Amelia and me to honor the betrothal made all those years ago. I understand you need someone you can trust in Milnos, someone bound by blood, loyal to the crown. Loyal to you."

Interrupting, Iver put up his hand to calm his son. "Son, you are nervous about the move and the marriage. It is a big step for someone at any age. You will have a year together in Milnos before..." Iver stopped short. The frustration on Kai's face must have caught his eye. "Do you need a moment to compose yourself?" He gestured towards Kai's white knuckles.

Unaware he was gripping the chair, Kai rubbed his hands together. "Father, Tolan's love for her is true, and she feels the same for him. Why trap us?"

"I know how Tolan feels towards Amelia," Iver replied. "It is why he continues to campaign to be stationed in Milnos. Just as I know that you care for Rayna. Everyone knows." Iver paused. "I warned you. Others warned you. Your duty commands you to honor my commitment. The future of our country depends on your loyalty."

Waving off his father's justification, Kai bellowed. "I cannot, *will not,* marry my sister. That is how I feel for Amelia—it would be wrong. And if I need another reason not to go, I am not your son. If anyone found out, it would tarnish your word." His words spewed like an angry wave.

Unhappy with how this was going, Kai rocked back into his seat. Nothing was coming out right. His emotions twisted each word. There had to be another way to say what he felt. No, he needed to let go of the emotional side and appeal to his father as a king.

Iver plopped into the sofa, visibly shaken by Kai's words. "Is that how you really feel? I know you are angry, but I never thought..." He brushed the front of his lips with his fingers. "I don't know what I thought. But all these years I have loved you as my own. You are my son, now and forever. Unless you feel different..." Iver tilted his head, waiting for his son's response.

Kai wiped his brow. Heat welled in his core. He needed to relax. "I'm sorry for my outburst. I do consider you my father, always and forever. But you know it is true. If somehow the truth came out, it could spell disaster for both of us. Diu, Nebea, everyone would question every decision you've ever made. The legitimacy of Aaron and Seth..." Kai crossed his arms. "I cannot deny my decision is influenced by my own feelings for Rayna. I want to be with the person I love. Like you chose my mother."

Shifting in his seat, Kai touched his chest. He could feel his mother's necklace rest against his chest. Searching for anything he thought would sway his father he shook his head. "Before you decide, allow me to offer one more consideration. Strategically, Tolan fits the role of King of Milnos. He is unquestionably loyal, with years of military experience and political connections. He has spent considerable time in Milnos, learning the area and their culture. His rank as captain means he could become a Kempery-man or a Duke, like his father. His strategic thinking during the battle of Port Anahita saved the city. He personally saved Aunt Helena and Uncle Kaeco. He is a decorated hero. His love for Amelia is true. His love for Diu is true."

That was all he could come up with—either his father would see reason, or Kai and Amelia would be trapped forever.

Iver's eyes drifted from one idea to the next. The room fell quiet. Only the crackle of the fire was left to challenge the silence. As Iver was often known to do, he paced around his study, calculating every possible outcome. Somehow movement aided him in finding clarity.

Kai considered his own words. His father had to know that if anyone ever questioned Kai's lineage, it would not bode well. They would both be held accountable. The news would tear the country apart. Even the best-kept secrets often find the light of day. The only question now was whether it was worth the risk.

Watching his father pace was nerve-racking. Kai knew he would have to accept whatever decision Iver made, even if that decision did not fall in his favor. The longer his father paced, the less confidence he had in his proposal.

There was a rap at the door. The Master General stepped into the room. "I trust I am not interrupting. Sire, I thought we could continue to go over the rebuilding of Port Anahita. You can inspect the rebuilding firsthand when you pass through in a few days. The repairs to the Intrepid are nearly finished."

Riffling through the table covered in maps, building diagrams, and material requests, Cazier turned to look at the serious nature of the room. He glanced back and forth between

Kai and Iver.

Iver ignored the disruption and continued contemplating. His pacing slowed. He stopped and placed his hand on his cabinet. Clearly having reached a decision, he responded. "Cazier, go and delay Duke Maxwell's departure to Milnos and assemble the council. Also, find Roark and Tolan Raebun. Bring everyone to the great hall."

Cazier nodded and left.

Afraid to speak or even move, Kai held his seat. He had to let this play out. If his father planned to lay this to rest today and force him to marry Amelia, he would do his duty. Tolan and Amelia would have to reconcile their feelings, as would he and Rayna. He let out a breath and with it, the control of his future. Alenga held his fate in her hands, and he needed to trust she knew best.

Iver opened his cabinet, retrieved a few small items, and tucked them into his vest pocket. "Let's go. Time to face this, my son," he said in a commanding tone.

Waiting for everyone to gather in the great hall, Kai looked around the room. Blue and gold Diu banners hung around the walls between the large arched windows. Sunlit stained-glass panels splashed color across the room. Iver sat clutching the armrest of his throne, while Kai remained standing on the bottom step of the dais.

First through the door was the Maxwell family. Amelia's expression turned to worry when she saw Kai standing before his father. "King Galloway," Regent Maxwell barged into the center of the room, "why have we been delayed? This is unacceptable..."

Before Maxwell could speak, Iver raised his hand to stop him. "We will wait for the others. I only plan to say this once." Maxwell's face turned sick with contempt.

Tolan entered the room followed by Dresnor and Admiral Raebun. Dresnor and Roark took their places beside Kai. Next came Nola, who slowly approached Iver, attempting to take her spot beside Iver. She had been on bed rest for weeks;

clearly still weak from a strange illness—which Kai knew all too well was his doing. He almost felt bad for her.

It would seem Riome might have taken it a bit too far to ensure Nola was subdued long enough to give Iver rest and clarity. Something Kai might have to thank Riome for later. Concerned for Nola's ability to stand, Kai came to her aid, helping her take her seat. While holding her stomach, she sat trying to exude her queenly composure and understand what was happening.

With Kempery-man Farwick, the Grand Duke Dante Carmello, Sigry, and Master General Adrian Cazier now in attendance, Kai knew this was it. It was time for his father to publicly finalize his decision. With one final prayer to Alenga, Kai took his place beside his father.

In an authoritative tone, Iver addresses the group. "Thank you all for coming. Many years ago, Lucas Maxwell, Regent of Milnos, and I sought to unite our two kingdoms. With no other male heir born in his family line, we made a betrothal for my son, Kai, to marry his daughter, Amelia, in their eighteenth year. I have gathered you all here today to finalize the union between Diu and Milnos."

Listening to his father command the hall, a lump formed in Kai's throat. He couldn't help but look at Tolan. Tolan's eyes were not angry, as he'd feared, but sad. Unable to return the look, Tolan crossed his arms and stared at the floor. Kai was certain, if his father, Roark, had not been standing behind him, Tolan would have walked out. Kai didn't blame him. If Kai could walk away from this, he would too.

Amelia's expression matched Tolan's. Sadness spilled out of her. Wet tears dampened her eyes and spilled down her cheeks. This was about to be the worst day of their lives. Kai had prayed to Alenga to change their fates. His greatest fear was about to come true. He would go to Milnos. He would marry Amelia and lose Rayna forever.

No matter what Tolan said, he would come to resent Kai. He would lose a dear friend today.

Beholding his father, Kai saw the heavy burden in Iver's eyes. He had never seen his father torn by decision. He could only hope the recent clarity of the hunting trip and Nola's sickness afforded him the ability to make his own decision.

Beside Iver, Nola seemed distressed. She weakly reached her hand over to touch Iver, and Kai felt his stomach turn as he watched her shaking hand. Fortunately, she could not bridge the gap between them before Iver stood and stepped to address the council.

The room remained silent as Iver stepped away from his throne. He took one step down the dais. "I have decided to promote the hero of the Battle of Port Anahita, Tolan Raebun, to Kempery-man for his strategic thinking on the battlefield, his courage, and more importantly, his loyalty to Diu." Iver motioned to Tolan. "Tolan Raebun, son of Duke Roark Raebun, Kempery-man of Diu, Admiral of Fort Pohaku, and Shannon Raebun, please step forward and bend the knee to your king."

Without question, Tolan stepped forward, as did his father a few paces behind. When they reached the bottom of the dais, Tolan glanced at Kai, his eyes a mix of optimism and concern. He knelt on one knee before his king.

"Tolan Raebun, do you accept the accolade of Kempery-man bestowed to you by Diu?" Iver asked.

"I accept my king's offering to become his champion, Kempery-man of Diu," Tolan responded.

"Do you pledge by your honor and all that we hold sacred? Will you conduct yourself with integrity and defend the Kingdom of Diu?"

"I pledge to be true and loyal to the Kingdom of Diu and all its subjects," Tolan responded.

"Who among us can vouch for the chivalrous virtue of this man?" Iver asked.

"My king, I, Duke Roark Raebun, Kempery-man of Diu and Admiral of Fort Pohaku, do affirm that Tolan Raebun holds himself to the highest standards. He is loyal to his king, respectful to your subjects, and his achievements in battle prove him to be duty-bound to your service." Roark gave a gracious bow.

Iver removed his sword from its scabbard. "Tolan Raebun, with my sword I dub thee Kempery-man, champion of Diu. Serve with veracity, compassion, and only draw your sword to defend others," he commanded.

As Iver spoke, Iver laid his sword flat on Tolan's right shoulder and then his left, before sheathing it once again at his side. "Arise Sir Kempery-man Tolan Raebun and accept this new fealty arm ring as proof of your rank and commitment to Diu."

Tolan stood, removed the plain silver arm ring from his wrist, and accepted the new arm ring. It was gold, silver, and copper intertwined with the head a wolf on the adjoining ends. Clamped around his wrist, Tolan looked up to his King. "I will wear this with honor and wield my sword with mercy and defend Diu with my dying breath. This I pledge to you, my King." Tolan bowed to Iver and turned to take the hand of his father, who stood proudly behind him.

"Now Tolan Raebun," Iver continued, "Kempery-man, I bestow another honor on you this day. It is through your affection for Amelia, I betroth you both, and upon her eighteenth year, you will be married."

Tolan could not hold back his joy. He turned and crossed to Amelia, taking her in his arms. He lifted her off the ground and smothered her in his embrace. Her own joy was evident by her smile and kicked up heels.

Regent Maxwell fumed. "Iver! How can you rescind your betrothal from a prince and offer my daughter to a Kempery-man? You would make him king over my homeland? My iron city. NO!" Maxwell thundered.

For a moment, everyone held their breath. Maxwell's public disregard for Iver's rank was unacceptable. While no longer a punishable offense, it was still frowned upon. Iver remained silent.

With only a nod to Tolan, Iver addressed the outburst. "Maxwell, you will council Tolan and introduce him to court.

When the time comes, Tolan will become king of Milnos with Amelia at his side. You accepted my offer to unite our two kingdoms, as you have no heir. Nothing has changed. We still want continued peace. Their marriage will sustain our relationship. I see no reason to trap our two children in a loveless union if another provides a more suitable match."

The speech concluded, Iver took the remaining steps down the dais, leaving Nola dumbstruck in her chair. Iver graciously nodded to Kai and joined the group in congratulating Tolan and Amelia. "Tolan, I advise you to take your unit with you to Milnos. They should become your internal security, your royal guard. Roark, send with your son at least one more contingent of men from Fort Pohaku to assist in the transition. I don't anticipate any challenge, but I prefer to be prepared."

Roark's chest puffed. "Yes, Sire, I will select the men myself."

"Terribly sorry, Tolan, to announce your nuptials to the lady before you could ask her. I am sure you can find a way to ask her officially when the time is right," Iver said, shaking Tolan's hand and pulling Amelia into a side hug. "We will miss Amelia. She is a charming young woman. May Alenga bless you both with years of happiness."

Not sure what to do, Kai held back and watched. It had been years since his father had made a decision this significant without consulting the council first. Farwick, Dresnor, and Cazier conversed quietly, but all seemed content with the decision. Sigry and Dante approached the group, seemingly indifferent to the conclusion.

Nola, however, seemed taken aback by the news as she approached Maxwell. She grasped his arm to steady herself. They stood conversing alone for several moments, and Kai noticed Maxwell holding her hand. *Odd*, Kai thought, noticing a tenderness between them.

Tolan overwhelmed with congratulatory offerings, broke through the group, and approached Kai. Instantly they shook hands and Tolan pulled him into a hug. "I know you had a hand in this. Thank you, my friend. I owe you my life."

At Tolan's side, Amelia extended a hand to Kai and leaned in, she kissed his cheek. "Thank you. We are blessed to have such a good friend. I will miss you dearly when we leave. I hope you will visit." Tears welled in her eyes once more, but they were tears of joy. "You will attend the wedding when the time comes."

Kai felt at a loss for words but choked out a response. "I will be there. I am happy for you both. You will make a fine king someday, Tolan. Watch your back and call on me if you ever need my help."

Before they could say more, the group swarmed the couple. Amelia's mother set kind eyes upon her daughter. Hugs and kisses, mixed with tears of joy. Kai was fairly certain Lady Grace only wanted her daughter to be happy. Lucas, however, remained stoic. He said nothing to his daughter or his future son-in-law. His future king.

In the wall, Kai sensed Riome. She waited, ever-present. He hoped with news about her time with Nola, and he knew they would need to put the next phase of their plan in place. They would need to eavesdrop on Nola and discover how she was brainwashing Iver.

When the crowd dispersed, Kai left the palace. He needed to see Rayna and tell her the news. He was free—they were free to be together. Like his father, he could marry who he wanted. She had to be the first person he told.

Hidden in the apple orchard, Kai gleaned the palace grounds for Rayna. She shined bright like a beacon. She was in the garden. Her dirt-covered hands prepared the soil for spring planting.

Wanting a moment alone, Kai folded his mind around his inner power. It would not take much. He pressed it inward; the pressure built and pushed back. Focused on reaching Rayna, he pushed the pulse with one thought attached—*come to me.*

In his mind, he saw her sit back on her heels and look towards the orchard. She knew he was there. To his delight, she dusted off her dirty hands and ran in his direction.

Anticipation bubbled within Kai, making it challenging to stand still. He paced while Rayna ran through the field. Unable to contain himself, he weaved through the trees to meet her. When her face came into view, he rushed to her. Words failed him. He could not contain his desire. Gently he wrapped his arm around her, and he kissed her the way he'd always wanted. No hesitation. Publicly. He felt free to love her and she him.

When he let her go, she blushed and pushed him toward the orchard. "What are you doing? Someone might see us."

"Let them see." Kai held her firm. "I love you, Rayna Kendrick, and I want the world to know."

He told her everything that had happened. He was free. He thanked Alenga for her blessings and kissed Rayna again. When he gave her a moment to breathe, she clung to him and buried her face in his chest. Her grip nearly crushed his ribs.

The heat from her fever burned through his shirt.

They needed to make a choice and soon.

CHAPTER 27

Nola's Secret

His birthday had been the usual fare: a family celebration in the great hall, a carriage ride around the city, and Linlou's creative handiwork in the Central City Gardens welcoming spring. Unfortunately, he was too sick to enjoy it. The entire day felt like a chore. Every step felt arduous. His splitting head hurt to the point of nausea. And he was now sensitive to daylight. His delicate blue eyes ached at the sight of sunlight.

Anxious to know what Riome learned from Nola, he searched for her. Maybe today she would have time. Leaving Smoke in his room, he made his way through the secret passageway to the tower and climbed to the seventh floor—Riome's level. Hot, he wiped the perspiration from his brow.

He rapped his knuckles on the oak door. *Knock, knock, knock.*

Inside her room, she sat perched in the window seat. Her view from the Master General's tower provided a view over the entire city below. Her look was all business when he entered. "Seems Iver's clarity has given you your freedom. I can't help but wonder if that was not your plan all along. Although, who could know Tolan's pivotal role in saving Iver's sister would gain him such unprecedented esteem. You've made

Tolan a king."

Kai shrugged his shoulders. "Right, who could know all that?" He closed the door behind himself. "Tolan is a good man, and he will make a great king." At least that was Kai's hope. He had no idea the state of things in Milnos, nor the challenges Regent Lucas Maxwell might provide given his love of power. Stepping down from over twenty years of rule would be difficult for anyone.

"Kai, I want to tell you a story." Riome offered him a seat. "You need to understand this treachery between Milnos and Diu is very old. When I was younger than you, I sailed alone to Bangloo. I lived on the streets to learn their language. I spent years in their spy school and heard rumors that spoke of conspiracy against Diu. Bangloo may have let Milnos go to end their part in the war, but Milnos has never let go of their desire to crush Diu. I cannot say for sure, but I believe the peace brokered by King Iver and Regent Maxwell is a ruse. Maxwell cannot be trusted." She took a deep breath before continuing.

"When I first applied to their secret finishing school for spies, they turned me away. Three times they turned me away. I was rat from the streets to them. From the beginning, I knew my calling. If I wanted to be able to go where I pleased. I needed to become anyone I pleased. To stand with kings and hide among maids, I needed to attend their school. To learn the art of fighting and swordplay or poisons and cures, I needed to attend their school. So, I shaved my head, I infiltrated their school, and I poisoned their master," she said coldly.

Riome was ruthlessness and grace wrapped in a beautiful woman. Her endless fury was frightening, yet her beauty, when she allowed it to shine, took your breath away. Even so, learning the history behind her beginnings was a shock to Kai.

"As the master lay dying, I displayed my disguises, revealing to him I was four people in one. Each had stood in his presence over the preceding days. Walked their halls. I had even spoken with him at length, and he did not know me. Needless to say, with his dying breath he signed my admission into their secret society. Not because I had proved myself worthy of their teaching through disguises, but because I proved my unyielding spirit. I was willing to do whatever it took. I understood, sometimes the means to an end is not always kind."

Kai's eyes bulged. "I had no idea."

Riome's expression turned crafty. "Once I joined their school, I continued to perfect the art of disguise, discernment, and weaponry. I excelled, much to the frustration of my teachers, who questioned my need to always be someone other than myself. I often came to class as my fellow scholars. I mimicked their behaviors and mastered their voices. They taught me sophistication and poise mixed with cunning and manipulation."

"And you chose this life?" Kai questioned.

"Let me explain the need for anonymity. Within the world, to this day, nobody knows the boy who trained in Bangloo was a girl. My face, my identity is a secret. I could stand with anyone from my time at the school, and they would not know who I was. I have seen some of those students in Nebea, Milnos, even here in Diu."

Kai wasn't sure why she was divulging her past. "Riome, I am sorry. I don't know what to say."

"Do not be sorry, Kai—I am not. Learn and become strong. It will save your life." Riome lowered her eyes.

Composed, she stared across at him with renewed intent. "I believe there are things at work around us, and we are the only ones who can stop it. You have no time left to be innocent. Change is coming for you, and you'd better be ready. That, in part, is why I push you. Train you. Not to mention in a year's time, Tolan and his precious Amelia will be wed living in Milnos." She paused, shaking her head. "Do you think they will welcome them with open arms? Her father may be old, but he still has fight in him yet. The man is power-hungry. I sense history repeating itself again and again around the Galloway line and its extended family. I mean to protect that—it is my purpose. We are a family, even though Iver is not your true father. Yes, I was listening that night. I know Keegan is your father."

Her words grew more intense as she spoke, and it inspired him. After the battle for Port Anahita, he was no longer the innocent prince. Still, he needed to be stronger. Fierce. "So, you don't care that I am not the prince of Diu? What about the fact that I am full Katori? Or that Keegan is my father?" He wasn't sure if that mattered, but he knew she would tell him the truth.

"Don't waste my time," she huffed, "prince or not. You are full Katori, and about to turn seventeen, now that is a concern. The timing is terrible. Remember, I lived there for over a decade. I know all their secrets. And I do mean all of them."

Of course, she knew everything. Kai rolled his eyes. "I am lucky to have you as my teacher. Thank you, Riome." He said, unsure what else he should say.

"Yes, well, don't thank me yet. As you know, I interrogated Nola. Not that she will recall the moment. The right potions can make you tell your life story and leave you hollow after the telling. This part is important."

"What did you learn?" Kai stared inquisitively, waiting for her reply.

"I am sure you will be as surprised to hear Nola's secret as I was. She is Nola Penier, older sister to Landon and illegitimate daughter to Bannon Penier, the Milnos king who killed Iver's father and uncle. When the event happened, she lived on Ahana. That is where the old king stashed her. His love child."

Riome's words drove home the last words Nola had said that night. *I'm your...* She meant to say, *sister*. All this time Nola knew precisely what she was doing here. She was plotting. As King Bannon's daughter, illegitimate or not, she must be out for revenge. How could she possibly love the man that put her father in the ground? Just cause or not, Nola must hate Iver on some level.

"What else have you learned?" Kai leaned in closer. "I know there is more. You hide it well when you choose, but your face says there is more to tell."

"There is more," she acknowledged. "Nola sees Landon in secret. She pays the guards well to let her visit. They talk every few days. Although I have not been privy to their conversations, I cannot believe she is happy letting him rot away in a dungeon. Now with Tolan going to Milnos, you will be left here. As far as anyone is concerned, you are the rightful heir to the Galloway throne. She cannot be happy, given her designs to have Aaron on the throne. On top of that, Iver and Nola plan to leave. They are not staying for King's day. He is taking her on his summer voyage."

"Yes, I know." Kai acknowledged. "And as I understand it, you will be joining them. Cazier told me."

She fingered her long hair. "Which is why tonight I will be listening to Nola from behind the secret passageway. I must learn what I can. I need to hear how she speaks to your father in private. You must be ready. We will need to swap off a few times. Cazier has sent Brannon ahead to Milnos, and Jarrod will be on Tolan and Amelia's ship as they sail around to Milnos. Spies for Diu. They will send word if they learn anything of note."

Kai furrowed his brow. "If we know her secret, what do you hope to gain by listening to her tonight? And why are we letting them sail anywhere? Cazier and Dante must be told."

"I have not shared this knowledge with my father. I need to learn her methods. If I am to undo the damage to your father, I must know how she suppresses him. After dinner, I will wait for them to return to their room. I will wait for them and listen within the hidden passage. Since Iver went hunting five weeks ago and her recent illness, this will be their first night together."

She stepped to the door and ushered him into the stairwell. Silently they entered the secret passageway. "We can switch off after four hours. If Cazier assumes the worst and arrests her, I might not be able to fully restore your father. She is able to manipulate him even if he seems clear-minded. Plus, I need to find her accomplices. There is no way she is doing this alone. Maxwell may have people in the city helping her. He is in on this, I am sure of it."

Hidden within the passageway above the library, she braced her hand against the stone wall. "Have courage. We will learn what we need. Get some rest and come to me in four hours." With nothing more, she stepped into the darkness.

Four hours later, Kai listened to the Mryken dogs venturing down the family hallway. Footfalls from the guards on patrol echoed down the stairwell. Swiftly he walked down the hallway to the nursery and entered. The door closed at his back; he sensed the guards pass on the other side of the door. He had made it without being seen. Inside the door, he calmed his breathing. Cautiously he passed Cordelia's bed. His little sister was fast asleep. Kendra was awake, yet she said nothing. She simply turned her head towards the secret panel and nodded.

Luckily, he had shared Riome's plan with Kendra beforehand. He did not want her alarmed by their movements within the walls. Even though he hated creeping through the nursery, it was the easiest access point into the hidden passage next to his father's room.

He released the latch and entered the narrow space between the two rooms. Riome stood poised on the stairs, blade in hand. When she saw Kai, she replaced the blade and descended the stairs into the pitch-black space. In his mind, he watched her slip through the music room. Stealthy as a shadow, she moved into the library; her movements were quick. Her ultimate destination was the Master General's tower and her room on the seventh floor.

Alone he sat in the dark, his back pressed against the cold stone, listening. Nothing more than the sound of breathing emanated from the king and queen's chamber. They were both sound asleep. He wondered if Riome had learned anything. Did she know how to help his father?

To pass the time, he let his mind wander about the palace. From room to room he searched for people, guards, and the Mryken. Everything was as it should be. Secure and silent. Bored, he took the time to meditate. He focused on his breathing and tried to clear his mind to relieve his throbbing headache.

He had no idea how long he sat. Normally he could sit for over an hour without difficulty. Tonight, everything ached. He twitched as he tried to find a comfortable posture. Stretching out his legs, he massaged his sore knees. Still uncomfortable, he twisted his back from side to side. The more he struggled, the hotter he became. He fanned his face with his hands. His pulse quickened. The narrow space felt stifling. His head swam in circles, and he passed out.

Kai felt a firm hand press against his mouth. "Wake up," he heard Riome whisper. Slowly he came to. Feverish, he leaned forward to get his bearings. Riome tugged at his arm and pulled him down the stairs. They crossed through the music room into the library. Still, she said nothing. She accessed the hidden passage. He stepped behind the panel and latched the painting in place. Quietly he marched up the stairs behind her.

While he used his sight, he noticed she ran her hand along the wall. It was her guide to know when to make the turn. She could not see as he did—she was only a Half-Light. The truth of being a Half-Light struck him with understanding.

Once within the safety of his room, she opened the balcony doors. A cool breeze chilled his room. "You have a problem. Alenga help you if you don't take care of it soon."

He knew full well what she meant. But did she really know, he wondered? Of course, she knew. Conhaspriga called to him. He had a choice to make. Go to Katori now or lose his gifts forever. The one thing he was sure of was that he didn't want to go without Rayna. He decided to test Riome's willingness to divulge her knowledge. "What do you mean?"

"Don't play dumb with me, Kai. You know full well what I

mean. The spirits call to you. You feel them. Don't deny them. The fever, the headaches. I can only imagine you are having dreams, too. Telling you where to go. Like I said. I know their secrets. I was raised there until I was old enough for them to know I was not full Katori."

Kai wanted to deny it. Pretend it wasn't real. How could he choose between the two? Leave his father. His friends. The only home he'd ever known. "I am fine. I just… I got too hot." He tried to convince her, but she was not having it.

She returned to the balcony, arms folded. Cool evening air drifted inside. "Come. Sit outside. The breeze will help your symptoms. Seriously, has nobody told you what you need to do? And when? You must complete your rite of passage before it is too late. My mother said they do not wish you to try, and they will try to stop you. You are Mariana and Iver's boy. You can do this."

"Did you know my mother? Were you in Katori when she was there?" His words came out more like a plea than a question.

"I am sorry, Kai, I was too young to know your mother. That and my mother kept me hidden. We lived in the highlands. She did not want me tested. She feared they would cast me out. Send us away. So, I left before the chiefs discovered me. Kai, I have faith in you. They will not make it easy, but I know you can outwit them. Think beyond their silly game. You have allies."

He shook his head. "You don't understand. I cannot leave my father. He needs me."

"Without your gifts, you can't stop what is coming. Yes, Iver needs you, but he needs this version of you. I am not saying your gifts make you better, but they do make you more useful. While I don't know the future, I can only trust in Alenga. She has served you well thus far. Why question her now?"

"What do you mean, they will not make it easy?" He thought about that. Her other comment struck him. "Allies.

You mean Kendra and Haygan. Haygan has not returned. Probably their doing. Kendra is trapped providing care for my siblings. How could she help?"

Riome shook her head. "Kendra's mate lives in the forest. On Eagle Peak. He will help you. My mother will help you. She remains outside of the city, near Sabastian. She spoke of another young man. Goes by the name of Liam. She has sent word to him. He waits for you to make your move." She nodded in agreement. "I believe you are right; I doubt Haygan will return. He is never this late."

He chuckled to himself. Riome really did make it her business to know everyone and everything. Still, he needed time to think. So did Rayna. She was going through the same thing. She would need to make a choice. Was she ready to leave her parents? He would need to ask her before he left. Before he made his own decision.

CHAPTER 28

Planting a Seed

There was always one place Kai could get away from the world. His room. When he closed his door, he noticed an open bottle of wine and two empty glasses on the sofa table. A cool breeze and sunshine drew his attention to his balcony.

Nola's golden hair blew in the breeze around her tall and slender frame. An uneasy feeling settled over Kai. Her being in his room uninvited was unusual. In fact, now that he thought about it, she had never been in this room, not that he could remember. He considered backing out, but she'd heard him enter.

"Kai, my dear, come and join me."

Cautiously he stepped outside and approached the railing at her side. "Queen Nola."

"What a lovely view you have. I had no idea you had this wonderful balcony. Dare I say it is almost as large as mine." She twisted around to face Kai.

She wasn't wrong. His view was spectacular. Still, he could not relax. Her duplicitous nature sickened him. There had to be a reason she was here. She wanted something. "How can I help you?" he asked warily.

"We never spend enough time together, Kai. You and me.

We did when you were younger." She touched his hand, and he recoiled.

"Sorry. I am dirty from horseback riding. I should get cleaned up."

"Oh, nonsense. Don't bother on my account. A little dirt never hurt anyone. Besides, it is a beautiful afternoon. Let us enjoy the sunshine while we have it." Nola turned her face skyward and closed her eyes.

Everything about this felt wrong, but Kai stayed. He listened to her babble about family and loyalty. Her songbird voice flitted through the air as she spoke of Aaron and his future and brotherly support. Kai desperately wanted to cover his ears. If she said it once, she said it multiple times. "You children are the future. Should anything happen to your father, I will need you, Kai. Promise me you will protect this family."

The thought of something happening to his father shook Kai. *What could she possibly mean? What were her plans?* He did not trust her. It was all he could do not to call the guards to lock her away. "Yes, Nola. I understand. I will do whatever I can to ensure the safety of my family."

He meant every word. He would do whatever he needed to do to save his father.

Her fake smile never made it to her eyes. "You know we are very proud of you, your father and I?" she crooned. "We know you will do the right thing for your family. Family means everything."

"Of course, Nola. I know my father commands me, and I will do as he wishes. I am ever loyal to Diu."

A soft exhale passed through her lips, and she wandered back into his room. Head down, Kai followed. *What more could she want? I need to rest.*

She poured them both a glass of wine and offered Kai a cup. "Here, let's sit."

Not wanting to be too close, he sat in the chair while she took the sofa. The smell of grapes lingered above his cup. Nola took a sip, and he did the same. "I must say, Kai, you have grown into a handsome young man." She nodded and took another sip.

Kai did the same.

"Thank you?" he responded, unsure what else to say.

"You keep yourself so busy these days, we hardly see you."

"My studies have been a priority." He nodded, sipping his wine and glaring at her over his glass.

Nola nodded. "Oh yes, your studies. Whatever do you plan to do, now that you are not going to Milnos? Surely you have a plan to occupy your time."

"I suppose," he responded, taking a larger gulp. "I will serve my father here, or wherever he sees fit to send me. I still have another year here with the professor."

"Yes, dear, of course. One year left."

He took another drink, hoping to send her on her way with his emptied cup. Silence filled the room with eerie tension. They sat there, neither saying a word. An uneasy feeling clouded Kai's mind. Anxious, he tried to stand. He felt detached from his body. Nola scooted towards him and touched his hand. Her eyes locked on his, her hand softly tracing tiny circles on his skin.

"You have a strong mind, Kai. Unlike any I have encountered. There, there," she rubbed his hand. "Relax now, and listen to my words."

Panic squeezed Kai's heart. He felt physically incapable of moving. With the little focus he had left, he gleaned the palace and searched for Kendra. He was in trouble, and he knew it. A lump formed in his throat. There was little time. With the smallest amount of energy, Kai pushed a thought through the palace—*Kendra.*

Nola's green eyes burned into his, and her words pierced his mind. Echoes of her voice danced in his head. "Oh, my dear, I will never be far from you. We are locked together, you and me. We are each other's future. I am the little bird in your ear. You will do as I say."

He could not shake her grasp on his attention. Obedience,

loyalty, and betrayal repeatedly glided off her tongue. As Nola gushed over the iron city of Milnos and its superiority over Diu, Kai lost his grasp on reality.

"Kai. Kai." He felt someone jostle him. "KAI." Kendra's face appeared in front of him.

"What?" he questioned, blinking several times.

"What's wrong? Are you alright?"

"What do you mean? I am fine. Why do you ask?" Confused, he glanced around his empty room.

Kendra's eyes swam with worry. "I was in the garden with your sister, and suddenly I heard a whisper on the wind. Your voice called to me." She knelt beside the chair he was sitting in.

Her eyes searched his, and she pressed the back of her hand to his forehead. "Are you sure you're alright?"

He licked his lips and detected the remnants of wine with his tongue. "I don't remember drinking…" he let his voice trail off.

"Kai. Can you hear me?" she shook him again.

He shook his head, again seeing Kendra, feeling confused by her presence. "Kendra. Yes, yes. I was just…" He looked around his room, confused.

"After I put your sister down for her nap in the nursery, I came to your room. You were staring off into nothing."

Kai felt as if he was lost in a fog. He didn't even remember coming to his room. His clothes reeked of the stables. Dirt covered his hands. He rubbed his head.

"Honestly, Kendra, I do not remember calling for you. Sure, I have done it in the past, testing my magic to bring you to me. But I don't remember anything after leaving the stables."

Kendra looked around his room. "What are you looking for?" she asked.

He wasn't sure himself. "It feels like there is a shadow over my mind. Like when you try to remember something but cannot."

"I am sorry I could not get here sooner. If it happens again, maybe we should speak with Sigry. Blacking out or losing time is not normal. I have never seen this reaction to the calling."

While he appreciated her concern, he simply could not remember what had happened. One minute he'd been in the stables, the next Kendra was shaking him. "I'm fine, Kendra. I just need to get cleaned up." He rose to his feet, but he was a little wobbly.

"Are you sure?" She caught his arm as he bumped into the chair.

"I'll be fine." He motioned for the pitcher of water on the table. "Just a little thirsty. My stomach feels uneasy."

Delighted to be of service, Kendra brought him a glass of water. "Here, drink."

"Thank you, Kendra." He gulped down the entire glassful. "I need to get cleaned up. I want to rest a little before my history test."

"Very well." With a bow, Kendra left.

CHAPTER 29

*H*ow do you tell your best friend goodbye? Kai wondered. He struggled with the question. They both had known this day was coming. Moving to Albey was all Shane had talked about these past few months. Shane had been his best friend four years now, and Kai hoped the right words would find him when the time came.

It was a long walk through the woods to Marduk's cabin. Smoke's silent footfalls padded a mere fifteen feet to his left. Rayna cheerfully held his hand while Dresnor walked a step behind, and Drew took the lead with Albey. His Kempery-men. Valiant protectors. Loyal friends. Everyone thought they were saying goodbye because Shane was moving, but they had no idea Kai's goodbye meant so much more.

Nearly every inch between the palace and their cabin held memories. Kai sniffed the air. The smell of roasting meat mixed with the smell of spring tree blossoms. A strange combination, he thought. The closer they came to the cabin, the stronger the scent. Smoked pig dominated the air. Laughter echoed in the trees.

Working with Markduk, Kai was surprised to find Drew's father, Lord Robert Henley. They were slowly flipping the large slit pig. They placed it back above the low burning firepit and turned to greet Kai and his men.

"Welcome. Glad you all could make it. Where's Finlee and Redmon?" Marduk asked.

"They are coming shortly, with a few extra guards for the night's ride back to the palace. I hope that's acceptable?" Kai asked, releasing Marduk's hand in exchange for Robert's. "Lord Henley, good to see you again. It seems you're a long way from home."

"Your Highness. Please call me Robert. Not as far as you think. I used to have a little cabin in the hills here when I was young, and I am building a new one for my nephews. Micha—Hunter Marduk has offered to teach my two young nephews the hunter's trade. Soldiering does not suit them. Besides, Micha will need help with Shane moving to Albey." He smiled at two young boys poking the fire. "Boys, come meet Prince Kai. This is Brian and Marcus."

Both boys stood half-frozen at the word prince. The eldest was not much older than he had been when he had first met Hunter Marduk. A strapping young man with a firm grip. The younger boy was a little round in the middle with a quirky smile. "Nice to meet you both." Kai nodded to both boys. Wordless, they greeted Kai and stepped away.

Near the cabin, Kai caught Shane's eye. His friend leaned against the cabin railing conversing with Julia. Julia gave Shane a nudge in Kai's direction before she took him by the hand and pulled the two young men together. "Thank you for coming, Your Highness." She bowed and released Shane's hand. Taking Rayna's hand, Julia pulled her away from Kai's side and left them alone.

"You are dressed rather nicely for a pig roast," Kai said poignantly. "Is there something I should know?"

Shane let his eyes leave Julia's departing form to face Kai. "Everything has happened kind of fast. Seems in a moment of excitement I have asked Julia to marry me, and she said yes! We plan to marry today. Her parents are over there." He gestured and released a breath he'd been holding. "I would hope to have you stand up with me."

"Wow, what can I say? You are my best friend—no, you are like a brother to me. It would be my honor to stand beside you."

"Thank you, Kai. It means a lot to have you here. If it were not for you, I might never have met Julia."

Kai looked around the clearing. "A wedding certainly explains all the flowers. Why didn't you tell me? I would have brought a gift or at least worn something more appropriate." Kai glanced at his rugged boots and dark clothing.

Shane laughed. "If you feel out of place, I can loan you a shirt. The wedding only came up this morning. Julia and her mother did all of this in just a few hours. I am leaving tomorrow, and I just couldn't leave her behind. I am sure you can relate." Shane nudged his chin in Rayna's direction.

Kai did indeed understand. He looked around the clearing. "Who will be performing the ceremony?"

"Lord Robert brought a chaplain. We want a simple ceremony, nothing like the Albey wedding. Though Julia insists on a few traditions."

"Prince Kai. Shane." Anna stepped up beside of her future son-in-law. "Julia has stepped inside to change her dress. If you two could prepare, we would like to get started."

Everyone gathered in the clearing north of the cabin. The foundation of Robert's cabin had been turned into a wedding platform decorated with pine garlands and white flowers. The warm spring sunshine filled the meadow with a delicate glow. Kai stood with Shane, and Rayna slowly climbed the stairs and took her place. Julia held her father's hand as they walked into the clearing and ascended the stairs. A simple moment in a simple glade.

Together everyone watched two friends stand ready to commit their lives to one another. A promise to love and care for one another forever. Tempted by the moment, Kai's eyes found Rayna's. He secretly wished this was their day.

The chaplain raised his hands in the air. "Today we come

together to celebrate the marriage between Shane and Julia." His voice carried wisdom and love. "We start with the giving of roses. Shane. Julia. Please accept this rose. Red is a symbol of your deep love for each other. May your marriage like this rose reflect the beauty in your union. This is the love and passion you promise to share with one another." Julia blushed as she and Shane held the flowers.

"The lavender rose I offer symbolizes your love at first sight. May this rose offer a daily reminder of your love and eagerness to grow your relationship."

Shane offered her the lavender rose. "Julia, I loved you the first time I saw you. You captured my heart." She tenderly took his rose and raised it to her nose. Their shared glances filled with enchantment.

The chaplain gestured. "Rayna offers you, a white rose. White, the purest of colors, represents innocence, purity, and charm. May it forever remind you of this new beginning." Rayna handed them the rose.

"Kai offers you a pink rose. The pink rose conveys gentleness, grace, and sweetness. May it inspire kind words and unconditional love." He paused for the exchange. "Now, to the loving couple, Micha offers an orange rose. Orange evokes energy and excitement. May it symbolize your desire and remind you of the attraction between you." Micha stepped back, giving his son a proud nod.

"Finally, the yellow rose offered by Anna. Bright and cheerful come to mind when seeing a yellow rose. Julia, your mother wishes this yellow rose creates warm feelings and provides happiness. May each yellow rose you see remind you of the joy you bring each other and the friendship you share.

"To the loving couple, I offer you this white ribbon. As you bind together your roses, so you also bind your lives together. May your love be constant and true. Today you become one in mind, heart, and family." Shane held the roses together, and Julia bound them with the white ribbon. Together they held their bundle.

Raising his hands to the sky, the chaplain blessed the couple. "May Alenga bless your marriage with peace and happiness. May your marriage deepen and enrich every facet of your lives. Trust in this, marriage understands and forgives life's unavoidable mistakes. It encourages and nurtures new life, new experiences, and new ways of expressing love through the seasons of life.

"May the promises you make to one another today be lived out to the end of your lives. You may now exchange your vows. Make your personal promise to love each other today, tomorrow, and forever."

Quietly Julia and Shane put their heads together and spoke softly into each other's ear. They shared their commitment and made their secret promises to each other. Finished, they offered Rayna their bundle of roses.

"Shane and Julia, as you hold hands, may you see the gift that they are to you. Let your hands keep you close, provide comfort, and remind you of this day. Today, you have chosen to seal your vows by exchanging rings. From the earliest times, the circle has been a sign of completeness. Endless symbols of commitment, much like your love for one another. They are a symbol of the words spoken today, and they are your reminders through time."

Shane took Julia's hand. Placing the ring on her finger, he said, "I give you this ring as a symbol of my love and faithfulness to you."

Julia took Shane's hand. Placing the ring on his finger, she said, "I give you this ring as a symbol of my love and faithfulness to you."

Pleased with the exchange, the chaplain placed his hands around the couple's joined hands. "Today you have pledged yourselves to a lifetime of caring for one another. May this commitment made in love, kept in faith, and lived in hope be eternally renewed. As you stand before us, it is our hope that you will go through life loving, trusting, and caring for one another, completely, and forever.

"Shane and Julia, from this moment forward, you will never be alone. Having pledged your fidelity to one another, to love, honor, and cherish one another in the presence of this gathering and by the grace of Alenga, it is my honor to now pronounce you husband and wife. You may seal your union with a kiss."

Shane gently cupped Julia's face and placed the most loving kiss on her lips. Leaning back, he looked into her eyes. "For today and always. You are my dearest love."

Julia blushed at his words. "I will hold dear your heart, as you hold mine. You are my dearest love." Then she kissed him again.

Happily, they turned to address the group, and everyone clapped and cheered for the couple. Shane's ear-to-ear grin was matched by Julia's.

"Let's eat," Shane declared, grabbing his wife's hand as they bounded down the steps, running through the woods to Marduk's clearing.

Gathered around the firepit, everyone relished good food and wine. Laughter and conversation surrounded the happy couple. A glint of gold caught Kai's eye. Julia blushed as she noticed her gold wedding band sparkle, reflecting the blaze of the firepit. The matching ring, a band of golden twists, decorated Shane's hand. He was deeply happy for his friends.

"Congratulations. When do you leave again?" Kai asked.

"First thing in the morning," Shane answered, clutching Julia's hand. "I have already moved everything dad offered me. Kinnon, Kempery-man Albey's brother, has been most gracious in providing anything I needed. I have to move Julia's few belongings—two trunks are all she owns." Shane's other hand gently stroked Smoke's head.

It was good to see his friend preparing for his future. The town of Albey would be his new life. Kai listened to all the details: the offer of land and a small cabin from Kinnon and a ready-made position for Julia with a local seamstress, they were all set to start their new adventure as man and wife.

After their evening concluded, everyone offered their good wishes and said their goodbyes. Surrounded by security, Kai walked hand-in-hand with Rayna back to the horses waiting at the forest's edge. It had been a beautiful day with a bittersweet ending. He hated the envy he felt as Shane and Julia began their new lives together. His life still felt beyond his control. While he was free to be with Rayna, their future was still uncertain and possibly out of reach.

Riding through the streets of Diu, Kai's Kempery-men kept a close eye on him and Rayna from a respectable distance. He was grateful the sounds of the city provided ample noise, allowing them to speak privately. "You seem to be having a good day. No headaches?" he asked.

She smiled pleasantly. "It was an exceptional day. I am thankful for the reprieve."

He reached over and gently squeezed her hand. "You know I want to spend my life with you? You are the love of my life. When the time is right, I hope to ask for your hand in marriage. If that is what you wish as well."

"Kai, you are my heart and soul. I know when the time is right, we will be together. That is my wish. First, we must decide if our future is here or in Katori. A decision I am nearly ready to make. I am grateful you have not pushed me to choose."

Entering the palace gatehouse, he slid from his horse and waited to respond. His men parted ways, giving them the privacy Kai so desperately desired, taking the horses. He led her down the road toward her home. "When you are ready, we will walk the road together, wherever it leads, hand-in-hand we will face our future."

"Thank you," she said, pulling him into a hug. "I think I need another night to speak to my parents. As you said, they have been very understanding. The burden is now on me to know my own heart." She stepped away, still holding his hand. "Goodnight, Kai."

Kai nodded in response. Then he pulled her back into his

arms and kissed her. He held the sweetness of their moment with his breath. In his soul, he felt the breeze slow down and the weight of time pressed on his heart. If only he could live in this moment forever. Slowly releasing his breath, he released her. "I love you, Rayna." Leading her by the hand, he walked her home and then returned to the palace.

CHAPTER 30

The Calling

Two days after Kai's seventeenth year, he stood on his bedroom balcony, savoring in the cool spring breeze on his skin. A decision crystallized in Kai's mind; he knew what he wanted. Now he waited for Rayna.

The palace was quiet. Peace seemed to have settled over Diu and security, and life was back to normal. Strangely enough, his father was on his way to Port Anahita to inspect the progress of the repairs. The lighthouse bell was being installed, and the new military base was well underway. After Iver inspected the new defenses, he and Nola would board a ship. Provided the weather was good and the trip proved bountiful, they would be home in about four to six months. This would be their first trip together since the twins were born. Along with Cordelia, Aaron and Seth would remain in Kendra's care.

Kai thought about leaving Diu. He thought about what he might have said to his father. Guilt over not telling his father his plans twisted Kai's stomach. Leaving Diu without telling Iver felt like a betrayal. Then there were his siblings; they were another sore spot on his soul. How could he explain his departure to them? How could he leave without saying goodbye?

Iver's safety out on the open sea concerned Kai. Even though he knew Riome would sail with them in secret, he still worried. Cazier had told Kai he personally saw to her assignment to Iver's ship, the Dominion. The memory of watching her cut off her long hair in order to pose as one of three cabin boys saddened him. Once again, her dedication was endless. The lengths she was willing to go to ensure their success was beyond measure.

Before he went to class, he took a quick moment with Kendra and she confirmed his concerns behind Haygan's failed return from his winter's stay in Katori. Sabastian told her he saw a large group of Katori in the Zabranen Forest. They were waiting for Kai. They knew he was coming. Never had Sabastian seen them move en masse. Usually, only a handful challenged a young one venturing home for Conhaspriga.

Kendra also confirmed this journey was never meant to be a challenge to keep a returnee out, only a test of their spirit to determine if they were guardian worthy. Fighting their way home tested their cunning. Their discernment in each phase proved their readiness to be more. Those wanting to become warriors trained to protect their homeland from outsiders.

This gathering confirmed Kai's assumptions. They aimed to keep him from completing his rite of passage. Although he did not really understand why he wondered if Rayna would be able to pass. Was she lumped in with him no matter what? Millions of possibilities ran through his mind. Kendra feared for him. It would all depend on who challenged him. More importantly, it would depend on how badly they were willing to keep him out.

Professor Greydon interrupted his thoughts. "Prince Kai, you are not looking well. Come here, young man." Greydon placed the back of his hand against Kai's forehead. "Dear me. You are burning with fever. Did you see Sigry before he left with your father?"

"Yes, sir, I did. I have been taking something he made with no success. He believes I could have what Nola had," Kai lied.

He knew what was wrong with him had nothing to do with her affliction. Although Sigry had insisted on giving him something for his fever, Kai knew what he had could not be cured with medication.

"Go. Take more of your medicine. Sleep. Take a few days to rest before returning to class, and do not worry about tomorrow's test. It can wait until you are better."

Back in his room, Kai laid across his bed. Like Rayna, he'd been having headaches. Now his low-grade fever was getting worse each day. Also, he had the same dream nearly every night. He wanted to talk to Haygan about the stone wall in his vision and the symbol carved into the stone. How was he to open the wall? He could not remember.

Kendra had been giving him water and insisted he had to make a choice: follow the calling or let his Katori heritage burn away. For now, he awaited Rayna's decision. She wanted to speak to her parents. She wanted to say goodbye, which he truly understood. Leaving without telling them would be wrong; it was why he felt so conflicted about going without telling his family.

He lay feverish in his bed. His thoughts drifted to Rayna. She too was having dreams and experiencing a wavering fever. He was only glad she had not been suffering since her birthday, whereas his birthday seemed to be a catalyst for his increased pain.

Exhausted, Kai closed his eyes and fell into a dream.

Kai's vision blossomed with dawn's rays dancing across white snow, and he felt bitter cold snow touch his face. His eyes squinted against the blinding whiteness, he found himself holding a white crystal climbing the snow-covered peaks of the Katori Mountains. The shadow of a man preceded him in the storm.

Through a cluster of ice-covered trees, he found a large

cave opening. Inside the nothingness, something waited. Heat pulsed within the walls. Hot breath blew into his face. The walls came alive with ambient blue light, and he came face to face with two enormous amber eyes.

Kai awoke with a gasp.

As he lay there dripping with sweat, his heart raced. He grabbed some paper on his side table to write down all the details of his dream. He'd taken to writing down his dreams; it was the only bit of advice from Sigry he'd followed. Not that he shared any during their sessions, but it was quite useful when trying to piece things together.

Finished jotting his notes, Kai looked around his room and realized he'd slept all day and into the night. On his way to his balcony, he took a deep breath and gleaned. His mind searched through the palace and the surrounding grounds. In the orchard, he found Rayna. *What could she be doing at this hour in the orchard?*

Concerned why she was awake, he dressed and sneaked out through the hidden passage, exiting in the kitchen. In the orchard, he found her on her knees, hugging a tree. "Are you alright, Rayna?" Kai knelt at her side.

"I don't think I am," she sobbed. "The dreams are getting more intense, and the fever is becoming unbearable. Again tonight, I saw the stone wall, and there was more. In the end, I was in the forest, holding a green heart-shaped crystal, surrounded by three girls. They spoke in rounds of broken sentences. Kai, I am frightened, but I still want to go." She was dripping with sweat and brought to tears.

"I think this is what Haygan meant about the gift burning itself out. We need to go, and we need to go now. Or suffer through this. Kendra says it could take weeks." Kai placed a hand on her shoulder. Heat emanated through her shirt. "Have you truly made your decision?" he asked, hoping she had come to the same conclusion. It was time to leave. He wanted this, but he would not force her to go.

She let go of the tree. Craggy bark indentions marked the

side of her face. "Have you?" Tears ran down her face, and she looked away. "I want to go, but how can I leave them? They need me. I love them too much to leave them. It would break their hearts."

Kai sat beside her and pulled her close. "Dori and Levi chose to be your parents. They want what is best for you. If you stay, you will resent them. At the very least you will spend your life wondering what might have been. Like me, they want you to be happy. Either way, I will respect your choice. And they will respect your choice."

She sat with her head on his shoulder and wiped the tears from her face. With a deep breath, she sat up. "You're right. If I don't follow my heart, I will resent them. Charlotte is here to help them. She is a great woman. They have always pushed me to follow my dreams. They told me to go. I told them I wanted to look for my birth parents and that I loved them. They will always be my parents, but I need to know why they left me." She shifted to her knees. "I'm ready. Ready to leave. I want to see this through."

"Here, let me help you." He stood and pulled Rayna to her feet. "I will speak with Dresnor. He can arrange for a boat to cross Baden Lake. We'll land north of Albey. You should tell your parents I am taking you to Albey because you've discovered a plant that can help us in your books. Then we will search for your parents. I have no idea when we will return. Make sure they understand we may travel to Katori before we return. This will be our cover story to everyone." He squeezed her hand.

It was only a few hours before dawn when Dresnor came to Kai's room. He had already told Kendra his plan, and she'd sent word to Sabastian and Yulia. They would do whatever they could to see he at least had the chance to try.

"Good, Philip, you're here," Kai said as Dresnor entered. "I need you to arrange passage across Baden Lake. Rayna has discovered an herb in her research that may cure our fever. She believes it is imperative that we leave straight away. Can you get us on a ship?" Kai paused to catch his breath and wipe the sweat from his brow.

Dresnor stepped forward. "Kai, are you sure you should be traveling? Perhaps I could go and retrieve the herb if you could provide a sketch and some idea of where to look."

"I appreciate the offer, but I don't believe we have that kind of time. We cannot risk you bringing back the wrong plant. And I believe freshness plays a part. By ship, we can be there mid-afternoon. I wish Rayna and I could travel alone, but we both know you would never let that happen."

Dresnor nodded in agreement. "You're right. I would not allow that, Your Highness."

The use of his rank told Kai a lot. "Let me be honest with you Dresnor, as it will help you explain it to the others. When we reach Albey, I will need to leave your care. According to Yulia, who will be coming with us, the Katori people may help us, but only if we come into the Zabranen Forest alone. After we are well, Rayna hopes to inquire about her birth parents. I have no idea when we will return. My current plan is to spend the summer in the mountains."

"Are we meant to sit idle while you travel without protection? I think not." Dresnor insisted.

"Dresnor, you cannot keep me from going. And if you think returning to Diu without me is wise, by all means, do so, but we are going. We have no choice—they have a cure, and we must go alone. Now, we both know you are going, and you will not return without me, as that might appear to some that you abandoned your post. So, I only want Kempery-man Albey and Captain Drew to go with us. They are the only ones without wives and children.

Kai hated asking Dresnor to leave Marabella. She meant the world to him, but he was honor-and-duty-bound to his service as a Kempery-man. "I will not waste my breath trying to convince you to stay." Kai pressed the side of his head, hoping to ease the pain. "I know you will not listen. Take the time, speak with Marabella. I am sorry there is no time to get your affairs in order. Thank you for your service, your friendship, and your loyalty."

Kai saw the depth of dedication and continued with a heavy heart. "I don't want to draw a lot of attention to our departure. I will inform Cazier, and he can tell Dante in the morning. Do not tell the boatman who they will be transporting until we depart. We leave at dawn."

"That is not enough men. What of Redmon? Scouts? Guards? I don't like this, Kai."

"Trust me. If I could leave all of you, I would, but you would only hunt me down. We need to go and go quickly. John will understand, he has a wife and child. I cannot ask him to choose. We need a fast ship. There will be little room for men and supplies. As I said, Yulia will also be traveling with us. We need to board a cutter. We need Dante's ship, the Dragaron. I leave it with you but get us on that ship," Kai said in a firm tone.

"Understood. I will give each of your men the choice."

Kendra knocked and entered his room. "Prince Kai, Kempery-man Dresnor. Please excuse my interruption. I have brought you some water. The food supplies you requested await your departure in the kitchen. Is there anything else I may prepare?" Kendra gracefully asked, with a curtsy to Kai for Dresnor's benefit.

Dresnor nodded slightly. "Prince Kai, I will see to your arrangements straight away. I will find you when we are ready to depart."

"Thank you, Kendra," Kai said before gulping down the water she'd brought him. "I have no idea how long we will be gone."

"I wish you well, Kai. I hope you make it. In all my years, I have never seen anyone wait this long, or the fever become this intense. You must hurry. Only take Dresnor with you into the woods. The less men with you, the better. When you reach the first waterfall, send him away. Do not let him go any further."

Her tone seemed sad, but her eyes were serious. "The Guardians will not let him enter the Zabranen Forest. Tell me you understand?" she asked with a frightened look in her eyes.

"I understand," he insisted. "I must speak with Cazier before I leave and inform him of Rayna's cure." Kai pushed out with his senses to search the palace for Cazier. Sure enough, he was in his office within the tower.

"Goodbye, Kendra." He wrapped her in a hug. "Please do me a favor. I've no time to check my room. Please clear my desk and burn whatever you deem necessary." He tossed his dream journals into the fire. He took the journal Rayna had given him and shoved it into his pack. "You and I both know if we make it, there is no telling when I will be allowed to come back."

The thought of leaving made his heart well with emotion. He only hoped he would return before his father so he would be able to explain why he left.

Kendra's eyes also filled with tears. "I will take good care of your family. You will make it, and we will see one another again, I promise you. Sabastian and Yulia await your departure on the docks. Yulia will sail with you and assist if she can." She wrapped him up in another tight hug and kissed his forehead. "Be well, little man."

Pack in hand, Kai stood outside Cazier's door and knocked. When the door opened, the look on his cousin's face told him it was painfully obvious to everyone he did not look well. "Kai, please come in, sit. My word, you look like you're burning up. Why do you call on me at this early hour? You should be in bed, or better still with a physician."

"Adrian, I need to tell you something. I leave within the hour by boat across Baden Lake for Albey. Dresnor is making my arrangements as we speak. It would seem Rayna has found a cure," Kai said, taking the offered seat. "The only catch is the plant we need means traveling into the Zabranen Forest. It may also mean dealing with the Katori. Yulia will travel with us. If the Katori people accept helping us, I do not know how long it will take. Also, we plan to search for Rayna's birth parents. It is my desire to spend the next six months in the Katori Mountains. Take care of my family until I can return." Kai looked out the window behind Cazier's desk to control his emotions. "Tell my father I love him, and I will return."

Cazier leaned forward in his chair and placed a hand on Kai's arm. "Sounds like you've made up your mind. Good luck. I will take care of your family. Riome will get to the bottom of Nola's duality, and my other spies will find out her true identity. Be well, cousin. I will miss our late-night talks. Send word when you can."

Cazier's words surprised him. He felt sure Riome would have told him by now that Nola was a Penier, Landon's older sister. Why had she kept that a secret? She was playing a dangerous game. Kai only hoped it would not get her killed. For now, he would trust in her methods and hope she found what she needed.

"I will send word when I can." Kai stepped back quietly and left the way he'd come.

Before leaving, he stopped by his room for one last look. There were so many things he wanted to take. Rayna's chess set sat neatly on the sofa table next to a stack of books he meant to read. Most of all he would miss the memories. Little moments he would cherish. His little sister Cordelia playing with Smoke, or Seth and Aaron's snowball fights on his balcony. Pulled from his reverie, Kai felt Seth enter.

Seth tugged at Kai's pack. "Are you going somewhere? Were you leaving without saying goodbye?" Seth asked in a sad, confused tone.

"Yes, Seth. I am leaving for Albey. I am sorry, I didn't want to wake you. Why are you up?"

Seth ignored the question. "Why Albey? You've already been there. I thought you would be home this summer. Especially now that you are not traveling to Milnos."

Kai hated to admit it, but Seth had always been his favorite brother. Seth was a clever boy, stirred by mischief. Curious about how the world flowed around him. Like Kai, Seth challenged the rules, questioned everything, and had become rather brave in recent years. Kai's departure would be painful for Seth, and he knew it. They shared similar interests and fed off each other's boldness.

It felt wrong to lie, but everyone needed to hear the same story. "You know I have not been well. I have learned there are herbs in the mountains near Albey that could help me get better. There are Katori people who know these plants and remedies. I am hopeful that if I can find them, they might be willing to help Rayna and me.

"How did Rayna get sick too?" asked Seth.

"Do you remember when your mother was sick, they kept her away from everyone?"

"Yes."

"The physicians want to avoid exposing the illness to others. I am afraid I did not stay away from Rayna when I got sick. Now she is also sick. Does that make sense?"

"It does."

"Come. Let me walk you back to your room." Kai dropped his pack and followed Seth.

It would possibly be the last time he would walk these halls. He would miss his family, but he would miss Seth most of all. It was a long and somber walk, and it made him feel a little better to spend this quiet moment with Seth. Outside Seth's door, he bent down. "Take care, Seth."

He hugged his brother. Seth's little arms locked around his neck. Although he wanted to say more, he dared not promise he would return. Sadly, his brother pushed open his door. Seth gave him one last look and closed his door. The moment clawed at Kai's heart. He hated leaving like this. Still, he turned on his heels to collect his things and meet his group.

Covered by the cowls of their cloaks, Kai and Rayna boarded the boat that would take them to Albey. His Kempery-men stood strategically onboard, and he was not a bit surprised to find Kempery-man Redmon among them. Kai gave them each a nod. Yulia was the last to board, and the boatman set out to open water.

A cutter was the fastest way to travel—a light ship with large sails and a streamlined hull. The Dragaron was not a fishing vessel or a supply runner. She was meant to move swiftly and carry news across Baden Lake. Dresnor had done well. The Dragaron was the quickest ship to get them to Albey.

It almost made him wonder what favors Dresnor had to offer to take Dante's ship for their use. The grand duke was a busy man, and his correspondence must flow through the land. Of course, there was the off chance Dresnor had not asked Dante; in which case they were all going to be in a heap of trouble. No matter, Kai thought, they would all settle their debt another day.

Happy to be out on the open water, Kai felt optimistic about their chances. The cold spring breeze felt good on his face. He removed his cloak and helped Rayna do the same. It felt good to have the weight off his shoulders and let the air dry his sweat-soaked shirt. The fresh spring air made him feel better than he had in days having been cooped up in the palace. The slight rocking motion of the ship gliding across the smooth morning water was nearly hypnotic.

Kai could almost feel the promise of uncertainty in the air. His future was wide open, and that thrilled him. For the first time in his life, he controlled his destiny. He could be anyone or anything he wanted. Caught in a wave of emotion, he felt torn by the life he was leaving behind and the future he wanted.

Was it wrong to choose his own path? His biggest fear was having Iver believe Kai had turned his back on everything his father had tried to create for him. Kai was not abandoning his family or the Diu people. He merely wanted to explore his Katori heritage. More importantly, he needed to find his mother. And his gifts and the Katori were his only option. He pressed his hand against her necklace hidden beneath his shirt. Ever since Iver had given it to him he'd worn it to keep it safe.

While his men stood clutching their cloaks for warmth against the spring breeze, Kai stood at the prow of the ship, Rayna at his side. His heart panged for the only home he'd ever known, and he glanced over his shoulder to watch the morning sun gleam off the white and gray stones of the palace high above Diu. He wondered if this would be the last time he ever saw his home.

Kai let his eyes linger on the Master General's tower. The tall white tower stood proud and strong against the early morning sky. His thoughts went to Cazier and Riome, his mentors. Cazier had become more than family, if that were possible. He would miss his guidance and Riome's intensity. He would miss so much about his life there. His city, with its layers of complexity and determination, those that thrived and those that worked diligently to scratch out a living.

Rayna shifted in his arms and offered him some water. Focused on their destination, he looked across the vast lake. The cold air returned his strength, and he felt hope for their success. This was the future he wanted, a life with Rayna by his side. A life in the real world, no longer sheltered by the Galloway name.

Dresnor leaned against the railing watching, always watching. Kai could almost see the wheels turning in his Kemperyman's mind. He could only guess at the questions that plagued him. Neither Dresnor nor Kai knew how this was going to end. They had no plan, no idea how they would explain Kai's departure. His unexplained disappearance into the Zabranen Forest would cause considerable disruption throughout the city.

Kai's men would be held accountable for his loss should he not return. They would be unable to return to Diu without him. He knew this, and so did they. Their loyalty to him was immeasurable. He could tell by the looks on their faces they knew this was a one-way trip, and the burden of his choice was now being carried by his men. Struck by the unyielding dedication, he approached them. Silently he shook the hand of each man. Uncertain was their future, yet they each chose to go with him.

He was blessed.

The End.

www.ingramcontent.com/pod-product-compliance
Lightning Source LLC
Chambersburg PA
CBHW071202100726

47908CB00002B/486